FOLK & FAIRY TALES

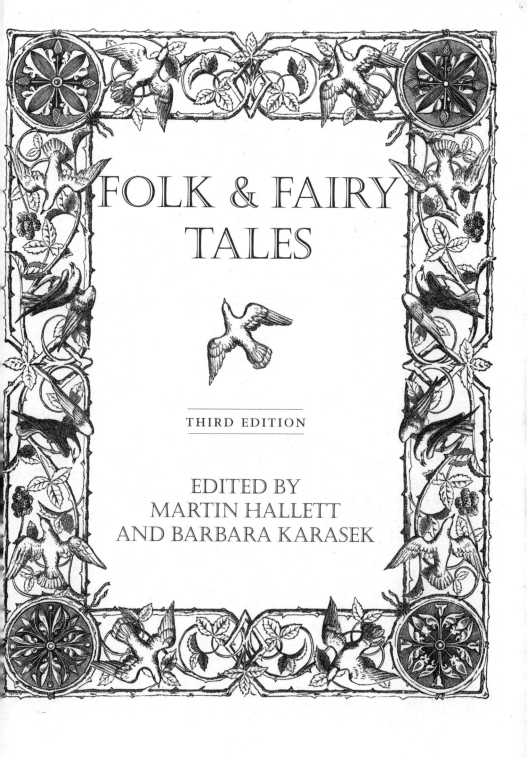

FOLK & FAIRY TALES

THIRD EDITION

EDITED BY
MARTIN HALLETT
AND BARBARA KARASEK

broadview press

National Library of Canada Cataloguing in Publication Data

Main entry under title:
  Folk and fairy tales

3rd ed.
Includes bibliographical references.
ISBN 1-55111-495-X

1. Fairy tales. 2. Tales. 3. Folk literature—History and criticism. I. Hallett, Martin, 1944- II. Karasek, Barbara, 1954-

PZ8.F65 2002   398.2   C2002-900796-8

Broadview Press Ltd. is an independent, international publishing house, incorporated in 1985.

North America:
P.O. Box 1243, Peterborough, Ontario, Canada K9J 7H5
3576 California Road, Orchard Park, NY 14127
TEL: (705) 743-8990; FAX: (705) 743-8353;
E-MAIL: customerservice@broadviewpress.com

United Kingdom:
Thomas Lyster Ltd.
Units 3 and 4a Ormskirk Industrial Park
Old Boundary Way, Burscough Road
Ormskirk, Lancashire L39 2YW
TEL: (01695) 575112; FAX: (01695) 570120; E-mail: books@tlyster.co.uk

Australia:
St. Clair Press, P.O. Box 287, Rozelle, NSW 2039
TEL: (02) 818-1942; FAX: (02) 418-1923

www.broadviewpress.com

Broadview Press gratefully acknowledges the financial support of the Book Publishing Industry Development Program, Ministry of Canadian Heritage, Government of Canada.

Text design and composition by George Kirkpatrick

PRINTED IN CANADA

TO MAITA AND JESSIKA—
FROM AN ONLY MODERATELY WICKED STEPFATHER
M.H.

TO MALIKA—
THE PRINCESS IN MY FAIRY TALE
B.K.

CONTENTS

PREFACE

THINGS change; things remain the same.

We hope that this truism has some application to this new edition of *Folk and Fairy Tales*—that the changes and additions we have made result in an anthology that is a yet more effective and enjoyable introduction to the study of fairy tales.

In preparing a new edition, we have been careful to remind ourselves that this book is, first and foremost, an *introduction*. From the very beginning, we have seen the typical reader of *Folk and Fairy Tales* as a student returning—somewhat sceptically—to the fairy tale for the first time since elementary school or kindergarten—or perhaps even professing to remember nothing about fairy tales that wasn't derived from a Disney movie. Thus, to revise our selection of tales or criticism purely for the sake of modernity would have been inappropriate; in striving for that elusive happy balance, we have tried to avoid making changes for change's sake.

At the same time, the valuable feedback that we have received from those who have used *Folk and Fairy Tales* in the classroom has helped us greatly in adjusting our selection of tales, both to introduce some lesser-known versions of famous tales and to encourage comparison between versions of one tale or categories of several.

Another change is to be found in the addition of a small selection of poetry. It is not representative of a huge body of work, but it demonstrates the continuing vitality of the fairy tale as a source of inspiration, not so much in terms of children's literature as in powerfully evocative imagery that works at an adult level.

The distinguished American critic Leslie Fiedler once observed that children's books introduce all the plots used in adult works and that adult responses are frequently based on forgotten or dimly remembered works from childhood. This is particularly true of fairy tales, which, in providing much of our earliest literary and imaginative experience, have surely exerted an enormous influence over us. The goal of this anthology, therefore, is to draw attention not only to the fascination inherent in the tales themselves, but also to the insights of some critics who have demonstrated, from a variety of perspectives—literary, psychological, and historical—that fairy tales have a complexity belied by their humble origins.

Furthermore, fairy tales can have great pedagogical value for teachers and students of literature. The increasing multi-culturalism of our society has brought with it many riches; at the same time, however, it presents a problem for the teacher who must endeavor to find some common ground for students from diverse cultural, social, and intellectual backgrounds. In this context, the fairy tale offers a unique opportunity to introduce students to a literary form that is familiar and simple, yet multi-dimensional. No student can claim to be wholly ignorant of fairy tales, but it is highly unlikely that he or she has ever gone beyond their surface simplicity to discover the surprisingly subtle complexities that lie beneath.

Because the pedagogical technique of challenging expectations has been a major principle influencing our choice and juxtaposition of tales, most of those selected will quickly be recognized as "classics." It must be pointed out, however, that despite their popularity, these well-known tales are not representative of the international body of fairy tales. We did not set out to make our selection comprehensive, since it was our feeling that the greatest advantage could be achieved by guiding students through familiar territory while introducing some new perspectives. It will be the students' task, then, to apply these and other critical approaches more widely, not only to other fairy tales, but also to the whole world of literature.

We have arranged the folk tales in groups that reflect similar motifs and themes, thus permitting the student to evaluate the effects of omissions, additions, and changes in versions of one tale and to examine the similarities among various tales. This analytical process may also be applied to the literary tales that follow. Such sensitivity to the text is a necessary step in developing the critical attitude demanded by all art and literature. Each group of tales is preceded by a short critical introduction that begins the process of placing the tale in context. We point out some of the issues that may well have inspired these stories in the first place and outline some of the reactions which they have in turn provoked. One of our objectives has been to show how the creative imagination has worked on and developed the fairy tale, as evidenced in the small sampling of contemporary stories. At the same time, such creative reworkings, whatever their medium (and the possibilities are endless), can only emerge from a profound understanding of the fairy tale's style, themes, and structure, as is further demonstrated in the section on illustration that is appended to the tales. To encourage further research, we have also included excerpts from influential critical works representative of different approaches to fairy tales, together with a selective bibliography.

INTRODUCTION

FAIRY tale is a term that is often used rather loosely. A dictionary tells us that it is a story about fairies (which is often not the case), or else that it is an unbelievable or untrue story (which reflects the rationalistic criticism to which the fairy tale has been subjected). This vagueness of definition has made the term something of a catch-all and, therefore, of limited usefulness: Lewis Carroll, for instance, described *Through the Looking-Glass* as a fairy tale, and Andrew Lang saw fit to include an abridged version of Book 1 of Swift's *Gulliver's Travels* in his *Blue Fairy Book*. So let us clarify the subject by introducing two more accurate terms: "folk tale" and "literary tale." Appreciating the essential difference between these two is like establishing North and South on a map; once we have those reference points, we can begin to look around with more confidence and can identify our position in relation to the literary landscape that surrounds us. And, as we shall discover, that task can sometimes turn out to be much more complex than we might expect.

"Folk tale" means exactly what it says: it's a tale of the folk. If we resort again to our dictionary, we learn that "folk" (when used as an adjective) signifies the common people of a nation; the important point to realize here is that the "common people" were, in the past, generally illiterate. Consequently, their tales were orally transmitted; in other words, they were passed down from generation to generation by word of mouth, until they were even-tually recorded and published by such famous individuals as

Charles Perrault (1628-1703) and Jacob and Wilhelm Grimm (1785-1863; 1786-1859). Because we hear so often of "Perrault's Fairy Tales" or of "Grimms' Fairy Tales," it's natural to assume that these men actually wrote them, but this isn't the case; while all three were highly accomplished literary men, none of them were fairy-tale writers. They wrote them *down*, which is quite a different thing—and they did it for quite different reasons, as we shall see.

In most cases, we have no idea how old folk tales are. Once a tale has been told, it is gone; no trace of it remains except in the memories of the teller and the audience. And for the great majority of people today, memory is a fickle instrument—we only have to think back to that examination, or to the last time we lost the shopping-list, to realize how quickly (and how thoroughly) we forget. We are thus confronted with the realization that the only authentic version of the folk tale is an oral version, and, since one telling will necessarily differ from the next, we must confer authenticity equally on all tellings, or—even more problematic—on the first telling alone, wherever and whenever that may have taken place.

Consider for a moment what happens when a tale is transposed from oral performance. Even if the collectors of earlier times had had modern tape-recorders at their disposal, they still could not have published the tales exactly as they had heard them, for the simple reason that spoken language is very different from written. The most judicious of collectors then had (and has) a task of making the tale "read" properly, which naturally involves the exercise of personal judgement and taste, thus imposing the "imprint" of this new intermediary. Moreover, the number of separate recorded versions of a single folk tale is sometimes quite amazing, reaching well into the hundreds. They come from all over the world, which presents us with some clues, and also some conundrums, about the universal use of story to help people come to terms with the fears, the challenges, and the mysteries that are all part of life.

The children's party-game "Broken Telephone" provides us with an idea of just how a folk tale may have evolved as it was passed on from generation to generation. The first player begins by whispering a phrase or sentence to his or her neighbor, who must then pass it on to the next, and so on until it reaches the last individual in the chain. Needless to say, in its progress from first to last, the words undergo some startling and often amusing changes, as they are variously misheard, misunderstood, or improved on. On the simplest level, the game entertains by allowing us to play around with language; on a more sophisticated level, we might see those changes as reflecting the preoccupations (conscious or otherwise) of the players. To put it another way, our moods, desires, and emotions will inevitably affect what is heard; we hear what we want (or expect) to hear. So it is with the folk tale; what we find there is—in part—a fragment of psychic history. An archeologist unearths a piece of pottery and uses his professional skill and knowledge to determine its significance and function in the wider context. In the same way, we can use our growing familiarity with folk tales to identify some of the psychological elements (the "preoccupations") that give each tale much of its energy and color.

The Grimm brothers might be described as archeologists of a sort—although contrary to what was once believed, they were rarely if ever involved with any "digs" that first discovered these tales among unlettered country folk. Such is the pre-eminence of the Grimms' collection that we tend to regard it as being almost as organic and timeless a phenomenon as the tales themselves. It is nevertheless a fact that in more recent times, controversy has swirled around the Grimms' methodology and motivation in assembling their collection. The image of the brothers roaming the German countryside, gathering the tales in remote villages and hamlets, is attractive but false; generally, they were contributed by literate, middle-class friends and relatives, who thus represent yet another intermediary stage between the genuine folk tale on the one hand and the literary tale on the other. In compiling the tales and revising them for publication, the scholarly brothers re-created them for their new audience—one radically different from the illiterate country folk amongst whom they originated. The brothers were at first more enthused by the cultural and his-torical aspects of folk tale, rather than by its potential as children's literature, although Wilhelm in particular revised later editions of their tales with a child audience increasingly in mind. The tenets of nationalism and Romanticism were the two driving forces behind their fascination with German tales. At the time when modern Germany was being forged out of a patchwork of tiny states and principalities, there was a growing need to answer a new question: what does it mean to be German? At the same time, the Grimms were responding to the contemporary Romantic creed that the true spirit of a people was to be found not in palaces or even cities, but in the countryside, far away from urban sophistication.

An entirely different motivation lay behind Charles Perrault's collection of tales, made over one hundred years earlier. Unlike the Grimms, he had no academic or socio-cultural purpose in mind; his less ambitious goal was to provide some quaint amusement for the royal court of Louis XIV, of which he was a member. As might be imagined, the lives of the aristocracy and the lives of the peasants in seventeenth-century France were literally worlds apart; nevertheless, Perrault's introduction of these tales of the peasants into educated society was, in its own way, a stroke of genius. Despite the absence of lofty motive, his work laid a major foundation-stone for what would become, over the next two hundred years, an enormous international museum.

Why use a word like "museum"? Because a museum is a place where you store and exhibit interesting dead things — and that is exactly what a folk tale is, once it is between the covers of a book. At that point, it has ceased to be an oral tale, since it is now "frozen" in print. It can no longer evolve with telling and re-telling; one reading will be exactly the same as any other. The change was inevitable, for as the illiterate became literate, so did their stories. In today's society, the status and role of the story-teller are rather different; he or she is as often to be found in the rarified atmosphere of library or classroom as in the lively informality of market-place or communal festivity.

It would be an exaggeration, however, to claim that the oral tale is entirely a thing of the past. Although the urban legend is much more localized and anecdotal than the fairy tale and is characterized by sensationalism and black humor, it too has its origins in some aspect of life that provokes anxiety or insecurity, such as our ambivalence toward technology or our suspicion that beneath the veneer of normalcy lurks chaos and madness. It is a poor cousin to the fairy tale, not least because its "orality" is short-lived, but it raises the intriguing question as to whether the Internet — often the favored means of transmission for urban legends — represents a kind of post-literate orality....

There is also a difference between what we might term "formal" and "informal" entertainment. "Formal" entertainment is that which we consciously seek out for ourselves, generally at some expense, such as a visit to the cinema or theater. There is a clear and traditional separation between performer and audience, in which the latter plays a passive role as consumer, purchasing the professional services of the entertainer. The story-teller, by contrast, belongs to a more intimate environment than that of the auditorium. If we look at "informal" entertainment, however, we find surroundings much more congenial to story-telling because the grouping (as opposed to audience) is likely to be spontaneous and transitory, such as at a cafeteria table or a party. This is not to suggest that there will be an exchange of folk tales (for reasons mentioned above), but there may well be some story-telling, albeit of a very local and personal nature. Nevertheless, the point can be made that that's probably the way in which many tales originated; the great majority died as quickly as they were born, a few managed a brief existence, and a tiny number contained that mysterious seed of insight, universality, or wisdom that allowed them to beat the odds and survive.

What is emerging, then, is the fact that the fairy tale must be seen as a continuum. At one extreme we find the oral folk tale, which by its very nature cannot be represented in this book. As we have already observed, the oral tale's transformation into literary form requires careful analysis not only of the tale itself, but also of the motives and values of those responsible for its metamorphosis. At the other extreme there is the literary tale, written by a specific person at a specific time, which allows us readily to place the tale in its original context, as we might do in examining any other literary work. In between these two poles, however, we have a virtually infinite number of permutations, as tradition blends with invention in the writer's mind.

If we take as an example the famous tale "Beauty and the Beast," included in this anthology, we can see the extent to which this interpolation can go — and the consequent difficulty we may have in deciding where the folk tale ends and the literary tale begins. Our version of the tale is by Madame Leprince de Beau-mont; it is generally accepted that she based her version on a much longer story by Madame de Villeneuve, who in turn had many possible sources for the theme. While it has the veneer of literary sophistication and elegance that is typical of the French tales as a group, its basic structure is clearly that of the folk tale; we only have to compare it with the other tales in the "Beastly Bride(groom)" section (in particular with Madame d'Aulnoy's "The White Cat") to appreciate that fact. Like Charles Perrault, these writers saw the folk tale as in need of "improvement," and as a result, the story of "Beauty and the Beast" tells us as much about eighteenth-century aristocratic manners and values as it does about a beautiful girl who is betrothed to a monster.

Even when we turn to the tales of Hans Christian Andersen (1805-1875), the link with folk tale remains strong. We perceive Andersen as a writer of fairy tales rather than as a collector, and we assume, therefore, that his tales were exclusively of his own invention. What we forget is that Andersen came from a poor, working-class background in which the oral folk tale was com-mon currency; consequently, his imagination was well primed before the world of literacy opened up new vistas of fancy to him. So it is hardly surprising to discover that several of Ander-sen's better-known tales (such as "The Tinderbox" and "The Nightingale") either allude to, or are re-tellings of, traditional sto-ries—some that he heard, and some that he later read. Thus, Andersen's literary contribution to the fairy tale differs from that of the Grimms in the sense that, while the latter were primarily concerned with presenting their tales in the most acceptable form to the German people, Andersen had a much more personal involvement with his tales. In his hands, a tale, whatever its source, became yet another opportunity for self-revelation. (It is no coincidence that he entitled one of his autobiographies *The Fairytale of My Life*.) As we have already seen, a knowledge of the historical context of the tales is an important element in our appreciation of them; in the case of Andersen and the other fairy-tale writers, that aspect becomes more specific, in the sense that we can now place the tales in a personal context as well as a social one.

The fact is that some rather unlikely minds have been drawn to express themselves through fairy tale, suggesting that the form retains a freedom and an energy that has survived the transformation of audience from rural simplicity to urban sophistication. For instance, what attraction could the fairy tale possibly have had for such an apparently worldly individual as Oscar Wilde (1854-1900)? Yet his tales show a great deal of craft and attention to detail, suggesting that they meant more to him that mere occasional pieces. Wilde, together with other well-known nineteenth-century writers such as Thackeray, MacDonald, Ruskin, and Dickens, regarded the fairy tale as just one of many literary forms to choose from, one with its own particular advantages and limitations.

There is no question, however, that all of these writers saw their primary audience as children; in several cases, their tales were composed with specific children in mind. Even Charles Perrault, at the end of the seventeenth century, was aware of the appeal of fairy tales for children, as is indicated by the frontispiece of the 1697 edition of *Histoires ou Contes du Temps passé, avec des Moralités*, with its inscription "Contes de ma Mère L'Oye" and its depiction of an old woman spinning while she tells her tales to a group of children. The conceit is extended by his addition of explicit morals to the tales, thus making them overtly cautionary in nature. Only their arch, ironic tone betrays his interest in appealing to a rather older, more sophisticated audience.

In England, the presence of the fairy tale in children's literature of the eighteenth century likewise depended on its ability to provide moral instruction. With its fantastic and sometimes violent and amoral content, the fairy tale was disapproved of by both the upholders of Puritan attitudes and the growing advocates of a more rational outlook, exemplified in the philosophy and educational theories of John Locke (which were influential during the eighteenth century). In their efforts to provide children with stories of virtue and piety, both the Rational Moralists and Sunday School Moralists of the late eighteenth and nineteenth centuries also looked upon this popular literature with a consternation verging on horror. In the periodical *The Guardian of Education*, its editor, the influential Sarah Trimmer, warned parents and governesses of the dangers of fairy tales:

A moment's consideration will surely be sufficient to convince people of the least reflection, of the danger, as well as the impropriety, of putting such books as these into the hands of little children, whose minds are susceptible to every impression; and who from the liveliness of their imaginations are apt to convert into realities whatever forcibly strikes their fancy.[1]

Despite this persistent disapproval, however, the tales were made available to eighteenth-century children through a somewhat less "respectable" source of reading material—chapbooks. The purveyors of this popular literature did not have the scruples of more reputable publishers, such as John Newbery, who sought to uphold the current educational theories of Locke. Chapbook publishers recognized the attraction of tales of fantasy and imagination and sought to provide them cheaply—generally by means of travelling pedlars—to the folk, child and adult alike. Thus the tale had, in a sense, come full circle. In being written down, it had been taken from the illiterate folk; now, as literacy was spreading slowly through the population, the tale could be returned—at a price—from whence it came.

During the early years of the nineteenth century, the Romantics countered the prevailing criticism of fairy tales and denounced the moralizing and utilitarian books that were being produced for children. In his affirmation of the value of fantasy in his early reading, the poet Samuel Taylor Coleridge reacted against the common disapproval of such literature:

Should children be permitted to read Romances, and Relations of Giants and Magicians and Genii?—I know all that has been said against it; but I have formed my faith in the affirmative—I know no other way of giving the mind a love of "the great" and "the Whole."[2]

1. Sarah Trimmer, "Nursery Tales," in *The Guardian of Education* 4 (1805) 74-75, as quoted in *Children and Literature: Views and Reviews*, ed. Virginia Haviland (Glenview, Ill.: Scott and Foresman, 1973) 7.

2. Earl Leslie Griggs, ed., *Collected Letters of Samuel Taylor Coleridge, 1785-1800* (Oxford: Clarendon Press, 1956) 1:354.

Although resistance to the fairy tale continued throughout the nineteenth century, when Grimms' fairy tales appeared in England in 1823, they were immediately popular. In the preface to his translation of the tales, Edgar Taylor criticized, in Romantic fashion, the prevailing educational goals and defended the value of fairy stories: "philosophy is made the companion of the nursery; we have lisping chemists and leading-string mathematicians ... Our imagination is surely as susceptible of improvement by exercise as our judgement and our memory."[1] His one stricture on imaginative stories was that they not interfere with moral education. Despite the acceptance of the Brothers Grimm's work, it would be another twenty years before the fairy tale was fully accepted as literature for children. During the 1840s, the appearance of Andersen's original fairy tales gave rise to the publication of a number of traditional folk-tale collections and imaginative stories for children. Thus, after centuries of criticism and banishment to the trade of the chapmen, fairy tales and fantasy itself finally achieved the status which they have never since lost—that of "approved" literature for children.

However, in the process of becoming so closely associated with children, fairy tales have all too often been dismissed as literature not worthy of serious attention on the part of adult readers. In his pioneering essay "On Fairy Stories," J.R.R. Tolkien, author of the fantasy works *The Hobbit* and *Lord of the Rings*, was among the first to point out that this association of fairy stories with children is an historical accident and that children "neither like fairy-stories more, nor understand them better than adults do; and no more than they like other things."[2] Tolkien saw fairy stories as a natural branch of literature, sharing the same qualities as may be found in many other branches.

It certainly can be argued that the fairy tale has regained an adult audience in recent times, as both the tales and the poems in the twentieth-century sections amply demonstrate. The surprise is in the fact that these tales have been out of favor for so long

1. Edgar Taylor, ed., *German Popular Stories* (London: John Camden Hotten, 1869) 90.

2. J.R.R. Tolkien, "On Fairy Stories," in *Tree and Leaf* (London: George Allen and Unwin, 1977) 38.

among older readers since, as Max Lüthi observes, fairy tales present us with both adult and child triumphing over their (and our) deepest fears and desires. Perhaps we have been the victims of our own rationalistic preconceptions of what a fairy tale actually is and what it has to say to us. It was only in 1976 that child psychologist Bruno Bettelheim pointed out that at each stage of our lives, fairy tales take on new significance and speak "simultaneously to all levels of the human personality, communicating in a manner which reaches the uneducated mind of the child as well as that of the sophisticated adult" (see p.379). In this respect, the fairy tale is unique.

In another sense, it is not. One conclusion that can be swiftly drawn from the sections that follow is that some folk tales come in an extraordinary number of versions. Consequently, to build an ambitious theory on the evidence of one version may well be to build a house of cards, for who is to say that this version is more authentic than any other? In some cases it may be possible to demonstrate that a particular version is the oldest of known variants — but is age the only criterion? Is it even possible to think of one particular version of a folk tale as definitive? For instance, in the version of "The Frog King" that we have used, the climax of the story comes when the princess throws the frog against the wall, and our commentary places emphasis on that moment (see Bruno Bettelheim's discussion, in *The Uses of Enchantment*). However, another well-known version is markedly different: the frog returns for three nights to sleep on the princess's pillow, "... but when the princess awoke on the following morning, she was astonished to see, instead of the frog, a handsome prince gazing on her with the most beautiful eyes that ever were seen ..." —and so the whole impact of the story is altered. Thus, any theory that we may devise applies in the first instance only to one version of a particular tale; the challenge then is to see if it retains its validity on being applied to other versions and other tales.

Moreover, pinning down the fairy tale has been made all the more difficult by other developments: the texts of many modern editions have been less heavily censored, and the accompanying illustrations often display a sophistication that inevitably raises questions about the nature of the intended reader. As a consequence of technical improvements that have made color illustration a viable part of any fairy-tale book, the artist has become as important as the writer, and so to the interpretive involvement of folk-tale recorders such as the Grimms, Perrault, and even Andersen, we must now add the contribution of the illustrators — and of course after the illustrators come the animators, bringing the extraordinary and all but overwhelming influence that the Walt Disney studios have had upon our understanding of the fairy tale.

LITTLE RED RIDING HOOD:
LOSS OF INNOCENCE

FOR what is unquestionably one of the classic folk-fairy tales, "Little Red Riding Hood" is more surprising for what it lacks than for what it contains. There is no royalty, no enchantment, no romance—just a talking wolf with a big appetite. How then has the heroine of this tale become as famous a figure as her more glamorous cousins, Sleeping Beauty, Cinderella, and Snow White? What is so remarkable about this stark little tale that describes the dramatic confrontation between an innocent little girl and a wicked wolf? How has it come about that the line "Grandmother, what big teeth you have!" is one of the most anticipated and familiar moments in all of Western literature, let alone fairy tale?

First of all, this is not a real wolf, and arguably neither child nor adult reader ever takes him as such. The first story in this section actually identifies him as a werewolf ("wer" is Old English for "man"), and, as Jack Zipes points out in his discussion of this version in *The Trials and Tribulations of Little Red Riding Hood*, "The direct forebears of Perrault's literary tale were not influenced by sun worship or Christian theology, but by the very material conditions of their existence and traditional pagan superstition. Little children were attacked and killed by animals and grown-ups in the woods and fields. Hunger often drove people to commit atrocious acts. In the 15th and 16th centuries, violence was difficult to explain on rational grounds. There was a strong superstitious belief in werewolves and witches, uncontrollable magical forces of nature, which threatened the lives of the peasant population ...

I

Consequently, the warning tale became part of a stock oral reper-
toire of storytellers."[1]

There are several intriguing aspects to the early version of the
tale "The Story of Grandmother." The representation of the two
paths through the forest as being made of needles and pins is no
doubt a play on the pine-needles that carpet the forest floor; it
may also be a sly reference to one of the domestic tasks that awaits
grown women. This tale also has a crudeness that suggests it is
closer to its folk origins than its successor written by Perrault
(Paul Delarue, the editor of the collection from which this tale
was taken, observes in his notes that " ... the common elements
that are lacking in [Perrault's] story are precisely those which
would have shocked the society of his period by their cruelness
[sic] ... and their impropriety").[2] Yet Perrault's tragic ending,
which catches the modern reader so much by surprise, is not in
fact peculiar to his version: Delarue tells us that it is also to be
found in the majority of folk variants extant at that time. Nevertheless, we can assume that such an ending suited Perrault's inten-
tions admirably, it being his ostensible concern to direct the tale to
a "younger" audience ("Children, especially pretty, nicely brought
-up young ladies, ought never to talk to strangers ...").

The ending of "The Story of Grandmother" catches our eye
because its happy ending comes about through the girl's practical
quick-wittedness. This is a quality that Perrault denies his heroine,
in keeping with his society's assumptions about female innocence
and vulnerability, which makes Little Red Riding Hood into the
wolf's unwitting accomplice. We must remember that Perrault
was a pioneer in recognizing the potential appeal of these tales
and transforming them from an oral to a literary form, even if his
initiative revealed a somewhat superior attitude in exploiting the
tales as quaint and novel amusement for the royal court of Louis
XIV. There can be little doubt that pleasing his aristocratic audience was much more important to him than providing the most
authentic version of the tales, unlike the Grimms, who saw folk
tales as a vital source of their cultural heritage.

---

1. Jack Zipes, *The Trials and Tribulations of Little Red Riding Hood* (South Hadley,
   Mass.: Bergin & Garvey, 1983) 6-7.
2. Paul Delarue, *The Borzoi Book of French Fairy Tales* (New York: Knopf, 1956).

What we also see in Perrault's version is the evolution of the werewolf into a metaphor: in adapting a gross folk tale to the more sophisticated tastes of the royal court, he chooses to remove all overt human aspects of his antagonist, relying simply on the powerful image of the wolf as predator and interloper. And what of the red riding hood, of which there is no mention in "The Story of Grandmother"? Perrault himself tells us that it's a "hood like the ones that fine ladies wear when they go riding," which suggests that he is trying to link the tale with the world of his audience. But why is it *red*? This time we are confronted with a color symbolic of sexuality, which again hints at Perrault's own interpretation of this tale.

When we turn to the Grimm Brothers' version, published over a hundred years later, we find a synthesis of the other two, with intriguing additions. The red garment remains, as does the wolf. Like Perrault, the Grimms choose to gloss over the cannibalistic snack that the girl unwittingly makes of her grandmother, and the "happy" ending has been restored, but only through the intervention of the paternalistic woodcutter, who must be introduced to rescue the helpless females. Nevertheless, it can be argued that the Grimm version is the most balanced, at least to modern eyes. The woodcutter presents an image of male goodness that counters the male wickedness of the wolf; the mother appears concerned about her daughter's correct behavior, if not her welfare—and the less familiar conclusion, describing the defeat of a second wolf through the strategy of a wiser little girl and her now-healthy grandmother, sends a very different message from Perrault's harsh ending.

The continual evolution of the folk tale as it travels from country to country (or even region to region) is well illustrated in an Italian version of this tale. An editorial note by its collector, Italo Calvino, should catch our attention: "I ... omitted an episode that would have been too gruesome in this meager text: the wolf kills the mother and makes a doorlatch cord out of her tendons, a meat pie out of her flesh, and wine out of her blood. The little girl, pulling on the doorlatch, says, 'What a soft cord you've put here, Mamma!' Then she eats the meat pie and drinks the wine, with comments in the same vein."[1] Calvino's fastidiousness comes too

---

1. Italo Calvino, *Italian Folktales* (New York: Pantheon, 1980) 720.

late for us, since we have already encountered similarly gory details in "The Story of Grandmother" with which we began this section. However, it again points up the importance of the role of the editor or teller, as he/she decides what to include and what to leave out. One interesting distinction is the fact that the little girl and her mother here are rescued not by a single good father-figure but by the townspeople at large. Does this tell us something about the close-knit nature of Italian society?

"The Chinese Red Riding Hoods" also reveals significant structural differences, yet, on closer examination, we may be surprised to discover just how much of the other versions it integrates. As in the previous tale, there are three girls rather than one; as in "The Story of Grandmother," the children escape from the wolf's clutches by means of a clever ruse; and his final demise is brought about by much the same strategy as in the conclusion to "Little Red Cap" — that is, by exploiting the greed that is central to the wolf's character.

In some respects, this Chinese version has a distinctly contemporary feel. The mother is described as a young widow who teaches her children carefully about the nature of the world, yet the time must come when her children will have to fend for themselves — and at that moment of crisis, the girls prove susceptible to the wolf's trickery. Despite their mistake, however, the sisters (led by the formidable Felice) are able to keep their wits about them and finally outsmart the deceitful wolf. The experience may have deprived them of at least some of their trust in those around them; by the same token, they will be less likely to be fooled a second time.

THE STORY OF GRANDMOTHER

THERE was once a woman who had some bread, and she said to her daughter: "You are going to carry a hot loaf and a bottle of milk to your grandmother."

The little girl departed. At the crossroads she met the *bzou*, who said to her:

"Where are you going?"

"I'm taking a hot loaf and a bottle of milk to my grandmother."

"What road are you taking," said the *bzou*, "the Needles Road or the Pins Road?"

"The Needles Road," said the little girl.

"Well, I shall take the Pins Road."

The little girl enjoyed herself picking up needles. Meanwhile the *bzou* arrived at her grandmother's, killed her, put some of her flesh in the pantry and a bottle of her blood on the shelf. The little girl arrived and knocked at the door.

"Push the door," said the *bzou*, "it's closed with a wet straw."

"Hello, Grandmother; I'm bringing you a hot loaf and a bottle of milk."

"Put them in the pantry. You eat the meat that's in it and drink a bottle of wine that is on the shelf."

As she ate there was a little cat that said: "A slut is she who eats the flesh and drinks the blood of her grandmother!"

"Undress, my child," said the *bzou*, "and come and sleep beside me."

"Where should I put my apron?"

"Throw it in the fire, my child; you don't need it any more."

"Where should I put my bodice?"

"Throw it in the fire, my child; you don't need it any more."

"Where should I put my dress?"

"Throw it in the fire, my child; you don't need it any more."

"Where should I put my skirt?"

"Throw it in the fire, my child; you don't need it any more."

"Where should I put my hose?"

"Throw it in the fire, my child; you don't need it any more."

"Oh, Grandmother, how hairy you are!"

"It's to keep me warmer, my child."

"Oh, Grandmother, those long nails you have!"

"It's to scratch me better, my child!"

"Oh, Grandmother, those big shoulders that you have!"

"All the better to carry kindling from the woods, my child."

"Oh Grandmother, those big ears that you have!"

"All the better to hear with, my child."

"Oh, Grandmother, that big mouth you have!"

"All the better to eat you with, my child!"

"Oh, Grandmother, I need to go outside to relieve myself."

"Do it in the bed, my child."

"No, Grandmother, I want to go outside."

"All right, but don't stay long."

The *bzou* tied a woolen thread to her foot and let her go out, and when the little girl was outside she tied the end of the string to a big plum tree in the yard. The *bzou* got impatient and said:

"Are you making cables?"

When he became aware that no one answered him, he jumped out of bed and saw that the little girl had escaped. He followed her, but he arrived at her house just at the moment she was safely inside.

LITTLE RED RIDING HOOD

Charles Perrault

ONCE upon a time there was a little village girl, the prettiest that had ever been seen. Her mother doted on her. Her grandmother was even fonder, and made her a little red hood, which became her so well that everywhere she went by the name of Little Red Riding Hood.

One day her mother, who had just made and baked some cakes, said to her:

"Go and see how your grandmother is, for I have been told that she is ill. Take her a cake and this little pot of butter."

Little Red Riding Hood set off at once for the house of her grandmother, who lived in another village.

On her way through a wood she met old Father Wolf. He would have very much liked to eat her, but dared not do so on account of some wood-cutters who were in the forest. He asked her where she was going. The poor child, not knowing that it was dangerous to stop and listen to a wolf, said:

"I am going to see my grandmother, and am taking her a cake and a pot of butter which my mother has sent to her."

"Does she live far away?" asked the Wolf.

"Oh yes," replied Little Red Riding Hood; "it is yonder by the mill which you can see right below there, and it is the first house in the village."

"Well now," said the Wolf, "I think I shall go and see her too. I will go by this path, and you by that path, and we will see who gets there first."

The Wolf set off running with all his might by the shorter road, and the little girl continued on her way by the longer road. As she went she amused herself by gathering nuts, running after the butterflies, and making nosegays of the wild flowers which she found.

The Wolf was not long in reaching the grandmother's house.

He knocked. *Toc Toc.*

"Who is there?"

"It is your granddaughter, Red Riding Hood," said the Wolf, disguising his voice, "and I bring you a cake and a little pot of butter as a present from my mother."

The worthy grandmother was in bed, not being very well, and cried out to him:

"Pull out the peg and the latch will fall."

The Wolf drew out the peg and the door flew open. Then he sprang upon the poor old lady and ate her up in less than no time, for he had been more than three days without food.

After that he shut the door, lay down in the grandmother's bed, and waited for Little Riding Hood.

Presently she came and knocked. *Toc Toc.*

"Who is there?"

Now Little Red Riding Hood on hearing the Wolf's gruff voice was at first frightened, but thinking that her grandmother had a bad cold, she replied:

"It is your granddaughter, Red Riding Hood, and I bring you a cake and a little pot of butter from my mother."

Softening his voice, the Wolf called out to her:

"Pull out the peg and the latch will fall."

Little Red Riding Hood drew out the peg and the door flew open.

When he saw her enter, the Wolf hid himself in the bed beneath the counterpane.

"Put the cake and the little pot of butter on the bin," he said, "and come up on the bed with me."

Little Red Riding Hood took off her cloak, but when she climbed up on the bed she was astonished to see how her grandmother looked in her nightgown.

"Grandmother dear!" she exclaimed, "what big arms you have!"

"The better to embrace you, my child!"
"Grandmother dear, what big legs you have!"
The better to run with, my child!"
"Grandmother dear, what big ears you have!"
"The better to hear with, my child!"
"Grandmother dear, what big eyes you have!"
"The better to see with, my child!"
"Grandmother dear, what big teeth you have!"
"The better to eat you with!"

With these words the wicked Wolf leapt upon Little Red Riding Hood and gobbled her up.

Moral

From this story one learns that children,
Especially young lasses,
Pretty, courteous and well-bred,
Do very wrong to listen to strangers,
And it is not an unheard thing
If the Wolf is thereby provided with his dinner.
I say Wolf, for all wolves
Are not of the same sort;
There is one kind with an amenable disposition
Neither noisy, nor hateful, nor angry,
But tame, obliging and gentle,
Following the young maids
In the streets, even into their homes.
Alas! who does not know that these gentle wolves
Are of all such creatures the most dangerous!

LITTLE RED CAP

Jacob and Wilhelm Grimm

ONCE there was a dear little girl whom everyone loved. Her grandmother loved her most of all and didn't know what to give the child next. Once she gave her a little red velvet cap, which was so becoming to her that she never wanted to wear anything else, and that was why everyone called her Little Red Cap. One day her mother said: "Look, Little Red Cap, here's a piece of cake and a bottle of wine. Take them to grandmother. She is sick and weak, and they will make her feel better. You'd better start now before it gets too hot; walk properly like a good little girl, and don't leave the path or you'll fall down and break the bottle and there won't be anything for grandmother. And when you get to her house, don't forget to say good morning, and don't go looking in all the corners."

"I'll do everything right," Little Red Cap promised her mother. Her grandmother lived in the wood, half an hour's walk from the village. No sooner had Little Red Cap set foot in the wood than she met the wolf. But Little Red Cap didn't know what a wicked beast he was, so she wasn't afraid of him. "Good morning, Little Red Cap," he said. "Thank you kindly, wolf." "Where are you going so early, Little Red Cap?" "To my grandmother's." "And what's that you've got under your apron?" "Cake and wine. We baked yesterday, and we want my grandmother, who's sick and weak, to have something nice that will make her feel better." "Where does your grandmother live, Little Red Cap?" "In the wood, fifteen or twenty minutes' walk from here, under the three big oak trees. That's where the house is. It has hazel hedges around it. You must know the place." "How young and tender she is!" thought the wolf. "Why, she'll be even tastier than the old woman. Maybe if I'm crafty enough I can get them both." So, after walking along for a short while beside Little Red Cap, he said: "Little Red Cap, open your eyes. What lovely flowers! Why don't you look around you? I don't believe you even hear how sweetly the birds are singing. It's so gay out here in the wood, yet you trudge along as solemnly as if you were going to school."

Little Red Cap looked up, and when she saw the sunbeams

dancing this way and that between the trees and the beautiful flowers all around her, she thought: "Grandmother will be pleased if I bring her a bunch of nice fresh flowers. It's so early now that I'm sure to be there in plenty of time." So she left the path and went into the wood to pick flowers. And when she had picked one, she thought there must be a more beautiful one farther on, so she went deeper and deeper into the wood. As for the wolf, he went straight to the grandmother's house and knocked at the door. "Who's there?" "Little Red Cap, bringing cake and wine. Open the door." "Just raise the latch," cried the grandmother, "I'm too weak to get out of bed." The wolf raised the latch and the door swung open. Without saying a single word he went straight to the grandmother's bed and gobbled her up. Then he put on her clothes and her nightcap, lay down in the bed, and drew the curtains.

Meanwhile Little Red Cap had been running about picking flowers, and when she had as many as she could carry she remembered her grandmother and started off again. She was surprised to find the door open, and when she stepped into the house she had such a strange feeling that she said to herself: "My goodness, I'm usually so glad to see grandmother. Why am I frightened today?" "Good morning," she cried out, but there was no answer. Then she went to the bed and opened the curtains. The grandmother had her cap pulled way down over her face, and looked very strange.

"Oh, grandmother, what big ears you have!"

"The better to hear you with."

"Oh, grandmother, what big eyes you have!"

"The better to see you with."

"Oh, grandmother, what big hands you have!"

"The better to grab you with."

"But, grandmother, what a dreadful big mouth you have!"

"The better to eat you with."

And no sooner had the wolf spoken than he bounded out of bed and gobbled up poor Little Red Cap.

When the wolf had stilled his hunger, he got back into bed, fell asleep, and began to snore very very loud. A hunter was just passing, and he thought: "How the old woman is snoring! I'd better go and see what's wrong." So he stepped into the house and went over to the bed and saw the wolf was in it. "You old sinner!" he said, "I've found you at last. It's been a long time." He levelled his musket and was just about to fire when it occurred to him that the wolf might have swallowed the grandmother and that there might still be a chance of saving her. So instead of firing, he took a pair of scissors and started cutting the sleeping wolf's belly open. After two snips, he saw the little red cap, and after another few snips the little girl jumped out, crying: "Oh, I've been so afraid! It was so dark inside the wolf!" And then the old grandmother came out, and she too was still alive, though she could hardly breathe. Little Red Cap ran outside and brought big stones, and they filled the wolf's belly with them. When he woke up, he wanted to run away, but the stones were so heavy that his legs wouldn't carry him and he fell dead.

All three were happy; the hunter skinned the wolf and went home with the skin, the grandmother ate the cake and drank the wine Little Red Cap had brought her and soon got well; and as for Little Red Cap, she said to herself: "Never again will I leave the path and run off into the wood when my mother tells me not to."

Another story they tell is that when Little Red Cap was taking another cake to her old grandmother another wolf spoke to her and tried to make her leave the path. But Little Red Cap was on her guard. She kept on going, and when she got to her grandmother's she told her how she had met a wolf who had bidden her good day but given her such a wicked look that "if it hadn't been on the open road he'd have gobbled me right up." "Well then," said the grandmother, "we'll just lock the door and he won't be able to get in." In a little while the wolf knocked and called out: "Open the door, grandmother, it's Little Red Cap. I've brought you some cake." But they didn't say a word and they didn't open the door. So Grayhead circled the house once or twice and finally jumped on the roof. His plan was to wait until evening when Little Red Cap would go home, and then he'd creep after her and gobble her up in the darkness. But the grandmother guessed what he had in mind. There was a big stone trough in front of the house, and she said to the child: "Here's a bucket, Little Red Cap. I cooked some sausages yesterday. Take the water I cooked them in and empty it into the trough." Little Red Cap carried water until the trough was full. The smell of the sausages rose up to the wolf's nostrils. He sniffed and looked down, and in the end he stuck his neck out so far that he couldn't keep his footing and began to slide. And he slid off the roof and slid straight into the big trough and was drowned. And Little Red Cap went happily home, and no one harmed her.

THE CHINESE RED RIDING HOODS

Isabelle C. Chang

"Beware of the wolf in sheep's clothing."

MANY years ago in China there lived a young widow with her three children. On their grandmother's birthday, the mother went to visit her.

"Felice," she cautioned her oldest daughter before she left, "you must watch over your sisters Mayling and Jeanne while I am gone. Lock the door and don't let anyone inside. I shall be back tomorrow."

A wolf who was hiding near the house at the edge of the woods overheard the news.

When it was dark he disguised himself as an elderly woman and knocked at the door of the three girls' house.

"Who is it?" called Felice.

"Felice, Mayling, and Jeanne, my treasures, it is your Grammie," answered the wolf as sweetly as possible.

"Grammie," said Felice through the door, "Mummy just went to see you!"

"It is too bad I missed her. We must have taken different roads," replied the crafty wolf.

"Grammie," asked Mayling, "why is your voice so different tonight?"

"Your old Grammie caught cold and is hoarse. Please let me in quickly, for it is drafty out here and the night air is very bad for me."

The tenderhearted girls could not bear to keep their grandmother out in the cold, so they unlatched the door and shouted,

"Grammie, Grammie!"

As soon as the wolf crossed the threshold, he blew out the candle, saying the light hurt his tired eyes. Felice pulled a chair forward for her grandmother. The wolf sat down hard on his tail hidden under the skirt.

"Ouch!" he exclaimed.

"Is something wrong, Grammie?" asked Felice.

"Nothing at all, my dear," said the wolf, bearing the pain silently.

Then Mayling and Jeanne wanted to sit on their Grammie's lap.

"What nice, plump children," said the wolf, holding Mayling on one knee and Jeanne on the other.

Soon the wolf said, "Grammie is tired and so are you children. Let's go to bed."

The children begged as usual to be allowed to sleep in the huge double bed with their Grammie.

Soon Jeanne felt the wolf's tail against her toes. "Grammie, what's that furry thing?" she asked.

"Oh, that's just the brush I always have by me to keep away mosquitoes and flies," answered the wolf.

Then Mayling felt the sharp claws of the wolf. "Grammie, what are these sharp things?"

"Go to sleep, dear, they are just Grammie's nails."

Then Felice lit the candle and caught a glimpse of the wolf's hairy face before he could blow out the light. Felice was frightened. She quickly grabbed hold of Jeanne and said, "Grammie, Jeanne is thirsty. She needs to get up to get a glass of water."

"Oh, for goodness sake," said the wolf, losing patience, "tell her to wait until later."

Felice pinched Jeanne so that she started to cry.

"All right, all right," said the wolf, "Jeanne may get up."

Felice thought quickly and said, "Mayling, hurry and help Jeanne get a glass of water!"

When the two younger ones had left the bedroom, Felice said, "Grammie, have you ever tasted our luscious gingko nuts?"

"What is a gingko nut?" asked the wolf.

"The meat of the gingko nut is softer and more tender than a firm baby and tastes like a delicious fairy food," replied Felice.

"Where can you get some?" asked the wolf, drooling.

"Those nuts grow on trees outside our house."

"Well, your Grammie is too old to climb trees now," sighed the wolf.

"Grammie, dear, I can pick some for you," said Felice sweetly.

"Will you, angel?" pleaded the wolf.

"Of course, I'll do it right now!" said Felice, leaping out of bed.

"Come back quickly," called the wolf after her.

Felice found Mayling and Jeanne in the other room. She told them about the wolf, and the three girls quickly decided to climb up the tallest gingko tree around their cottage.

The wolf waited and waited, but no one came back. Then he got up and went outside and shouted, "Felice, Mayling, Jeanne, where are you?"

"We're up in the tree, eating gingko nuts," called Felice.

"Throw some down for me," yelled the wolf.

"Ah, Grammie, we just remembered Mummy telling us that gingkos are fairy nuts. They change when they leave the tree. You'll just have to climb up and eat these mouth-watering nuts here."

The wolf was raging as he paced back and forth under the tree.

Then Felice said, "Grammie, I just had an idea. There is a clothesbasket by the door with a long clothesline inside. Tie one end to the handle and throw the end of the rope up to me. We shall pull you up here."

The wolf happily went to get the clothesbasket.

Felice pulled hard on the rope. When the basket was halfway up, she let go, and the wolf fell to the ground badly bruised.

"Boo hoo, hoo!" cried Felice, pretending to be very sorry. "I did not have enough strength to pull poor Grammie up!"

"Don't cry, Sister," said Mayling, "I'll help you pull Grammie up!"

The greedy wolf got into the basket again.

Felice and Mayling pulled with all their might. The wolf was two thirds up the tree before they let go of the rope. Down he fell with a crash. He began to scold.

"Grammie, Grammie, please don't get so upset," begged Jeanne. "I'll help my sisters to pull you all the way this time."

"All right, but mind you be very careful or I'll bite your heads off!" screeched the wolf.

The three children pulled with all their strength.

"Heave ho, heave ho!" they sang in rhythm as they hauled the wolf up slowly till he was thirty feet high. He was just beyond reach of a branch when Felice coughed and everyone let go of the rope. As the basket spun down, the wolf let out his last howl.

When the children were unable to get any answer to their calls of "Grammie," they slid down the tree and ran into the house, latched the door and soon went to sleep.

THE WOLF AND THE THREE GIRLS

Italo Calvino

ONCE there were three sisters who worked in a certain town. Word reached them one day that their mother, who lived in Borgoforte, was deathly ill. The oldest sister therefore filled two baskets with four bottles of wine and four cakes and set out for Borgoforte. Along the way she met the wolf, who said to her, "Where are you going in such haste?"

"To Borgoforte to see Mamma, who is gravely ill."

"What's in those baskets?"

"Four bottles of wine and four cakes."

"Give them to me, or else—to put it bluntly—I'll eat you."

The girl gave the wolf everything and went flying back home to her sisters. Then the middle girl filled her baskets and left for Borgoforte. She too met the wolf.

"Where are you going in such haste?"

"To Borgoforte to see Mamma, who is gravely ill."

"What's in those baskets?"

"Four bottles of wine and four cakes."

"Give them to me, or else—to put it bluntly—I'll eat you."

So the second sister emptied her baskets and ran home. Then the youngest girl said, "Now it's my turn." She prepared the baskets and set out. There was the wolf.

"Where are you going in such haste?"

"To Borgoforte to see Mamma, who is gravely ill."

"What's in those baskets?"

"Four bottles of wine and four cakes."

"Give them to me, or else — to put it bluntly — I'll eat you."

The little girl took a cake and threw it to the wolf, who had his mouth open. She had made the cake especially for him and filled it with nails. The wolf caught it and bit into it, pricking his palate all over. He spat out the cake, leaped back, and ran off, shouting, "You'll pay for that!"

Taking certain short cuts known only to him, the wolf ran ahead and reached Borgoforte before the little girl. He slipped into the sick mother's house, gobbled her up, and took her place in bed.

The little girl arrived, found her mother with the sheet drawn up to her eyes, and said, "How dark you've become, Mamma!"

"That's because I've been sick so much, my child," said the wolf.

"How big your head has become, Mamma!"

"That's because I've worried so much, my child."

"Let me hug you, Mamma," said the little girl, and the wolf gobbled her up whole.

With the little girl in his belly, the wolf ran out of the house. But the townspeople, seeing him come out, chased him with pitchforks and shovels, cornered him and killed him. They slit him open at once and out came mother and daughter still alive. The mother got well, and the little girl went back and said to her sisters, "Here I am, safe and sound!"

SLEEPING BEAUTY:
WAITING FOR MR. RIGHT

Now we turn to three versions of another famous tale: "Sleeping Beauty." As in the previous section, there can be little doubt that the earlier version (or versions) had a definite influence upon its successors—but in this case, the result of that influence is clearly different. In the versions of "Little Red Riding Hood," we can see the process of literary refinement in the tale's elaboration; now that same process takes the opposite tack, as the tale undergoes significant shrinkage (particularly between Perrault and the Grimms) in the effort to make the tale suitable for its ever-younger audience.

Despite the obvious differences between these versions, the central image of the enchanted sleep remains constant and is arguably the key to the popularity of the tale. So the question arises: how could an image of extended inactivity be so crucial to the tale's success? One answer, as P.L. Travers points out in an insightful essay on this tale,[1] is that the central image of a sleeping

---

1. P.L. Travers, *About the Sleeping Beauty*, (New York: McGraw-Hill, 1975) 59-61.
   Travers takes pains to remind us of the multi-faceted nature of the symbol, which she illustrates most effectively in a list of famous sleepers whose concerns often have little to do with growing up:

   > The idea of the sleeper, of somebody hidden from mortal eye, waiting until the time shall ripen has always been dear to the folkly mind— Snow White asleep in her glass coffin, Brynhild behind her wall of fire, Charlemagne in the heart of France, King Arthur in the Isle of

princess awaiting the prince who will bring her (and her whole world) back to life has powerful mythic overtones of death and resurrection. On a more human level, the image is a metaphor of growing up: in each case, the heroine falls asleep as a naive girl and awakens as a mature young woman on the threshold of marriage and adult responsibility. For cultural reasons, the metaphor is generally seen as gender-specific, in that sleep denotes the decorous passivity expected of the virtuous young female — a characteristic that undoubtedly attracted nineteenth-century approval of this tale (see Anne Thackeray Ritchie's version, p.261). By contrast, the young male must demonstrate his maturity through deeds of daring, manifested most effectively in Perrault's version of the tale.

Giambattista Basile (1575-1632) was a minor Neapolitan courtier and soldier who in some respects resembles his more famous French successor, Charles Perrault. Both men recognized the vitality and appeal of folk tales and set out to bring them to a new audience, adapting and embellishing them as literary style and social decorum demanded. It becomes quickly apparent, however, that Basile's tales are not only sophisticated but distinctly *adult* in appeal; their content, tone, and overall structure hearken back to Boccaccio and Chaucer rather than anticipate the fairy-tale collections that follow. Basile's version of "Sleeping Beauty" is a story of rape, adultery, sexual rivalry, and attempted cannibalism — a far cry from what we have come to expect in this famous tale!

Comparing Basile's tale with Perrault's "Sleeping Beauty in the Wood" provides a fascinating glimpse into the evolution of a tale in its literary form, as the Frenchman sets about revising it to match *his* assumptions about what a fairy tale is and who will read

---

Avalon, Frederick Barbarossa under his mountain in Thuringia. Muchukunda, the Hindu King, slept through eons till he was awakened by the Lord Krishna; Oisin of Ireland dreamed in Tir n'an Og for over three hundred years. Psyche in her magic sleep is a type of Sleeping Beauty, Sumerian Ishtar in the underworld may be said to be another. Holga the Dane is sleeping and waiting, and so, they say, is Sir Francis Drake. Quetzalcoatl of Mexico and Virochocha of Peru are both sleepers. Morgan le Fay of France and England and Dame Holle of Germany are sleeping in raths and cairns. (51)

(or hear) it. In a nutshell, it might be said that Perrault's approach is rather more subtle than that of his Neapolitan predecessor. Clearly, Perrault wants no part of Basile's evident delight in the salacious aspects of his story. While as a royal courtier he was doubtless no stranger to confrontations between jealous wives and beautiful mistresses, his tale suggests that discretion and a sophisticated cynicism are now the rule in dealing with such matters; social diplomat that he is, Perrault favors the oblique comment, the aside that demonstrates the wit of the writer and makes an accomplice of the reader. Thus Perrault's prince refrains—at least at the moment of discovery—from all physical contact with the sleeping princess (he is simply present when the enchantment reaches full term, whereas the spell-breaking kiss bestowed by the Grimms' prince implies an arousal that is sexual in nature). We may detect more than a trace of archness, however, when Perrault tells us that the young couple "... slept but little ... The princess, indeed, had not much need of sleep...." Likewise, through his use of symbolism, Perrault finds a way to sublimate the sexual rivalry that gives Basile's more realistic tale much of its impact. In Perrault's version, the King's tigerish wife becomes the Prince's ogress mother, which allows the retention of several significant elements (such as the cannibalism motif), while further deflecting the violence of the tale with a characteristic touch of sly humor: her decision to eat one of Sleeping Beauty's children is horrific, of course—but there is a certain Gallic *savoir-faire* in her instruction to her steward to "... serve her with piquant sauce...."

To modern eyes, Perrault's alteration of the tale clearly invites a Freudian interpretation, as the Prince's mother wages her ruthless campaign to destroy all rivals for her son's affections. As suggested above, his sequel contains an intriguing insight into *male* maturation, counterpointing Sleeping Beauty's transformation by sleep. The crisis of this episode is brought on by the Prince's assumption that his ascension to kingship is the external confirmation of his personal maturity; he therefore chooses this moment to reveal the existence of his wife and children to his mother. "Some time afterwards," we are told, in an apparent *non-sequitur* that speaks volumes, "the king declared war on his neighbor, the Emperor Cantalabutte." Given the Prince's awareness of his mother's

predilections, how are we to explain such a decision? Is his departure an indication of his naivety, in that he has no inkling of the
rivalry that he leaves behind him—or is he in fact so aware of it
that he reckons there is more peace to be found in the middle of a
battlefield?

After all the excitement of the two earlier versions, it comes as
something of a surprise to realize that the much shorter, blander
version by the Brothers Grimm is by far the best-known—perhaps for the very reason that the Grimms chose not to darken the
blue sky of romance with the storm-clouds of jealousy and sexual
rivalry that may loom up in human relationships (although as we
noted above, theirs is the version in which Sleeping Beauty's
awakening has the clearest sexual connotation). Yet only a
moment's thought is necessary to appreciate why they may have
made the editorial decision to end the story there; once again, the
central importance of the intended audience asserts itself. Perrault's claims notwithstanding, it was only with the Grimms that
the folk tale unequivocally entered the child's domain, and the
Grimms took their responsibility seriously. Consequently, no trace
of Basile's hand remains, and little enough of Perrault's either: a
comparison of the gifts presented to Sleeping Beauty by the fairies
in the Perrault and Grimm versions offers an intriguing insight
into the different worlds from which these tales come. At the
same time, it might be said that in the Grimms' version we see the
tale stripped down to its narrative core, revealing most clearly its
oral evolution.

SOLE, LUNA, E TALIA
(SUN, MOON, AND TALIA)

Giambattista Basile

THERE was once a great king who, on the birth of his daughter—
to whom he gave the name of Talia—commanded all the wise
men and seers in the kingdom to come and tell him what her
future would be. These wise men, after many consultations, came
to the conclusion that she would be exposed to great danger from
a small splinter in some flax. Thereupon the King, to prevent any

unfortunate accident, commanded that no flax or hemp or any other similar material should ever come into his house.

One day when Talia was grown up she was standing by the window, and saw an old woman pass who was spinning. Talia had never seen a distaff and spindle, and was therefore delighted with the dancing of the spindle. Prompted by curiosity, she had the old woman brought up to her, and taking the distaff in her hand, began to draw out the thread; but unfortunately a splinter in the hemp got under her fingernail, and she immediately fell dead upon the ground. At this terrible catastrophe the old woman fled from the room, rushing precipitously down the stairs. The stricken father, after having paid for this bucketful of sour wine with a barrelful of tears, left the dead Talia seated on a velvet chair under an embroidered canopy in the palace, which was in the middle of a wood. Then he locked the door and left forever the house which had brought him such evil fortune, so that he might entirely obliterate the memory of his sorrow and suffering.

It happened some time after that a falcon of a king who was out hunting in these parts flew in at the window of this house. As the bird did not return when called back, the King sent someone to knock at the door, thinking the house was inhabited. When they had knocked a long time in vain, the King sent for a vine-dresser's ladder, so that he might climb up himself and see what was inside. He climbed up and went in, and was astonished at not finding a living being anywhere. Finally he came to the room in which sat Talia as if under a spell.

The King called to her, thinking she was asleep; but since nothing he did or said brought her back to her senses, and being on fire with love, he carried her to a couch and, having gathered the fruits of love, left her lying there. Then he returned to his own kingdom and for a long time entirely forgot the affair.

Nine months later, Talia gave birth to two children, a boy and a girl, two splendid pearls. They were looked after by two fairies, who had appeared in the palace, and who put the babies to their mother's breast. Once, when one of the babies wanted to suck, it could not find the breast, but got into its mouth instead the finger that had been pricked. This the baby sucked so hard that it drew out the splinter, and Talia was roused as if from a deep sleep. When she saw the two jewels at her side, she clasped them to her breast and held them as dear as life; but she could not understand what had happened, and how she came to be alone in the palace with two children, having everything she required to eat brought to her without seeing anyone.

One day the King bethought himself of the adventure of the fair sleeper, and took the opportunity of another hunting expedition to go and see her. Finding her awake and with two prodigies of beauty, he was overpowered with joy. He told Talia what had happened and they made a great compact of friendship, and he remained several days in her company. Then he left her, promising to come again and take her back with him to his kingdom. When he reached his home he was forever talking of Talia and her children. At meals the names of Talia, Sun, and Moon (these were the children's names) were always on his lips; when he went to bed he was always calling one or the other.

The Queen had already had some glimmering of suspicion on account of her husband's long absence when hunting; and hearing his continued calling on Talia, Sun, and Moon, burned with a heat very different from the sun's heat, and calling the King's secretary, said to him: "Listen, my son, you are between Scylla and Charybdis, between the doorpost and the door, between the poker and the grate. If you tell me with whom it is that my husband is in love, I will make you rich; if you hide the truth from me, you shall never be found again, dead or alive." The man, on the one hand moved by fear, and on the other egged on by interest, which is a bandage over the eyes of honour, a blinding of justice and a cast horseshoe to faith, told the Queen all, calling bread bread and wine wine.

Then she sent the same secretary in the King's name to tell Talia that he wished to see his children. Talia was delighted and sent the children. But the Queen, as soon as she had possession of them, with the heart of a Medea, ordered the cook to cut their throats and to make them into hashes and sauces and give them to their unfortunate father to eat.

The cook, who was tender-hearted, was filled with pity on seeing these two golden apples of beauty, and gave them to his wife to hide and prepared two kids, making a hundred different dishes of them. When the hour for dinner arrived, the Queen had the dishes brought in, and whilst the King was eating and enjoying them, exclaiming: "How good this is, by the life of Lanfusa! How tasty this is, by the soul of my grandmother!" she kept encouraging him, saying: "Eat away, you are eating what is your own." The first two or three times the King paid no attention to these words, but as she kept up the same strain of music, he answered: "I know very well I am eating what is my own; you never brought anything into the house." And getting up in a rage, he went off to a villa not far away to cool his anger down.

The Queen, not satisfied with what she thought she had already done, called the secretary again, and sent him to fetch Talia herself, pretending that the King was expecting her. Talia came at once, longing to see the light of her eyes and little guessing that it was fire that awaited her. She was brought before the Queen, who, with the face of a Nero all inflamed with rage, said to her; "Welcome, Madame Troccola (busybody)! So you are the fine piece of goods, the fine flower my husband is enjoying! You are the cursed bitch that makes my head go round! Now you have got into purgatory, and I will make you pay for all the harm you have done me!"

Talia began to excuse herself, saying it was not her fault and that the King had taken possession of her territory whilst she was sleeping. But the Queen would not listen to her, and commanded that a great fire should be lit in the courtyard of the palace and that Talia should be thrown into it.

The unfortunate Talia, seeing herself lost, threw herself on her knees before the Queen, and begged that at least she should be given time to take off the clothes she was wearing. The Queen, not out of pity for her, but because she wanted to save the clothes, which were embroidered with gold and pearls, said: "Undress — that I agree to."

Talia began to undress, and for each garment that she took off she uttered a shriek. She had taken off her dress, her skirt, and bodice and was about to take off her petticoat, and to utter her last cry, and they were just going to drag her away to reduce her to lye ashes, which they would throw into boiling water to wash Charon's breeches with, when the King saw the spectacle and rushed up to learn what was happening. He asked for his children, and heard from his wife, who reproached him for his betrayal of her, how she had made him eat them himself.

The King abandoned himself to despair. "What!" he cried, "am I the wolf of my own sheep?" Alas, why did my veins not recognise the fountain of their own blood? You renegade Turk, this barbarous deed is the work of your hands? Go, you shall get what you deserve; there will be no need to send such a tyrant-faced one to the Colosseum to do penance!"

So saying, he ordered that the Queen should be thrown into the fire lighted for Talia, and that the secretary should be thrown in, too, for he had been her handle in this cruel game and the weaver of this wicked web. He would have had the same done to the cook who, as he thought, had cut up his children; but the cook threw himself at the King's feet, saying: "Indeed, my lord, for such a service there should be no other reward than a burning furnace; no pension but a spike-thrust from behind; no entertainment but that of being twisted and shrivelled in the fire; neither could there be any greater honour than for me, a cook, to have my ashes mingle with those of a queen. But this is not the thanks I expect for having saved your children from that spiteful dog who wished to kill them and return to your body what came from it."

The King was beside himself when he heard these words; it seemed to him as if he must be dreaming and that he could not believe his ears. Turning to the cook, he said: "If it is true that you have saved my children, you may be sure I will not leave you turning spits in the kitchen. You shall be in the kitchen of my heart, turning my will just as you please, and you shall have such rewards that you will account yourself the luckiest man in the world."

Whilst the King was speaking, the cook's wife, seeing her husband's difficulties, brought Sun and Moon up to their father, who, playing at the game of three with his wife and children, made a ring of kisses, kissing first one and then the other. He gave a handsome reward to the cook and made him Gentleman of the Bedchamber. Talia became his wife, and enjoyed a long life with her husband and children, finding it to be true that:

> *Lucky people, so tis said,*
> *Are blessed by Fortune whilst in bed.*

THE SLEEPING BEAUTY IN THE WOOD

Charles Perrault

ONCE upon a time there lived a king and queen who were grieved, more grieved than words can tell, because they had no children. They tried the waters of every country, made vows and pilgrimages, and did everything that could be done, but without result. At last, however, the queen found that her wishes were fulfilled, and in due course she gave birth to a daughter.

A grand christening was held, and all the fairies that could be found in the realm (they numbered seven in all) were invited to be godmothers to the little princess. This was done so that by means of the gifts which each in turn would bestow upon her (in accordance with the fairy custom of those days) the princess might be endowed with every imaginable perfection.

When the christening ceremony was over, all the company returned to the king's palace, where a great banquet was held in honour of the fairies. Places were laid for them in magnificent style, and before each was placed a solid gold casket containing a spoon, fork, and knife of fine gold, set with diamonds and rubies. But just as all were sitting down to table an aged fairy was seen to enter, whom no one had thought to invite—the reason being that for more than fifty years she had never quitted the tower in which she lived, and people had supposed her to be dead or bewitched.

By the king's orders a place was laid for her, but it was impossible to give her a golden casket like the others, for only seven had been made for the seven fairies. The old creature believed that she was intentionally slighted, and muttered threats between her teeth.

She was overheard by one of the young fairies, who was seated near by. The latter, guessing that some mischievous gift might be bestowed upon the little princess, hid behind the tapestry as soon as the company left the table. Her intention was to be the last to speak, and so to have the power of counteracting, as far as possible, any evil which the old fairy might do.

Presently the fairies began to bestow their gifts upon the princess. The youngest ordained that she should be the most beautiful person in the world; the next, that she should have the temper of an angel; the third, that she should do everything with wonderful grace; the fourth, that she should dance to perfection; the fifth, that she should sing like a nightingale; and the sixth, that she should play every kind of music with the utmost skill.

It was now the turn of the aged fairy. Shaking her head, in token of spite rather than of infirmity, she declared that the princess should prick her hand with a spindle, and die of it. A shudder ran through the company at this terrible gift. All eyes were filled with tears.

But at this moment the young fairy stepped forth from behind the tapestry.

"Take comfort your Majesties," she cried in a loud voice; "your daughter shall not die. My power, it is true, is not enough to undo all that my aged kinswoman has decreed: the princess will indeed prick her hand with a spindle. But instead of dying she shall merely fall into a profound slumber that will last a hundred years. At the end of that time a king's son shall come to awaken her."

The king, in an attempt to avert the unhappy doom pronounced by the old fairy, at once published an edict forbidding all persons, under pain of death, to use a spinning-wheel or keep a spindle in the house.

At the end of the fifteen or sixteen years the king and queen happened one day to be away, on pleasure bent. The princess was running about the castle, and going upstairs from room to room she came at length to a garret at the top of a tower, where an old serving-woman sat alone with her distaff, spinning. This good woman had never heard speak of the king's proclamation forbidding the use of spinning-wheels.

"What are you doing, my good woman?" asked the princess.

"I am spinning, my pretty child," replied the dame, not knowing who she was.

"Oh, what fun!" rejoined the princess; "how do you do it? Let me try and see if I can do it equally well."

Partly because she was too hasty, partly because she was a little heedless, but also because the fairy decree had ordained it, no sooner had she seized the spindle than she pricked her hand and fell down in a swoon.

In great alarm the good dame cried out for help. People came

26

running from every quarter to the princess. They threw water on her face, chafed her with their hands, and rubbed her temples with the royal essence of Hungary. But nothing would restore her.

Then the king, who had been brought upstairs by the commotion, remembered the fairy prophecy. Feeling certain that what had happened was inevitable, since the fairies had decreed it, he gave orders that the princess should be placed in the finest apartment in the palace, upon a bed embroidered in gold and silver.

You would have thought her an angel, so fair was she to behold. The trance had not taken away the lovely colour of her complexion. Her cheeks were delicately flushed, her lips like coral. Her eyes, indeed, were closed, but her gentle breathing could be heard, and it was therefore plain that she was not dead. The king commanded that she should be left to sleep in peace until the hour of her awakening should come.

When the accident happened to the princess, the good fairy who had saved her life by condemning her to sleep a hundred years was in the kingdom of Mataquin, twelve thousand leagues away. She was instantly warned of it, however, by a little dwarf who had a pair of seven-league boots, which are boots that enable one to cover seven leagues at a single step. The fairy set off at once, and within an hour her chariot of fire, drawn by dragons, was seen approaching.

The king handed her down from her chariot, and she approved of all that he had done. But being gifted with great powers of foresight, she bethought herself that when the princess came to be awakened, she would be much distressed to find herself all alone in the old castle. And this is what she did.

She touched with her wand everybody (except the king and queen) who was in the castle — governesses, maids of honour, ladies-in-waiting, gentlemen, officers, stewards, cooks, scullions, errand boys, guards, porters, pages, footmen. She touched likewise all the horses in the stables, with their grooms, the big mastiffs in the courtyard, and little Puff, the pet dog of the princess, who was lying on the bed beside his mistress. The moment she had touched them they all fell asleep, to awaken only at the same moment as their mistress. Thus they would always be ready with their service whenever she should require it. The very spits before the fire, loaded with partridges and pheasants, subsided into slumber, and the fire as well. All was done in a moment, for the fairies do not take long over their work.

Then the king and queen kissed their dear child, without waking her, and left the castle. Proclamations were issued, forbidding any approach to it, but these warnings were not needed, for within a quarter of an hour there grew up all round the park so vast a quantity of trees big and small, with interlacing brambles and thorns, that neither man nor beast could penetrate them. The tops alone of the castle towers could be seen, and these only from a distance. Thus did the fairy's magic contrive that the princess, during all the time of her slumber, should have nought whatever to fear from prying eyes.

At the end of a hundred years the throne had passed to another family from that of the sleeping princess. One day the king's son chanced to go a-hunting that way, and seeing in the distance some towers in the midst of a large and dense forest, he asked what they were. His attendants told him in reply the various stories which they had heard. Some said there was an old castle haunted by ghosts, others that all the witches of the neighbourhood held their revels there. The favourite tale was that in the castle lived an ogre, who carried thither all the children whom he could catch. There he devoured them at his leisure, and since he was the only person who could force a passage through the wood nobody had been able to pursue him.

While the prince was wondering what to believe, an old peasant took up the tale.

"Your Highness," said he, "more than fifty years ago I heard my father say that in this castle lies a princess, the most beautiful that has ever been seen. It is her doom to sleep there for a hundred years, and then to be awakened by a king's son, for whose coming she waits."

This story fired the young prince. He jumped immediately to the conclusion that it was for him to see so gay an adventure through, and impelled alike by the wish for love and glory, he resolved to set about it on the spot.

Hardly had he taken a step towards the wood when the tall trees, the brambles and the thorns, separated of themselves and made a path for him. He turned in the direction of the castle, and espied it at the end of a long avenue. This avenue he entered, and was surprised to notice that the trees closed up again as soon as he had passed, so that none of his retinue was able to follow him. A young and gallant prince is always brave, however; so he continued on his way, and presently reached a large fore-court.

The sight that now met his gaze was enough to fill him with an icy fear. The silence of the place was dreadful, and death seemed all about him. The recumbent figures of men and animals had all the appearance of being lifeless, until he perceived by the pimply noses and ruddy faces of the porters that they merely slept. It was plain, too, from their glasses, in which were still some dregs of wine, that they had fallen asleep while drinking.

The prince made his way into a great courtyard, paved with marble, and mounting the staircase entered the guardroom. Here the guards were lined up on either side in two ranks, their muskets on their shoulders, snoring their hardest. Through several apartments crowded with ladies- and gentlemen-in-waiting, some seated, some standing, but all asleep, he pushed on. and so came at last to a chamber which was decked all over with gold. There he encountered the most beautiful sight he had ever seen. Reclining upon a bed, the curtains of which on every side were drawn back, was a princess of seemingly some fifteen or sixteen summers, whose radiant beauty had an almost unearthly lustre.

Trembling in his admiration he drew near and went on his knees beside her. At the same moment, the hour of disenchantment having come, the princess awoke, and bestowed upon him a look more tender than a first glance might seem to warrant.

"Is it you, dear prince?" she said; "you have been long in coming!"

Charmed by these words, and especially by the manner in which they were said, the prince scarcely knew how to express his delight and gratification. He declared that he loved her better than he loved himself. His words were faltering, but they pleased the more for that. The less there is of eloquence, the more there is of love.

Her embarrassment was less than his, and that is not to be wondered at, since she had had time to think of what she would say to him. It seems (although the story says nothing about it) that the good fairy had beguiled her long slumber with pleasant dreams.

To be brief, after four hours of talking they had not succeeded in uttering one half of the things they had to say to each other.

Now the whole palace had awakened with the princess. Every one went about his business, and since they were not all in love they presently began to feel mortally hungry. The lady-in-waiting, who was suffering like the rest, at length lost patience, and in a loud voice called out to the princess that supper was served.

The princess was already fully dressed, and in most magnificent style. As he helped her to rise, the prince refrained from telling her that her clothes, with the straight collar which she wore, were like those to which his grandmother had been accustomed. And in truth, they in no way detracted from her beauty.

They passed into an apartment hung with mirrors, and were there served with supper by the stewards of the household, while the fiddles and oboes played some old music—and played it remarkably well, considering they had not played at all for just upon a hundred years. A little later, when supper was over, the chaplain married them in the castle chapel, and in due course, attended by the courtiers in waiting, they retired to rest.

They slept but little, however. The princess, indeed, had not much need of sleep, and as soon as morning came the prince took his leave of her. He returned to the city, and told his father, who was awaiting him with some anxiety, that he had lost himself while hunting in the forest, but had obtained some black bread and cheese from a charcoal-burner, in whose hovel he had passed the night. His royal father, being of an easy-going nature, believed the tale, but his mother was not so easily hoodwinked. She noticed that he now went hunting every day, and that he always had an excuse handy when he had slept two or three nights from home. She felt certain, therefore, that he had some love affair.

Two whole years passed since the marriage of the prince and princess, and during that time they had two children. The first, a daughter, was called "Dawn," while the second, a boy, was named "Day," because he seemed even more beautiful than his sister.

Many a time the queen told her son that he ought to settle down in life. She tried in this way to make him confide in her, but he did not dare to trust her with his secret. Despite the affection which he bore her, he was afraid of his mother, for she came of a race of ogres, and the king had only married her for her wealth.

It was whispered at the Court that she had ogrish instincts, and that when little children were near her she had the greatest difficulty in the world to keep herself from pouncing on them.

No wonder the prince was reluctant to say a word.

But at the end of two years the king died, and the prince found himself on the throne. He then made public announcement of his marriage, and went in state to fetch his royal consort from her castle. With her two children beside her she made a triumphal entry into the capital of her husband's realm.

Some time afterwards the king declared war on his neighbour, the Emperor Cantalabutte. He appointed the queen-mother as regent in his absence, and entrusted his wife and children to her care.

He expected to be away at the war for the whole of the summer, and as soon as he was gone the queen-mother sent her daughter-in-law and the two children to a country mansion in the forest. This she did that she might be able the more easily to gratify her horrible longings. A few days later she went there herself, and in the evening summoned the chief steward.

"For my dinner to-morrow," she told him, "I will eat little Dawn."

"Oh, Madam!" exclaimed the steward.

"That is my will," said the queen; and she spoke in the tones of an ogre who longs for raw meat.

"You will serve her with piquant sauce," she added.

The poor man, seeing plainly that it was useless to trifle with an ogress, took his big knife and went up to little Dawn's chamber. She was at that time four years old, and when she came running with a smile to greet him, flinging her arms round his neck and coaxing him to give her some sweets, he burst into tears, and let the knife fall from his hand.

Presently he went down to the yard behind the house, and slaughtered a young lamb. For this he made so delicious a sauce that his mistress declared she had never eaten anything so good.

At the same time the steward carried little Dawn to his wife, and bade the latter hide her in the quarters which they had below the yard.

Eight days later the wicked queen summoned her steward again.

"For my supper," she announced, "I will eat little Day."

The steward made no answer, being determined to trick her as he had done previously. He went in search of little Day, whom he found with a tiny foil in his hand, making brave passes—though he was but three years old—at a big monkey. He carried him off to his wife, who stowed him away in hiding with little Dawn. To the ogress the steward served up, in place of Day, a young kid so tender that she found it surprisingly delicious.

So far, so good. But there came an evening when this evil queen again addressed the steward.

"I have a mind," she said, "to eat the queen with the same sauce as you served with her children."

This time the poor steward despaired of being able to practice another deception. The young queen was twenty years old, without counting the hundred years she had been asleep. Her skin, though white and beautiful, had become a little tough, and what animal could he possibly find that would correspond to her? He made up his mind that if he would save his own life he must kill the queen, and went upstairs to her apartment determined to do the deed once and for all. Goading himself into a rage he drew his knife and entered the young queen's chamber, but a reluctance to give her no moment of grace made him repeat respectfully the command which he had received from the queen-mother.

"Do it! do it!" she cried, baring her neck to him; "carry out the order you have been given! Then once more I shall see my children, my poor children that I loved so much!"

Nothing had been said to her when the children were stolen away, and she believed them to be dead.

The poor steward was overcome by compassion. "No, no, Madam," he declared; "you shall not die, but you shall certainly see your children again. That will be in my quarters, where I have hidden them. I shall make the queen eat a young hind in place of you, and thus trick her once more."

Without more ado he led her to his quarters, and leaving her there to embrace and weep over her children, proceeded to cook a hind with such art that the queen-mother ate it for her supper with as much appetite as if it had indeed been the young queen.

The queen-mother felt well satisfied with her cruel deeds, and planned to tell the king, on his return, that savage wolves had devoured his consort and his children. It was her habit, however, to prowl often about the courts and alleys of the mansion, in the hope of scenting raw meat, and one evening she heard the little boy Day crying in a basement cellar. The child was weeping because his mother had threatened to whip him for some naughtiness, and she heard at the same time the voice of Dawn begging forgiveness for her brother.

The ogress recognised the voices of the queen and her children, and was enraged to find she had been tricked. The next morning, in tones so affrighting that all trembled, she ordered a huge vat to be brought into the middle of the courtyard. This she filled with vipers and toads, with snakes and serpents of every kind, intending to cast into it the queen and her children, and the steward and his wife and serving-girl. By her command these were brought forward, with their hands tied behind their backs.

There they were, and her minions were making ready to cast them into the vat, when into the courtyard rode the king! Nobody had expected him so soon, but he had travelled post-haste. Filled with amazement, he demanded to know what this horrible spectacle meant. None dared tell him, and at that moment the ogress, enraged at what confronted her, threw herself head foremost into the vat, and was devoured on the instant by the hideous creatures she had placed in it.

The king could not but be sorry, for after all she was his mother; but it was not long before he found ample consolation in his beautiful wife and children.

Moral

To wait a bit in choosing a husband
Rich, courteous, genteel and kind;
That is understandable enough.
But to wait a hundred years, and all the time asleep,
Not many maidens would be found with such patience.
This story, however, seems to prove
That marriage bonds,
Even though they be delayed, are none the less blissful,
And that one loses nothing by waiting.
But maidens yearn for the wedding joys

With so much ardour
That I have neither strength nor the heart
To preach this moral to them.

BRIER ROSE

Jacob and Wilhelm Grimm

LONG, long ago there lived a king and a queen, who said day after day: "Ah, if only we had a child!" but none ever came. Then one day when the queen was sitting in her bath a frog crawled out of the water and said to her: "You will get your wish; before a year goes by, you will bring a daughter into the world." The frog's prediction came true. The queen gave birth to a baby girl who was so beautiful that the king couldn't get over his joy and decided to give a great feast. He invited not only his relatives, friends, and acquaintances, but also the Wise Women, for he wanted them to feel friendly toward his child. There were thirteen Wise Women in his kingdom, but he only had twelve golden plates for them to eat from, so one of them had to stay home. The feast was celebrated in great splendour and when it was over the Wise Women gave the child their magic gifts; one gave virtue, the second beauty, the third wealth, and so on, until they had given everything a person could wish for in this world. When the eleventh had spoken, the thirteenth suddenly stepped in. She had come to avenge herself for not having been invited, and without a word of greeting, without so much as looking at anyone, she cried out in a loud voice: "When she is fifteen, the princess will prick her finger on a spinning wheel and fall down dead." Then without another word she turned around and left the hall. Everyone was horror-stricken. But the twelfth Wise Woman, who still had her wish to make, stepped forward, and since she couldn't undo the evil spell but only soften it, she said: "The princess will not die, but only fall into a deep hundred-year sleep."

The king, who wanted to guard his beloved child against such a calamity, sent out an order that every spindle in the whole kingdom should be destroyed. All the Wise Women's wishes for the child came true: she grew to be so beautiful, so modest, so sweet-tempered and wise that no one who saw her could help loving her. The day she turned fifteen the king and the queen happened to be away from home and she was left alone. She went all over the castle, examining room after room, and finally she came to an old tower. She climbed a narrow winding staircase, which led to a little door with a rusty key in the lock. She turned the key, the door sprang open, and there in a small room sat an old woman with a spindle, busily spinning her flax. "Good day, old woman," said the princess. "What are you doing?" "I'm spinning," said the old woman, nodding her head. "And what's the thing that twirls around so gaily?" the princess asked. With that she took hold of the spindle and tried to spin, but no sooner had she touched it than the magic spell took effect and she pricked her finger.

The moment she felt the prick she fell down on the bed that was in the room and a deep sleep came over her. And her sleep spread to the entire palace. The king and queen had just come home, and when they entered the great hall they fell asleep and the whole court with them. The horses fell asleep in the stables, the dogs in the courtyard, the pigeons on the roof, and the flies on the wall. Even the fire on the hearth stopped flaming and fell asleep, and the roast stopped crackling, and the cook, who was about to pull the kitchen boy's hair because he had done something wrong, let go and fell asleep. And the wind died down, and not a leaf stirred on the trees outside the castle.

All around the castle a brier hedge began to grow. Each year it grew higher until in the end it surrounded and covered the whole castle and there was no trace of a castle to be seen, not even the flag on the roof. The story of Brier Rose, as people called the beautiful sleeping princess, came to be told far and wide, and from time to time a prince tried to pass through the hedge into the castle. But none succeeded, for the brier bushes clung together as though they had hands, so the young men were caught and couldn't break loose and died a pitiful death. After many years another prince came to the country and heard an old man telling about the brier hedge that was said to conceal a castle, where a beautiful princess named Brier Rose had been sleeping for a hundred years, along with the king and the queen and their whole court. The old man had also heard from his grandfather that a number of princes had tried to pass through the brier hedge and had got caught in it and died a pitiful death. Then the young man said: "I'm not afraid. I will go and see the beautiful Brier Rose." The good man did his best to dissuade him, but the prince wouldn't listen.

It so happened that the hundred years had passed and the day had come for Brier Rose to wake up. As the king's son approached the brier hedge, the briers turned into big beautiful flowers, which opened of their own accord and let him through, then closed behind him to form a hedge again. In the courtyard he saw the horses and mottled hounds lying asleep, and on the roof pigeons were roosting with their heads under their wings. When he went into the castle, the flies were asleep on the wall, the cook in the kitchen was still holding out his hand as though to grab the kitchen boy, and the maid was sitting at the table with a black hen in front of her that needed plucking. Going farther, he saw the whole court asleep in the great hall, and on the dais beside the throne lay the king and the queen. On he went, and everything was so still that he could hear himself breathe. At last he came to the tower and opened the door to the little room where Brier Rose was sleeping. There she lay, so beautiful that he couldn't stop looking at her, and he bent down and kissed her. No sooner had his lips touched hers than Brier Rose opened her eyes, woke up, and smiled sweetly. They went downstairs together, and then the king and the queen and the whole court woke up, and they all looked at each other in amazement. The horses in the courtyard stood up and shook themselves; the hounds jumped to their feet and wagged their tails; the pigeons on the roof took their heads from under their wings, looked around and flew off into the fields; the flies on the wall started crawling, the fire in the kitchen flamed up and cooked the meal; the roast began to crackle again, the cook boxed the kitchen boy's ear so hard that he howled, and the maid plucked the chicken. The prince and Brier Rose were married in splendour, and they lived happily to the end of their lives.

CINDERELLA: DON'T JUDGE A BOOK BY ITS COVER

WE conclude the comparative sections with a consideration of three versions of "Cinderella" which, with "Little Red Riding Hood" and "Sleeping Beauty," might be described as the core of the Western fairy-tale canon. As with the two previous tales, the abiding popularity of "Cinderella" raises the inevitable question: what is the explanation behind such success?

Part of the answer lies in the popular phrase: "hers (or his!) is a real Cinderella story." It signifies that the individual has risen from obscurity and oppression to success and celebrity, perhaps with the implication that the good fortune is well-deserved. There can be little doubt that the attraction of this tale has a lot to do with its theme of virtue revealed and rewarded: it invites us to recall times when we felt ourselves unappreciated and rejected and to share Cinderella's satisfaction at being discovered as a true princess. (As we shall see later on, Hans Andersen taps into much the same feeling in "The Ugly Duckling.")

At this point, we should not be surprised to discover that Perrault's Cinderella is a rather passive young lady, no stranger to self-denial; she goes out of her way to assist her obnoxious stepsisters in preparing for the ball while denying that she has any right to such pleasures ("It would be no place for me..."). On their departure, Cinderella collapses in tears, provoking the appearance of a fairy-tale *deus ex machina* in the shape of her fairy godmother, who provides her with all the accoutrements necessary for an impressive entry into high society.

The Grimms' Ashputtle responds to the situation rather differently. Instead of playing the helpless martyr, she makes it clear to her stepmother that she too wishes to go to the ball and is prepared to do whatever is necessary to get there. As a rule, Nature plays a more significant role in the Grimms' tales than in those of Perrault, and that is the case here. Ashputtle's virtue is rewarded by the assistance of the natural world, manifested both in the embodied spirit of her dead mother and in the birds who complete the impossible tasks that she is set by her stepmother. The natural world is also responsible for identifying and punishing vice, observable when the stepsisters attempt to trick the prince into marriage.

Speaking of the prince, it is worth noting that, in both "Cinderella" and "Ashputtle," his role is less than heroic. In the former, he sends a servant to find the owner of the glass slipper, while in the latter, he is so out of touch with his surroundings (and hence with his feelings?) that he is fooled not once but twice by the stepsisters; it takes the intervention of the two doves to draw his attention to their bleeding feet. Thus far, we have found little enough reason to be impressed by the courage and maturity of the fairy-tale prince.

If Ashputtle is a more assertive heroine than her predecessor, then Cap o' Rushes eclipses the pair of them. Jacobs' tale contains some obvious differences from the other two, the most immediately apparent being the absence of a wicked stepmother and stepsisters. The opening episode bears a striking resemblance, of course, to the scene in Shakespeare's *King Lear* in which the king's youngest daughter, Cordelia, offers as honest and plain an answer to her father as Cap o' Rushes — with the same consequence. The point here, however, is that in Cap o' Rushes we have a resourceful, determined heroine who reacts to her rejection by creating a plan and following it through to a successful conclusion that not only brings her a husband but also reconciles her to her father. Although less well-known, this tale is a significant variant of the Cinderella story, which can also be found in many collections, including those of the Grimm Brothers ("All-Fur") and Charles Perrault ("Donkeyskin").

CINDERELLA

Charles Perrault

Once upon a time there was a worthy man who married for his second wife the haughtiest, proudest woman that had ever been seen. She had two daughters, who possessed their mother's temper and resembled her in everything. Her husband, on the other hand, had a young daughter, who was of an exceptionally sweet and gentle nature. She got this from her mother, who had been the nicest person in the world.

The wedding was no sooner over than the stepmother began to display her bad temper. She could not endure the excellent qualities of this young girl, for they made her own daughters appear more hateful than ever. She thrust upon her all the meanest tasks about the house. It was she who had to clean the plates and the stairs, and sweep out the rooms of the mistress of the house and her daughters. She slept on a wretched mattress in a garret at the top of the house, while the sisters had rooms with parquet flooring, and beds of the most fashionable style, with mirrors in which they could see themselves from top to toe.

The poor girl endured everything patiently, not daring to complain to her father. The latter would have scolded her, because he was entirely ruled by his wife. When she had finished her work she used to sit amongst the cinders in the corner of the chimney, and it was from this habit that she came to be commonly known as Cinder-clod. The younger of the two sisters, who was not quite so spiteful as the elder, called her Cinderella. But her wretched clothes did not prevent Cinderella from being a hundred times more beautiful than her sisters, for all their resplendent garments.

It happened that the king's son gave a ball, and he invited all persons of high degree. The two young ladies were invited amongst others, for they cut a considerable figure in the country. Not a little pleased were they, and the question of what clothes and what mode of dressing the hair would become them best took up all their time. And all this meant fresh trouble for Cinderella, for it was she who went over her sisters' linen and ironed their ruffles. They could talk of nothing else but the fashions in clothes.

"For my part," said the elder, "I shall wear my dress of red velvet, with the Honiton lace."

"I have only my everyday petticoat," said the younger, "but to make up for it I shall wear my cloak with the golden flowers and my necklace of diamonds, which are not so bad."

They sent for a good hairdresser to arrange their doublefrilled caps, and bought patches at the best shop.

They summoned Cinderella and asked her advice, for she had good taste. Cinderella gave them the best possible suggestions, and even offered to dress their hair, to which they gladly agreed.

While she was thus occupied they said:

"Cinderella, would you not like to go to the ball?"

"Ah, but you fine young ladies are laughing at me. It would be no place for me."

"That is very true, people would laugh to see a cinder-clod in the ballroom."

Any one else but Cinderella would have done their hair amiss, but she was good-natured, and she finished them off to perfection. They were so excited in their glee that for nearly two days they ate nothing. They broke more than a dozen laces through drawing their stays tight in order to make their waists more slender, and they were perpetually in front of a mirror.

At last the happy day arrived. Away they went, Cinderella watching them as long as she could keep them in sight. When she could no longer see them she began to cry. Her godmother found her in tears, and asked what was troubling her.

"I should like — I should like ——"

She was crying so bitterly that she could not finish the sentence.

Said her godmother, who was a fairy:

"You would like to go to the ball, would you not?"

"Ah, yes," said Cinderella, sighing.

"Well, well," said her godmother, "promise to be a good girl and I will arrange for you to go."

She took Cinderella into her room and said:

"Go into the garden and bring me a pumpkin."

Cinderella went at once and gathered the finest that she could find. This she brought to her godmother, wondering how a pumpkin could help in taking her to the ball.

40

Her godmother scooped it out, and when only the rind was left, struck it with her wand. Instantly the pumpkin was changed into a beautiful coach, gilded all over.

Then she went and looked in the mouse-trap, where she found six mice all alive. She told Cinderella to lift the door of the mouse-trap a little, and as each mouse came out she gave it a tap with her wand, whereupon it was transformed into a fine horse. So that here was a fine team of six dappled mouse-grey horses.

But she was puzzled to know how to provide a coachman.

"I will go and see," said Cinderella, "if there is not a rat in the rat-trap. We could make a coachman of him."

"Quite right," said her godmother, "go and see."

Cinderella brought in the rat-trap, which contained three big rats. The fairy chose one specially on account of his elegant whiskers.

As soon as she had touched him he turned into a fat coachman with the finest moustachios that ever were seen.

"Now go into the garden and bring me the six lizards which you will find behind the water-butt."

No sooner had they been brought than the godmother turned them into six lackeys, who at once climbed up behind the coach in their braided liveries, and hung on there as if they had never done anything else all their lives.

Then said the fairy godmother:

"Well, there you have the means of going to the ball. Are you satisfied?" *Now has the means,*

"Oh, yes, but am I to go like this in my ugly clothes?"

Her godmother merely touched her with her wand, and on the instant her clothes were changed into garments of gold and silver cloth, bedecked with jewels. After that her godmother gave her a pair of glass slippers, the prettiest in the world.

Thus altered, she entered the coach. Her godmother bade her not to stay beyond midnight whatever happened, warning her that *Test 2.* if she remained at the ball a moment longer, her coach would again become a pumpkin, her horses mice, and her lackeys lizards, while her old clothes would reappear upon her once more.

She promised her godmother that she would not fail to leave the ball before midnight, and away she went, beside herself with delight.

The king's son, when he was told of the arrival of a great princess whom nobody knew, went forth to receive her. He handed her down from the coach, and led her into the hall where the company was assembled. At once there fell a great silence. The dancers stopped, the violins played no more, so rapt was the attention which everybody bestowed upon the superb beauty of the unknown guest. Everywhere could be heard in confused whispers:

"Oh, how beautiful she is!"

The king, old man as he was, could not take his eyes off her, and whispered to the queen that it was many a long day since he had seen any one so beautiful and charming.

All the ladies were eager to scrutinise her clothes and the dressing of her hair, being determined to copy them on the morrow, provided they could find materials so fine, and tailors so clever.

The king's son placed her in the seat of honour, and at once begged the privilege of being her partner in a dance. Such was the grace with which she danced that the admiration of all was increased.

A magnificent supper was served, but the young prince could eat nothing, so taken up was he with watching her. She went and sat beside her sisters, and bestowed numberless attentions upon them. She made them share with her the oranges and lemons which the king had given her — greatly to their astonishment, for they did not recognise her.

While they were talking, Cinderella heard the clock strike a quarter to twelve. She at once made a profound curtsey to the company, and departed as quickly as she could.

As soon as she was home again she sought out her godmother, and having thanked her, declared that she wished to go upon the morrow once more to the ball, because the king's son had invited her.

While she was busy telling her godmother all that had happened at the ball, her two sisters knocked at the door. Cinderella let them in.

"What a long time you have been in coming!" she declared, rubbing her eyes and stretching herself as if she had only just awakened. In real truth she had not for a moment wished to sleep since they had left.

"If you had been at the ball," said one of the sisters, "you would not be feeling weary. There came a most beautiful princess, the most beautiful that has ever been seen, and she bestowed numberless attentions upon us, and gave us her oranges and lemons." —→

kind + beautiful

Cinderella was overjoyed. She asked them the name of the princess, but they replied that no one knew it, and that the king's son was so distressed that he would give anything in the world to know who she was.

Cinderella smiled, and said she must have been beautiful indeed.

"Oh, how lucky you are. Could I not manage to see her? Oh, please, Javotte, lend me the yellow dress which you wear every day."

"Indeed!" said Javotte, "that is a fine idea. Lend my dress to a grubby cinder-clod like you — you must think me mad!"

sisters cruel

Cinderella had expected this refusal. She was in no way upset, for she would have been very greatly embarrassed had her sister been willing to lend the dress.

The next day the two sisters went to the ball, and so did Cinderella, even more splendidly attired than the first time.

The king's son was always at her elbow, and paid her endless compliments.

The young girl enjoyed herself so much that she forgot her godmother's bidding completely, and when the first stroke of midnight fell upon her ears, she thought it was no more than eleven o'clock.

She rose and fled as nimbly as a fawn. The prince followed her, but could not catch her. She let fall one of her glass slippers, however, and this the prince picked up with tender care.

she did it on purpose.

When Cinderella reached home she was out of breath, without coach, without lackeys, and in her shabby clothes. Nothing remained of all her splendid clothes save one of the little slippers, the fellow to the one which she had let fall.

Inquiries were made of the palace doorkeepers as to whether they had seen a princess go out, but they declared they had seen no one leave except a young girl, very ill-clad, who looked more like a peasant than a young lady.

When her two sisters returned from the ball, Cinderella asked them if they had again enjoyed themselves, and if the beautiful lady had been there. They told her that she was present, but had fled away when midnight sounded, and in such haste that she had let fall one of her little glass slippers, the prettiest thing in the world. They added that the king's son, who picked it up, had done nothing but gaze at it for the rest of the ball, from which it was plain that he was deeply in love with its beautiful owner.

They spoke the truth. A few days later, the king's son caused a proclamation to be made by trumpeters, that he would take for wife the owner of the foot which the slipper would fit.

They tried it first on the princesses, then on the duchesses and the whole of the Court, but in vain. Presently they brought it to the home of the two sisters, who did all they could to squeeze a foot into the slipper. This, however, they could not manage.

Cinderella was looking on and recognised her slipper:

"Let me see," she cried, laughingly, "if it will not fit me."

Her sisters burst out laughing, and began to gibe at her, but the equerry who was trying on the slipper looked closely at Cinderella. Observing that she was very beautiful he declared that the claim was quite a fair one, and that his orders were to try the slipper on every maiden. He bade Cinderella sit down, and on putting the slipper to her little foot he perceived that the latter slid in without trouble, and was moulded to its shape like wax.

Great was the astonishment of the two sisters at this, and greater still when Cinderella drew from her pocket the other little slipper. This she likewise drew on.

At that very moment her godmother appeared on the scene. She gave a tap with her wand to Cinderella's clothes, and transformed them into a dress even more magnificent than her previous ones.

The two sisters recognised her for the beautiful person whom they had seen at the ball, and threw themselves at her feet, begging her pardon for all the ill-treatment she had suffered at their hands.

Cinderella raised them, and declaring as she embraced them that she pardoned them with all her heart, bade them to love her well in future.

She was taken to the palace of the young prince in all her new array. He found her more beautiful than ever, and was married to her a few days afterwards.

Cinderella was as good as she was beautiful. She set aside apart-

44

ments in the palace for her two sisters, and married them the very same day to two gentlemen of high rank about the Court.

Moral

Beauty in a maid is an extraordinary treasure;
One never tires of admiring it.
But what we mean by graciousness
Is beyond price and still more precious.
It was this which her godmother gave Cinderella,
Teaching her to become a Queen.
(So the moral of this story goes.)
Lasses, this is a better gift than looks so fair
For winning over a heart successfully.
Graciousness is the true gift of the Fairies.
Without it, one can do nothing;
With it, one can do all!

Another Moral

It is surely a great advantage
To have spirit and courage,
Good breeding and common sense,
And other qualities of this sort,
Which are the gifts of Heaven!
You will do well to own these;
But for success, they may well be in vain
If, as a final gift, one has not
The blessing of godfather or godmother.

ASHPUTTLE

Jacob and Wilhelm Grimm

A RICH man's wife fell sick and, feeling that her end was near, she called her only daughter to her bedside and said: "Dear child, be good and say your prayers; God will help you, and I shall look down on you from heaven and always be with you." With

45

that she closed her eyes and died. Every day the little girl went out to her mother's grave and wept, and she went on being good and saying her prayers. When winter came, the snow spread a white cloth over the grave, and when spring took it off, the man remarried.

His new wife brought two daughters into the house. Their faces were beautiful and lily-white, but their hearts were ugly and black. That was the beginning of a bad time for the poor stepchild. "Why should this silly goose sit in the parlour with us?" they said. "People who want to eat bread must earn it. Get into the kitchen where you belong!" They took away her fine clothes and gave her an old gray dress and wooden shoes to wear. "Look at the haughty princess in her finery!" they cried and, laughing, led her to the kitchen. From then on she had to do all the work, getting up before daybreak, carrying water, lighting fires, cooking and washing. In addition the sisters did everything they could to plague her. They jeered at her and poured peas and lentils into the ashes, so that she had to sit there picking them out. At night, when she was tired out with work, she had no bed to sleep in but had to lie in the ashes by the hearth. And they took to calling her Ashputtle because she always looked dusty and dirty.

One day when her father was going to the fair, he asked his two stepdaughters what he should bring them. "Beautiful dresses," said one. "Diamonds and pearls," said the other. "And you, Ashputtle. What would you like?" "Father," she said, "break off the first branch that brushes against your hat on your way home, and bring it to me." So he bought beautiful dresses, diamonds and pearls for his two stepdaughters, and on the way home, as he was riding through a copse, a hazel branch brushed against him and knocked off his hat. So he broke off the branch and took it home with him. When he got home, he gave the stepdaughters what they had asked for, and gave Ashputtle the branch. After thanking him, she went to her mother's grave and planted the hazel sprig over it and cried so hard that her tears fell on the sprig and watered it. It grew and became a beautiful tree. Three times a day Ashputtle went and sat under it and wept and prayed. Each time a little white bird came and perched on the tree, and when Ashputtle made a wish the little bird threw down what she had wished for.

Now it so happened that the king arranged for a celebration. It was to go on for three days and all the beautiful girls in the kingdom were invited, in order that his son might choose a bride. When the two stepsisters heard that they had been asked, they were delighted. They called Ashputtle and said: "Comb our hair, brush our shoes, and fasten our buckles. We're going to the wedding at the king's palace." Ashputtle obeyed, but she wept, for she too would have liked to go dancing, and she begged her stepmother to let her go. "You little sloven!" said the stepmother. "How can you go to a wedding when you're all dusty and dirty?" How can you go dancing when you have neither dress nor shoes?" But when Ashputtle begged and begged, the stepmother finally said: "Here, I've dumped a bowlful of lentils in the ashes. If you can pick them out in two hours, you may go." The girl went out the back door to the garden and cried out: "O tame little doves, O turtledoves, and all the birds under heaven, come and help me put

> the good ones in the pot
> the bad ones in your crop."

Two little white doves came flying through the kitchen window, and then came the turtledoves, and finally all the birds under heaven came flapping and fluttering and settled down by the ashes. The doves nodded their little heads and started in, peck peck peck peck, and all the others started in, peck peck peck peck, and they sorted out all the good lentils and put them in the bowl. Hardly an hour had passed before they finished and flew away. Then the girl brought the bowl to her stepmother, and she was happy, for she thought she'd be allowed to go to the wedding. But the stepmother said: "No, Ashputtle. You have nothing to wear and you don't know how to dance; the people would only laugh at you." When Ashputtle began to cry, the stepmother said: "If you can pick two bowlfuls of lentils out of the ashes in an hour, you may come." And she thought: "She'll never be able to do it." When she had dumped the two bowlfuls of lentils in the ashes, Ashputtle went out the back door to the garden and cried out: "O tame little doves, O turtledoves, and all the birds under heaven, come and help me put

the good ones in the pot
the bad ones in your crop."

Then two little white doves came flying through the kitchen window, and then came the turtledoves, and finally all the birds under
heaven came flapping and fluttering and settled down by the
ashes. The doves nodded their little heads and started in, peck
peck peck peck, and they sorted out all the good lentils and put
them in the bowls. Before half an hour had passed, they had
finished and they all flew away. Then the girl brought the bowls
to her stepmother, and she was happy, for she thought she'd be
allowed to go to the wedding. But her stepmother said. "It's no
use. You can't come, because you have nothing to wear and you
don't know how to dance. We'd only be ashamed of you." Then
she turned her back and hurried away with her two proud daughters.

When they had all gone out, Ashputtle went to her mother's
grave. She stood under the hazel tree and cried:

"Shake your branches, little tree,
Throw gold and silver down on me."

Whereupon the bird tossed down a gold and silver dress and slippers embroidered with silk and silver. Ashputtle slipped into the
dress as fast as she could and went to the wedding. Her sisters and
stepmother didn't recognize her. She was so beautiful in her gold-
en dress that they thought she must be the daughter of some foreign king. They never dreamed it could be Ashputtle, for they
thought she was sitting at home in her filthy rags, picking lentils
out of the ashes. The king's son came up to her, took her by the
hand and danced with her. He wouldn't dance with anyone else
and he never let go of her hand. When someone else asked for a
dance, he said: "She is my partner."

She danced until evening, and then she wanted to go home.
The king's son said: "I'll go with you, I'll see you home," for he
wanted to find out whom the beautiful girl belonged to. But she
got away from him and slipped into the dovecote. The king's son
waited until her father arrived, and told him the strange girl had
slipped into the dovecote. The old man thought: "Could it be

48

Ashputtle?" and he sent for an ax and a pick and broke into the dovecote, but there was no one inside. When they went indoors, Ashputtle was lying in the ashes in her filthy clothes and a dim oil lamp was burning on the chimney piece, for Ashputtle had slipped out the back end of the dovecote and run to the hazel tree. There she had taken off her fine clothes and put them on the grave, and the bird had taken them away. Then she had put her gray dress on again, crept into the kitchen and lain down in the ashes.

Next day when the festivities started in again and her parents and stepsisters had gone, Ashputtle went to the hazel tree and said:

> "Shake your branches, little tree,
> Throw gold and silver down on me."

Whereupon the bird threw down a dress that was even more dazzling than the first one. And when she appeared at the wedding, everyone marvelled at her beauty. The king's son was waiting for her. He took her by the hand and danced with no one but her. When others came and asked her for a dance, he said: "She is my partner." When evening came, she said she was going home. The king's son followed her, wishing to see which house she went into, but she ran away and disappeared into the garden behind the house, where there was a big beautiful tree with the most wonderful pears growing on it. She climbed among the branches as nimbly as a squirrel and the king's son didn't know what had become of her. He waited until her father arrived and said to him: "The strange girl has got away from me and I think she has climbed up in the pear tree." Her father thought: "Could it be Ashputtle?" He sent for an ax and chopped the tree down, but there was no one in it. When they went into the kitchen, Ashputtle was lying there in the ashes as usual, for she had jumped down on the other side of the tree, and put on her filthy gray dress.

On the third day, after her parents and sisters had gone, Ashputtle went back to her mother's grave and said to the tree:

> "Shake your branches, little tree,
> Throw gold and silver down on me."

Whereupon the bird threw down a dress that was more radiant

than either of the others, and the slippers were all gold. When she appeared at the wedding, the people were too amazed to speak. The king's son danced with no one but her, and when someone else asked her for a dance, he said: "She is my partner."

When evening came, Ashputtle wanted to go home, and the king's son said he'd go with her, but she slipped away so quickly that he couldn't follow. But he had thought up a trick. He had arranged to have the whole staircase brushed with pitch, and as she was running down it the pitch pulled her left slipper off. The king's son picked it up, and it was tiny and delicate and all gold. Next morning he went to the father and said: "No girl shall be my wife but the one this golden shoe fits." The sisters were overjoyed, for they had beautiful feet. The eldest took the shoe to her room to try it on and her mother went with her. But the shoe was too small and she couldn't get her big toe in. So her mother handed her a knife and said: "Cut your toe off. Once you're queen you won't have to walk any more." The girl cut her toe off, forced her foot into the shoe, gritted her teeth against the pain, and went out to the king's son. He accepted her as his bride-to-be, lifted her up on his horse, and rode away with her. But they had to pass the grave. The two doves were sitting in the hazel tree and they cried out:

> "Roocoo, roocoo,
> There's blood in the shoe.
> The foot's too long, the foot's too wide,
> That's not the proper bride."

He looked down at her foot and saw the blood spurting. At that he turned his horse around and took the false bride home again. "No," he said, "this isn't the right girl; let her sister try the shoe on." The sister went to her room and managed to get her toes into the shoe, but her heel was too big. So her mother handed her a knife and said: "Cut off a chunk of your heel. Once you're queen you won't have to walk any more." The girl cut off a chunk of her heel, forced her foot into the shoe, gritted her teeth against the pain, and went out to the king's son. He accepted her as his bride-to-be, lifted her up on his horse, and rode away with her. As they passed the hazel tree, the two doves were sitting there, and they cried out:

> "Roocoo, roocoo,
> There's blood in the shoe.
> The foot's too long, the foot's too wide,
> That's not the proper bride."

He looked down at her foot and saw that blood was spurting from her shoe and staining her white stocking all red. He turned his horse around and took the false bride home again. "This isn't the right girl, either," he said. "Haven't you got another daughter?" "No," said the man, "there's only a puny little kitchen drudge that my dead wife left me. She couldn't possibly be the bride." "Send her up," said the king's son, but the mother said: "Oh no, she's much too dirty to be seen." But he insisted and they had to call her. First she washed her face and hands, and when they were clean, she went upstairs and curtsied to the king's son. He handed her the golden slipper and sat down on a footstool, took her foot out of her heavy wooden shoe, and put it into the slipper. It fitted perfectly. And when she stood up and the king's son looked into her face, he recognized the beautiful girl he had danced with and cried out: "This is my true bride!" The stepmother and the two sisters went pale with fear and rage. But he lifted Ashputtle up on his horse and rode away with her. As they passed the hazel tree, the two white doves called out:

Identity Revealed.

> "Roocoo, roocoo,
> No blood in the shoe.
> Her foot is neither long nor wide,
> This one is the proper bride."

Then they flew down and alighted on Ashputtle's shoulders, one on the right and one on the left, and there they sat.

On the day of Ashputtle's wedding, the two stepsisters came and tried to ingratiate themselves and share in her happiness. On the way to church the elder was on the right side of the bridal couple and the younger on the left. The doves came along and pecked out one of the elder sister's eyes and one of the younger sister's eyes. Afterward, on the way out, the elder was on the left side and the younger on the right, and the doves pecked out both the remaining eyes. So both sisters were punished with blindness to the end of their days for being so wicked and false.

CAP O' RUSHES

Joseph Jacobs

WELL, there was once a very rich gentleman, and he'd three daughters, and he thought he'd see how fond they were of him. So he says to the first, "How much do you love me, my dear?"

"Why," says she, "as I love my life."

"That's good," says he.

So he says to the second, "How much do *you* love me, my dear?"

"Why," says she, "better nor all the world."

"That's good," says he.

So he says to the third, "How much do *you* love me, my dear?"

"Why, I love you as fresh meat loves salt," says she.

Well, but he was angry. "You don't love me at all," says he, "and in my house you stay no more." So he drove her out there and then, and shut the door in her face.

Well, she went away on and on till she came to a fen, and there she gathered a lot of rushes and made them into a kind of a sort of a cloak with a hood, to cover her from head to foot, and to hide her fine clothes. And then she went on and on till she came to a great house.

"Do you want a maid?" says she.

"No, we don't," said they.

"I haven't nowhere to go," says she; "and I ask no wages, and do any sort of work," says she.

"Well," said they, "if you like to wash the pots and scrape the saucepans you may stay," said they.

So she stayed there and washed the pots and scraped the saucepans and did all the dirty work. And because she gave no name they called her "Cap o' Rushes."

Well, one day there was to be a great dance a little way off, and the servants were allowed to go and look on at the grand people.

Cap o' Rushes said she was too tired to go, so she stayed at home.

But when they were gone she offed with her cap o' rushes, and cleaned herself, and went to the dance. And no one there was so finely dressed as she.

Well, who should be there but her master's son, and what should he do but fall in love with her the minute he set eyes on her. He wouldn't dance with any one else.

But before the dance was done Cap o' Rushes slipped off, and away she went home. And when the other maids came back she was pretending to be asleep with her cap o' rushes on.

Well, next morning they said to her, "You did miss a sight, Cap o' Rushes!"

"What was that?" says she.

"Why, the beautifullest lady you ever see, dressed right gay and ga'. The young master, he never took his eyes off her."

"Well, I should have liked to have seen her," says Cap o' Rushes.

"Well, there's to be another dance this evening, and perhaps she'll be there."

But, come the evening, Cap o' Rushes said she was too tired to go with them. Howsoever, when they were gone she offed with her cap o' rushes and cleaned herself, and away she went to the dance.

The master's son had been reckoning on seeing her, and he danced with no one else, and never took his eyes off her. But, before the dance was over, she slipt off, and home she went, and when the maids came back she pretended to be asleep with her cap o' rushes on.

Next day they said to her again, "Well, Cap o' Rushes, you should ha' been there to see the lady. There she was again, gay and ga', and the young master he never took his eyes off her."

"Well, there," says she, "I should ha' liked to ha' seen her."

"Well," says they, "there's a dance again this evening, and you must go with us, for she's sure to be there."

Well, come this evening, Cap o' Rushes said she was too tired to go, and do what they would she stayed at home. But when they were gone she offed with her cap o' rushes and cleaned herself, and away she went to the dance.

The master's son was rarely glad when he saw her. He danced

with none but her and never took his eyes off her. When she wouldn't tell him her name, nor where she came from, he gave her a ring and told her if he didn't see her again he should die.

Well, before the dance was over, off she slipped, and home she went, and when the maids came home she was pretending to be asleep with her cap o' rushes on.

Well, next day they says to her, "There, Cap o' Rushes, you didn't come last night, and now you won't see the lady, for there's no more dances."

"Well I should have rarely liked to have seen her," says she.

The master's son he tried every way to find out where the lady was gone, but go where he might, and ask whom he might, he never heard anything about her. And he got worse and worse for the love of her till he had to keep his bed.

"Make some gruel for the young master," they said to the cook. "He's dying for the love of the lady." The cook she set about making it when Cap o' Rushes came in.

"What are you a-doing of?" says she.

"I'm going to make some gruel for the young master," says the cook, "for he's dying for love of the lady."

"Let me make it," says Cap o' Rushes.

Well, the cook wouldn't at first, but at last she said yes, and Cap o' Rushes made the gruel. And when she had made it she slipped the ring into it on the sly before the cook took it upstairs.

The young man he drank it and then he saw the ring at the bottom.

"Send for the cook," says he.

So up she comes.

"Who made this gruel here?" says he.

"I did," says the cook, for she was frightened.

And he looked at her.

"No, you didn't," says he. "Say who did it, and you shan't be harmed."

"Well, then, 'twas Cap o' Rushes," says she.

"Send Cap o' Rushes here," says he.

So Cap o' Rushes came.

"Did you make my gruel?" says he.

"Yes, I did," says she.

"Where did you get this ring?" says he.

54

"From him that gave it me," says she.

"Who are you, then?" says the young man.

"I'll show you," says she. And she offed with her cap o' rushes, and there she was in her beautiful clothes.

Well, the master's son he got well very soon, and they were to be married in a little time. It was to be a very grand wedding, and every one was asked far and near. And Cap o' Rushes' father was asked. But she never told anybody who she was.

But before the wedding she went to the cook, and says she:

"I want you to dress every dish without a mite o' salt."

"That'll be rare nasty," says the cook.

"That doesn't signify," says she.

"Very well," says the cook.

Well, the wedding-day came, and they were married. And after they were married all the company sat down to the dinner. When they began to eat the meat, it was so tasteless they couldn't eat it. But Cap o' Rushes' father tried first one dish and then another, and then he burst out crying.

"What is the matter?" said the master's son to him.

"Oh!" says he, "I had a daughter. And I asked her how much she loved me. And she said 'As much as fresh meat loves salt.' And I turned her from my door, for I thought she didn't love me. And now I see she loved me best of all. And she may be dead for aught I know."

"No, father, here she is!" says Cap o' Rushes. And she goes up to him and puts her arms round him.

And so they were all happy ever after.

DAMSELS IN
DISTRESS

THIS section, along with several tales in the previous sections, suggests why much feminist criticism has been levelled at the folk-fairy tale. Each of the heroines exhibits varying degrees of passivity and must ultimately be rescued and then fulfilled by marriage. So why, we may ask, does this kind of tale so often focus on the girl? After all, marriage is an event that should involve male and female equally. The answer is that in our society as in many others, marriage has not been a celebration of equality. In some cultures, a bride may still be chosen for her husband on grounds that have little to do with her own preference, and it is not so very long ago that wifely obedience was dropped from the Christian marriage vows. The social inequality of the sexes runs as a central thread through tale after tale, although there is often an intriguing contrast between the conventional female role and the actual behavior of some heroines, as we shall see. However, given the social prejudices through which these stories have been filtered and the gender-roles that they reflect, this pattern should not surprise us too much: we were well into the second half of the twentieth century, in fact, before serious efforts were made (in the form of the feminist fairy tale) to redress the sexual stereotypes that are firmly entrenched in many traditional tales. Quite apart from the innate originality and inventiveness of the narratives themselves, the popular success of such tales as "Sleeping Beauty," "Cinderella," and "Snow White" may have been equally attributable to the preconceptions and values of nineteenth-century readers.

Looked at from another perspective, however, passivity often manifests itself as, or else brings about, a spiritual isolation—and that encounter with the self leads toward the maturity of adulthood. Thus Snow White finding her way in the forest, Rapunzel languishing in a lonely tower, and the princess in "The Goose Girl" discovering how it feels to be a serving-girl are all vital stages in the acquisition of self-knowledge.

Feminist criticism has not only directed our attention to the role of the young heroine, but also to other intriguing facets of the female presence in these tales. Contrasting the innocence and helplessness of the young heroine, for example, is the cunning and malice of a powerful older woman, a character who is all the more sinister because her villainy is often insidious and psychological in nature; she will readily resort to trickery and deceit to gain her ends. This is arguably the most obvious example of inter-generational conflict, which is one of the central issues in the folk-fairy tale, reflecting the fear of the older woman being superceded and made irrelevant by her younger rival.

The father-figure, by contrast, is either absent or plays a subservient role, and the younger male, the prince, benefits more often from good timing than from bravery; in none of these stories does he win his bride through the performance of heroic deeds. He is often as passive as she: the prince in "Snow White," having fallen in love with a beautiful but lifeless image, is provided with a wife literally by accident, while Rapunzel's prince (admittedly after enduring some maturity-enhancing misery in the forest) stumbles upon his wife in just as accidental a fashion.

Some different perspectives emerge in "The Goose Girl," which juxtaposes aristocratic presumption and working-class ambition in a memorable encounter between princess and serving-girl. Here the villain is not an older woman but a poorer one. Further, in this tale it is the old king who shows the presence of mind to discover the truth and then act upon it. Despite these unusual features, however, the princess herself is a classic case: her ultimate good fortune can be attributed to little except her innate innocence. Since the folk-fairy tale is essentially conservative in its values, it comes as no surprise to see order restored and the servant harshly punished for her audacity. At the same time, a modern reader may be forgiven for feeling a certain sympathy for the servant as she attempts to improve her lot—a viewpoint that is in fact explored by Emma Donoghue in her re-telling of the story "The Tale of the Handkerchief" (p.306). Certainly "The Goose Girl" provides us with an ideal transition, as damsel in distress is confronted by girl with gumption!

It is worth noting that almost all of the tales we have read to this point deal with the difficulties and dangers involved in becoming a woman, many of which are created by those who should be facilitating the transition. The fact is that the complexities of the parent-child relationship provide a primary source for the fairy-tale plot. With surprising frequency, an effort is made by a parent (or step-parent, or surrogate) to prevent the inevitable, although not always with wicked motive. In the first section, for example, we saw how Little Red Riding Hood's mother's natural desire to shelter her daughter ultimately becomes a destructive force, when the child is sent defenceless into the waiting jaws of the Wolf. ("The poor child, not knowing that it was dangerous to stop and listen to a wolf..."). Likewise in the "Sleeping Beauty" variants, the same instinct causes the father to attempt to insulate his daughter from harsh reality, with the same consequence.

It is significant that each tale ends with the celebration of marriage, denoting that the heroine has survived the loss of childhood innocence and is now ready for initiation into the privileged status of adulthood. Here, perhaps, is one reason for the enduring popularity of the folk-fairy tale: it offers vital reassurance to the reader/listener that while the road to maturity is both long and difficult, the goal of self-fulfillment awaits those who persevere.

SNOW WHITE

Jacob and Wilhelm Grimm

ONCE in midwinter when the snowflakes were falling from the sky like feathers, a queen sat sewing at the window, with an ebony frame. And as she was sewing and looking out at the snowflakes, she pricked her finger with her needle and three drops of blood fell on the snow. The red looked so beautiful on the white snow that she thought to herself: "If only I had a child as white as snow and as red as blood and as black as the wood of my window frame." A little while later she gave birth to a daughter, who was as white as snow and as red as blood, and her hair was as black as ebony. They called her Snow White, and when she was born, the queen died.

A year later the king took a second wife. She was beautiful, but she was proud and overbearing, and she couldn't bear the thought that anyone might be more beautiful than she. She had a magic mirror, and when she went up to it and looked at herself, she said:

> "Mirror, Mirror, here I stand.
> Who is the fairest in the land?"

and the mirror answered:

> "You, O Queen, are the fairest in the land."

That set her mind at rest, for she knew the mirror told the truth.

But as Snow White grew, she became more and more beautiful, and by the time she was seven years old she was as beautiful as the day and more beautiful than the queen herself. One day when the queen said to her mirror:

> "Mirror, Mirror, here I stand.
> Who is the fairest in the land?"

the mirror replied:

> "You, O Queen, are the fairest here,
> But Snow White is a thousand times more fair."

The Queen gasped, and turned yellow and green with envy. Every time she laid eyes on Snow White after that she hated her so much that her heart turned over in her bosom. Envy and pride grew like weeds in her heart, until she knew no peace by day or by night. Finally she sent for a huntsman and said: "Get that child out of my sight. Take her into the forest and kill her and bring me her lungs and her liver to prove you've done it." The huntsman obeyed. He took the child out into the forest, but when he drew his hunting knife and prepared to pierce Snow White's innocent heart, she began to cry and said: "Oh, dear huntsman, let me live. I'll run off through the wild woods and never come home again." Because of her beauty the huntsman took pity on her and said: "All right, you poor child. Run away." To himself, he thought: "The wild beasts will soon eat her," but not having to kill her was a great weight off his mind all the same. Just then a young boar came bounding out of the thicket. The huntsman thrust his knife into it, took the lungs and liver and brought them to the queen as proof that he had done her bidding. The cook was ordered to salt and stew them, and the godless woman ate them, thinking she was eating Snow White's lungs and liver.

Meanwhile the poor child was all alone in the great forest. She was so afraid that she looked at all the leaves on the trees and didn't know what to do. She began to run, she ran over sharp stones and through brambles, and the wild beasts passed by without harming her. She ran as long as her legs would carry her and then, just before nightfall, she saw a little house and went in to rest. Inside the house everything was tiny, but wonderfully neat and clean. There was a table spread with a white cloth, and on the table there were seven little plates, each with its own knife, fork, and spoon, and seven little cups. Over against the wall there were seven little beds all in a row, covered with spotless white sheets. Snow White was very hungry and thirsty, but she didn't want to eat up anyone's entire meal, so she ate a bit of bread and vegetables from each plate and drank a sip of wine from each cup. Then she was so tired that she lay down on one of the beds, but none of the beds quite suited her; some were too long and some were too short, but the seventh was just right. There she stayed and when she had said her prayers she fell asleep.

When it was quite dark, the owners of the little house came home. They were seven dwarfs who went off to the mountains every day with their picks and shovels, to mine silver. They lit their seven little candles, and when the light went up they saw someone had been there, because certain things had been moved. The first said: "Who has been sitting in my chair?" The second: "Who has been eating off my plate?" The third: "Who has taken a bite of my bread?" The fourth: "Who has been eating some of my vegetables?" The fifth: "Who has been using my fork?" The sixth:

"Who has been cutting with my knife?" And the seventh: "Who has been drinking out of my cup?" Then the first looked around, saw a little hollow in his bed and said: "Who has been lying in my bed?" The others came running, and cried out: "Somebody has been lying in my bed too." But when the seventh looked at his bed, he saw Snow White lying there asleep. He called the others, who came running. They cried out in amazement, went to get their seven little candles, and held them over Snow White: "Heavens above!" they cried. "Heavens above! What a beautiful child!" They were so delighted they didn't wake her but let her go on sleeping in the little bed. The seventh dwarf slept with his comrades, an hour with each one, and then the night was over.

Next morning Snow White woke up, and when she saw the seven dwarfs she was frightened. But they were friendly and asked: "What's your name?" "My name is Snow White," she said. "How did you get to our house?" the dwarfs asked. And she told them how her stepmother had wanted to kill her, how the huntsman had spared her life, and how she had walked all day until at last she found their little house. The dwarfs said: "If you will keep house for us, and do the cooking and make the beds and wash and sew and knit, and keep everything neat and clean, you can stay with us and you'll want for nothing." "Oh, yes," said Snow White. "I'd love to." So she stayed and kept the house in order, and in the morning they went off to the mountains to look for silver and gold, and in the evening they came home again and dinner had to be ready. But all day Snow White was alone, and the kindly dwarfs warned her, saying: "Watch out for your stepmother. She'll soon find out you're here. Don't let anyone in."

After eating Snow White's lungs and liver, the queen felt sure she was again the most beautiful of all. She went to her mirror and said:

> "Mirror, Mirror, here I stand.
> Who is the fairest in the land?"

And the mirror replied:

> "You, O Queen, are the fairest here,
> But Snow White, who has gone to stay

With the seven dwarfs far, far away,
Is a thousand times more fair."

The queen gasped. She knew the mirror told no lies and she realized that the huntsman had deceived her and that Snow White
was still alive. She racked her brains for a way to kill her, because
she simply had to be the fairest in the land, or envy would leave
her no peace. At last she thought up a plan. She stained her face
and dressed like an old peddler woman, so that no one could have
recognized her. In this disguise she made her way across the seven
mountains to the house of the seven dwarfs, knocked at the door
and cried out: "Pretty things for sale! For sale!" Snow White
looked out of the window and said: "Good day, old woman, what
have you got to sell?" "Nice things, nice things!" she replied.
"Laces, all colors," and she took out a lace woven of bright-col-
ored silk. "This woman looks so honest," thought Snow White.
"It must be all right to let her in." So she unbolted the door and
bought the pretty lace. "Child!" said the old woman, "you look a
fright. Come, let me lace you up properly." Suspecting nothing,
Snow White stepped up and let the old woman put in the new
lace. But she did it so quickly and pulled the lace so tight that
Snow White's breath was cut off and she fell down as though
dead. "Well, well," said the queen, "you're not the fairest in the
land now." And she hurried away.

A little while later, at nightfall, the seven dwarfs came home.
How horrified they were to see their beloved Snow White lying
on the floor! She lay so still they thought she was dead. They lifted her up, and when they saw she was laced too tightly, they cut
the lace. She breathed just a little, and then little by little she came
to life. When the dwarfs heard what had happened, they said:
"That old peddler woman was the wicked queen and no one else.
You've got to be careful and never let anyone in when we're
away."

When the wicked woman got home, she went to her mirror
and asked:

"Mirror, Mirror, here I stand.
Who is the fairest in the land?"

And the mirror answered as usual:

"You, O Queen, are the fairest here,
But Snow White, who has gone to stay
With the seven dwarfs far, far away,
Is a thousand times more fair."

When she heard that, it gave her such a pang that the blood rushed to her heart, for she realized that Snow White had revived. "Never mind," she said. "I'll think up something now that will really destroy you," and with the help of some magic spells she knew she made a poisoned comb. Then she disguised herself and took the form of another old woman. And again she made her way over the seven mountains to the house of the seven dwarfs, knocked at the door and said: "Pretty things for sale! For sale!" Snow White looked out and said: "Go away. I can't let anyone in." "You can look, can't you?" said the old woman, taking out the poisoned comb and holding it up. The child liked it so well that she forgot everything else and opened the door. When they had agreed on the price, the old woman said: "Now I'll give your hair a proper combing." Suspecting nothing, poor Snow White stood still for the old woman, but no sooner had the comb touched her hair than the poison took effect and she fell into a dead faint. "There, my beauty," said the wicked woman. "It's all up with you now." And she went away. But luckily it wasn't long till nightfall. When the seven dwarfs came home and found Snow White lying on the floor as though dead, they immediately suspected the step-mother. They examined Snow White and found the poisoned comb, and no sooner had they pulled it out than she woke up and told them what had happened. Again they warned her to be on her guard and not to open the door to anyone.

When the queen got home she went to her mirror and said:

"Mirror, Mirror, here I stand.
Who is the fairest in the land?"

And the mirror answered as before:

"You, O Queen, are the fairest here,

64

But Snow White, who has gone to stay
With the seven dwarfs far, far away,
Is a thousand times more fair."

When she heard the mirror say that, she trembled and shook with rage. "Snow White must die!" she cried out. "Even if it costs me my own life." Then she went to a secret room that no one else knew about and made a very poisonous apple. It looked so nice on the outside, white with red cheeks, that anyone who saw it would want it; but anyone who ate even the tiniest bit of it would die. When the apple was ready, she stained her face and disguised herself as a peasant woman. And again she made her way across the seven mountains to the house of the seven dwarfs. She knocked at the door and Snow White put her head out of the window. "I can't let anyone in," she said. "The seven dwarfs won't let me." "It doesn't matter," said the peasant woman. "I only want to get rid of these apples. Here, I'll make you a present of one." "No," said Snow White. "I'm not allowed to take anything." "Are you afraid of poison?" said the old woman. "Look, I'm cutting it in half. You eat the red cheek and I'll eat the white cheek." But the apple had been so cleverly made that only the red cheek was poisoned. Snow White longed for the lovely apple, and when she saw the peasant woman taking a bite out of it she couldn't resist. She held out her hand and took the poisonous half. And no sooner had she taken a bite than she fell to the floor dead. The queen gave her a cruel look, laughed a terrible laugh, and said: "White as snow, red as blood, black as ebony. The dwarfs won't revive you this time." And when she got home and questioned the mirror:

"Mirror, Mirror, here I stand.
Who is the fairest in the land?"

The mirror answered at last:

"You, O Queen, are the fairest in the land."

Then her envious heart was at peace, insofar as an envious heart can be at peace.

When the dwarfs came home at nightfall, they found Snow

65

White lying on the floor. No breath came out of her mouth and she was really dead. They lifted her up, looked to see if they could find anything poisonous, unlaced her, combed her hair, washed her in water and wine, but nothing helped; the dear child was dead, and dead she remained. They laid her on a bier, and all seven sat down beside it and mourned, and they wept for three whole days. Then they were going to bury her, but she still looked fresh and alive, and she still had her beautiful red cheeks. "We can't lower her into the black earth," they said, and they had a coffin made out of glass, so that she could be seen from all sides, and they put her into it and wrote her name in gold letters on the coffin, adding that she was a king's daughter. Then they put the coffin on the hilltop, and one of them always stayed there to guard it. And the birds came and wept for Snow White, first an owl, then a raven, and then a dove.

Snow White lay in her coffin for years and years. She didn't rot, but continued to look as if she were asleep, for she was still as white as snow, as red as blood, and as black as ebony. Then one day a prince came to that forest and stopped for the night at the dwarfs' house. He saw the coffin on the hilltop, he saw lovely Snow White inside it, and he read the gold letters on the coffin. He said to the dwarfs: "Let me have the coffin, I'll pay you as much as you like for it." But the dwarfs replied: "We wouldn't part with it for all the money in the world." "Then give it to me," he said, "for I can't go on living unless I look at Snow White. I will honor and cherish her forever." Then the dwarfs took pity on him and gave him the coffin. The prince's servants hoisted it up on their shoulders and as they were carrying it away they stumbled over a root. The jolt shook the poisoned core, which Snow White had bitten off, out of her throat, and soon she opened her eyes, lifted the coffin lid, sat up, and was alive again. "Oh!" she cried. "Where am I?" "With me!" the prince answered joyfully. Then he told her what had happened and said: "I love you more than anything in the world; come with me to my father's castle and be my wife." Snow White loved him and went with him, and arrangements were made for a splendid wedding feast.

Snow White's wicked stepmother was among those invited to the wedding. When she had put on her fine clothes, she went to her mirror and said:

"Mirror, Mirror, here I stand.
Who is the fairest in the land?"

And the mirror answered:

"You, O Queen, are the fairest here.
But the young queen is a thousand times more fair."

At that the wicked woman spat out a curse. She was so horror-stricken she didn't know what to do. At first she didn't want to go to the wedding, but then she couldn't resist; she just had to go and see the young queen. The moment she entered the hall she recognized Snow White, and she was so terrified that she just stood there and couldn't move. But two iron slippers had already been put into glowing coals. Someone took them out with a pair of tongs and set them down in front of her. She was forced to step into the red-hot shoes and dance till she fell to the floor dead.

RAPUNZEL

Jacob and Wilhelm Grimm

ONCE after a man and wife had long wished in vain for a child, the wife had reason to hope that God would grant them their wish. In the back of their house there was a little window that looked out over a wonderful garden, full of beautiful flowers and vegetables. But there was a high wall around the garden, and no one dared enter it because it belonged to a witch, who was very powerful and everyone was afraid of her. One day the wife stood at this window, looking down into the garden, and her eyes lit on a bed of the finest rapunzel, which is a kind of lettuce. And it looked so fresh and green that she longed for it and her mouth watered. Her craving for it grew from day to day, and she began to waste away because she knew she would never get any. Seeing her so pale and wretched, her husband took fright and asked: "What's the matter with you, dear wife?" "Oh," she said, "I shall die unless I get some rapunzel to eat from the garden behind our house." Her husband, who loved her, thought: "Sooner than let my wife

die, I shall get her some of that rapunzel, cost what it may." As
night was falling, he climbed the wall into the witch's garden, took
a handful of rapunzel, and brought it to his wife. She made it into
a salad right away and ate it hungrily. But it tasted so good, so very
good, that the next day her craving for it was three times as great.
Her husband could see she would know no peace unless he paid
another visit to the garden. So at nightfall he climbed the wall
again, but when he came down on the other side he had an awful
fright, for there was the witch right in front of him. "How dare
you!" she said with an angry look. "How dare you sneak into my
garden like a thief and steal my rapunzel! I'll make you pay dearly
for this." "Oh, please," he said, "please temper justice with mercy. I
only did it because I had to. My wife was looking out of the window, and when she saw your rapunzel she felt such a craving for it
that she would have died if I hadn't got her some." At that the
witch's anger died down and she said: "If that's how it is, you may
take as much rapunzel as you wish, but on one condition: that you
give me the child your wife will bear. It will have a good life and
I shall care for it like a mother." In his fright, the man agreed to
everything, and the moment his wife was delivered, the witch
appeared, gave the child the name of Rapunzel, and took her
away.

Rapunzel grew to be the loveliest child under the sun. When
she was twelve years old, the witch took her to the middle of the
forest and shut her up in a tower that had neither stairs nor door,
but only a little window at the very top. When the witch wanted
to come in, she stood down below and called out:

> "Rapunzel, Rapunzel,
> Let down your hair for me."

Rapunzel had beautiful long hair, as fine as spun gold. When she
heard the witch's voice, she undid her braids and fastened them to
the window latch. They fell to the ground twenty ells down, and
the witch climbed up on them.

A few years later it so happened that the king's son was passing
through the forest. When he came to the tower, he heard someone singing, and the singing was so lovely that he stopped and listened. It was Rapunzel, who in her loneliness was singing to pass

the time. The prince wanted to go up to her and he looked for a
door but found none. He rode away home, but the singing had so
touched his heart that he went out into the forest every day and
listened. Once as he was standing behind a tree, he saw a witch
come to the foot of the tower and heard her call out:

"Rapunzel, Rapunzel,
Let down your hair."

Whereupon Rapunzel let down her braids, and the witch climbed
up to her. "Aha," he thought, "if that's the ladder that goes up to
her, then I'll try my luck too." And next day, when it was beginning to get dark, he went to the tower and called out:

"Rapunzel, Rapunzel,
Let down your hair."

A moment later her hair fell to the ground and the prince
climbed up.

At first Rapunzel was dreadfully frightened, for she had never
seen a man before, but the prince spoke gently to her and told her
how he had been so moved by her singing that he couldn't rest
easy until he had seen her. At that Rapunzel lost her fear, and
when he asked if she would have him as her husband and she saw
he was young and handsome, she thought: "He will love me better
than my old godmother." So she said yes and put her hand in his
hand. "I'd gladly go with you," she said, "but how will I ever get
down? Every time you come, bring a skein of silk and I'll make a
ladder with it. When it's finished, I'll climb down, and you will
carry me home on your horse." They agreed that in the meantime
he would come every evening, because the old witch came during
the day. The witch noticed nothing until one day Rapunzel said
to her: "Tell me, Godmother, how is it that you're so much harder
to pull up than the young prince? With him it hardly takes a
minute." "Wicked child!" cried the witch. "What did you say? I
thought I had shut you away from the world, but you've deceived
me." In her fury she seized Rapunzel's beautiful hair, wound it
several times around her left hand and picked up a pair of scissors
in her right hand. Snippety-snap went the scissors, and the lovely

braids fell to the floor. Then the heartless witch sent poor Rapunzel to a desert place, where she lived in misery and want.

At dusk on the day she had sent Rapunzel away, she fastened the severed braids to the window latch, and when the prince came and called:

> "Rapunzel, Rapunzel,
> Let down your hair."

she let the hair down. The prince climbed up, but instead of his dearest Rapunzel, the witch was waiting for him with angry, poisonous looks. "Aha!" she cried. "You've come to take your darling wife away, but the bird is gone from the nest, she won't be singing any more; the cat has taken her away and before she's done she'll scratch your eyes out too. You've lost Rapunzel, you'll never see her again." The prince was beside himself with grief, and in his despair he jumped from the tower. It didn't kill him, but the brambles he fell into scratched his eyes out and he was blind. He wandered through the forest, living on roots and berries and weeping and wailing over the loss of his dearest wife. For several years he wandered wretchedly, until at last he came to the desert place where Rapunzel was living in misery with the twins she had born—a boy and a girl. He heard a voice that seemed familiar, and when he approached Rapunzel recognized him, fell on his neck and wept. Two of her tears dropped on his eyes, which were made clear again, so that he could see as well as ever. He took her to his kingdom, where she was welcomed with rejoicing, and they lived happy and contented for many years to come.

THE GOOSE GIRL

Jacob and Wilhelm Grimm

THERE was once an old queen, whose husband had long been dead, and she had a beautiful daughter. When the princess was old enough, she was betrothed to a king's son who lived far away, and soon it was time for the marriage. The princess prepared to set out for the distant kingdom, and the queen packed all manner of precious things, jewels and goblets and gold and silver plate, in short, everything required for a royal dowry, for she loved her child with all her heart. And she also gave her a waiting maid to keep her company on the way and see to it that she reached her bridegroom safely. They were both given horses for the journey, and the princess's horse, whose name was Fallada, could talk. When it was time for them to go, the old mother went to her bedchamber, took a knife, and cut her finger till it bled. She let three drops of blood fall on a snippet of white cloth, which she gave her daughter, saying: "Take good care of this. You will need it on your journey."

After a sorrowful leavetaking the princess put the snippet of cloth in her bodice, mounted her horse, and rode away to her betrothed. When they had ridden an hour, she was thirsty and said to her waiting maid: "I'm thirsty. Get down from your horse, take the golden cup you've brought and bring me some water from the brook." The waiting maid answered: "If you're thirsty, go and serve yourself. Lie down over the brook and drink. I don't choose to wait on you." The princess was so thirsty that she dismounted, bent over the brook and drank. The maid wouldn't even let her use her golden cup. "Poor me!" she sighed. And the three drops of blood replied: "If your mother knew of this, it would break her heart." But the princess was meek. She said nothing and remounted. They rode on for a few miles, but it was a hot day, the sun was scorching, and soon she was thirsty again. They came to a stream and again she said to her waiting maid: "Get down and bring me some water in my golden cup," for she had long forgotten the girl's wicked words. But the waiting maid answered even more haughtily than before: "If you're thirsty, go and drink. I don't choose to wait on you." And again the princess was so thirsty that she dismounted. She lay down over the flowing water, wept, and said: "Poor me!" And again the drops of blood replied: "If your mother knew of this, it would break her heart." As she bent over the stream, drinking, the snippet of cloth with the three drops of blood on it fell out of her bodice and flowed away with the stream. In her great distress she didn't notice, but the waiting maid had seen the cloth fall and gloated, for now she had power over the bride who, without the drops of blood, became weak and helpless. When the princess was going to remount the horse

71

named Fallada, the maid said: "I'll take Fallada. My nag is good enough for you." And the princess had to put up with it. Then the waiting maid spoke harshly to her, saying: "Now give me your royal garments and take these rags for yourself." After that she made her swear under the open sky never to breathe a word of all this to a living soul at court, and if she hadn't sworn, the waiting maid would have killed her on the spot. But Fallada saw it all and took good note.

Then the waiting maid mounted Fallada and the true bride mounted the wretched nag, and on they rode until they reached the royal palace. There was great rejoicing at their arrival. The prince ran out to meet them and, taking the waiting maid for his bride, lifted her down from her saddle and led her up the stairs, while the real princess was left standing down below. The old king looked out of the window and saw how delicate and lovely she was, whereupon he went straight to the royal apartments and asked the bride about the girl in the courtyard, the one who had come with her. "Oh, I picked her up on the way to keep me company. Give her some work to keep her out of mischief." But the old king had no work for her and couldn't think of any, so he said: "There's a little boy who tends the geese, she can help him." So the true bride had to help the little gooseherd, whose name was Conrad.

After a while the false bride said to the young king: "Dearest husband, I beg you, do me a favor." "I shall be glad to," he replied. "Then send for the knacker and make him cut the head off the horse that brought me here. The beast infuriated me on the way." The truth was that she was afraid the horse would tell everyone what she had done to the princess. So it was arranged, and when the true princess heard that the faithful Fallada was to die, she secretly promised the knacker some money in return for a small service. At the edge of the town there was a big dark gateway through which she passed morning and evening with the geese. Would he nail Fallada's head to the wall of the gateway, so that she could see it every day? The knacker promised to do it, and after cutting the head off, he nailed it to the wall of the dark gateway.

Early in the morning when she and little Conrad drove the geese through the gateway, she said as she passed by:

"Oh, poor Fallada, hanging there,"

and the head answered:

"Oh, poor princess in despair,
If your dear mother knew,
Her heart would break in two."

After that she didn't open her mouth, and they drove the geese out into the country. When they reached a certain meadow, she sat down and undid her hair, which was pure gold, and little Conrad looked on. He loved the way her hair glistened in the sun and tried to pull some out for himself. Whereupon she said:

"Blow, wind, blow,
Take Conrad's hat and make it go
Flying here and flying there.
And make him run until I've done
Combing and braiding my hair
And putting it up in a bun."

Then a wind came up that sent little Conrad's hat flying far and wide, and he had to run after it. By the time he got back she had finished her combing and braiding, and he couldn't get himself any hair. That made him angry and he stopped talking to her. And so they tended the geese until evening, and then they went home.

Next morning as they drove the geese through the dark gateway, the princess said:

"Oh, poor Fallada, hanging there,"

and Fallada replied:

"Oh, poor princess in despair,
If your dear mother knew,
Her heart would break in two."

When they reached the meadow, she again sat down and combed out her hair. Again Conrad ran and tried to grab at it, and again she said:

> "Blow, wind, blow,
> Take Conrad's hat and make it go
> Flying here and flying there.
> And make him run until I've done
> Combing and braiding my hair
> And putting it up in a bun."

The wind blew and lifted the hat off his head and blew it far away. Little Conrad had to run after it, and by the time he got back, she had put her hair up and he couldn't get hold of it. And so they tended the geese until evening.

When they got home that evening, little Conrad went to the old king and said: "I don't want to tend geese with that girl any more." "Why not?" the old king asked. "Because she aggravates me from morning till night." "Tell me just what she does," said the old king. "Well," said the boy, "in the morning, when we drive the geese through the dark gateway, there's a horse's head on the wall. She always speaks to it and says:

> "Oh, poor Fallada, hanging there,"

and the head answers:

> "Oh, poor princess in despair,
> If your dear mother knew,
> Her heart would break in two."

And little Conrad went on to tell the old king what happened in the meadow and how he had to run after his hat in the wind.

The old king ordered him to go out again with the geese next day, and in the morning he himself sat down near the dark gateway and heard the princess talking with Fallada's head. And then he followed her into the meadow and hid behind a bush. With his own eyes he soon saw the goose girl and the little gooseherd coming along with their flock. And after a while he saw her sit down and undo her glistening golden hair. Once again she said:

> "Blow, wind, blow,
> Take Conrad's hat and make it go
> Flying here and flying there.
> And make him run until I've done
> Combing and braiding my hair
> And putting it up in a bun."

Then a gust of wind carried little Conrad's hat away, and he had to run and run, and meanwhile the girl quietly combed and braided her hair. The old king saw it all and went back to the palace unseen, and when the goose girl got home that evening, he called her aside and asked her why she did all those things: "I mustn't tell you that," she said. "I can't pour out my heart to anyone, because under the open sky I swore not to. I'd have been killed if I hadn't." He argued and kept at her, but he couldn't get anything out of her. So finally he said: "If you won't tell me, then pour out your heart to this cast-iron stove." With that he left her and she crawled into the cast-iron stove, and wept and wailed and poured out her heart: "Here I sit, forsaken by the whole world," she said. "And yet I'm a king's daughter. A false waiting maid forced me to give her my royal garments and took my place with my bridegroom, and now I'm a goose girl, obliged to do menial work. If my dear mother knew, her heart would break in two." The old king was standing outside with his ear to the stove-pipe, and he heard everything she said. He came back in and told her to come out of the stove. They dressed her in royal garments, and she was so beautiful that it seemed a miracle. The old king called his son and told him he had the wrong bride, that she was only a waiting maid, and that the one standing there, who had been the goose girl, was the right one. The young king was overjoyed when he saw how beautiful and virtuous she was. A great banquet was made ready, and all the courtiers and good friends were invited. At the head of the table sat the bridegroom. The princess was on one side of him and the waiting maid on the other, but the waiting maid was dazzled by the princess and didn't recognize her in her sparkling jewels. When they had finished eating and drinking and were all in good spirits, the old king put a riddle to the waiting

75

maid: What, he asked, would a woman deserve who had deceived her master in such and such a way? He went on to tell the whole story and ended by asking: "What punishment does such a woman deserve?" The false bride replied: "She deserves no better than to have her clothes taken off and to be shut up stark naked in a barrel studded with sharp nails on the inside. And two white horses should be harnessed to it and made to drag her up street and down until she is dead." "You are that woman!" said the old king. "You have pronounced your own sentence, and that is what will be done to you." When the sentence had been carried out, the young king married the right bride, and they ruled the kingdom together in peace and happiness.

GIRLS WITH GUMPTION

THERE is no denying that the tales in this section are less well-known than most of those that have gone before. The question is whether that is simply a coincidence, or whether these tales have remained in relative obscurity because they depict the heroine in roles that have not met with the approval of the editors, publishers, and cultural critics who have exerted considerable control over what is made available, particularly in relation to children. We have already seen how Perrault chose to adapt "Little Red Riding Hood" to address his own concerns about sexual impropriety; similarly, Wilhelm Grimm, who took primary responsibility for editing later editions of the Grimm tales, was also concerned enough to adapt them to accord with current views about what was suitable for the eyes of children.

This evolution of a gender stereotype can be seen quite clearly if one compares the first tale, Basile's "Petrosinella," with its better-known successor from the Brothers Grimm, "Rapunzel" (see previous section). In the latter, the central character's role is that of innocent victim whose suffering renders her saint-like and thereby justifies a happy reunion with her prince. Basile's heroine plays a much more decisive role in pursuing her marital destiny; there is no hint of the excessive emotionalism that suffuses the conclusion of "Rapunzel."

"Clever Gretel" reminds us that not all fairy tales are about kings and queens, palaces and princes, for here the central character is a servant, a representative of the folk. Nevertheless, its appeal remains that of wish-fulfillment, just as in the tales of glamor and romance, for the point about Gretel is that she is smart, not to mention self-indulgent and sassy. Much classist and sexist fun is to be had as she pulls the wool over the eyes of her ineffectual master, while doing considerable damage to his wine-cellar at the same time.

While there is an obvious argument for placing the Norwegian tale "East of the Sun, West of the Moon" in the "Beastly Bride(groom)" section, we have nevertheless chosen to include it here because it contains such a dramatic reversal of gender roles. Although the young woman is at least partly responsible for the abduction of her lover, her determination to rectify the situation results in her undertaking an odyssey of reconciliation that puts most would-be heroes to shame. Here again it is the mother who, out of a combination of jealousy and distrust, proves more foe than friend to her daughter. Nevertheless, if we take this long and dangerous journey as a measure of our heroine's love and maturity, its successful conclusion augurs well for her future relationship.

The final tale in this section is altogether of a darker hue. Taken from Joseph Jacobs' *English Fairy Tales*, it illustrates the essentially *derivative* nature of the folk tale, forever simmering in the communal psychic stockpot — what J.R.R. Tolkien refers to as the "Cauldron of Story." As with the previous tale, it is the memorable character of the young woman that justifies its inclusion here. The similarity of plot to "Bluebeard" (see "Villains") is striking, but, unlike her French counterpart, Lady Mary is not about to permit others to determine her fate. The repetition in the story gives it a chilling, ritualistic quality as it moves inexorably to its nightmarish climax.

PETROSINELLA

Giambattista Basile

THERE was once a pregnant woman called Pascadozia who, standing before a window which overlooked the garden of an ogress, saw a fine bed of parsley and was seized with so great a desire to have some that she nearly fainted. Unable to resist the desire, as soon as she saw the ogress go out, she went down to the garden and took a handful.

When the ogress came home again she started to prepare a parsley soup, and finding that someone had been at her bed, exclaimed: "Let me break my neck if I don't discover this bird of prey and make him repent. I'll teach people to eat off their own platter and not meddle with other people's pots!"

The poor pregnant woman continued to go down into the garden from time to time, till one day she ran into the ogress, who, furious and exasperated, said: "Now I have caught you at it, you swindling thief! Pray, do you pay the rent of this garden that you come so boldly to help yourself to my plants? By my faith, you won't have to go as far as Rome to do penance!"

The unfortunate Pascadozia began to excuse herself, saying it was not through gluttony or greed that she had been prompted by the devil to this wrongful act, but because she was pregnant and feared there might be a crop of parsley on the face of her child when it was born; the ogress, she added, ought rather to be grateful that she hadn't given her the sore eye.[1]

"The bride wants more than mere words!" replied the ogress; "you won't get round me with this chatter. Your life's work is over unless you promise to give me the child that is to be born to you, boy or girl, whichever it shall be."

To escape from the danger in which she stood, the poor woman promised this and made an oath, placing one hand on the other; then the ogress let her go.

When her time came, Pascadozia gave birth to the most beautiful baby girl, a joy to behold, and she gave her the name of Petrosinella,[2] for on her breast was a mark like a fine sprig of parsley.

The child grew day by day, and when she was seven years old she started going to school. Every day as she crossed the road the little girl met the ogress, who each time said: "Tell your mother to remember her promise!"

The unfortunate mother was worried so often with this mes-

---

1. According to popular belief, whoever failed to gratify the wish of a pregnant woman was punished with what was called the "orzaiuolo," a swelling and redness of the eyelids.

2. Prezzemolina. From "petrosino" (*prezzemolo*), both meaning parsley.

sage that, having no courage for further resistance, she at last said to the child: "If you meet the same old woman and she reminds you of that accursed promise, answer: 'You can take her!'"

Petrosinella, who was ignorant of what had happened, when she next met the ogress innocently replied as her mother had suggested. The ogress at once seized her by the hair and dragged her into a wood which was never entered by the horses of the Sun, for they had no grazing rights in those shadowy pastures. Then she put her into a tower with neither door nor stairs and only one little window, which with her magic she had caused to spring up in the wood. By this window the ogress let herself in and out of the tower, using Petrosinella's long long hair just as a ship's boy uses the ropes when he climbs up and down the mast.

Now one day when the ogress had gone out and Petrosinella had let down her tresses to the sun,[1] the King's son happened to pass by the tower. When he saw these golden banners hanging from the window calling to his soul to enlist under Love's standard, and saw these precious waves surrounding the face of a siren enchanting every heart, he fell desperately in love with so much beauty and sent a message of sighs begging for a place in her favour. So successful was he that when he kissed his hand to her, Petrosinella nodded back; when he bowed, she smiled and answered all this flattering offers and promises with thanks and gracious words of hope.

This went on for several days and the two became so friendly that they made an arrangement to meet. This was to take place at night when the Moon plays at hide and seek with the Stars, and Petrosinella was to give the ogress a draught of opium and to drag the Prince up by means of her rope of hair.

At the appointed time the Prince came to the tower and gave a whistle, which was to be the signal, and Petrosinella let down her tresses; he seized them with both hands, and calling "Pull," was drawn up to the little window through which he sprang into the room and there feasted with that sprig of parsley at the banquet of love. Before the Sun had bid his horses spring through the hoop

---

1. It was the custom at this time for women to bleach their hair in some mixture and then to expose it for many hours to the sun, protecting the forehead with a band of straw.

of the Zodiac, he let himself down by the same golden ladder and went his way.

As this proceeding was repeated several times, it was noticed by a gossip of the ogress, and she, interfering with what was no concern of hers, warned the ogress to be on the look-out, for Petrosinella and a youth were in love with one another and she feared, from the buzzing of that big fly as he went in and out, that things had gone pretty far; also she thought those two wouldn't be waiting till May[1] before they were flitting, carrying off with them all there was in the house.

The ogress thanked her gossip for her timely warning and said she would take care to stop Petrosinella, but that as a matter of fact it was quite impossible for her to escape, because she had put a spell upon her by which, unless she had in her hand the three acorns which were hidden in a beam in the kitchen, she could not get out of the house.

Whilst these two were talking together, Petrosinella, who had rather suspected the gossip, kept her ears on the stretch and heard the whole of the conversation. And when Night spread her dark robes out over the sky to air them and keep them from the moth, and the Prince arrived as usual, she made him climb up into the beams, where he soon found the acorns. These, because she had been enchanted by the ogress, she already knew how to use. Then, having knotted a rope ladder, they both climbed down it to the foot of the tower and took to their heels towards the city.

But the gossip saw them run away and at once began to call the ogress, shrieking so loud that she woke her up. As soon as she heard that Petrosinella had escaped, down came the ogress by the rope ladder which had been left fastened to the little window, and rushed after the lovers.

When the two saw her at their heels, galloping faster than a runaway horse, they thought they were lost. But Petrosinella remembered the acorns and threw one down. Immediately out sprang a great Corsican hound,—oh my goodness! such a terrible sight,—and barking furiously and with open jaws he made for the ogress as if to swallow her in one mouthful. But she, more cun-

---

1. That is, before May 4, which is still, according to the old custom, the day for removals and changing houses in Naples.

ning than the devil, took some bread out of her pocket and threw it to the dog, which allayed his fury and made him hang his tail. Then she continued her pursuit of the two fugitives, who, seeing her coming, threw down the second acorn. Out of this came a ferocious lion, who, lashing the ground with his tail, shaking his mane and opening his jaws two feet wide, made ready to gobble up the ogress. But she, turning round and seeing an ass grazing in the field, tore off its skin, which she threw over herself and then rushed at the lion, who, taking her for an ass, was so frightened that he is still running away. Saved a second time in this way, she again went after the young couple, who, hearing the sound of her great boots and seeing the cloud of dust that she raised to the sky, were warned of her approach. Petrosinella threw down the third acorn, and this time out came a wolf who, when he saw the ogress still wrapped in the ass's skin which she had kept on lest the lion should follow her, gave her no time to adopt another device but swallowed her down, ass's skin and all.

So the lovers were freed from their troubles and continued their way at leisure till they came to the kingdom of the Prince. Here, with the consent of his father, the Prince made Petrosinella his wife and found that after many hardships,

> *In one hour safe in port, one can forget*
> *A hundred years on stormy seas.*

CLEVER GRETEL

Jacob and Wilhelm Grimm

There was once a cook by the name of Gretel, who wore shoes with red heels, and when she went out in them she wiggled and waggled happily, and said to herself: "My, what a pretty girl I am." And when she got home again, she'd be in such a good humor that she'd take a drink of wine, and then, as wine whets the appetite, she'd taste all the best parts of what she was cooking until she was full, and say: "A cook has to know how her cooking tastes."

One day her master said to her: "Gretel, I'm having a guest for

dinner. I want you to make us two nice roast chickens." "Yes, master, I'll be glad to," said Gretel. She slit the chickens' throats, scald-
ed, plucked, and spitted them, and toward evening put them over
the fire to roast. The chickens began to brown and were almost
done, but the guest hadn't arrived. Gretel called in to her master:
"If your guest doesn't come soon, I'll have to take the chickens off
the fire, but it would be a crying shame not to eat them now,
while they're at their juiciest best." "In that case," said the master,
"I'll go and get him myself." The moment his back was turned,
she put the spit with the chickens on it to one side. "Standing
over the fire so long makes a body sweat," she thought, "and
sweating makes a body thirsty. How do I know when they'll get
here? In the meantime I'll hop down to the cellar and have a little
drink." Down she ran, filled a jug from the barrel, said: "God bless
it to your use, Gretel," and took a healthy swig. "Wine goes with
wine," she said, "and never should they part," and took a healthier
swig. Then she went upstairs, put the chickens back on the fire,
brushed them with butter, and gave the spit a few lively turns. But
the chickens smelled so good that she thought: "Maybe they're
not seasoned quite right, I'd better taste them." She touched her
fingers to one, licked them, and cried out: "Oh, how delicious
these chickens are! It's a crying shame not to eat them this
minute!" She went to the window to see if the master and his
guest were coming, but there was no one in sight. She went back
to the chickens and thought: "That wing is burning. There's only
one way to stop it." So she cut the wing off and ate it. It hit the
spot, and when she had finished she thought: "I'll have to take the
other one off too, or the master will see that something's missing."
After doing away with the two wings, she went back to the window to look for her master. No master in sight, so then she had an
idea. "How do I know? Maybe they're not coming. Maybe
they've stopped at a tavern." She gave herself a poke: "Come on,
Gretel. Don't be a spoilsport. One has been cut into; have another
drink and finish it up. Once it's gone, you won't have anything to
worry about. Why waste God's blessings?" Again she hopped
down to the cellar, took a good stiff drink, and polished off the
one chicken with joy in her heart. When one chicken was gone
and there was still no sign of the master, Gretel looked at the other
and said: "Where the one is, there the other should be. Chickens

83

go in pairs, and what's good enough for one is good enough for the other. And besides, another drink won't hurt me any." Whereupon she took an enormous drink and started the second chicken on its way to rejoin the first.

She was still eating lustily when her master came along and called out: "Quick, Gretel. Our guest will be here in a minute." "Oh, yes, sir," said Gretel. "I'll serve you in a jiffy." The master looked in to make sure the table was properly set, took his big carving knife, and began to sharpen it in the pantry. The guest was a well-bred man. When he got to the house, he knocked softly. Gretel hurried to the door and looked out. When she saw the guest, she put her finger to her lips and said: "Sh-sh! Quick, go away! If my master catches you, you're done for. Do you know why he invited you to dinner? Because he wants to cut your ears off. Listen! That's him sharpening his knife!" The guest heard the master whetting his knife and ran down the steps as fast as his legs could carry him. But Gretel wasn't through yet. She ran screaming to her master: "A fine guest you brought into the house!" she cried. "Why, what's the matter, Gretel? What do you mean?" "I mean," she said, "that just as I was getting ready to serve up the chickens he grabbed them and ran away with them." "That's a fine way to behave," said the master, grieved at the loss of his fine chickens. "If he'd only left me one of them! Then at least I'd have something to eat." "Stop! Stop!" he shouted, but the guest pretended not to hear. So still holding his knife the master ran after him, crying out: "Just one! Just one!" meaning that the guest should leave him one chicken and not take both. But the guest thought the master had decided to content himself with one ear, and seeing that he wanted to take both his ears home with him, he ran as if someone had made a fire under his feet.

EAST OF THE SUN AND WEST OF THE MOON

Asbjørnsen and Moe

ONCE upon a time there was a poor husbandman who had many children and little to give them in the way either of food or clothing. They were all pretty, but the prettiest of all was the youngest

84

daughter, who was so beautiful that there were no bounds to her beauty.

So once—it was late on a Thursday evening in autumn, and wild weather outside, terribly dark, and raining so heavily and blowing so hard that the walls of the cottage shook again—they were all sitting together by the fireside, each of them busy with something or other, when suddenly someone rapped three times against the window-pane. The man went out to see what could be the matter, and when he got out there stood a great big white bear.

"Good-evening to you," said the White Bear.

"Good-evening," said the man.

"Will you give me your youngest daughter?" said the White Bear; "if you will, you shall be as rich as you are now poor."

Truly the man would have had no objection to being rich, but he thought to himself: "I must first ask my daughter about this," so he went in and told them that there was a great white bear outside who had faithfully promised to make them all rich if he might but have the youngest daughter.

She said no, and would not hear of it; so the man went out again, and settled with the White Bear that he should come again next Thursday evening, and get her answer. Then the man persuaded her, and talked so much to her about the wealth that they would have, and what a good thing it would be for herself, that at last she made up her mind to go, and washed and mended all her rags, made herself as smart as she could, and held herself in readiness to set out. Little enough had she to take away with her.

Next Thursday evening the White Bear came to fetch her. She seated herself on his back with her bundle, and thus they departed. When they had gone a great part of the way, the White Bear said: "Are you afraid?"

"No, that I am not," said she.

"Keep tight hold of my fur, and then there is no danger," said he.

And thus she rode far, far away, until they came to a great mountain. Then the White Bear knocked on it, and a door opened, and they went into a castle where there were many brilliantly lighted rooms which shone with gold and silver, likewise a large hall in which there was a well-spread table, and it was so magnificent that it would be hard to make anyone understand how splendid it was. The White Bear gave her a silver bell, and told her that when she needed anything she had but to ring this bell, and what she wanted would appear. So after she had eaten, and night was drawing near, she grew sleepy after her journey, and thought she would like to go to bed. She rang the bell, and scarcely had she touched it before she found herself in a chamber where a bed stood ready made for her, which was as pretty as anyone could wish to sleep in. It had pillows of silk, and curtains of silk fringed with gold, and everything that was in the room was of gold or silver; but when she had lain down and put out the light a man came and lay down beside her, and behold it was the White Bear, who cast off the form of a beast during the night. She never saw him, however, for he always came after she had put out her light, and went away before daylight appeared.

So all went well and happily for a time, but then she began to be very sad and sorrowful, for all day long she had to go about alone; and she did so wish to go home to her father and mother and brothers and sisters. Then the White Bear asked what it was that she wanted, and she told him that it was so dull there in the mountain, and that she had to go about all alone, and that in her parents' house at home there were all her brothers and sisters, and it was because she could not go to them that she was so sorrowful.

"There might be a cure for that," said the White Bear, "if you would but promise me never to talk with your mother alone, but only when the others are there too; for she will take hold of your hand," he said, "and will want to lead you into a room to talk with you alone; but that you must by no means do, or you will bring great misery on both of us."

So one Sunday the White Bear came and said that they could now set out to see her father and mother, and they journeyed thither, she sitting on his back, and they went a long, long way, and it took a long, long time; but at last they came to a large white farmhouse, and her brothers and sisters were running outside it, playing, and it was so pretty that it was a pleasure to look at it.

"Your parents dwell here now," said the White Bear; "but do not forget what I said to you, or you will do much harm both to yourself and me."

"No, indeed," said she, "I shall never forget;" and as soon as she was at home the White Bear turned round and went back again.

There were such rejoicings when she went in to her parents that it seemed as if they would never come to an end. Everyone thought that he could never be sufficiently grateful to her for all she had done for them all. Now they had everything that they wanted, and everything was as good as it could be. They all asked her how she was getting on where she was. All was well with her too, she said; and she had everything that she could want. What other answers she gave I cannot say, but I am pretty sure that they did not learn much from her. But in the afternoon, after they had dined at mid-day, all happened just as the White Bear had said. Her mother wanted to talk with her alone in her own chamber. But she remembered what the White Bear had said, and would on no account go. "What we have to say can be said at any time," she answered. But somehow or other her mother at last persuaded her, and she was forced to tell the whole story. So she told how every night a man came and lay down beside her when the lights were all put out, and how she never saw him, because he always went away before it grew light in the morning, and how she continually went about in sadness, thinking how happy she would be if she could but see him, and how all day long she had to go about alone, and it was so dull and solitary. "Oh!" cried the mother, in horror, "you are very likely sleeping with a troll! But I will teach you a way to see him. You shall have a bit of one of my candles, which you can take away with you hidden in your breast. Look at him with that when he is asleep, but take care not to let any tallow drop upon him."

So she took the candle, and hid it in her breast, and when evening drew near the White Bear came to fetch her away. When they had gone some distance on their way, the White Bear asked her if everything had not happened just as he had foretold, and she could not own but that it had. "Then, if you have done what your mother wished," said he, "you have brought great misery on both of us." "No," she said, "I have not done anything at all." So when she had reached home and had gone to bed it was just the same as it had been before, and a man came and lay down beside her, and late at night, when she could hear that he was sleeping, she got up and kindled a light, lit her candle, let her light shine on him, and saw him, and he was the handsomest prince that eyes had ever beheld, and she loved him so much that it seemed to her that she must die if she did not kiss him that very moment. So she did kiss him; but while she was doing it she let three drops of hot tallow fall upon his shirt, and he awoke. "What have you done now?" said he; "you have brought misery on both of us. If you had but held out for the space of one year I should have been free. I have a stepmother who has bewitched me so that I am a white bear by day and a man by night; but now all is at an end between you and me, and I must leave you, and go to her. She lives in a castle which lies east of the sun and west of the moon, and there too is a princess with a nose which is three ells long, and she now is the one whom I must marry."

She wept and lamented, but all in vain, for go he must. Then she asked him if she could not go with him. But no, that could not be. "Can you tell me the way then, and I will seek you — that I may surely be allowed to do!"

"Yes, you may do that," said he; "but there is no way thither. It lies east of the sun and west of the moon, and never would you find your way there."

When she awoke in the morning both the Prince and the castle were gone, and she was lying on a small green patch in the midst of a dark, thick wood. By her side lay the self-same bundle of rags which she had brought with her from her own home. So when she had rubbed the sleep out of her eyes, and wept till she was weary, she set out on her way, and thus she walked for many and many a long day, until at last she came to a great mountain. Outside it an aged woman was sitting, playing with a golden apple. The girl asked her if she knew the way to the Prince who lived with his stepmother in the castle which lay east of the sun and west of the moon, and who was to marry a princess with a nose which was three ells long. "How do you happen to know about him?" enquired the old woman; "maybe you are she who ought to have had him." "Yes, indeed, I am," she said. "So it is you, then?" said the old woman; "I know nothing about him but that he dwells in a castle which is east of the sun and west of the moon. You will be a long time in getting to it, if ever you get to it at all; but you shall have the loan of my horse, and then you can ride on it to an old woman who is a neighbor of mine: perhaps she can tell you about him. When you have got there you must just strike the horse beneath the left ear and bid it go home again; but you may take the golden apple with you."

So the girl seated herself on the horse, and rode for a long, long way, and at last she came to the mountain, where an aged woman was sitting outside with a gold carding-comb. The girl asked her if she knew the way to the castle which lay east of the sun and west of the moon; but she said what the first old woman had said: "I know nothing about it, but that it is east of the sun and west of the moon, and that you will be a long time in getting to it, if ever you get there at all; but you may have the loan of my horse, and then you can ride on it to an old woman who lives the nearest to me: perhaps she may know where the castle is, and when you have got to her you may just strike the horse beneath the left ear and bid it go home again." Then she gave her the gold carding-comb, for it might, perhaps, be of use to her, she said.

So the girl seated herself on the horse, and rode a wearisome long way onwards again, and after a very long time she came to a great mountain, where an aged woman was sitting, spinning at a golden spinning-wheel. Of this woman, too, she enquired if she knew the way to the Prince, and where to find the castle which lay east of the sun and west of the moon. But it was only the same thing once again. "Maybe it was you who should have had the Prince," said the old woman. "Yes, indeed, I should have been the one," said the girl. But this old crone knew the way no better than the others—it was east of the sun and west of the moon, she knew that, "and you will be a long time in getting to it, if ever you get to it at all," she said; "but you may have the loan of my horse, and I think you had better ride to the East Wind, and ask him: perhaps he may know where the castle is, and will blow you thither. But when you have got to him you must just strike the horse beneath the left ear, and he will come home again." And then she gave her the golden spinning-wheel, saying: "Perhaps you may find that you have a use for it."

The girl had to ride for a great many days, and for a long and wearisome time, before she got there; but at last she did arrive, and then she asked the East Wind if he could tell her the way to the Prince who dwelt east of the sun and west of the moon. "Well," said the East Wind, "I have heard tell of the Prince, and of his castle, but I do not know the way to it, for I have never blown so far;

but, if you like, I will go with you to my brother the West Wind: he may know that, for he is much stronger than I am. You may sit on my back, and then I can carry you there." So she seated herself on his back, and they did go so swiftly! When they got there, the East Wind went in and said that the girl whom he had brought was the one who ought to have had the Prince up at the castle which lay east of the sun and west of the moon, and that now she was travelling about to find him again, so he had come there with her, and would like to hear if the West Wind knew whereabouts the castle was. "No," said the West Wind; "so far as that have I never blown: but if you like I will go with you to the South Wind, for he is much stronger than either of us, and he has roamed far and wide, and perhaps he can tell you what you want to know. You may seat yourself on my back, and then I will carry you to him."

So she did this, and journeyed to the South Wind, neither was she very long on the way. When they had got there, the West Wind asked him if he could tell her the way to the castle that lay east of the sun and west of the moon, for she was the girl who ought to marry the Prince who lived there. "Oh, indeed!" said the South Wind, "is that she? Well," said he, "I have wandered about a great deal in my time, and in all kinds of places, but I have never blown so far as that. If you like, however, I will go with you to my brother the North Wind; he is the oldest and strongest of all of us, and if he does not know where it is no one in the whole world will be able to tell you. You may sit upon my back, and then I will carry you there." So she seated herself on his back, and off he went from his house in great haste, and they were not long on the way. When they came near the North Wind's dwelling, he was so wild and frantic that they felt cold gusts a long while before they got there. "What do you want?" he roared out from afar, and they froze as they heard. Said the South Wind: "It is I, and this is she who should have had the Prince who lives in the castle which lies east of the sun and west of the moon. And now she wishes to ask you if you have ever been there, and can tell her the way, for she would gladly find him again."

"Yes," said the North Wind, "I know where it is. I once blew an aspen leaf there, but I was so tired that for many days afterwards I was not able to blow at all. However, if you really are anxious to go there, and are not afraid to go with me, I will take you on my back, and try if I can blow you there."

"Get there I must," said she; "and if there is any way of going I will; and I have no fear, no matter how fast you go."

"Very well then," said the North Wind; "but you must sleep here to-night, for if we are ever to get there we must have the day before us."

The North Wind woke her betimes next morning, and puffed himself up, and made himself so big and so strong that it was frightful to see him, and away they went, high up through the air, as if they would not stop until they had reached the very end of the world. Down below there was such a storm! It blew down woods and houses, and when they were above the sea the ships were wrecked by hundreds. And thus they tore on and on, and a long time went by, and then yet more time passed, and still they were above the sea, and the North Wind grew tired, and more tired, and at last so utterly weary that he was scarcely able to blow any longer, and he sank and sank, lower and lower, until at last he went so low that the crests of the waves dashed against the heels of the poor girl he was carrying. "Art thou afraid?" said the North Wind. "I have no fear," said she; and it was true. But they were not very, very far from land, and there was just enough strength left in the North Wind to enable him to throw her on to the shore, immediately under the windows of a castle which lay east of the sun and west of the moon; but then he was so weary and worn out that he was forced to rest for several days before he could go to his own home again.

Next morning she sat down beneath the walls of the castle to play with the golden apple, and the first person she saw was the maiden with the long nose, who was to have the Prince. "How much do you want for that gold apple of yours, girl?" said she, opening the window. "It can't be bought either for gold or money," answered the girl. "If it cannot be bought either for gold or money, what will buy it? You may say what you please," said the Princess.

"Well, if I may go to the Prince who is here, and be with him to-night, you shall have it," said the girl who had come with the North Wind. "You may do that," said the Princess, for she had made up her mind what she would do. So the Princess got the golden apple, but when the girl went up to the Prince's apartment that night he was asleep, for the Princess had so contrived it. The poor girl called to him, and shook him, and between whiles she wept; but she could not wake him. In the morning, as soon as day dawned, in came the Princess with the long nose, and drove her out again. In the daytime she sat down once more beneath the windows of the castle, and began to card with her golden carding-comb; and then all happened as it had happened before. The princess asked her what she wanted for it, and she replied that it was not for sale, either for gold or money, but that if she could get leave to go to the Prince, and be with him during the night, she should have it. But when she went up to the Prince's room he was again asleep, and, let her call him, or shake him, or weep as she would, he still slept on, and she could not put any life in him. When daylight came in the morning, the Princess with the long nose came too, and once more drove her away. When day had quite come, the girl seated herself under the castle windows, to spin with her golden spinning-wheel, and the Princess with the long nose wanted to have that also. So she opened the window, and asked what she would take for it. The girl said what she had said on each of the former occasions — that it was not for sale either for gold or for money, but if she could get leave to go to the Prince who lived there, and be with him during the night, she should have it.

"Yes," said the Princess, "I will gladly consent to that."

But in that place there were some Christian folk who had been carried off, and they had been sitting in the chamber which was next to that of the Prince, and had heard how a woman had been in there who had wept and called on him two nights running, and they told the Prince of this. So that evening, when the Princess came once more with her sleeping-drink, he pretended to drink, but threw it away behind him, for he suspected that it was a sleep-ing-drink. So, when the girl went into the Prince's room this time he was awake, and she had to tell him how she had come there. "You have come just in time," said the Prince, "for I should have been married to-morrow; but I will not have the long-nosed Princess, and you alone can save me. I will say that I want to see what my bride can do, and bid her wash the shirt which has the three drops of tallow on it. This she will consent to do, for she does not know that it is you who let them fall on it; but no one can wash them out but one born of Christian folk: it cannot be done by one of a pack of trolls; and then I will say that no one shall ever be my bride but the woman who can do this, and I know that you can." There was great joy and gladness between them all that night, but the next day, when the wedding was to take place, the Prince said, "I must see what my bride can do." "That you may do," said the stepmother.

"I have a fine shirt which I want to wear as my wedding shirt, but three drops of tallow have got upon it which I want to have washed off, and I have vowed to marry no one but the woman who is able to do it. If she cannot do that, she is not worth having."

Well, that was a very small matter, they thought, and agreed to do it. The Princess with the long nose began to wash as well as she could, but, the more she washed and rubbed, the larger the spots grew. "Ah! you can't wash at all," said the old troll-hag, who was her mother. "Give it to me." But she too had not had the shirt very long in her hands before it looked worse still, and, the more she washed it and rubbed it, the larger and blacker grew the spots.

So the other trolls had to come and wash, but, the more they did, the blacker and uglier grew the shirt, until at length it was as black as if it had been up the chimney. "Oh," cried the Prince, "not one of you is good for anything at all! There is a beggar-girl sitting outside the window, and I'll be bound that she can wash better than any of you! Come in, you girl there!" he cried. So she came in. "Can you wash this shirt clean?" he cried. "Oh! I don't know," she said; "but I will try." And no sooner had she taken the shirt and dipped it in the water than it was white as driven snow, and even whiter than that. "I will marry you," said the Prince.

Then the old troll-hag flew into such a rage that she burst, and the Princess with the long nose and all the little trolls must have burst too, for they have never been heard of since. The Prince and his bride set free all the Christian folk who were imprisoned there, and took away with them all the gold and silver that they could carry, and moved far away from the castle which lay east of the sun and west of the moon.

MR. FOX

Joseph Jacobs

LADY MARY was young, and Lady Mary was fair. She had two brothers, and more lovers than she could count. But of them all, the bravest and most gallant, was a Mr. Fox, whom she met when she was down at her father's country-house. No one knew who Mr. Fox was; but he was certainly brave, and surely rich, and of all her lovers, Lady Mary cared for him alone. At last it was agreed upon between them that they should be married. Lady Mary asked Mr. Fox where they should live, and he described to her his castle, and where it was; but, strange to say, did not ask her, or her brothers to come and see it.

So one day, near the wedding-day, when her brothers were out, and Mr. Fox was away for a day or two on business, as he said, Lady Mary set out for Mr. Fox's castle. And after many searchings, she came at last to it, and a fine strong house it was, with high walls and a deep moat. And when she came up to the gateway she saw written on it:

Be bold, be bold.

But as the gate was open, she went through it, and found no one there. So she went up to the doorway, and over it she found written:

Be bold, be bold, but not too bold.

Still she went on, till she came into the hall, and went up the broad stairs till she came to a door in the gallery, over which was written:

Be bold, be bold, but not too bold,
Lest that your heart's blood should run cold.

But Lady Mary was a brave one, she was, and she opened the door, and what do you think she saw ? Why, bodies and skeletons of beautiful young ladies all stained with blood. So Lady Mary thought it was high time to get out of that horrid place, and she closed the door, went through the gallery, and was just going down the stairs, and out of the hall, when who should she see through the window, but Mr. Fox dragging a beautiful young lady along from the gateway to the door. Lady Mary rushed downstairs, and hid herself behind a cask, just in time, as Mr. Fox came in with the poor young lady who seemed to have fainted. Just as he got near Lady Mary, Mr. Fox saw a diamond ring glittering on the finger of the young lady he was dragging, and he tried to pull it off. But it was tightly fixed, and would not come off, so Mr. Fox cursed and swore, and drew his sword, raised it and brought it down upon the hand of the poor lady. The sword cut off the hand, which jumped up into the air, and fell of all places in the world into Lady Mary's lap. Mr. Fox looked about a bit, but did not think of looking behind the cask, so at last he went on dragging the young lady up the stairs into the Bloody Chamber.

As soon as she heard him pass through the gallery, Lady Mary crept out of the door, down through the gateway, and ran home as fast as she could.

Now it happened that the very next day the marriage contract of Lady Mary and Mr. Fox was to be signed, and there was a splendid breakfast before that. And when Mr. Fox was seated at table opposite Lady Mary, he looked at her. "How pale you are this morning, my dear." "Yes," said she, "I had a bad night's rest last night. I had horrible dreams." "Dreams go by contraries," said Mr. Fox; "but tell us your dream, and your sweet voice will make the time pass till the happy hour comes."

"I dreamed," said Lady Mary, "that I went yestermorn to your castle, and I found it in the woods, with high walls, and a deep moat, and over the gateway was written:

Be bold, be bold.

"But it is not so, nor it was not so," said Mr. Fox.
"And when I came to the doorway over it was written:

Be bold, be bold, but not too bold.

"It is not so, nor it was not so," said Mr. Fox.

"And then I went upstairs, and came to a gallery, at the end of which was a door, on which was written:

Be bold, be bold, but not too bold,
Lest that your heart's blood should run cold.

"It is not so, nor it was not so," said Mr. Fox.

"And then—and then I opened the door, and the room was filled with bodies and skeletons of poor dead women, all stained with their blood."

"It is not so, nor it was not so. And God forbid it should be so," said Mr. Fox.

"I then dreamed that I rushed down the gallery, and just as I was going down the stairs, I saw you, Mr. Fox, coming up to the hall door, dragging after you a poor young lady, rich and beautiful."

"It is not so, nor it was not so. And God forbid it should be so," said Mr. Fox.

"I rushed downstairs, just in time to hide myself behind a cask, when you, Mr. Fox, came in dragging the young lady by the arm. And, as you passed me, Mr. Fox, I thought I saw you try and get off her diamond ring, and when you could not, Mr. Fox, it seemed to me in my dream, that you out with your sword and hacked off the poor lady's hand to get the ring."

"It is not so, nor it was not so. And God forbid it should be so," said Mr. Fox, and was going to say something else as he rose from his seat, when Lady Mary cried out:

"But it is so, and it was so. Here's hand and ring I have to show," and pulled out the lady's hand from her dress, and pointed it straight at Mr. Fox.

At once her brothers and her friends drew their swords and cut Mr. Fox into a thousand pieces.

BEASTLY
BRIDE(GROOM)

A FEATURE of virtually all tales that contain animal characters is the unquestioned acceptance of communication between human and animal. One explanation that we have already considered (see "Loss of Innocence") is that the animal is actually the symbolic representation of a particular aspect of the human character, since the fairy tale is first and foremost about people. The essential quality of an animal is its *otherness*; the ability to communicate notwithstanding, the animal represents the unknown, a denizen of the dark world of instinct.

For the immature young woman depicted in many folk–fairy tales, marriage represents at best a challenge, at worst a threat. She may have succeeded in retaining her innocence, but as a consequence of that fact, the prospect of sexual union with a male is a step into the disturbing unknown — which explains why the male often takes the form of an animal. While marriage represents elevation into womanhood, it brings with it also all the anxieties and even revulsion often associated with initiation into sexuality. Thus Beauty is terrified by the prospect of a Beast, and the princess in "The Frog King," in hurling the frog against the wall, is finally responding to her anger and disgust at her importunate suitor.

As we would expect, the theme of love is introduced in all four tales in this section, but from some rather unexpected angles. In "Beauty and the Beast," for example, the story deals with the gradual development of a daughter's love to embrace both father

97

and husband, while in the somewhat similar "Bearskin," love grows out of the youngest daughter's insight that a man's deeds mean more than his appearance. In "The Frog King," love is only made possible by an act of violent self-assertion that is also a declaration of independence, while in "The White Cat," it comes through a prince's acceptance of and trust in a female's power.

In "Beauty and the Beast" and "The White Cat," we have examples of what are termed "salon" tales. They were written by two aristocratic Frenchwomen, Madame Leprince de Beaumont and Madame la Comtesse d'Aulnoy, both of whom were contemporaries of Charles Perrault and important contributors to the literary salons of that time. The fairy tale was much in vogue at the beginning of the eighteenth century, and the aristocratic perspective is clearly visible in the satirical tone and opulent description that characterize these tales. Suggestive of the role these salons played for their predominantly female adherents, we see another instance of role-reversal in "The White Cat" (cf. "East of the Sun, West of the Moon"); the youngest prince's good fortune is entirely attributable to the assistance of the White Cat, and in that respect the tale may be seen as an interesting contrast to "Beauty and the Beast." We cannot fail to notice the animal's gender is of major consequence. Despite the Beast's unfailing courteousness and generosity, his physical presence remains daunting; he exudes sensuality and passion. The White Cat, while sharing the Beast's expensive tastes in household effects, presents a very different image: as mild as the Beast is ferocious, as delicate as he is overwhelming.

The inclusion of "Bearskin" in this section takes a liberty, in that although the soldier is obviously not an *animal* bridegroom, his circumstances surely reveal a continuum; he is simply not under enchantment like the others. This Grimm tale is as gritty in its setting as the French tales are ornate; the desperation of the soldier is indicated in the arrival of the Devil in search of a soul, the reference to whom draws our attention to the Christian influence that is to be found in a number of Grimm tales.

BEAUTY AND THE BEAST

Madame Leprince de Beaumont

ONCE upon a time there lived a merchant who was exceedingly rich. He had six children — three boys and three girls — and being a sensible man he spared no expense upon their education, but engaged tutors of every kind for them. All his daughters were pretty, but the youngest especially was admired by everybody. When she was small she was known simply as 'the little beauty,' and this name stuck to her, causing a great deal of jealousy on the part of her sisters.

This youngest girl was not only prettier than her sisters, but very much nicer. The two elder girls were very arrogant as a result of their wealth; they pretended to be great ladies, declining to receive the daughters of other merchants, and associating only with people of quality. Every day they went off to balls and theatres, and for walks in the park, with many a gibe at their little sister, who spent much of her time in reading good books.

Now these girls were known to be very rich, and in consequence were sought in marriage by many prominent merchants. The two eldest said they would never marry unless they could find a duke, or at least a count. But Beauty — this, as I have mentioned, was the name by which the youngest was known — very politely thanked all who proposed marriage to her, and said that she was too young at present, and that she wished to keep her father company for several years yet.

Suddenly the merchant lost his fortune, the sole property which remained to him being a small house in the country, a long way from the capital. With tears he broke it to his children that they would have to move to this house, where by working like peasants they might just be able to live.

The two elder girls replied that they did not wish to leave the town, and that they had several admirers who would be only too happy to marry them, notwithstanding their loss of fortune. But the simple maidens were mistaken: their admirers would no longer look at them, now that they were poor. Everybody disliked them on account of their arrogance, and folks declared that they did not deserve pity: in fact, that it was a good thing their pride had had a fall—a turn at minding sheep would teach them how to play the fine lady! "But we are very sorry for Beauty's misfortune," everybody added; "she is such a dear girl, and was always so considerate to poor people: so gentle, and with such charming manners!"

There were even several worthy men who would have married her, despite the fact that she was now penniless; but she told them she could not make up her mind to leave her poor father in his misfortune, and that she intended to go with him to the country, to comfort him and help him to work. Poor Beauty had been very grieved at first over the loss of her fortune, but she said to herself:

"However much I cry, I shall not recover my wealth, so I must try to be happy without it."

When they were established in the country the merchant and his family started working on the land. Beauty used to rise at four o'clock in the morning, and was busy all day looking after the house, and preparing dinner for the family. At first she found it very hard, for she was not accustomed to work like a servant, but at the end of a couple of months she grew stronger, and her health was improved by the work. When she had leisure she read, or played the harpsichord, or sang at her spinning-wheel.

Her two sisters, on the other hand, were bored to death; they did not get up till ten o'clock in the morning, and they idled about all day. Their only diversion was to bemoan the beautiful clothes they used to wear and the company they used to keep. "Look at our little sister," they would say to each other; "her tastes are so low and her mind so stupid that she is quite content with this miserable state of affairs."

The good merchant did not share the opinion of his two daughters, for he knew that Beauty was more fitted to shine in company than her sisters. He was greatly impressed by the girl's good qualities, and especially by her patience—for her sisters, not content with leaving her all the work of the house, never missed an opportunity of insulting her.

They had been living for a year in this seclusion when the merchant received a letter informing him that a ship on which he had some merchandise had just come safely home. The news nearly turned the heads of the two elder girls, for they thought that at last they would be able to quit their dull life in the country. When they saw their father ready to set out they begged him to bring them back dresses, furs, caps, and finery of every kind. Beauty asked for nothing, thinking to herself that all the money which the merchandise might yield would not be enough to satisfy her sisters' demands.

"You have not asked me for anything," said her father.

"As you are so kind as to think of me," she replied, "please bring me a rose, for there are none here."

Beauty had no real craving for a rose, but she was anxious not to seem to disparage the conduct of her sisters. The latter would have declared that she purposely asked for nothing in order to be different from them.

The merchant duly set forth; but when he reached his destination there was a law-suit over his merchandise, and after much trouble he returned poorer than he had been before. With only thirty miles to go before reaching home, he was already looking forward to the pleasure of seeing his children again, when he found he had to pass through a large wood. Here he lost himself. It was snowing horribly; the wind was so strong that twice he was thrown from his horse, and when night came on he made up his mind he must either die of hunger and cold or be eaten by the wolves that he could hear howling all about him.

Suddenly he saw, at the end of a long avenue of trees, a strong light. It seemed to be some distance away, but he walked towards it, and presently discovered that it came from a large palace, which was all lit up.

The merchant thanked heaven for sending him this help, and hastened to the castle. To his surprise, however, he found no one about in the courtyards. His horse, which had followed him, saw a large stable open and went in; and on finding hay and oats in readiness the poor animal, which was dying of hunger, set to with a will. The merchant tied him up in the stable, and approached the house, where he found not a soul. He entered a large room; here there was a good fire, and a table laden with food, but with a place laid for one only. The rain and snow had soaked him to the skin, so he drew near the fire to dry himself. "I am sure," he remarked to himself, "that the master of this house or his servants will forgive the liberty I am taking; doubtless they will be here soon."

He waited some considerable time; but eleven o'clock struck and still he had seen nobody. Being no longer able to resist his hunger he took a chicken and devoured it in two mouthfuls, trembling. Then he drank several glasses of wine, and becoming bolder ventured out of the room. He went through several magnificently furnished apartments, and finally found a room with a very good bed. It was now past midnight, and as he was very tired he decided to shut the door and go to bed.

It was ten o'clock the next morning when he rose, and he was greatly astonished to find a new suit in place of his own, which had been spoilt. "This palace," he said to himself, "must surely belong to some good fairy, who has taken pity on my plight."

He looked out of the window. The snow had vanished, and his eyes rested instead upon arbours of flowers—a charming spectacle. He went back to the room where he had supped the night before, and found there a little table with a cup of chocolate on it. "I thank you, Madam Fairy," he said aloud, "for being so kind as to think of my breakfast."

Having drunk his chocolate the good man went forth to look for his horse. As he passed under a bower of roses he remembered that Beauty had asked for one, and he plucked a spray from a mass of blooms. The very same moment he heard a terrible noise, and saw a beast coming towards him which was so hideous that he came near to fainting.

"Ungrateful wretch!" said the Beast, in a dreadful voice; "I have saved your life by receiving you into my castle, and in return you steal that which I love better than anything in the world—my roses. You shall pay for this with your life! I give you fifteen minutes to make your peace with Heaven."

The merchant threw himself on his knees and wrung his hands. "Pardon, my lord!" he cried; "one of my daughters had asked for a rose, and I did not dream I should be giving offence by picking one."

"I am not called 'my lord,'" answered the monster, "but 'The Beast.' I have no liking for compliments, but prefer people to say what they think. Do not hope therefore to soften me by flattery.

You have daughters, you say; well, I am willing to pardon you if one of your daughters will come, of her own choice, to die in your place. Do not argue with me—go! And swear that if your daughters refuse to die in your place you will come back again in three months."

The good man had no intention of sacrificing one of his daughters to this hideous monster, but he thought that at least he might have the pleasure of kissing them once again. He therefore swore to return, and the Beast told him he could go when he wished. "I do not wish you to go empty-handed," he added; "return to the room where you slept; you will find there a large empty box. Fill it with what you will; I will have it sent home for you."

With these words the Beast withdrew, leaving the merchant to reflect that if he must indeed die, at all events he would have the consolation of providing for his poor children.

He went back to the room where he had slept. He found there a large number of gold pieces, and with these he filled the box the Beast had mentioned. Having closed the latter, he took his horse, which was still in the stable, and set forth from the palace, as melancholy now as he had been joyous when he entered it.

The horse of its own accord took one of the forest roads, and in a few hours the good man reached his own little house. His children crowded round him, but at sight of them, instead of welcoming their caresses, he burst into tears. In his hand was the bunch of roses which he had brought for Beauty, and he gave it to her with these words:

"Take these roses, Beauty; it is dearly that your poor father will have to pay for them."

Thereupon he told his family of the dire adventure which had befallen him. On hearing the tale the two elder girls were in a great commotion, and began to upbraid Beauty for not weeping as they did. "See to what her smugness has brought this young chit," they said; "surely she might strive to find some way out of this trouble, as we do! But oh, dear me, no; her ladyship is so determined to be different that she can speak of her father's death without a tear!"

"It would be quite useless to weep," said Beauty. "Why should I lament my father's death? He is not going to die. Since the monster agrees to accept a daughter instead, I intend to offer myself to appease his fury. It will be a happiness to do so, for in dying I shall have the joy of saving my father, and of proving to him my devotion."

"No, sister," said her three brothers; "you shall not die; we will go in quest of this monster, and will perish under his blows if we cannot kill him."

"Do not entertain any such hopes, my children," said the merchant; "the power of this Beast is so great that I have not the slightest expectation of escaping him. I am touched by the goodness of Beauty's heart, but I will not expose her to death. I am old and have not much longer to live; and I shall merely lose a few years that will be regretted only on account of you, my dear children."

"I can assure you, father," said Beauty, "that you will not go to this palace without me. You cannot prevent me from following you. Although I am young I am not so very deeply in love with life, and I would rather be devoured by this monster than die of the grief which your loss would cause me." Words were useless. Beauty was quite determined to go to this wonderful palace, and her sisters were not sorry, for they regarded her good qualities with deep jealousy.

The merchant was so taken up with the sorrow of losing his daughter that he forgot all about the box which he had filled with gold. To his astonishment, when he had shut the door of his room and was about to retire for the night, there it was at the side of his bed! He decided not to tell his children that he had become so rich, for his elder daughters would have wanted to go back to town, and he had resolved to die in the country. He did confide his secret to Beauty, however, and the latter told him that during his absence they had entertained some visitors, amongst whom were two admirers of her sisters. She begged her father to let them marry; for she was of such a sweet nature that she loved them, and forgave them with all her heart the evil they had done her.

When Beauty set off with her father the two heartless girls rubbed their eyes with an onion, so as to seem tearful; but her brothers wept in reality, as did also the merchant. Beauty alone did not cry, because she did not want to add to their sorrow.

The horse took the road to the palace, and by evening they espied it, all lit up as before. An empty stable awaited the nag, and when the good merchant and his daughter entered the great hall, they found there a table magnificently laid for two people. The merchant had not the heart to eat, but Beauty, forcing herself to appear calm, sat down and served him. Since the Beast had provided such splendid fare, she thought to herself, he must presumably be anxious to fatten her up before eating her.

When they had finished supper they heard a terrible noise. With tears the merchant bade farewell to his daughter, for he knew it was the Beast. Beauty herself could not help trembling at the awful apparition, but she did her best to compose herself. The Beast asked her if she had come of her own free will, and she timidly answered that such was the case.

"You are indeed kind," said the Beast, "and I am much obliged to you. You, my good man, will depart to-morrow morning, and you must not think of coming back again. Good-bye, Beauty!"

"Good-bye, Beast!" she answered.

Thereupon the monster suddenly disappeared.

"Daughter," said the merchant, embracing Beauty, "I am nearly dead with fright. Let me be the one to stay here!"

"No, father," said Beauty, firmly, "you must go to-morrow morning, and leave me to the mercy of Heaven. Perhaps pity will be taken on me."

They retired to rest, thinking they would not sleep at all during the night, but they were hardly in bed before their eyes were closed in sleep. In her dreams there appeared to Beauty a lady, who said to her:

"Your virtuous character pleases me, Beauty. In thus undertaking to give your life to save your father you have performed an act of goodness which shall not go unrewarded."

When she woke up Beauty related this dream to her father. He was somewhat consoled by it, but could not refrain from loudly giving vent to his grief when the time came to tear himself away from his beloved child.

As soon as he had gone Beauty sat down in the great hall and began to cry. But she had plenty of courage, and after imploring divine protection she determined to grieve no more during the short time she had yet to live.

She was convinced that the Beast would devour her that night, but made up her mind that in the interval she would walk about and have a look at this beautiful castle, the splendour of which she could not but admire.

Imagine her surprise when she came upon a door on which were the words "Beauty's Room"! She quickly opened this door, and was dazzled by the magnificence of the appointments within. "They are evidently anxious that I should not be dull," she murmured, as she caught sight of a large bookcase, a harpsichord, and several volumes of music. A moment later another thought crossed her mind. "If I had only a day to spend here," she reflected, "such provision would surely not have been made for me."

This notion gave her fresh courage. She opened the bookcase, and found a book in which was written, in letters of gold:

"Ask for anything you wish: you are mistress of all here."

"Alas!" she said with a sigh, "my only wish is to see my poor father, and to know what he is doing."

As she said this to herself she glanced at a large mirror. Imagine her astonishment when she perceived her home reflected in it, and saw her father just approaching. Sorrow was written on his face; but when her sisters came to meet him it was impossible not to detect, despite the grimaces with which they tried to simulate grief, the satisfaction they felt at the loss of their sister. In a moment the vision faded away, yet Beauty could not but think that the Beast was very kind, and that she had nothing much to fear from him.

At midday she found the table laid, and during her meal she enjoyed an excellent concert, though the performers were invisible. But in the evening, as she was about to sit down at the table, she heard the noise made by the Beast, and quaked in spite of herself.

"Beauty," said the monster to her, "may I watch you have your supper?"

"You are master here," said the trembling Beauty.

"Not so," replied the Beast; "it is you who are mistress; you have only to tell me to go, if my presence annoys you, and I will go immediately. Tell me, now, do you not consider me very ugly?"

"I do," said Beauty, "since I must speak the truth; but I think you are also very kind."

"It is as you say," said the monster; "and in addition to being ugly, I lack intelligence. As I am well aware, I am a mere beast."

"It is not the way with stupid people," answered Beauty, "to admit a lack of intelligence. Fools never realise it."

"Sup well, Beauty," said the monster, "and try to banish dullness from your home—for all about you is yours, and I should be sorry to think you were not happy."

"You are indeed kind," said Beauty. "With one thing, I must own, I am well pleased, and that is your kind heart. When I think of that you no longer seem to be ugly."

"Oh yes," answered the Beast, "I have a good heart, right enough, but I am a monster."

"There are many men," said Beauty, "who make worse monsters than you, and I prefer you, notwithstanding your looks, to those who under the semblance of men hide false, corrupt, and ungrateful hearts."

The Beast replied that if only he had a grain of wit he would compliment her in the grand style by way of thanks; but that being so stupid he could only say he was much obliged.

Beauty ate with a good appetite, for she now had scarcely any fear of the Beast. But she nearly died of fright when he put this question to her:

"Beauty, will you be my wife?"

For some time she did not answer, fearing lest she might anger the monster by her refusal. She summoned up courage at last to say, rather fearfully, "No, Beast!"

The poor monster gave forth so terrible a sigh that the noise of it went whistling through the whole palace. But to Beauty's speedy relief the Beast sadly took his leave and left the room, turning several times as he did so to look once more at her. Left alone, Beauty was moved by great compassion for this poor Beast. "What a pity he is so ugly," she said, "for he is so good."

Beauty passed three months in the palace quietly enough. Every evening the Beast paid her a visit, and entertained her at supper by a display of much good sense, if not with what the world calls wit. And every day Beauty was made aware of fresh kindnesses on the part of the monster. Through seeing him often she had become accustomed to his ugliness, and far from dreading the moment of his visit, she frequently looked at her watch to see if it was nine o'clock, the hour when the Beast always appeared.

One thing alone troubled Beauty; every evening, before retiring to bed, the monster asked her if she would be his wife, and seemed overwhelmed with grief when she refused. One day she said to him:

"You distress me, Beast. I wish I could marry you, but I cannot deceive you by allowing you to believe that that can ever be. I will always be your friend—be content with that."

"Needs must," said the Beast. "But let me make the position plain. I know I am very terrible, but I love you very much, and I shall be very happy if you will only remain here. Promise that you will never leave me."

Beauty blushed at these words. She had seen in her mirror that her father was stricken down by the sorrow of having lost her, and she wished very much to see him again. "I would willingly promise to remain with you always," she said to the Beast, "but I have so great a desire to see my father again that I shall die of grief if you refuse me this boon."

"I would rather die myself than cause you grief," said the monster. "I will send you back to your father. You shall stay with him, and your Beast shall die of sorrow at your departure."

"No, no," said Beauty, crying; "I like you too much to wish to cause your death. I promise you I will return in eight days. You have shown me that my sisters are married, and that my brothers have joined the army. My father is all alone; let me stay with him one week."

"You shall be with him to-morrow morning," said the Beast. "But remember your promise. All you have to do when you want to return is to put your ring on a table when you are going to bed. Good-bye, Beauty!"

As usual, the Beast sighed when he said these last words, and Beauty went to bed quite down-hearted at having grieved him.

When she awoke the next morning she found she was in her father's house. She rang a little bell which stood by the side of her bed, and it was answered by their servant, who gave a great cry at sight of her. The good man came running at the noise, and was overwhelmed with joy at the sight of his dear daughter. Their embraces lasted for more than a quarter of an hour. When their transports had subsided, it occurred to Beauty that she had no clothes to put on; but the servant told her that she had just discovered in the next room a chest full of dresses trimmed with gold and studded with diamonds. Beauty felt grateful to the Beast for this attention, and having selected the simplest of the gowns she bade the servant pack up the others, as she wished to send them as presents to her sisters. The words were hardly out of her mouth when the chest disappeared. Her father expressed the opinion that the Beast wished her to keep them all for herself, and in a trice dresses and chest were back again where they were before.

When Beauty had dressed she learned that her sisters, with their husbands, had arrived. Both were very unhappy. The eldest had wedded an exceedingly handsome man, but the latter was so taken up with his own looks that he studied them from morning to night, and despised his wife's beauty. The second had married a man with plenty of brains, but he only used them to pay insults to everybody — his wife first and foremost.

The sisters were greatly mortified when they saw Beauty dressed like a princess, and more beautiful than the dawn. Her caresses were ignored, and the jealousy which they could not stifle only grew worse when she told them how happy she was. Out into the garden went the envious pair, there to vent their spleen to the full.

"Why should this chit be happier than we are?" each demanded of the other; "are we not much nicer than she is?"

"Sister," said the elder, "I have an idea. Let us try to persuade her to stay here longer than the eight days. Her stupid Beast will fly into a rage when he finds she has broken her word, and will very likely devour her."

"You are right, sister," said the other; "but we must make a great fuss of her if we are to make the plan successful."

With this plot decided upon they went upstairs again, and paid such attention to their little sister that Beauty wept for joy. When the eight days had passed the two sisters tore their hair, and showed such grief over her departure that she promised to remain another eight days.

Beauty reproached herself, nevertheless, with the grief she was causing to the poor Beast; moreover, she greatly missed not seeing him. On the tenth night of her stay in her father's house she dreamed that she was in the palace garden, where she saw the

Beast lying on the grass nearly dead, and that he upbraided her for her ingratitude. Beauty woke up with a start, and burst into tears.

"I am indeed very wicked," she said, "to cause so much grief to a Beast who has shown me nothing but kindness. Is it his fault that he is so ugly, and has so few wits? He is good, and that makes up for all the rest. Why did I not wish to marry him? I should have been a good deal happier with him than my sisters are with their husbands. It is neither good looks nor brains in a husband that make a woman happy; it is beauty of character, virtue, kindness. All these qualities the Beast has. I admit I have no love for him, but he has my esteem, friendship, and gratitude. At all events I must not make him miserable, or I shall reproach myself all my life."

With these words Beauty rose and placed her ring on the table.

Hardly had she returned to her bed than she was asleep, and when she woke the next morning she saw with joy that she was in the Beast's palace. She dressed in her very best on purpose to please him, and nearly died of impatience all day, waiting for nine o'clock in the evening. But the clock struck in vain: no Beast appeared. Beauty now thought she must have caused his death, and rushed about the palace with loud despairing cries. She looked everywhere, and at last, recalling her dream, dashed into the garden by the canal, where she had seen him in her sleep. There she found the poor Beast lying unconscious, and thought he must be dead. She threw herself on his body, all her horror of his looks forgotten, and feeling his heart still beat, fetched water from the canal and threw it on his face.

The Beast opened his eyes and said to Beauty:

"You forgot your promise. The grief I felt as having lost you made me resolve to die of hunger; but I die content since I have the pleasure of seeing you once more."

"Dear Beast, you shall not die," said Beauty; "you shall live and become my husband. Here and now I offer you my hand, and swear that I will marry none but you. Alas, I fancied I felt only friendship for you, but the sorrow I have experienced clearly proves to me that I cannot live without you."

Beauty had scarce uttered these words when the castle became ablaze with lights before her eyes: fireworks, music—all proclaimed a feast. But these splendours were lost on her: she turned to her dear Beast, still trembling for his danger.

Judge of her surprise now! At her feet she saw no longer the Beast, who had disappeared, but a prince, more beautiful than Love himself, who thanked her for having put an end to his enchantment. With good reason were her eyes riveted upon the prince, but she asked him nevertheless where the Beast had gone.

"You see him at your feet," answered the prince. "A wicked fairy condemned me to retain that form until some beautiful girl should consent to marry me, and she forbade me to betray any sign of intelligence. You alone in all the world could show yourself susceptible to the kindness of my character, and in offering you my crown I do but discharge the obligation that I owe you."

In agreeable surprise Beauty offered her hand to the handsome prince, and assisted him to rise. Together they repaired to the castle, and Beauty was overcome with joy to find, assembled in the hall, her father and her entire family. The lady who had appeared to her in her dream had had them transported to the castle.

"Beauty," said this lady (who was a celebrated fairy), "come and receive the reward of your noble choice. You preferred merit to either beauty or wit, and you certainly deserve to find these qualities combined in one person. It is your destiny to become a great queen, but I hope that the pomp of royalty will not destroy your virtues. As for you, ladies," she continued, turning to Beauty's two sisters, "I know your hearts and the malice they harbour. Your doom is to become statues, and under the stone that wraps you round to retain all your feelings. You will stand at the door of your sister's palace, and I can visit no greater punishment upon you than that you shall be witnesses of her happiness. Only when you recognise your faults can you return to your present shape, and I am very much afraid that you will be statues for ever. Pride, ill-temper, greed, and laziness can all be corrected, but nothing short of a miracle will turn a wicked and envious heart."

In a trice, with a tap of her hand, the fairy transported them all to the prince's realm, where his subjects were delighted to see him again. He married Beauty, and they lived together for a long time in happiness the more perfect because it was founded on virtue.

THE WHITE CAT

Madame la Comtesse d'Aulnoy

ONCE upon a time there was a king who had three sons, who were all so clever and brave that he began to be afraid that they would want to reign over the kingdom before he was dead. Now the King, though he felt that he was growing old, did not at all wish to give up the government of his kingdom while he could still manage it very well, so he thought the best way to live in peace would be to divert the minds of his sons by promises which he could always get out of when the time came for keeping them.

So he sent for them all, and, after speaking to them kindly, he added:

"You will quite agree with me, my dear children, that my great age makes it impossible for me to look after my affairs of state as carefully as I once did. I begin to fear that this may affect the welfare of my subjects, therefore I wish that one of you should succeed to my crown; but in return for such a gift as this it is only right that you should do something for me. Now, as I think of retiring into the country, it seems to me that a pretty, lively, faithful little dog would be very good company for me; so, without any regard for your ages, I promise that the one who brings me the most beautiful little dog shall succeed me at once."

The three Princes were greatly surprised by their father's sudden fancy for a little dog, but as it gave the two younger ones a chance they would not otherwise have had of being king, and as the eldest was too polite to make any objection, they accepted the commission with pleasure. They bade farewell to the King, who gave them presents of silver and precious stones, and appointed to meet them at the same hour, in the same place, after a year had passed, to see the little dogs they had brought for him.

Then they went together to a castle which was about a league from the city, accompanied by all their particular friends, to whom they gave a grand banquet, and the three brothers promised to be friends always, to share whatever good fortune befell them, and not to be parted by any envy or jealousy; and so they set out, agreeing to meet at the same castle at the appointed time, to present themselves before the King together. Each one took a different road, and the two eldest met with many adventures; but it is about the youngest that you are going to hear. He was young, and gay, and handsome, and knew everything that a prince ought to know; and as for his courage, there was simply no end to it.

Hardly a day passed without his buying several dogs—big and little, greyhounds, mastiffs, spaniels, and lapdogs. As soon as he had bought a pretty one he was sure to see a still prettier, and then he had to get rid of all the others and buy that one, as, being alone, he found it impossible to take thirty or forty thousand dogs about with him. He journeyed from day to day, not knowing where he was going, until at last, just at nightfall, he reached a great, gloomy forest. He did not know his way, and, to make matters worse, it began to thunder, and the rain poured down. He took the first path he could find, and after walking for a long time he fancied he saw a faint light, and began to hope that he was coming to some cottage where he might find shelter for the night. At length, guided by the light, he reached the door of the most splendid castle he could have imagined. This door was of gold covered with carbuncles, and it was the pure red light which shone from them that had shown him the way through the forest. The walls were of the finest porcelain in all the most delicate colours, and the Prince saw that all the stories he had ever read were pictured upon them; but as he was quite terribly wet, and the rain still fell in torrents, he could not stay to look about any more, but came back to the golden door. There he saw a deer's foot hanging by a chain of diamonds, and he began to wonder who could live in this magnificent castle.

"They must feel very secure against robbers," he said to himself. "What is to hinder anyone from cutting off that chain and digging out those carbuncles, and making himself rich for life?"

He pulled the deer's foot, and immediately a silver bell sounded and the door flew open, but the Prince could see nothing but numbers of hands in the air, each holding a torch. He was so much surprised that he stood quite still, until he felt himself pushed forward by other hands, so that, though he was somewhat uneasy, he could not help going on. With his hand on his sword, to be prepared for whatever might happen, he entered a hall paved with lapis-lazuli, while two lovely voices sang:

The hands you see floating above
Will swiftly your bidding obey;
If your heart dreads not conquering Love,
In this place you may fearlessly stay.

The Prince could not believe that any danger threatened him when he was welcomed in this way, so, guided by the mysterious hands, he went towards a door of coral, which opened of its own accord, and he found himself in a vast hall of mother-of-pearl, out of which opened a number of other rooms, glittering with thousands of lights, and full of such beautiful pictures and precious things that the Prince felt quite bewildered. After passing through sixty rooms the hands that conducted him stopped, and the Prince saw a most comfortable-looking arm-chair drawn up close to the chimney-corner; at the same moment the fire lighted itself, and the pretty, soft, clever hands took off the Prince's wet, muddy clothes, and presented him with fresh ones made of the richest stuffs, all embroidered with gold and emeralds. He could not help admiring everything he saw, and the deft way in which the hands waited on him, though they sometimes appeared so suddenly that they made him jump.

When he was quite ready—and I can assure you that he looked very different from the wet and weary Prince who had stood outside in the rain, and pulled the deer's foot—the hands led him to a splendid room, upon the walls of which were painted the histories of Puss in Boots and a number of other famous cats. The table was laid for supper with two golden plates, and golden spoons and forks, and the sideboard was covered with dishes and glasses of crystal set with precious stones. The Prince was wondering who the second place could be for, when suddenly in came about a dozen cats carrying guitars and rolls of music, who took their places at one end of the room, and under the direction of a cat who beat time with a roll of paper began to mew in every imaginable key, and to draw their claws across the strings of the guitars, making the strangest kind of music that could be heard. The Prince hastily stopped up his ears, but even then the sight of these comical musicians sent him into fits of laughter.

"What funny thing shall I see next?" he said to himself, and instantly the door opened, and in came a tiny figure covered by a long black veil. It was conducted by two cats wearing black mantles and carrying swords, and a large party of cats followed, who brought in cages full of rats and mice.

The Prince was so much astonished that he thought he must be dreaming, but the little figure came up to him and threw back its veil, and he saw that it was the loveliest little white cat it is possible to imagine. She looked very young and very sad, and in a sweet little voice that went straight to his heart she said to the Prince:

"King's son, you are welcome; the Queen of the Cats is glad to see you."

"Lady Cat," replied the Prince, "I thank you for receiving me so kindly, but surely you are no ordinary pussy-cat? Indeed, the way you speak and the magnificence of your castle prove it plainly."

"King's son," said the White Cat, "I beg you to spare me these compliments, for I am not used to them. But now," she added, "let supper be served, and let the musicians be silent, as the Prince does not understand what they are saying."

So the mysterious hands began to bring in the supper, and first they put on the table two dishes, one containing stewed pigeons and the other a fricassée of fat mice. The sight of the latter made the Prince feel as if he could not enjoy his supper at all; but the White Cat seeing this assured him that the dishes intended for him were prepared in a separate kitchen, and he might be quite certain that they contained neither rats nor mice; and the Prince felt so sure that she would not deceive him that he had no more hesitation in beginning. Presently he noticed that on the little paw that was next him the White Cat wore a bracelet containing a portrait, and he begged to be allowed to look at it. To his great surprise he found it represented an extremely handsome young man, who was so like himself that it might have been his own portrait! The White Cat sighed as he looked at it, and seemed sadder than ever, and the Prince dared not ask any questions for fear of displeasing her; so he began to talk about other things, and found that she was interested in all the subjects he cared for himself, and seemed to know quite well what was going on in the world. After supper they went into another room, which was fitted up as a theatre, and the cats acted and danced for their amusement, and then the White Cat said good-night to him, and the hands conducted him into a room he had not seen before, hung with tapestry worked with butterflies' wings of every colour; there were mirrors that reached from the ceiling to the floor, and a little white bed with curtains of gauze tied up with ribbons. The Prince went to bed in silence, as he did not quite know how to begin a conversation with the hands that waited on him, and in the morning he was awakened by a noise and confusion outside his window, and the hands came and quickly dressed him in hunting costume. When he looked out all the cats were assembled in the courtyard, some leading greyhounds, some blowing horns, for the White Cat was going out hunting. The hands led a wooden horse up to the Prince, and seemed to expect him to mount it, at which he was very indignant; but it was no use for him to object, for he speedily found himself upon its back, and it pranced gaily off with him.

The White Cat herself was riding a monkey, which climbed even up to the eagles' nests when she had a fancy for the young eaglets. Never was there a pleasanter hunting party, and when they returned to the castle the Prince and the White Cat supped together as before, but when they had finished she offered him a crystal goblet, which must have contained a magic draught, for, as soon as he had swallowed its contents, he forgot everything, even the little dog that he was seeking for the King; and only thought how happy he was to be with the White Cat! And so the days passed, in every kind of amusement, until the year was nearly gone. The Prince had forgotten all about meeting his brothers: he did not even know what country he belonged to; but the White Cat knew when he ought to go back, and one day she said to him:

"Do you know that you have only three days left to look for the little dog for your father, and your brothers have found lovely ones?"

Then the Prince suddenly recovered his memory, and cried:

"What can have made me forget such an important thing? my whole fortune depends upon it; and even if I could in such a short time find a dog pretty enough to gain me a kingdom, where should I find a horse who could carry me all that way in three days?" And he began to be very vexed. But the White Cat said to him: "King's son, do not trouble yourself; I am your friend, and will make everything easy for you. You can still stay here for a day, as the good wooden horse can take you to your country in twelve hours."

"I thank you, beautiful Cat," said the Prince; "but what good will it do me to get back if I have not a dog to take to my father?"

"See here," answered the White Cat, holding up an acorn; "there is a prettier one in this than in the Dog-star!"

"Oh! White Cat dear," said the Prince, "how unkind you are to laugh at me now!"

"Only listen," she said, holding the acorn to his ear.

And inside it he distinctly heard a tiny voice say: "Bow-wow!"

The Prince was delighted, for a dog that can be shut up in an acorn must be very small indeed. He wanted to take it out and look at it, but the White Cat said it would be better not to open the acorn till he was before the King, in case the tiny dog should be cold on the journey. He thanked her a thousand times, and said good-bye quite sadly when the time came for him to set out.

"The days have passed so quickly with you," he said, "I only wish I could take you with me now."

But the White Cat shook her head and sighed deeply in answer.

After all the Prince was the first to arrive at the castle where he had agreed to meet his brothers, but they came soon after, and stared in amazement when they saw the wooden horse in the courtyard jumping like a hunter.

The Prince met them joyfully, and they began to tell him all their adventures; but he managed to hide from them what he had been doing, and even led them to think that a turnspit dog which he had with him was the one he was bringing for the King. Fond as they all were of one another, the two eldest could not help being glad to think that their dogs certainly had a better chance. The next morning they started in the same chariot. The elder brothers carried in baskets two such tiny, fragile dogs that they hardly dared to touch them. As for the turnspit, he ran after the chariot, and got so covered with mud that one could hardly see what he was like at all. When they reached the palace everyone crowded round to welcome them as they went into the King's great hall; and when the two brothers presented their little dogs nobody could decide which was the prettier. They were already arranging between themselves to share the kingdom equally, when the youngest stepped forward, drawing from his pocket the acorn the White Cat had given him. He opened it quickly, and there upon a white cushion they saw a dog so small that it could easily have been put through a ring. The Prince laid it upon the ground, and it got up at once and began to dance. The King did not know what to say, for it was impossible that anything could be prettier than this little creature. Nevertheless, as he was in no hurry to part with his crown, he told his sons that, as they had been so successful the first time, he would ask them to go once again, and seek by land and sea for a piece of muslin so fine that it could be drawn through the eye of a needle. The brothers were not very willing to set out again, but the two eldest consented because it gave them another chance, and they started as before. The youngest again mounted the wooden horse, and rode back at full speed to his beloved White Cat. Every door of the castle stood wide open, and every window and turret was illuminated, so it looked more wonderful than before. The hands hastened to meet him, and led the wooden horse off to the stable, while he hurried in to find the White Cat. She was asleep in a little basket on a white satin cushion, but she very soon started up when she heard the Prince, and was over-joyed at seeing him once more.

"How could I hope that you would come back to me, King's son?" she said. And then he stroked and petted her, and told her of his successful journey, and how he had come back to ask her help, as he believed that it was impossible to find what the King demanded. The White Cat looked serious, and said she must think what was to be done, but that, luckily, there were some cats in the castle who could spin very well, and if anybody could manage it they could, and she would set them the task herself.

And then the hands appeared carrying torches, and conducted the Prince and the White Cat to a long gallery which overlooked the river, from the windows of which they saw a magnificent display of fireworks of all sorts; after which they had supper, which the Prince liked even better than the fireworks, for it was very late, and he was hungry after his long ride. And so the days passed quickly as before; it was impossible to feel dull with the White Cat, and she had quite a talent for inventing new amusements — indeed, she was cleverer than a cat has any right to be. But when the Prince asked her how it was that she was so wise, she only said:

"King's son, do not ask me; guess what you please. I may not tell you anything."

The Prince was so happy that he did not trouble himself at all about the time, but presently the White Cat told him that the year was gone, and that he need not be at all anxious about the piece of muslin, as they had made it very well.

"This time," she added, "I can give you a suitable escort;" and on looking out into the courtyard the Prince saw a superb chariot of burnished gold, enamelled in flame colour with a thousand different devices. It was drawn by twelve snow-white horses, harnessed four abreast; their trappings were of flame-coloured velvet, embroidered with diamonds. A hundred chariots followed, each drawn by eight horses, and filled with officers in splendid uniforms, and a thousand guards surrounded the procession. "Go!" said the White Cat, "and when you appear before the King in such state he surely will not refuse you the crown which you deserve. Take this walnut, but do not open it until you are before him, then you will find in it the piece of stuff you asked me for."

"Lovely Blanchette," said the Prince, "how can I thank you properly for all your kindness to me? Only tell me that you wish it, and I will give up for ever all thought of being king, and will stay here with you always."

"King's son," she replied, "it shows the goodness of your heart that you should care so much for a little white cat, who is good for nothing but to catch mice; but you must not stay."

So the Prince kissed her little paw and set out. You can imagine how fast he travelled when I tell you that they reached the King's palace in just half the time it had taken the wooden horse to get there. This time the Prince was so late that he did not try to meet his brothers at their castle, so they thought he could not be coming, and were rather glad of it, and displayed their pieces of muslin to the King proudly, feeling sure of success. And indeed the stuff was very fine, and would go through the eyes of a very large needle; but the King, who was only too glad to make a difficulty, sent for a particular needle, which was kept among the Crown jewels, and had such a small eye that everybody saw at once that it was impossible that the muslin should pass through it.

The Princes were angry, and were beginning to complain that it was a trick, when suddenly the trumpets sounded and the youngest Prince came in. His father and brothers were quite astonished at his magnificence, and after he had greeted them he took the walnut from his pocket and opened it, fully expecting to find the piece of muslin, but instead there was only a hazel-nut. He cracked it, and there lay a cherry-stone. Everybody was looking on, and the King was chuckling to himself at the idea of finding the piece of muslin in a nutshell.

However, the Prince cracked the cherry-stone, but everyone laughed when he saw it contained only its own kernel. He opened that and found a grain of wheat, and in that was a millet seed. Then he himself began to wonder, and muttered softly:

"White Cat, White Cat, are you making fun of me?"

In an instant he felt a cat's claw give his hand quite a sharp scratch, and hoping that it was meant as an encouragement he opened the millet seed, and drew out of it a piece of muslin four hundred ells long, woven with the loveliest colours and most wonderful patterns; and when the needle was brought it went through the eye six times with the greatest ease! The king turned pale, and the other Princes stood silent and sorrowful, for nobody could deny that this was the most marvellous piece of muslin that was to be found in the world.

Presently the King turned to his sons, and said, with a deep sigh:

"Nothing could console me more in old age than to realise your willingness to gratify my wishes. Go then once more, and whoever at the end of a year can bring back the loveliest princess shall be married to her, and shall, without further delay, receive the crown, for my successor must certainly be married." The Prince considered that he had earned the kingdom fairly twice over, but still he was too well bred to argue about it, so he just went back to his gorgeous chariot, and, surrounded by his escort, returned to the White Cat faster than he had come. This time she was expecting him, the path was strewn with flowers, and a thousand braziers were burning scented woods which perfumed the air. Seated in a gallery from which she could see his arrival, the White Cat waited for him. "Well, King's son," she said, "here you are once more, without a crown." "Madam," said he, "thanks to your generosity

I have earned one twice over; but the fact is that my father is so loth to part with it that it would be no pleasure to me to take it."

"Never mind," she answered; "it's just as well to try and deserve it. As you must take back a lovely princess with you next time I will be on the look-out for one for you. In the meantime let us enjoy ourselves; to-night I have ordered a battle between my cats and the river rats, on purpose to amuse you." So this year slipped away even more pleasantly than the preceding ones. Sometimes the Prince could not help asking the White Cat how it was she could talk.

"Perhaps you are a fairy," he said. "Or has some enchanter changed you into a cat?"

But she only gave him answers that told him nothing. Days go by so quickly when one is very happy that it is certain the Prince would never have thought of its being time to go back, when one evening as they sat together the White Cat said to him that if he wanted to take a lovely princess home with him the next day he must be prepared to do as she told him.

"Take this sword," she said, "and cut off my head!"

"I!" cried the Prince, "I cut off your head! Blanchette darling, how could I do it?"

"I entreat you to do as I tell you, King's son," she replied.

The tears came into the Prince's eyes as he begged her to ask him anything but that—to set him any task she pleased as a proof of his devotion, but to spare him the grief of killing his dear Pussy. But nothing he could say altered her determination, and at last he drew his sword, and desperately, with a trembling hand, cut off the little white head. But imagine his astonishment and delight when suddenly a lovely princess stood before him, and, while he was still speechless with amazement, the door opened and a goodly company of knights and ladies entered, each carrying a cat's skin! They hastened with every sign of joy to the Princess, kissing her hand and congratulating her on being once more restored to her natural shape. She received them graciously, but after a few minutes begged that they would leave her alone with the Prince, to whom she said:

"You see, Prince, that you were right in supposing me to be no ordinary cat. My father reigned over six kingdoms. The Queen, my mother, whom he loved dearly, had a passion for travelling and exploring, and when I was only a few weeks old she obtained his permission to visit a certain mountain of which she had heard many marvellous tales, and set out, taking with her a number of her attendants. On the way they had to pass near an old castle belonging to the fairies. Nobody had even been into it, but it was reported to be full of the most wonderful things, and my mother remembered to have heard that the fairies had in their garden such fruits as were to be seen and tasted nowhere else. She began to wish to try them for herself, and turned her steps in the direction of the garden. On arriving at the door, which blazed with gold and jewels, she ordered her servants to knock loudly, but it was useless; it seemed as if all the inhabitants of the castle must be asleep or dead. Now the more difficult it became to obtain the fruit, the more the Queen was determined that have it she would. So she ordered that they should bring ladders, and get over the wall into the garden; but though the wall did not look very high, and they tied the ladders together to make them very long, it was quite impossible to get to the top.

"The Queen was in despair, but as night was coming on she ordered that they should encamp just where they were, and went to bed herself, feeling quite ill, she was so disappointed. In the middle of the night she was suddenly awakened, and saw to her surprise a tiny, ugly old woman seated by her bedside, who said to her:

"'I must say that we consider it somewhat troublesome of your Majesty to insist upon tasting our fruit; but, to save you any annoyance, my sisters and I will consent to give you as much as you can carry away, on one condition—that is, that you shall give us your little daughter to bring up as our own.'

"'Ah! my dear madam,' cried the Queen, 'is there nothing else that you will take for the fruit? I will give you my kingdoms willingly.'

"'No,' replied the old fairy, 'we will have nothing but your little daughter. She shall be as happy as the day is long, and we will give her everything that is worth having in fairy-land, but you must not see her again until she is married.'

"'Though it is a hard condition,' said the Queen, 'I consent, for I shall certainly die if I do not taste the fruit, and so I should lose my little daughter either way.'

"So the old fairy led her into the castle, and, though it was still the middle of the night, the Queen could see plainly that it was far more beautiful than she had been told, which you can easily believe, Prince," said the White Cat, "when I tell you that it was this castle that we are now in. 'Will you gather the fruit yourself, Queen?' said the old fairy, 'or shall I call it to come to you?'

"'I beg you to let me see it come when it is called,' cried the Queen; 'that will be something quite new.' The old fairy whistled twice, then she cried:

"'Apricots, peaches, nectarines, cherries, plums, pears, melons, grapes, apples, oranges, lemons, gooseberries, strawberries, raspberries, come!'

"And in an instant they came tumbling in, one over another, and yet they were neither dusty nor spoilt, and the Queen found them quite as good as she had fancied them. You see they grew upon fairy trees.

"The old fairy gave her golden baskets in which to take the fruit away, and it was as much as four hundred mules could carry. Then she reminded the Queen of her agreement, and led her back to the camp, and next morning she went back to her kingdom; but before she had gone very far she began to repent of her bargain, and when the King came out to meet her she looked so sad that he guessed that something had happened, and asked what was the matter. At first the Queen was afraid to tell him, but when, as soon as they reached the palace, five frightful little dwarfs were sent by the fairies to fetch me, she was obliged to confess what she had promised. The King was very angry, and had the Queen and myself shut up in a great tower and safely guarded, and drove the little dwarfs out of his kingdom; but the fairies sent a great dragon who ate up all the people he met, and whose breath burnt up everything as he passed through the country; and at last, after trying in vain to rid himself of the monster, the King, to save his subjects, was obliged to consent that I should be given up to the fairies. This time they came themselves to fetch me, in a chariot of pearl drawn by sea-horses, followed by the dragon, who was led with chains of diamonds. My cradle was placed between the old fairies, who loaded me with caresses, and away we whirled through the air to a tower which they had built on purpose for me. There I grew up surrounded with everything that was beautiful and rare, and learning everything that is ever taught to a princess, but without any companions but a parrot and a little dog, who could both talk; and receiving every day a visit from one of the old fairies, who came mounted upon the dragon. One day, however, as I sat at my window I saw a handsome young prince, who seemed to have been hunting in the forest which surrounded my prison, and who was standing and looking up at me. When he saw that I observed him he saluted me with great deference. You can imagine that I was delighted to have some one new to talk to, and in spite of the height of my window our conversation was prolonged till night fell, then my prince reluctantly bade me farewell. But after that he came again many times, and at last I consented to marry him, but the question was how I was to escape from my tower. The fairies always supplied me with flax for my spinning, and by great diligence I made enough cord for a ladder that would reach to the foot of the tower; but, alas! just as my prince was helping me to descend it, the crossest and ugliest of the old fairies flew in. Before he had time to defend himself my unhappy lover was swallowed up by the dragon. As for me, the fairies, furious at having their plans defeated, for they intended me to marry the king of the dwarfs and I utterly refused, changed me into a white cat. When they brought me here I found all the lords and ladies of my father's court awaiting me under the same enchantment, while the people of lesser rank had been made invisible, all but their hands.

"As they laid me under the enchantment the fairies told me all my history, for until then I had quite believed that I was their child, and warned me that my only chance of regaining my natural form was to win the love of a prince who resembled in every way my unfortunate lover."

"And you have won it, lovely Princess," interrupted the Prince.

"You are indeed wonderfully like him," resumed the Princess—"in voice, in features, and everything; and if you really love me all my troubles will be at an end."

"And mine too," cried the Prince, throwing himself at her feet, "if you will consent to marry me."

"I love you already better than anyone in the world," she said; "but now it is time to go back to your father, and we shall hear what he says about it."

So the Prince gave her his hand and led her out, and they mounted the chariot together; it was even more splendid than before, and so was the whole company. Even the horses' shoes were of rubies with diamond nails, and I suppose that is the first time such a thing was ever seen.

As the Princess was as kind and clever as she was beautiful, you may imagine what a delightful journey the Prince found it, for everything the Princess said seemed to him quite charming.

When they came near the castle where the brothers were to meet, the Princess got into a chair carried by four of the guards; it was hewn out of one splendid crystal, and had silken curtains, which she drew round her that she might not be seen.

The Prince saw his brothers walking upon the terrace, each with a lovely princess, and they came to meet him, asking if he had also found a wife. He said that he had found something much rarer—a little white cat! At which they laughed very much, and asked him if he was afraid of being eaten up by mice in the palace. And then they set out together for the town. Each prince and princess rode in a splendid carriage; the horses were decked with plumes of feathers, and glittered with gold. After them came the youngest prince, and last of all the crystal chair, at which everybody looked with admiration and curiosity. When the courtiers saw them coming they hastened to tell the King.

"Are the ladies beautiful?" he asked anxiously.

And when they answered that nobody had ever before seen such lovely princesses he seemed quite annoyed.

However, he received them graciously, but found it impossible to choose between them.

Then turning to his youngest son he said:

"Have you come back alone, after all?"

"Your Majesty," replied the Prince, "will find in that crystal chair a little white cat, which has such soft paws, and mews so prettily, that I am sure you will be charmed with it."

The King smiled, and went to draw back the curtains himself, but at a touch from the Princess the crystal shivered into a thousand splinters, and there she stood in all her beauty; her fair hair floated over her shoulders and was crowned with flowers, and her softly falling robe was of the purest white. She saluted the King gracefully, while a murmur of admiration rose from all around.

"Sire," she said, "I am not come to deprive you of the throne you fill so worthily. I have already six kingdoms, permit me to bestow one upon you, and upon each of your sons. I ask nothing but your friendship, and your consent to my marriage with your youngest son; we shall still have three kingdoms left for ourselves."

The King and all the courtiers could not conceal their joy and astonishment, and the marriage of the three Princes was celebrated at once. The festivities lasted several months, and then each king and queen departed to their own kingdom and lived happily ever after.

THE FROG KING
OR IRON HEINRICH

Jacob and Wilhelm Grimm

IN olden times, when wishing still helped, there lived a king, whose daughters were all beautiful, but the youngest was so beautiful that even the sun, who had seen many things, was filled with wonder every time he shone upon her face. Not far from the king's palace there was a great, dark forest, and under an old lime tree in the forest there was a spring. When the weather was very hot, the princess went out to the forest and sat near the edge of the cool spring. And when the time hung heavy on her hands, she took a golden ball, threw it into the air and caught it. It was her favorite plaything.

One day it so happened that when she held out her little hand to catch the golden ball, the ball passed it by, fell to the ground, and rolled straight into the water. The princess followed the ball with her eyes, but it disappeared, and the spring was deep, so deep that you couldn't see the bottom. She began to cry; she cried louder and louder, she was inconsolable. As she was lamenting, someone called out to her: "What's the matter, princess? Why, to hear you wailing, a stone would take pity." She looked to see where the voice came from and saw a frog sticking his big ugly head out of the water. "Oh, it's you, you old splasher," she said. "I'm crying because my ball has fallen into the spring." "Stop crying," said the frog. "I believe I can help you, but what will you give me if I bring you your plaything?" "Anything you like, dear frog," she said. "My clothes, my beads, my jewels, even the golden crown I'm wearing." The frog replied: "I don't want your clothes, your beads and jewels, or your golden crown. But if you will love me, if you will let me be your companion and playmate, and sit at your table and eat from your golden plate and drink from your golden cup and sleep in your bed, if you promise me that, I'll go down and fetch you your golden ball." "Oh yes," she said, "I promise you anything you want, if only you'll bring me my ball." But she thought: "What nonsense that silly frog talks; he lives in the water with other frogs and croaks; how can he be a companion to anybody?"

Once the frog had her promise, he put his head down and dived, and in a little while he came swimming back to the surface. He had her golden ball in his mouth and he tossed it onto the grass. When she saw her beautiful plaything, the princess was very happy. She picked it up and ran off with it. "Wait, wait," cried the frog. "Take me with you, I can't run like you." He croaked and he croaked at the top of his lungs, but it did him no good. The princess didn't listen. She hurried home and soon forgot the poor frog. There was nothing he could do but go back down into his spring.

The next day, when she had sat down to table with the king and all his courtiers and was eating from her golden plate, something came hopping *plip plop, plip plop,* up the marble steps. When it reached the top, it knocked at the door and cried out: "Princess, youngest princess, let me in." She ran to see who was there, and when she opened the door, she saw the frog. She closed the door as fast as she could and went back to the table. She was frightened to death. The king saw that her heart was going pit-a-pat and said: "What are you afraid of, my child? Is there a giant outside come to take you away?" "Oh no," she said. "It's not a giant, but only a nasty frog." "What does a frog want of you?" "O father dear, yesterday when I was playing beside the spring in the forest, my golden ball fell in the water. And because I was crying so, the frog got it for me, and because he insisted, I promised he could be my companion. I never thought he'd get out of his spring. And now he's outside and he wants to come in after me." Then the frog knocked a second time and cried out:

"Princess, youngest princess,
Let me in.
Don't you remember what
You promised yesterday
By the cool spring?
Princess, youngest princess,
Let me in."

Then the king said: "When you make a promise, you must keep it; just go and let him in." She went and opened the door; the frog hopped in and followed close at her heels. There he sat and cried out: "Lift me up beside you." She didn't know what to do, but the king ordered her to obey. Once the frog was on the chair, he wanted to be on the table, and once he was on the table, he said: "Now push your golden plate up closer to me, so we can eat together." She did as he asked, but anyone could see she wasn't happy about it. The frog enjoyed his meal, but almost every bite stuck in the princess's throat. Finally he said: "I've had enough to eat and now I'm tired, so carry me to your room and prepare your silken bed. Then we'll lie down and sleep." The princess began to cry. She was afraid of the cold frog; she didn't dare touch him and now he wanted to sleep in her lovely clean bed. But the king grew angry and said: "He helped you when you were in trouble and you mustn't despise him now." Then she picked him up between thumb and forefinger, carried him upstairs, and put him down in a corner. But when she lay down in the bed, he came crawling over and said: "I'm tired. I want to sleep as much as you do; pick me up or I'll tell your father." At that she grew very angry, picked him up and dashed him against the wall with all her might. "Now you'll get your rest, you nasty frog."

But when he fell to the floor, he wasn't a frog any longer; he was a king's son with beautiful smiling eyes. At her father's bidding, he became her dear companion and husband. He told her that a wicked witch had put a spell on him and that no one but she alone could have freed him from the spring, and that they would go to his kingdom together the next day. Then they fell asleep and in the morning when the sun woke them a carriage drove up, drawn by eight white horses in golden harness, with white ostrich plumes on their heads, and behind it stood the young king's servant, the faithful Heinrich. Faithful Heinrich had been so sad when his master was turned into a frog that he had had three iron bands forged around his heart, to keep it from bursting with grief and sadness. The carriage had come to take the young king back to his kingdom. Faithful Heinrich lifted the two of them in and sat down again in back, overjoyed that his master had been set free. When they had gone a bit of the way, the prince heard a cracking sound behind him, as though something had broken. He turned around and cried out:

> "Heinrich, the carriage is falling apart."
> "No, master, it's only an iron ring.
> I had it forged around my heart
> For fear that it would break in two
> When, struck by cruel magic, you
> Were turned to a frog in a forest spring."

Once again and yet once again, the cracking was heard, and each time the king's son thought the carriage was falling to pieces, but it was only the bands snapping and falling away from faithful Heinrich's heart, because his master had been set free and was happy.

BEARSKIN

Jacob and Wilhelm Grimm

THERE was once a young fellow who enlisted as a soldier, fought bravely, and was always foremost when the bullets were flying thick and fast. As long as the war lasted, he was well off, but when peace was made, he was given his discharge and his captain told him he could go wherever he pleased. His parents were dead and he had no home, so he went to his brothers and asked them to take him in until the war started up again. But his brothers were hardhearted men. "Why should we?" they said. "What use can you be to us? Go and shift for yourself." The soldier had nothing but his gun. He slung it over his shoulder and started out. Soon he came to a great heath, where all he could see was a circle of trees.

Feeling very sad, he sat down under the trees and thought about his dismal fate. "I have no money," he said to himself. "The only trade I've ever learned is soldiering, and now that peace has been made they don't need me any more. I can see I'm going to starve." Suddenly he heard a rustling, and when he looked around a stranger was standing there. He was wearing a green coat and was very handsome, but he had a horrid-looking cloven hoof. "I know what your trouble is," said the man. "I'll give you as much money and wealth as you can possibly use, but first I must know that you're not afraid, because I don't want to spend my money for nothing." "Would I be a soldier if I were afraid?" said the soldier. "Put me to the test." "All right," said the man. "Look behind you." When the soldier turned around, a big growling bear was coming toward him. "Oho!" cried the soldier. "When I get through tickling your nose, you won't feel like growling any more." Whereupon he took aim and shot the bear in the muzzle. The bear fell down and lay still, and the stranger said: "I can see you've got plenty of courage, but there is one more condition you'll have to meet." "If it won't harm my immortal soul," said the soldier, who knew perfectly well whom he was dealing with. "If it does, I won't have anything to do with it." "You'll judge that for yourself," said Greencoat. "In the next seven years you musn't wash or comb your beard or hair, or cut your nails, or say so much as a single paternoster. I'm going to give you a coat and a clock, and you must wear them all that time. If you die before the seven years are out you'll be mine, but if you live you'll be free for the rest of your life, and rich to boot." The soldier thought of his dire poverty, remembered how often he had faced death, and decided to risk it. The Devil took off his green coat, handed it to the soldier, and said: "If you reach into your pocket when you're wearing this coat, your hand will always be full of money." Then he stripped off the bear's skin and said: "This will be your cloak and your bed. Because of it, people will call you Bearskin." And with that, the Devil vanished.

The soldier put the coat on, reached into his pocket, and found that the Devil had been telling the truth. Then he threw the bearskin over his shoulders, went out into the world and enjoyed himself, neglecting nothing that gave him pleasure and cost money. It wasn't so bad during the first year, but by the second he was looking like a monster. His face was almost entirely covered with hair, his beard was matted like felt, his fingernails were claws, there was so much dirt on his face that if cress had been sown in it, it would have sprouted. Everyone who caught sight of him ran away, but since wherever he went he gave money to the poor to pray that he wouldn't die before the seven years were out, and since he always paid well, he could count on finding lodgings. In the fourth year he came to an inn and the innkeeper didn't want to take him in or even let him sleep in the stable, because he was afraid the sight of him would make the horses skittish. When Bearskin reached into his pocket and brought out a handful of ducats, the innkeeper took pity on him and gave him a room at the back of the house, but, for fear of bringing the inn into ill repute, made him promise not to show his face.

As he was sitting there alone, wishing with all his heart that the seven years were over, he heard someone lamenting in the next room. Now Bearskin had a kind heart. He opened the door and there was an old man, weeping bitterly and wringing his hands. At the sight of Bearskin, the old man jumped up and started to run away, but when he heard a human voice he stopped and listened and finally, in answer to Bearskin's soft words, told him the reason for his despair. Little by little his fortune had dwindled, he and his daughters were reduced to starvation, he was too poor to pay the innkeeper, and he was going to be thrown into prison. "If that's all it is," said Bearskin, "you can stop worrying. I have plenty of money." He sent for the innkeeper, paid him, and put a purse full of gold into the unhappy man's pocket.

When the old man saw that his troubles were over, he didn't know how to show his gratitude. "Come with me," he said. "My daughters are miracles of beauty. Choose one of them for your wife. When she hears what you've done for me, she won't refuse. It's true, you look rather weird, but she'll set you to rights." The idea appealed to Bearskin and he went with the old man. When the eldest daughter saw him, she was so horrified that she screamed and ran away. The second stood still and examined him from top to toe, but then she said: "How can I marry a man who doesn't even look human? I'd sooner have taken the shaved bear who was here once, passing himself off as a man. He at least was wearing a hussar's uniform and white gloves. If it were only his ugliness, I could get used to it." But the youngest said: "Dear father, he must be a good man, to have helped you in your need. If you've promised him a wife in return, your promise must be kept." Unfortunately Bearskin's face was covered with dirt and hair, or you'd have seen how his heart leaped for joy when he heard those words. He took a ring from his finger, broke it in two, gave her one half, and kept the other half for himself. On her half he wrote his name and on his half he wrote her name, and he asked her to take good care of her half. Then he bade her farewell saying: "I shall have to wander for another three years. If I don't come back then, you will be free, for I shall be dead. But pray God to keep me alive."

The poor girl dressed all in black, and the tears came to her eyes when she thought of her betrothed. All she got from her sisters was mockery. "Better be careful," said the eldest. "If you hold out your hand, he'll crush it in his paw." "Watch out," said the second, "bears love sweets. If he likes you, he'll eat you up." "Be sure to do what he wants," said the eldest, "or he'll start to growl." And the second: "The wedding will be merry, though. Bears are such good dancers." But the bride made no answer and nothing they said could ruffle her. Meanwhile Bearskin wandered from place to place, helping people as much as he could, and giving generously to the poor so they would pray for him. Finally, when the last day of the seven years dawned, he went back to the heath and sat down inside the circle of trees. Soon the wind whistled and the Devil stood before him. He gave Bearskin a glum look, tossed him his old coat and asked to have his green one back. "Not so fast," said Bearskin. "First you must clean me up." Like it or not, the Devil had to bring water, give Bearskin a good scrubbing, comb his hair and cut his nails. When that was done, he looked like a dashing soldier and was much more handsome than before.

When the Devil had left him, Bearskin felt light of heart. He went to the town, bought a splendid velvet coat, seated himself in a carriage drawn by four white horses, and rode to the house of his betrothed. No one recognized him. The father took him for a general, led him to the room where his daughters were sitting, and showed him to a place between his two elder daughters. They poured wine for him, put the tastiest morsels before him, and thought they had never in all their lives seen a handsomer man.

His betrothed, who was sitting across from him in her black dress, didn't raise her eyes or say a word. When at last he asked the father if he would give him one of his daughters for a wife, the two eldest jumped up, ran to their rooms and put on their best clothes, for each of them thought she was the chosen one. As soon as he was alone with his betrothed, the stranger took out his half ring, dropped it into a glass of wine and passed it across the table to her. She took the wine and drank it, and when she found the half ring at the bottom of her glass, her heart leaped. She took the other half, which she had been wearing on a ribbon round her neck, put the two together, and saw that the two parts fitted together perfectly. Whereupon he said: "I am your betrothed. I was Bearskin when you saw me last, but by the grace of God I have regained my human form and been made clean again." He went over to her, took her in his arms and kissed her. Just then the two sisters came back in all their finery, and when they saw that the handsome man had chosen the youngest and heard that he was Bearskin, they ran out of the house in a rage. The eldest drowned herself in the well, the other hanged herself from a tree. That evening there was a knock at the door, and when the bride-groom opened, it was the Devil in his green coat. "You see," he said, "now I've got two souls in exchange for your one."

THE CHILD
AS HERO

As we have seen, the folk-fairy tale did not begin life as the exclusive property of children, for the simple reason that it was originally told by and for adults, which explains what many would now consider its occasionally unsuitable subject-matter. We must remember that the concept of childhood has only emerged over the last three to four centuries; in earlier times, childhood was simply not perceived as being a distinct period of life. The explanation for this is partly economic and partly psychological in nature. Among the peasantry, children represented a natural resource, but of a kind that required years of nurturing before any return could be expected, years during which the child was actually a drain on scarce resources, with no guarantee that he or she would live long enough to repay such an investment. In a world of such hardship, it is reasonable to speculate that the emotional attachment between parent and child was sometimes less intense than in our own world of relative affluence and leisure. This social and psychological insignificance makes it all the more surprising that children are as well-represented in the folk-fairy tale as they are. However, the point must be made that although many of the tales we have read so far *begin* with childhood, their major emphasis is upon the transition to adulthood. The tales in this section are distinguished by the fact that their focus is specifically upon childhood, with little or no reference to later life.

There is a deep-seated ambivalence toward children reflected in folk-fairy tales. These tales are about children not so much

135

because they are perceived as interesting or entertaining characters (as is generally the assumption today), but rather because they are representatives of the upcoming generation, prospective claimants of adult privilege and status. On the one hand, there are tales in which love and protectiveness toward offspring is expressed— more often, it may be added, in tales about the rich than about the poor—although the over-protectiveness found in such tales as "Little Red Riding Hood" and "Sleeping Beauty" can be seen as leading to unhappy consequences. On the other hand, there is fear and resentment of the child as a potential rival (as we saw in "Damsels in Distress"). It is no coincidence, then, that in all three of the tales in this section the conflict is generational and represents the "rite of passage" that the child or children must undergo to achieve adult status.

The beginnings of these tales depict physical hardship and that is surely based in historical fact. Poverty and famine are experiences that few of us have suffered at first hand, and so we have little conception of the profound effects they have on those afflicted. So, while we may brand the mother of Hansel and Gretel as cold-hearted and cruel, we cannot deny that she is responding to a harsh reality in a pragmatic fashion. Indeed, the same dire situation is outlined at the beginning of "Molly Whuppie" in so offhand a fashion as to suggest that this kind of thing happens all the time. Is it possible that the roots of these tales (connected as they clearly are) reach back to a time when children were, in such extreme circumstances, seen as expendable? In "Jack and the Beanstalk," the situation is reversed, with the widowed mother at the mercy of her immature, good-for-nothing son; while there is certainly no evil intent here, the prospect is nevertheless the same—imminent starvation.

The similarity of structure continues into the second phase of the tales, wherein the realistic gives way to the fantastic, and the child-characters must quickly learn to fend for themselves or perish in the attempt. That they succeed in overcoming the adult characters who oppose them should be seen as a practical acknowledgement of the way the world works, rather than as a glorification of intrepid youth. Any notion of the child as natural adventurer and hero was simply incompatible with the attitudes toward childhood that prevailed in earlier times.

Not surprisingly, Freudian critics such as Bruno Bettelheim have much to say about these visceral conflicts between child and adult which, by virtue of being played out in the realm of the imaginary, sublimate anxiety-creating aggression and rivalry into a form that the listener/reader can accept and resolve. Hansel and Gretel return home (escaping the fantasy-world via an obviously symbolic body of water) to discover that their mother has died in their absence. The link between mother and witch seems obvious, and although the children choose to return home, one senses that they are now more likely to look after their father, rather than the reverse.

For his part, Jack comes back the same way he left, but as a dramatically different person—the Jack who kills the giant and bestows wealth and security upon his mother is no longer an aimless, impulsive boy. As with "Molly Whuppie," however, we must confront the moral question that arises from Jack's thefts from the giant, the last of which seems particularly gratuitous, in that his wealth is assured by his possession of the hen that lays the golden eggs. Some versions of this tale present it as a matter of revenge: Jack's father is absent from the story because he has been killed by the giant, and so Jack is simply reclaiming his own. In the case of *this* version, the explanation must be that we judge motive according to the folk tale's simple—even primitive—moral code: the giant is by nature wicked (as his earlier behavior has amply revealed) and therefore his possessions must be ill-gotten. If Jack or Molly has the youthful audacity to make the attempt, then to the victor go the spoils. The new generation has passed the test and takes its rightful place until it in turn finds itself cast in the role of giant or witch, and the struggle begins anew.

HANSEL AND GRETEL

Jacob and Wilhelm Grimm

AT the edge of a large forest there lived a poor woodcutter with his wife and two children. The little boy's name was Hansel, and the little girl's was Gretel. There was never much to eat in the house, and once, in time of famine, there wasn't even enough

bread to go around. One night the woodcutter lay in bed thinking, tossing and turning with worry. All at once he sighed and said
to his wife: "What's to become of us? How can we feed our poor
children when we haven't even got enough for ourselves?" His
wife answered: "Husband, listen to me. Tomorrow at daybreak
we'll take the children out to the thickest part of the forest and
make a fire for them and give them each a piece of bread. Then
we'll leave them and go about our work. They'll never find the
way home again and that way we'll be rid of them." "No, Wife,"
said the man. "I won't do it. How can I bring myself to leave my
children alone in the woods? The wild beasts will come and tear
them to pieces." "You fool!" she said. "Then all four of us will
starve. You may as well start planing the boards for our coffins."
And she gave him no peace until he consented. "But I still feel
badly about the poor children," he said.

The children were too hungry to sleep, and they heard what
their stepmother said to their father. Gretel wept bitter tears and
said: "Oh, Hansel, we're lost." "Hush, Gretel," said Hansel. "Don't
worry. I'll find a way." When the old people had fallen asleep, he
got up, put on his little jacket, opened the bottom half of the
Dutch door, and crept outside. The moon was shining bright, and
the pebbles around the house glittered like silver coins. Hansel
crouched down and stuffed his pocket full of them. Then he went
back and said to Gretel: "Don't worry, little sister. Just go to sleep,
God won't forsake us," and went back to bed.

At daybreak, before the sun had risen, the woman came and
woke the two children. "Get up, you lazybones. We're going to
the forest for wood." Then she gave each a piece of bread and said:
"This is for your noonday meal. Don't eat it too soon, because
there won't be any more." Gretel put the bread under her apron,
because Hansel had pebbles in his pocket. Then they all started
out for the forest together. When they had gone a little way,
Hansel stopped still and looked back in the direction of their
house, and every so often he did it again. His father said: "Hansel,
why do you keep looking back and lagging behind? Wake up and
don't forget what your legs are for." "Oh, father," said Hansel, "I'm
looking for my white kitten; he's sitting on the roof, trying to bid
me good-bye." The woman said: "You fool, that's not your white
kitten. It's the morning sun shining on the chimney." But Hansel

hadn't been looking at his kitten. Each time, he had taken a shiny pebble from his pocket and dropped it on the ground.

When they came to the middle of the forest, the father said: "Start gathering wood, children, and I'll make a fire to keep you warm." Hansel and Gretel gathered brushwood till they had a little pile of it. The brushwood was kindled and when the flames were high enough the woman said: "Now, children, lie down by the fire and rest. We're going into the forest to cut wood. When we're done, we'll come back and get you."

Hansel and Gretel sat by the fire, and at midday they both ate their pieces of bread. They heard the strokes of an ax and thought their father was nearby. But it wasn't an ax, it was a branch he had tied to a withered tree, and the wind was shaking it to and fro. After sitting there for some time, they became so tired that their eyes closed and they fell into a deep sleep. When at last they awoke, it was dark night. Gretel began to cry and said: "How will we ever get out of this forest?" But Hansel comforted her: "Just wait a little while. As soon as the moon rises, we'll find the way." And when the full moon had risen, Hansel took his little sister by the hand and followed the pebbles, which glistened like newly minted silver pieces and showed them the way. They walked all night and reached their father's house just as day was breaking. They knocked at the door, and when the woman opened it and saw Hansel and Gretel, she said: "Wicked children! Why did you sleep so long in the forest? We thought you'd never get home." But their father was glad, for he had been very unhappy about deserting them.

A while later the whole country was again stricken with famine, and the children heard their mother talking to their father in bed at night: "Everything has been eaten up. We still have half a loaf of bread, and when that's gone there will be no more. The children must go. We'll take them still deeper into the forest, and this time they won't find their way home; it's our only hope." The husband was heavy-hearted, and he thought: "It would be better if I shared the last bite with my children." But the woman wouldn't listen to anything he said; she only scolded and found fault. Once you've said yes, it's hard to say no, and so it was that the woodcutter gave in again.

But the children were awake; they had heard the conversation.

When the old people had fallen asleep, Hansel got up again. He wanted to pick up some more pebbles, but the woman had locked the door and he couldn't get out. But he comforted his little sister and said: "Don't cry, Gretel. Just go to sleep, God will help us."

Early in the morning the woman came and got the children out of bed. She gave them their pieces of bread, but they were smaller than the last time. On the way to the forest, Hansel crumbled his bread in his pocket. From time to time he stopped and dropped a few crumbs on the ground. "Hansel," said his father, "why are you always stopping and looking back? Keep moving." "I'm looking at my little pigeon," said Hansel. "He's sitting on the roof, trying to bid me good-bye." "Fool," said the woman. "That's not your little pigeon, it's the morning sun shining on the chimney." But little by little Hansel strewed all his bread on the ground.

The woman led the children still deeper into the forest, to a place where they had never been in all their lives. Again a big fire was made, and the mother said: "Just sit here, children. If you get tired, you can sleep awhile. We're going into the forest to cut wood, and this evening when we've finished we'll come and get you." At midday Gretel shared her bread with Hansel, who had strewn his on the ground. Then they fell asleep and the afternoon passed, but no one came for the poor children. It was dark night when they woke up, and Hansel comforted his little sister. "Gretel," he said, "just wait till the moon rises; then we'll see the breadcrumbs I strewed and they'll show us the way home." When the moon rose, they started out, but they didn't find any breadcrumbs, because the thousands of birds that fly around in the forests and fields had eaten them all up. Hansel said to Gretel: "Don't worry, we'll find the way," but they didn't find it. They walked all night and then all day from morning to night, but they were still in the forest, and they were very hungry, for they had nothing to eat but the few berries they could pick from the bushes. And when they were so tired their legs could carry them no farther, they lay down under a tree and fell asleep.

It was already the third morning since they had left their father's house. They started out again, but they were getting deeper and deeper into the forest, and unless help came soon, they were sure to die of hunger and weariness. At midday, they saw a lovely snowbird sitting on a branch. It sang so beautifully that they stood still and listened. When it had done singing, it flapped its wings and flew on ahead, and they followed until the bird came to a little house and perched on the roof. When they came closer, they saw that the house was made of bread, and the roof was made of cake and the windows of sparkling sugar. "Let's eat," said Hansel, "and the Lord bless our food. I'll take a piece of the roof. You, Gretel, had better take some of the window; it's sweet." Hansel reached up and broke off a bit of the roof to see how it tasted, and Gretel pressed against the windowpanes and nibbled at them. And then a soft voice called from inside:

> "Nibble nibble, little mouse,
> Who's that nibbling at my house?"

The children answered:

> "The wind so wild,
> The heavenly child,"

and went right on eating. Hansel liked the taste of the roof, so he tore off a big chunk, and Gretel broke out a whole round windowpane and sat down on the ground to enjoy it. All at once the door opened, and an old, old woman with a crutch came hobbling out. Hansel and Gretel were so frightened they dropped what they were eating. But the old woman wagged her head and said: "Oh, what dear children! However did you get here? Don't be afraid, come in and stay with me. You will come to no harm." She took them by the hand and led them into her house. A fine meal of milk and pancakes, sugar, apples, and nuts was set before them. And then two little beds were made up clean and white, and Hansel and Gretel got into them and thought they were in heaven.

But the old woman had only pretended to be so kind. Actually she was a wicked witch, who waylaid children and had built her house out of bread to entice them. She killed, cooked, and ate any child who fell into her hands, and that to her was a feast day. Witches have red eyes and can't see very far, but they have a keen sense of smell like animals, so they know when humans are coming. As Hansel and Gretel approached, she laughed her wicked laugh and said with a jeer: "Here come two who will never get away from me." Early in the morning, when the children were still asleep, she got up, and when she saw them resting so sweetly with their plump red cheeks, she muttered to herself: "What tasty morsels they will be!" She grabbed Hansel with her scrawny hand, carried him to a little shed, and closed the iron-barred door behind him. He screamed for all he was worth, but much good it did him. Then she went back to Gretel, shook her awake, and cried: "Get up, lazybones. You must draw water and cook something nice for your brother. He's out in the shed and we've got to fatten him up. When he's nice and fat, I'm going to eat him." Gretel wept bitterly, but in vain; she had to do what the wicked witch told her.

The best of food was cooked for poor Hansel, but Gretel got nothing but crayfish shells. Every morning the old witch crept to the shed and said: "Hansel, hold out your finger. I want to see if you're getting fat." But Hansel held out a bone. The old woman had weak eyes and couldn't see it; she thought it was Hansel's finger and wondered why he wasn't getting fat. When four weeks had gone by and Hansel was as skinny as ever, her impatience got the better of her and she decided not to wait any longer. "Ho there, Gretel," she cried out. "Go and draw water and don't dawdle. Skinny or fat, I'm going to butcher Hansel tomorrow and cook him." Oh, how the little girl wailed at having to carry the water, and how the tears flowed down her cheeks! "Dear God," she cried, "oh, won't you help us? If only the wild beasts had eaten us in the forest, at least we'd have died together." "Stop that blubbering," said the witch. "It won't do you a bit of good."

Early in the morning Gretel had to fill the kettle with water and light the fire. "First we'll bake," said the old witch. "I've heated the oven and kneaded the dough." And she drove poor Gretel out to the oven, which by now was spitting flames. "Crawl in," said the witch, "and see if it's hot enough for the bread." Once Gretel was inside, she meant to close the door and roast her, so as to eat her too. But Gretel saw what she had in mind and said: "I don't know how. How do I get in?" "Silly goose," said the old woman. "The opening is big enough. Look. Even I can get in." She crept to the opening and stuck her head in, whereupon Gretel gave her a push that sent her sprawling, closed the iron door and fastened the bolt. Eek! How horribly she screeched! But Gretel ran away and the wicked witch burned miserably to death.

Gretel ran straight to Hansel, opened the door of the shed, and cried: "Hansel, we're saved! The old witch is dead." Hansel hopped out like a bird when someone opens the door of its cage. How happy they were! They hugged and kissed each other and danced around. And now that there was nothing to be afraid of, they went into the witch's house and in every corner there were boxes full of pearls and precious stones. Hansel stuffed his pockets full of them and said: "These will be much better than pebbles," and Gretel said: "I'll take some home too," and filled her apron with them. "We'd better leave now," said Hansel, "and get out of this bewitched forest." When they had walked a few hours, they came to a big body of water. "How will we ever get across" said Hansel. "I don't see any bridge." "And there's no boat, either," said Gretel, "but over there I see a white duck. She'll help us across if I ask her." And she cried out:

> "Duckling, duckling, here is Gretel,
> Duckling, duckling, here is Hansel,
> No bridge or ferry far and wide—
> Duckling, come and give us a ride."

Sure enough, the duck came over to them and Hansel sat down on her back and told his sister to sit beside him. "No," said Gretel, "that would be too much for the poor thing; let her carry us one at a time." And that's just what the good little duck did. And when they were safely across and had walked a little while, the forest began to look more and more familiar, and finally they saw their father's house in the distance. They began to run, and they flew into the house and threw themselves into their father's arms. The poor man hadn't had a happy hour since he had left the children in the forest, and in the meantime his wife had died. Gretel opened out her little apron, the pearls and precious stones went bouncing around the room, and Hansel reached into his pockets and tossed out handful after handful. All their worries were over, and they lived together in pure happiness. My story is done, see the mouse run; if you catch it, you may make yourself a great big fur cap out of it.

MOLLY WHUPPIE

Joseph Jacobs

ONCE upon a time there was a man and a wife had too many children, and they could not get meat for them, so they took the three youngest and left them in a wood. They travelled and travelled and could see never a house. It began to be dark, and they were hungry. At last they saw a light and made for it; it turned out to be a house. They knocked at the door, and a woman came to it, who said: "What do you want?" They said: "Please let us in and give us something to eat." The woman said: "I can't do that, as my man is a giant, and he would kill you if he comes home." They begged hard. "Let us stop for a little while," said they, "and we will go away before he comes." So she took them in, and set them down before the fire, and gave them milk and bread; but just as they had begun to eat a great knock came to the door, and a dreadful voice said:

> "Fee, fie, fo, fum,
> I smell the blood of some earthly one.

Who have you there wife?" "Eh," said the wife, "it's three poor lassies cold and hungry, and they will go away. Ye won't touch 'em, man." He said nothing, but ate up a big supper, and ordered them to stay all night. Now he had three lassies of his own, and they were to sleep in the same bed with the three strangers. The youngest of the three strange lassies was called Molly Whuppie, and she was very clever. She noticed that before they went to bed the giant put straw ropes round her neck and her sisters', and round his own lassies' necks he put gold chains. So Molly took care and did not fall asleep, but waited till she was sure every one was sleeping sound. Then she slipped out of the bed, and took the straw ropes off her own and her sisters' necks, and took the gold chains off the giant's lassies. She then put the straw ropes on the giant's lassies and the gold on herself and her sisters, and lay down. And in the middle of the night up rose the giant, armed with a great club, and felt for the necks with the straw. It was dark. He took his own lassies out of bed on to the floor, and battered them until they were dead, and then lay down again, thinking he had managed finely, Molly thought it time she and her sisters were off and away, so she wakened them and told them to be quiet, and they slipped out of the house. They all got out safe, and they ran and ran, and never stopped until morning, when they saw a grand house before them. It turned out to be a king's house: so Molly went in, and told her story to the king. He said: "Well, Molly, you are a clever girl, and you have managed well; but, if you would manage better, and go back, and steal the giant's sword that hangs on the back of his bed, I would give your eldest sister my eldest son to marry." Molly said she would try. So she went back, and managed to slip into the giant's house, and crept in below the bed. The giant came home, and ate up a great supper, and went to bed. Molly waited until he was snoring, and she crept out, and reached over the giant and got down the sword; but just as she got it out over the bed it gave a rattle, and up jumped the giant, and Molly ran out at the door and the sword with her; and she ran, and he ran, till they came to the "Bridge of one hair "; and she got over, but he couldn't, and he says, "Woe worth ye, Molly Whuppie! never ye come again." And she says: "Twice yet, carle," quoth she, "I'll come to Spain." So Molly took the sword to the king, and her sister was married to his son.

Well, the king he says: "Ye've managed well, Molly; but if ye would manage better, and steal the purse that lies below the giant's pillow, I would marry your second sister to my second son." And Molly said she would try. So she set out for the giant's house, and slipped in, and hid again below the bed, and waited till the giant had eaten his supper, and was snoring sound asleep. She slipped out, and slipped her hand below the pillow, and got out the purse; but just as she was going out the giant wakened, and ran after her; and she ran, and he ran, till they came to the "Bridge of one hair," and she got over, but he couldn't, and he said, "Woe worth ye, Molly Whuppie! never you come again." "Once yet, carle," quoth she, "I'll come to Spain." So Molly took the purse to the king, and her second sister was married to the king's second son.

After that the king says to Molly: "Molly, you are a clever girl, but if you would do better yet, and steal the giant's ring that he wears on his finger, I will give you my youngest son for yourself." Molly said she would try. So back she goes to the giant's house, and hides herself below the bed. The giant wasn't long ere he came home, and, after he had eaten a great big supper, he went to his bed, and shortly was snoring loud. Molly crept out and reached over the bed, and got hold of the giant's hand, and she pulled and she pulled until she got off the ring; but just as she got it off the giant got up, and gripped her by the hand, and he says: "Now I have caught you, Molly Whuppie, and, if I had done as much ill to you as ye have done to me, what would ye do to me?"

Molly says: "I would put you into a sack, and I'd put the cat inside wi' you, and the dog aside you, and a needle and thread and a shears, and I'd hang you up upon the wall, and I'd go to the wood, and choose the thickest stick I could get, and I would come home, and take you down, and bang you till you were dead."

"Well, Molly," says the giant, "I'll just do that to you."

So he gets a sack, and puts Molly into it, and the cat and the dog beside her, and a needle and thread and shears, and hangs her up upon the wall, and goes to the wood to choose a stick.

Molly she sings out: "Oh, if ye saw what I see."

"Oh," says the giant's wife, "what do ye see, Molly?"

But Molly never said a word but, "Oh, if ye saw what I see!"

The giant's wife begged that Molly would take her up into the sack till she would see what Molly saw. So Molly took the shears and cut a hole in the sack, and took out the needle and thread with her, and jumped down and helped the giant's wife up into the sack, and sewed up the hole.

The giant's wife saw nothing, and began to ask to get down again; but Molly never minded, but hid herself at the back of the door. Home came the giant, and a great big tree in his hand, and he took down the sack, and began to batter it. His wife cried, "It's me, man;" but the dog barked and the cat mewed, and he did not know his wife's voice. But Molly came out from the back of the door, and the giant saw her, and he after her; and he ran and she ran, till they came to the "Bridge of one hair," and she got over but he couldn't; and he said, "Woe worth you, Molly Whuppie! never you come again." "Never more, carle," quoth she, "will I come again to Spain."

So Molly took the ring to the king, and she was married to his youngest son, and she never saw the giant again.

JACK AND THE BEANSTALK

Joseph Jacobs

THERE was once upon a time a poor widow who had an only son named Jack, and a cow named Milky-white. And all they had to live on was the milk the cow gave every morning, which they carried to the market and sold. But one morning Milky-white gave no milk, and they didn't know what to do.

"What shall we do, what shall we do?" said the widow, wringing her hands.

"Cheer up, mother, I'll go and get work somewhere," said Jack.

"We've tried that before, and nobody would take you," said his mother; "we must sell Milky-white and with the money start shop, or something."

"All right, mother," says Jack; "it's market-day today, and I'll soon sell Milky-white, and then we'll see what we can do."

So he took the cow's halter in his hand, and off he started. He hadn't gone far when he met a funny-looking old man, who said to him: "Good morning, Jack."

"Good morning to you," said Jack, and wondered how he knew his name.

"Well, Jack, and where are you off to?" said the man.

"I'm going to market to sell our cow here."

"Oh, you look the proper sort of chap to sell cows," said the man; "I wonder if you know how many beans make five."

"Two in each hand and one in your mouth," says Jack, as sharp as a needle.

"Right you are," says the man, "and here they are, the very beans themselves," he went on, pulling out of his pocket a number of strange-looking beans. "As you are so sharp," says he, "I don't mind doing a swap with you — your cow for these beans."

"Go along," says Jack; "wouldn't you like it?"

"Ah! you don't know what these beans are," said the man; "if you plant them over-night, by morning they grow right up to the sky."

"Really?" said Jack; "you don't say so."

"Yes, that is so, and if it doesn't turn out to be true you can have your cow back."

"Right," says Jack, and hands him over Milky-white's halter and pockets the beans.

Back goes Jack home, and as he hadn't gone very far it wasn't dusk by the time he got to his door.

"Back already, Jack?" said his mother; "I see you haven't got Milky-white, so you've sold her. How much did you get for her?"

"You'll never guess, mother," says Jack.

"No, you don't say so. Good boy! Five pounds, ten, fifteen, no, it can't be twenty."

"I told you you couldn't guess. What do you say to these beans; they're magical, plant them over-night and—"

"What! " says Jack's mother, "have you been such a fool, such a dolt, such an idiot, as to give away my Milky-white, the best milker in the parish, and prime beef to boot, for a set of paltry beans? Take that! Take that! Take that! And as for your precious beans here they go out of the window. And now off with you to bed. Not a sup shall you drink, and not a bit shall you swallow this very night."

So Jack went upstairs to his little room in the attic, and sad and sorry he was, to be sure, as much for his mother's sake, as for the loss of his supper.

At last he dropped off to sleep.

When he woke up, the room looked so funny. The sun was shining into part of it, and yet all the rest was quite dark and shady. So Jack jumped up and dressed himself and went to the window. And what do you think he saw? Why, the beans his mother had thrown out of the window into the garden, had sprung up into a big beanstalk which went up and up and up till it reached the sky. So the man spoke truth after all.

The beanstalk grew up quite close past Jack's window, so all he had to do was to open it and give a jump on to the beanstalk which ran up just like a big ladder. So Jack climbed, and he climbed and he climbed and he climbed and he climbed and he climbed and he climbed till at last he reached the sky. And when he got there he found a long broad road going as straight as a dart. So he walked along and he walked along and he walked along till he came to a great big tall house, and on the doorstep there was a great big tall woman.

"Good morning, mum," says Jack, quite polite-like. "Could you be so kind as to give me some breakfast?" For he hadn't had anything to eat, you know, the night before and was as hungry as a hunter.

"It's breakfast you want, is it?" says the great big tall woman, "it's breakfast you'll be if you don't move off from here. My man is an ogre and there's nothing he likes better than boys broiled on toast. You'd better be moving on or he'll soon be coming."

"Oh! please mum, do give me something to eat, mum. I've had nothing to eat since yesterday morning, really and truly, mum," says Jack. "I may as well be broiled as die of hunger."

Well, the ogre's wife was not half so bad after all. So she took Jack into the kitchen, and gave him a hunk of bread and cheese and a jug of milk. But Jack hadn't half finished these when thump! thump! thump! the whole house began to tremble with the noise of some one coming.

"Goodness gracious me! It's my old man," said the ogre's wife, "what on earth shall I do? Come along quick and jump in here." And she bundled Jack into the oven just as the ogre came in.

He was a big one, to be sure. At his belt he had three calves strung up by the heels, and he unhooked them and threw them down on the table and said: "Here, wife, broil me a couple of these for breakfast. Ah! what's this I smell?

> Fee-fi-fo-fum,
> I smell the blood of an Englishman,
> Be he alive, or be he dead
> I'll have his bones to grind my bread."

"Nonsense dear," said his wife, "you're dreaming. Or perhaps you smell the scraps of that little boy you liked so much for yesterday's dinner. Here, you go and have a wash and tidy up, and by the time you come back your breakfast'll be ready for you."

So off the ogre went, and Jack was just going to jump out of the oven and run away when the woman told him not. "Wait till he's asleep," says she; "he always has a doze after breakfast."

Well, the ogre had his breakfast, and after that he goes to a big chest and takes out of it a couple of bags of gold, and down he sits and counts till at last his head began to nod and he began to snore till the whole house shook again.

Then Jack crept out on tiptoe from his oven, and as he was passing the ogre he took one of the bags of gold under his arm, and off he pelters till he came to the beanstalk, and then he threw down the bag of gold, which of course fell into his mother's garden, and then he climbed down and climbed down till at last he got home and told his mother and showed her the gold and said: "Well, mother, wasn't I right about the beans? They are really magical, you see."

So they lived on the bag of gold for some time, but at last they came to the end of it, and Jack made up his mind to try his luck once more up at the top of the beanstalk. So one fine morning he rose up early, and got on to the beanstalk, and he climbed and he climbed and he climbed and he climbed and he climbed and he climbed till at last he came out on to the road again and up to the great big tall house he had been to before. There, sure enough, was the great big tall woman a-standing on the doorstep.

"Good morning, mum," says Jack, as bold as brass, "could you be so good as to give me something to eat?"

"Go away, my boy," said the big tall woman, "or else my man will eat you for breakfast. But aren't you the youngster who came here once before? Do you know, that very day, my man missed one of his bags of gold."

"That's strange, mum," said Jack, "I dare say I could tell you something about that, but I'm so hungry I can't speak till I've had something to eat."

Well the big tall woman was so curious that she took him in and gave him something to eat. But he had scarcely begun munching it as slowly as he could when thump! thump! thump! they heard the giant's footstep, and his wife hid Jack away in the oven.

All happened as it did before. In came the ogre as he did before, said: "Fee-fi-fo-fum," and had his breakfast of three broiled oxen. Then he said: "Wife, bring me the hen that lays the golden eggs." So she brought it, and the ogre said: "Lay," and it laid an egg all of gold. And then the ogre began to nod his head, and to snore till the house shook.

Then Jack crept out of the oven on tiptoe and caught hold of the golden hen, and was off before you could say "Jack Robinson." But this time the hen gave a cackle which woke the ogre, and just as Jack got out of the house he heard him calling: "Wife, wife, what have you done with my golden hen?"

And the wife said: "Why, my dear?"

But that was all Jack heard, for he rushed off to the beanstalk and climbed down like a house on fire. And when he got home he showed his mother the wonderful hen, and said "Lay" to it; and it laid a golden egg every time he said "Lay."

Well, Jack was not content, and it wasn't very long before he determined to have another try at his luck up there at the top of the beanstalk. So one fine morning, he rose up early, and got on to the beanstalk, and he climbed and he climbed and he climbed and he climbed till he got to the top. But this time he knew better than to go straight to the ogre's house. And when he got near it, he waited behind a bush till he saw the ogre's wife come out with a pail to get some water, and then he crept into the house and got into the copper. He hadn't been there long when he heard thump! thump! thump! as before, and in come the ogre and his wife.

"Fee-fi-fo-fum, I smell the blood of an Englishman," cried out the ogre. "I smell him, wife, I smell him."

"Do you, my dearie?" says the ogre's wife. "Then, if it's that little rogue that stole your gold and the hen that laid the golden eggs he's sure to have got into the oven." And they both rushed to the oven. But Jack wasn't there, luckily, and the ogre's wife said: "There you are again with your fee-fi-fo-fum. Why of course it's the boy you caught last night that I've just broiled for your breakfast. How forgetful I am, and how careless you are not to know the difference between live and dead after all these years."

So the ogre sat down to the breakfast and ate it, but every now and then he would mutter: "Well, I could have sworn—" and he'd get up and search the larder and the cupboards and everything, only, luckily, he didn't think of the copper.

After breakfast was over, the ogre called out: "Wife, wife, bring me my golden harp." So she brought it and put it on the table before him. Then he said: "Sing!" and the golden harp sang most beautifully. And it went on singing till the ogre fell asleep, and commenced to snore like thunder.

Then Jack lifted up the copper-lid very quietly and got down like a mouse and crept on hands and knees till he came to the table, when up he crawled, caught hold of the golden harp and dashed with it towards the door. But the harp called out quite loud: "Master! Master!" and the ogre woke up just in time to see Jack running off with his harp.

Jack ran as fast as he could, and the ogre came rushing after, and would soon have caught him only Jack had a start and dodged him a bit and knew where he was going. When he got to the beanstalk the ogre was not more than twenty yards away when suddenly he saw Jack disappear like, and when he came to the end of the road he saw Jack underneath climbing down for dear life. Well, the ogre didn't like trusting himself to such a ladder, and he stood and waited, so Jack got another start. But just then the harp cried out: "Master! Master!" and the ogre swung himself down on to the beanstalk, which shook with his weight. Down climbs Jack, and after him climbed the ogre. By this time Jack had climbed down and climbed down and climbed down till he was very near- ly home. So he called out: "Mother! Mother! bring me an axe, bring me an axe." And his mother came rushing out with the axe in her hand, but when she came to the beanstalk she stood stock still with fright for there she saw the ogre with his legs just through the clouds.

But Jack jumped down and got hold of the axe and gave a chop at the beanstalk which cut it half in two. The ogre felt the beanstalk shake and quiver so he stopped to see what was the mat- ter. Then Jack gave another chop with the axe, and the beanstalk was cut in two and began to topple over. Then the ogre fell down and broke his crown, and the beanstalk came toppling after.

Then Jack showed his mother his golden harp, and what with showing that and selling the golden eggs, Jack and his mother became very rich, and he married a great princess, and they lived happy ever after.

BRAIN OVER
BRAWN

THE theme of the underdog overcoming great odds is found in tales the world over and is as popular today as ever. We don't have to look far to find an explanation, once we remind ourselves that these tales originated with the folk; stories in which superior size and strength is rendered impotent by superior cunning must have held an immediate appeal to people who lived with constant reminders of their own political and economic powerlessness. To express discontent with their lot in any direct manner would be to invite swift and cruel retribution, and so frustrations had to be released imaginatively rather than actively. In this respect, the tales in this section surely provide a kind of socio-political therapy; the flippant and even exuberant manner in which the underdog/protagonist sets about the task of exploiting the stupidity of his opponent must have provided a very pointed satisfaction.

The nature of the protagonists in this section deserves some consideration, in that none of them can accurately be described as good, at least in the conventional sense. There is an ambiguous quality to the first two tales, which can be traced in part to the strong hint of amorality shown by their "heroes" in pursuit of their respective goals. We find ourselves both amused and taken aback by the effrontery of Puss in Boots as he threatens the peasantry, or of the tailor as he sets out to bamboozle the world with an embroidery of the truth that is both literal and figurative. Yet we should not be surprised by these tales' implicit assumption that cunning is a virtue. The people among whom these tales evolved had little reason to expect any material change for the better in their lives; for them, prosperity and success were no more than dreams. (Two of the protagonists in this section are endeavoring to save their skins, in fact.) Thus, it is easy to understand how the character who has the wit and audacity to seize the main chance when it comes along is not to be censored for a lack of honesty or sensitivity.

Several critics — Bruno Bettelheim prominent among them — have pointed out that this kind of tale can also be interpreted on a psychological level, in terms of the conflict between generations; from this perspective, the giant or ogre is the authoritarian father-figure whose dull-witted truculence is no match for the energy and ambition of the young. The fact that the protagonists in this section are respectively an adult, a cat, and a pig is not inconsistent with this view; in each tale, small is pitted against large, and the two non-human characters nevertheless manifest some aspect of inferiority: one is a domesticated, the other a farm animal.

In the previous section we noted the surprising passivity of many of the males who are nevertheless cast in the role of rescuer. Here, however, we meet a young male who acquires fame and fortune entirely through the assistance of a helpful animal, his only contribution being to allow himself to be dissuaded from eating the cat and making a muff with his pelt! All that is necessary to guarantee our "hero" his success, it appears, is his willingness to relinquish his assumed "rational" superiority in favor of his helper's intuition — what in the modern world would be termed "street-smarts." It turns into a very profitable partnership, which is surely part of the point: the miller's son is open to unorthodox solutions to his problems, and the cat needs an opportunity to show off his skills. Indeed, the mutually beneficial relationship between these two provides some insight into the symbolic uses of animals in fairy tale.

PUSS IN BOOTS

Charles Perrault

A CERTAIN miller had three sons, and when he died the sole worldly goods which he bequeathed to them were his mill, his ass, and his cat. This little legacy was very quickly divided up, and you may be quite sure that neither notary nor attorney were called in to help, for they would speedily have grabbed it all for themselves.

The eldest son took the mill, and the second son took the ass. Consequently all that remained for the youngest son was the cat, and he was not a little disappointed at receiving such a miserable portion.

"My brothers," said he, "will be able to get a decent living by joining forces, but for my part, as soon as I have eaten my cat and made a muff out of his skin, I am bound to die of hunger."

These remarks were overheard by Puss, who pretended not to have been listening, and said very soberly and seriously:

"There is not the least need for you to worry, Master. All you have to do is to give me a pouch, and get a pair of boots made for me so that I can walk in the woods. You will find then that your share is not so bad after all."

Now this cat had often shown himself capable of performing cunning tricks. When catching rats and mice, for example, he would hide himself amongst the meal and hang downwards by the feet as though he were dead. His master, therefore, though he did not build too much on what the cat had said, felt some hope of being assisted in his miserable plight.

On receiving the boots which he had asked for, Puss gaily pulled them on. Then he hung the pouch round his neck, and holding the cords which tied it in front of him with his paws, he sallied forth to a warren where rabbits abounded. Placing some bran and lettuce in the pouch, he stretched himself out and lay as if dead. His plan was to wait until some young rabbit, unlearned in worldly wisdom, should come and rummage in the pouch for the eatables which he had placed there.

Hardly had he laid himself down when things fell out as he wished. A stupid young rabbit went into the pouch, and Master Puss, pulling the cords tight, killed him on the instant.

Well satisfied with his capture, Puss departed to the king's palace. There he demanded an audience, and was ushered upstairs. He entered the royal apartment, and bowed profoundly to the king.

"I bring you, Sire," said he, "a rabbit from the warren of the marquis of Carabas (such was the title he invented for his master), which I am bidden to present to you on his behalf."

"Tell your master," replied the king, "that I thank him, and am pleased by his attention."

Another time the cat hid himself in a wheatfield, keeping the mouth of his bag wide open. Two partridges ventured in, and by pulling the cords tight he captured both of them. Off he went and presented them to the king, just as he had done with the rabbit from the warren. His Majesty was not less gratified by the brace of partridges, and handed the cat a present for himself.

For two or three months Puss went on in this way, every now and again taking to the king, as a present from his master, some game which he had caught. There came a day when he learned that the king intended to take his daughter, who was the most beautiful princess in the world, for an excursion along the river bank.

"If you will do as I tell you," said Puss to his master, "your fortune is made. You have only to go and bathe in the river at the spot which I shall point out to you. Leave the rest to me."

The marquis of Carabas had no idea what plan was afoot, but did as the cat had directed.

While he was bathing the king drew near, and Puss at once began to cry out at the top of his voice:

"Help! help! the marquis of Carabas is drowning!"

At these shouts the king put his head out of the carriage window. He recognised the cat who had so often brought him game, and bade his escort go speedily to the help of the marquis of Carabas.

While they were pulling the poor marquis out of the river, Puss approached the carriage and explained to the king that while his master was bathing robbers had come and taken away his clothes, though he had cried "Stop, thief!" at the top of his voice. As a matter of fact, the rascal had hidden them under a big stone. The king at once commanded the keepers of his wardrobe to go and select a suit of his finest clothes for the marquis of Carabas.

The king received the marquis with many compliments, and as the fine clothes which the latter had just put on set off his good looks (for he was handsome and comely in appearance), the king's daughter found him very much to her liking. Indeed, the marquis of Carabas had not bestowed more than two or three respectful but sentimental glances upon her when she fell madly in love with him. The king invited him to enter the coach and join the party.

Delighted to see his plan so successfully launched, the cat went on ahead, and presently came upon some peasants who were mowing a field.

"Listen, my good fellows," said he; "if you do not tell the king that the field which you are mowing belongs to the marquis of Carabas, you will all be chopped up into little pieces like mincemeat."

In due course the king asked the mowers to whom the field on which they were at work belonged.

"It is the property of the marquis of Carabas," they all cried with one voice, for the threat from Puss had frightened them.

"You have inherited a fine estate," the king remarked to Carabas.

"As you see for yourself, Sire," replied the marquis; "this is a meadow which never fails to yield an abundant crop each year."

Still travelling ahead, the cat came upon some harvesters.

"Listen, my good fellows," said he; "if you do not declare that every one of these fields belongs to the marquis of Carabas, you will all be chopped up into little bits like mincemeat."

The king came by a moment later, and wished to know who was the owner of the fields in sight.

"It is the marquis of Carabas," cried the harvesters.

At this the king was more pleased than ever with the marquis.

Preceding the coach on its journey, the cat made the same threat to all whom he met, and the king grew astonished at the great wealth of the marquis of Carabas.

Finally Master Puss reached a splendid castle, which belonged to an ogre. He was the richest ogre that had ever been known, for all the lands through which the king had passed were part of the castle domain.

The cat had taken care to find out who this ogre was, and what powers he possessed. He now asked for an interview, declaring that he was unwilling to pass so close to the castle without having the honour of paying his respects to the owner.

The ogre received him as civilly as an ogre can, and bade him sit down.

"I have been told," said Puss, "that you have the power to change yourself into any kind of animal—for example, that you can transform yourself into a lion or an elephant."

"That is perfectly true," said the ogre, curtly; "and just to prove it you shall see me turn into a lion."

Puss was so frightened on seeing a lion before him that he sprang on to the roof—not without difficulty and danger, for his boots were not meant for walking on tiles.

Perceiving presently that the ogre had abandoned his transformation, Puss descended, and owned to having been thoroughly frightened.

"I have also been told," he added, "but I can scarcely believe it, that you have the further power to take the shape of the smallest animals—for example, that you can change yourself into a rat or a mouse. I confess that to me it seems quite impossible."

"Impossible?" cried the ogre; "you shall see!" And in the same moment he changed himself into a mouse, which began to run about the floor. No sooner did Puss see it than he pounced on it and ate it.

Presently the king came along, and noticing the ogre's beautiful mansion desired to visit it. The cat heard the rumble of the coach as it crossed the castle drawbridge, and running out to the courtyard cried to the king:

"Welcome, your Majesty, to the castle of the marquis of Carabas!"

"What's that?" cried the king. "Is this castle also yours, marquis? Nothing could be finer than this courtyard and the buildings which I see all about. With your permission we will go inside and look round."

The marquis gave his hand to the young princess, and followed the king as he led the way up the staircase. Entering a great hall they found there a magnificent collation. This had been prepared by the ogre for some friends who were to pay him a visit that very day. The latter had not dared to enter when they learned that the king was there.

The king was now quite as charmed with the excellent qualities of the marquis of Carabas as his daughter. The latter was completely captivated by him. Noting the great wealth of which the marquis was evidently possessed, and having quaffed several cups of wine, he turned to his host, saying:

"It rests with you, marquis, whether you will be my son-in-law."

The marquis, bowing very low, accepted the honour which the king bestowed upon him. The very same day he married the princess.

Puss became a personage of great importance, and gave up hunting mice, except for amusement.

Moral

> No matter how great may be the advantages
> Of enjoying a rich inheritance,
> Coming down from father to son,
> Most young people will do well to remember
> That industry, knowledge and a clever mind
> Are worth more than mere gifts from others.

Another Moral

> If a miller's son, in so short a time,
> Can win the heart of a Princess,
> So that she gazes at him with lovelorn eyes,
> Perhaps it is the clothes, the appearance, and youthfulness
> That are seldom the indifferent means
> Of inspiring love!

THE BRAVE LITTLE TAILOR

Jacob and Wilhelm Grimm

ONE summer morning a little tailor was sitting on his table near the window. He was in high good humor and sewed with all his might. A peasant woman came down the street, crying out: "Good jam—cheap!" That sounded sweet to the tailor's ears. He stuck his shapely little head out of the window and cried: "Up here, my good woman, you'll find a buyer." The woman hauled her heavy baskets up the three flights of stairs to the tailor's and he made her unpack every single pot. He examined them all, lifted them up, sniffed at them, and finally said: "This looks like good jam to me; weigh me out three ounces, my good woman, and if it comes to a quarter of a pound you won't find me complaining." The woman, who had hoped to make a good sale, gave him what he asked for, and went away grumbling and very much out of sorts. "God bless this jam and give me health and strength," cried the little tailor. Whereupon he took bread from the cupboard, cut a slice straight across the loaf, and spread it with jam. "I bet this won't taste bitter," he said, "but before biting into it I'm going to finish my jacket." He put the bread down beside him and went on with his sewing, taking bigger and bigger stitches in his joy. Meanwhile, the flies that had been sitting on the wall, enticed by the sweet smell, came swarming down on the jam. "Hey, who invited you?" cried the little tailor and shooed the unbidden guests away. But the flies, who didn't understand his language, refused to be dismissed and kept coming in greater and greater numbers. Finally, at the end of his patience, the tailor took a rag from the catchall under his table. "Just wait! I'll show you!" he cried, and struck out at them unmercifully. When he stopped and counted, no less than seven flies lay dead with their legs in the air. He couldn't help admiring his bravery. "What a man I am!" he cried. "The whole town must hear of this." And one two three, he cut out a belt for himself, stitched it up, and embroidered on it in big letters: "Seven at one blow!" Then he said: "Town, my foot! The whole world must hear of it!" And for joy his heart wagged like a lamb's tail.

The tailor put on his belt and decided to go out into the world, for clearly his shop was too small for such valor. Before leaving, he ransacked the house for something to take with him, but all he could find was an old cheese, so he put that in his pocket. Just outside the door, he caught sight of a bird that had got itself caught in the bushes, and the bird joined the cheese in his pocket. Ever so bravely he took to the road, and because he was light and nimble, he never seemed to get tired. Up into the mountains he went, and when he reached the highest peak he found an enormous giant sitting there taking it easy and enjoying the view. The little tailor went right up to him; he wasn't the least bit afraid. "Greetings, friend," he said. "Looking out at the great world, are you? Well, that's just where I'm headed for, to try my luck. Would you care to go with me?" The giant looked at the tailor contemptuously and said: "You little pipsqueak! You miserable nobody!" "Is that so?" said the little tailor, unbuttoning his coat and showing the giant his belt. "Read that! That'll show you what kind of man I am!" When he had read what was written — "Seven at one blow!" — the giant thought somewhat better of the little man. All the same, he decided to put him to the test, so he picked up a stone and squeezed it until drops of water appeared. "Do that," he said, "if you've got the strength." "That?" said the tailor. "Why, that's child's play for a man like me." Whereupon he reached into his pocket, took out the soft cheese, and squeezed it until the whey ran out. "What do you think of that?" he cried. "Not so bad, eh?" The giant didn't know what to say; he couldn't believe the little man was so strong. So he picked up a stone and threw it so high that the eye could hardly keep up with it: "All right, you little runt, let's see you do that." "Nice throw," said the tailor, "but it fell to the ground in the end. Watch me throw one that won't ever come back." Whereupon he reached into his pocket, took out the bird, and tossed it into the air. Glad to be free, the bird flew up and away and didn't come back. "Well," said the tailor. "What do you think of that?" "I've got to admit you can throw," said the giant, "but now let's see what you can carry." Pointing at a big oak tree that lay felled on the ground, he said: "If you're strong enough, help me carry this tree out of the forest." "Glad to," said the little man. "You take the trunk over your shoulder, and I'll carry the branches; they're the heaviest part." The giant took the trunk over his shoulder, and the tailor sat down on a branch, so that the giant, who couldn't look around, had to carry the whole tree and the tailor to boot. The tailor felt so chipper in his comfortable back seat that he began to whistle "Three Tailors Went a-Riding," as though hauling trees were child's play to a man of his strength. After carrying the heavy load for quite some distance, the giant was exhausted. "Hey!" he cried out, "I've got to drop it." The tailor jumped nimbly down, put his arms around the tree as if he'd been carrying it, and said to the giant: "I wouldn't have thought a tiny tree would be too much for a big man like you."

They went on together until they came to a cherry tree. The giant grabbed the crown where the cherries ripen soonest, pulled it down, handed it to the tailor, and bade him eat. But the tailor was much too light to hold the tree down. When the giant let go, the crown snapped back into place and the tailor was whisked high into the air. When he had fallen to the ground without hurting himself, the giant cried out: "What's the matter? You mean you're not strong enough to hold that bit of a sapling?" "Not strong enough? How can you say such a thing about a man who did for seven at one blow? I jumped over that tree because the hunters down there were shooting into the thicket. Now you try. See if you can do it." The giant tried, but he couldn't get over the tree and got stuck in the upper branches. Once again the little tailor had won out.

"All right," said the giant. "If you're so brave, let me take you to our cave to spend the night with us." The little tailor was willing and went along with him. When they got to the cave, the other giants were sitting around the fire. Each one was holding a roasted sheep in his hands and eating it. The little tailor looked around and thought: "This place is a good deal roomier than my workshop." The giant showed him a bed and told him to lie down and sleep. But the bed was too big for the little tailor, so instead of getting into it, he crept into a corner. At midnight, when the giant thought the tailor must be sound asleep, he got up, took a big iron bar and split the bed in two with one stroke. That will settle the little runt's hash, he thought. At the crack of dawn the giants started into the forest. They had forgotten all about the little tailor. All at once he came striding along as chipper and bold as you please. The giants were terrified. They thought he would kill them all, and ran away as fast as their legs would carry them.

The little tailor went his way. After following his nose for many days he came to the grounds of a king's palace. Feeling tired, he lay down in the grass and went to sleep, and while he was sleeping some courtiers came along. They examined him from all sides and read the inscription on his belt: "Seven at one blow!" "Goodness," they said, "what can a great war hero like this be doing here in peacetime? He must be some great lord." They went and told the king. "If war should break out," they said, "a man like that would come in very handy. Don't let him leave on any account." This struck the king as good advice, and he sent one of his courtiers to offer the tailor a post in his army. The courtier went back to the sleeper, waited until he stretched his limbs and opened his eyes, and made his offer. "That's just what I came here for," said the tailor. "I'll be glad to enter the king's service." So he was received with honor and given apartments of his own.

But the soldiers, who were taken in by the little tailor, wished him a thousand miles away. "What will become of us?" they asked. "If we quarrel with him and he strikes, seven of us will fall at one blow. We won't last long at that rate." So they took counsel together, went to the king and asked to be released from his service. Because, they said, "we can't hope to keep up with a man who does for seven at one blow." The king was sad to be losing all his faithful servants because of one and wished he had never laid eyes on him. He'd have been glad to get rid of him, but he didn't dare dismiss him for fear the great hero might strike him and all his people dead and seize the throne for himself. He thought and thought, and at last he hit on an idea. He sent word to the little tailor that since he was such a great hero he wanted to make him an offer. There were two giants living in a certain forest, and they were murdering, looting, burning, and laying the country waste. No one dared go near them for fear of his life. If the hero should conquer and kill these two giants, the king would give him his only daughter to wife, with half his kingdom as her dowry. And, moreover, the king would send a hundred knights to back him up. "Sounds like just the thing for me," thought the little tailor. "It's not every day that somebody offers you a beautiful princess and half a kingdom." "It's a deal," he replied. "I'll take care of those giants, and I won't need the hundred knights. You can't expect a man who does for seven at one blow to be afraid of two."

The little tailor started out with the hundred knights at his heels. When they got to the edge of the forest, he said to his companions: "Stay here. I'll attend to the giants by myself." Then he bounded into the woods, peering to the right and to the left. After a while he caught sight of the two giants, who were lying under a tree asleep, snoring so hard that the branches rose and fell. Quick as a flash the little tailor picked up stones, filled both his pockets with them, and climbed the tree. Halfway up, he slid along a branch until he was right over the sleeping giants. Then he picked out one of the giants and dropped stone after stone on his chest. For a long while the giant didn't notice, but in the end he woke up, gave his companion a poke, and said: "Why are you hitting me?" "You're dreaming," said the other. "I'm not hitting you." When they had lain down to sleep again, the tailor dropped a stone on the second giant. "What is this?" he cried. "Why are you pelting me?" "I'm not pelting you!" the first grumbled. They argued awhile, but they were too tired to keep it up and finally their eyes closed again. Then the little tailor took his biggest stone and threw it with all his might at the first giant's chest. "This is too much!" cried the giant, and jumping up like a madman he pushed his companion so hard against the tree that it shook. The other repaid him in kind and they both flew into such a rage that they started pulling up trees and belaboring each other until they both lay dead on the ground. The little tailor jumped down. "Lucky they didn't pull up the tree I was sitting in," he said to himself. "I'd have had to jump into another like a squirrel. But then we tailors are quick." He drew his sword, gave them both good thrusts in the chest, and went back to the knights. "The job is done," he said. "I've settled their hash. But it was a hard fight. They were so desperate they pulled up trees to fight with, but how could that help them against a man who does for seven at one blow!" "Aren't you even wounded?" the knights asked. "I should say not!" said the tailor. "Not so much as a scratch." The knights wouldn't believe him, so they rode into the forest, where they found the giants lying in pools of blood, with uprooted trees all around them.

The little tailor went to the king and demanded the promised reward, but the king regretted his promise and thought up another way to get rid of the hero. "Before I give you my daughter and half my kingdom," he said, "you will have to perform one more task. There's a unicorn loose in the forest and he's doing a good deal of damage. You will have to catch him first." "If the two giants didn't scare me, why would I worry about a unicorn? Seven at one blow is my meat." Taking a rope and an ax, he went into the forest, and again told the knights who had been sent with him to wait on the fringe. He didn't have long to look. In a short while the unicorn came along and rushed at the tailor, meaning to run him straight through with his horn. "Not so fast!" said the tailor. "It's not as easy as all that." He stood still, waited until the unicorn was quite near him, and then jumped nimbly behind a tree. The unicorn charged full force and rammed into the tree. His horn went in and stuck so fast that he hadn't the strength to pull it out. He was caught. "I've got him," said the tailor. He came out from behind the tree, put the rope around the unicorn's neck, and, taking his ax, chopped the wood away from the horn. When that was done, he led the beast to the king.

But the king was still unwilling to grant him the promised reward and made a third demand. Before the wedding he wanted the tailor to capture a wild boar which had been ravaging the forest, and said the royal huntsmen would help him. "Gladly," said the little tailor. "It's child's play." He didn't take the huntsmen into the forest with him, and they were just as pleased, for several times the boar had given them such a reception that they had no desire to seek him out. When the boar caught sight of the tailor, he gnashed his teeth, foamed at the mouth, made a dash at him, and would have lain him out flat if the nimble hero hadn't escaped into a nearby chapel. The boar ran in after him, but the tailor jumped out of the window, ran around the chapel and slammed the door. The infuriated beast was much too heavy and clumsy to jump out of the window, and so he was caught. The little tailor ran back to the huntsmen and told them to go and see the captive with their own eyes. He himself went to the king, who had to keep his promise this time, like it or not, and give him his daughter and half the kingdom. If he had known that, far from being a war hero, the bridegroom was only a little tailor, he would have been even unhappier than he was. And so the wedding was celebrated with great splendor and little joy, and a tailor became a king.

One night the young queen heard her husband talking in his

sleep. "Boy," he said, "hurry up with that jerkin you're making and get those breeches mended or I'll break my yardstick over your head." Then she knew how he had got his start in life. Next morning she went to her father, told him her tale of woe, and begged him to help her get rid of a husband who had turned out to be a common tailor. The king bade her take comfort and said: "Leave the door of your bedroom unlocked tonight. My servants will be waiting outside. Once he's asleep they'll go in, tie him up, and put him aboard a ship bound for the end of the world." The young queen was pleased, but the armor-bearer, who was devoted to the hero, heard the whole conversation and told him all about the plot. "They won't get away with that!" said the little tailor. That night he went to bed with his wife at the usual hour. When she thought he was asleep, she got up, opened the door, and lay down again. The little tailor, who was only pretending to be asleep, cried out in a loud voice: "Boy, hurry up with that jerkin you're making and get those breeches mended or I'll break my yardstick over your head. I've done for seven at one blow, killed two giants, brought home a unicorn, and captured a wild boar. And now I'm expected to be afraid of these scoundrels at my door." When they heard that, the servants were terrified. Not one of them dared lay hands on him and they ran as if the hosts of hell had been chasing them. And so the little tailor went on being king for the rest of his days.

THE STORY OF THE THREE LITTLE PIGS

Joseph Jacobs

> *Once upon a time when pigs spoke rhyme*
> *And monkeys chewed tobacco,*
> *And hens took snuff to make them tough,*
> *And ducks went quack, quack, quack, O!*

THERE was an old sow with three little pigs, and as she had not enough to keep them, she sent them out to seek their fortune. The first that went off met a man with a bundle of straw, and said to him:

"Please, man, give me that straw to build me a house."

Which the man did, and the little pig built a house with it. Presently came along a wolf, and knocked at the door, and said:

"Little pig, little pig, let me come in."

To which the pig answered:

"No, no, by the hair of my chiny chin chin."

The wolf then answered to that:

"Then I'll huff, and I'll puff, and I'll blow your house in."

So he huffed, and he puffed, and he blew his house in, and ate up the little pig.

The second little pig met a man with a bundle of furze, and said:

"Please, man, give me that furze to build a house."

Which the man did, and the pig built his house. Then along came the wolf, and said:

"Little pig, little pig, let me come in."

"No, no, by the hair of my chiny chin chin."

"Then I'll puff, and I'll huff, and I'll blow your house in."

So he huffed, and he puffed, and he puffed, and he huffed, and at last he blew the house down, and he ate up the little pig.

The third little pig met a man with a load of bricks, and said:

"Please, man, give me those bricks to build a house with."

So the man gave him the bricks, and he built his house with them. So the wolf came, as he did to the other little pigs, and said:

"Little pig, little pig, let me come in."

"No, no, by the hair of my chiny chin chin."

"Then I'll huff, and I'll puff, and I'll blow your house in."

Well, he huffed, and he puffed, and he huffed and he puffed, and he puffed and huffed; but he could *not* get the house down. When he found that he could not, with all his huffing and puffing, blow the house down, he said:

"Little pig, I know where there is a nice field of turnips."

"Where?" said the little pig.

"Oh, in Mr. Smith's Home-field, and if you will be ready to-morrow morning I will call for you, and we will go together, and get some for dinner."

"Very well," said the little pig, "I will be ready. What time do you mean to go?"

"Oh, at six o'clock."

Well, the little pig got up at five, and got the turnips before the wolf came (which he did about six) and who said:

"Little pig, are you ready?"

The little pig said: "Ready! I have been and come back again, and got a nice potful for dinner."

The wolf felt very angry at this, but thought that he would be up to the little pig somehow or other, so he said:

"Little pig, I know where there is a nice apple-tree."

"Where?" said the pig.

"Down at Merry-garden," replied the wolf, "and if you will not deceive me I will come for you, at five o'clock to-morrow and get some apples."

Well, the little pig bustled up the next morning at four o'clock, and went off for the apples, hoping to get back before the wolf came; but he had further to go, and had to climb the tree, so that just as he was coming down from it, he saw the wolf coming, which, as you may suppose, frightened him very much. When the wolf came up he said:

"Little pig, what! are you here before me? Are they nice apples?"

"Yes, very," said the little pig. "I will throw you down one."

And he threw it so far, that, while the wolf was gone to pick it up, the little pig jumped down and ran home. The next day the wolf came again, and said to the little pig:

"Little pig, there is a fair at Shanklin this afternoon, will you go?"

"Oh yes," said the pig, "I will go; what time shall you be ready?"

"At three," said the wolf. So the little pig went off before the time as usual, and got to the fair, and bought a butter-churn, which he was going home with, when he saw the wolf coming. Then he could not tell what to do. So he got into the churn to hide, and by so doing turned it round, and it rolled down the hill with the pig in it, which frightened the wolf so much, that he ran home without going to the fair. He went to the little pig's house, and told him how frightened he had been by a great round thing which came down the hill past him. Then the little pig said:

"Hah, I frightened you, then. I had been to the fair and bought a butter-churn, and when I saw you, I got into it, and rolled down the hill."

Then the wolf was very angry indeed, and declared he *would* eat up the little pig, and that he would get down the chimney after him. When the little pig saw what he was about, he hung on the pot full of water, and made up a blazing fire, and, just as the wolf was coming down, took off the cover, and in fell the wolf; so the little pig put on the cover again in an instant, boiled him up, and ate him for supper, and lived happy ever afterwards.

VILLAINS

OBVIOUSLY there is no shortage of villains in the folk-fairy tale, since the black-and-white simplicity of its dramatic structure produces the clearest of distinctions between protagonist and antagonist. We will not find in the folk-fairy tale the kind of psychological analysis typical of the modern omniscient narrator, but once we remind ourselves how concrete the tale often is, we can easily perceive that in many cases the inner self is expressed through action or visual images. In other words, we are very rarely told what a character is thinking, and such editorial comment as Perrault is prone to offer must be seen as extraneous to the tale proper. At the simplest level, then, goodness is equated with beauty and wickedness with ugliness. As we have already observed, however, the equation is often more complex, as in the instance of Snow White's stepmother, whose beauty is all the more disturbing because it conceals her wickedness. Although this externalization reflects a simplistic brand of logic, the two tales in this section illustrate very effectively how much subtlety and insight can be conveyed through use of this "simple" convention.

These two tales are distinctive to the extent that the villain is the central character, if only in the sense that his influence (rather than his presence) dominates the story. In each case he eventually gets his comeuppance, although not without leaving behind a certain moral murkiness that characterizes these tales and gives them a distinctly modern "feel." This is particularly true of Perrault's

"Bluebeard," in part because the central character is a wealthy businessman (not a common fairy-tale profession!), and also because the theme of this tale strikes as raw a nerve today as it ever may have done in the past, constantly reminded as we are of the primitive forces of psychopathic rage. Consequently, this tale has a realism that sets it apart from other tales (including the other tale in this section). Some regard it as having a historical origin — in *The Classic Fairy Tales*, the Opies nominate two possible candidates — suggesting that the basis of a fairy tale is to be found in the combustible mixture of reality and imagination. Indeed, our ongoing fascination with the mysteries of the aberrant mind is well-documented; from Jack the Ripper to Adolf Hitler, from Lady Macbeth to Hannibal Lecter, we find it difficult to avert our eyes from those who would lead us into the moral abyss.

In its dramatic inevitability, "Bluebeard" may usefully be compared to "Little Red Riding Hood": in each tale the central female character falls victim to a rapacious male, and in each there is the same chilling sense of doom as the trap is sprung. One way in which the tales differ, however, is in the level of symbolism: unlike the "human" wolf, Bluebeard appears to be a normal person in every respect except the color of his beard. The story hinges on our readiness to rationalize away what we would prefer not to see, even when the evidence is, so to speak, staring us in the face: "…everything went so gaily that the younger daughter began to think the master of the house had not so very blue a beard after all…."

Rumpelstiltskin also seems to have his "human" side, despite clearly being of nether-worldly (and thus wicked) origin. We must resist the temptation to interpret his sympathy for the Queen's predicament as evidence of a heart of gold; his name (sometimes translated into English as "Spindleshanks") is as clear an indicator as Bluebeard's beard that he is truly a villain. His generosity must be seen in the light of its deceitful and exploitative motive; his "guess-my-name" offer to the Queen is based on the conviction that he is setting her an impossible task.

One aspect that these tales have in common is their lack of any "heroic" character; neither the wife in "Bluebeard" nor the Queen in "Rumpelstiltskin" is a very prepossessing figure. The Queen is perhaps more of a victim than the wife, who, the tale implies, is at least partly to blame for her predicament; however, it can be argued how much either character has earned the happy ending. Be that as it may, justice demands that the villains be punished and their victims compensated for the suffering to which they have been subjected. Indeed, their terrible experiences result in a new maturity, as is particularly evident in Bluebeard's wife, whose generosity toward her family and her marriage to a worthy gentleman bespeak a very different frame of mind from that in which she entered her first marriage!

The ambivalent feelings that both these tales provoke in us suggest that our identification with the characters is more complex than is customary in the folk-fairy tale. In each instance, our sympathies are drawn in different directions at different points in the story. Few of us can, in all honesty, deny the attractiveness of the riches with which Bluebeard seduces his young wife (proof positive of his dastardly scheme) and the irresistibility of the desire to know what lies behind that closet door—she surely acts for us all in opening it. Yet once she has done so, she bears the guilt alone, and we have the luxury of watching in horrified fascination as her disobedience is discovered. Similarly, we can identify with the Queen's acceptance of the bargain offered to her by Rumpelstiltskin, since she is left with no alternative. But when the time comes to face the consequences, we again assume the voyeuristic role, torn as we are (an appropriate turn of phrase, considering the story's ending!) between the natural desire of the Queen to keep her baby and Rumpelstiltskin's apparent benevolence in granting her another chance.

Even though the nature of these tales may preclude the kind of unequivocal identification that is invited by characters like Cinderella or Snow White, there can be little doubt that these darker tales provide us with some powerful imaginative experiences, in particular the fearful loneliness and anticipation of the victim. The moral confusion that characterizes these tales demands an unusually careful scrutiny of motive and circumstance, in order to appreciate the justice of the final outcome.

BLUE BEARD

Charles Perrault

ONCE upon a time there was a man who owned splendid town and country houses, gold and silver plate, tapestries and coaches gilt all over. But the poor fellow had a blue beard, and this made him so ugly and frightful that there was not a woman or girl who did not run away at sight of him.

Amongst his neighbours was a lady of high degree who had two surpassingly beautiful daughters. He asked for the hand of one of these in marriage, leaving it to their mother to choose which should be bestowed upon him. Both girls, however, raised objections, and his offer was bandied from one to the other, neither being able to bring herself to accept a man with a blue beard. Another reason for their distaste was the fact that he had already married several wives, and no one knew what had become of them.

In order that they might become better acquainted, Blue Beard invited the two girls, with their mother and three or four of their best friends, to meet a party of young men from the neighbourhood at one of his country houses. Here they spent eight whole days, and throughout their stay there was a constant round of picnics, hunting and fishing expeditions, dances, dinners, and luncheons; and they never slept at all, through spending all the night in playing merry pranks upon each other. In short, everything went so gaily that the younger daughter began to think the master of the house had not so very blue a beard after all, and that he was an exceedingly agreeable man. As soon as the party returned to town their marriage took place.

At the end of a month Blue Beard informed his wife that important business obliged him to make a journey into a distant part of the country, which would occupy at least six weeks. He begged her to amuse herself well during his absence, and suggested that she should invite some of her friends and take them, if she liked, to the country. He was particularly anxious that she should enjoy herself thoroughly.

"Here," he said, "are the keys of the two large storerooms, and here is the one that locks up the gold and silver plate which is not in everyday use. This key belongs to the strong-boxes where my gold and silver is kept, this to the caskets containing my jewels; while here you have the master-key which gives admittance to all the apartments. As regards this little key, it is the key of the small room at the end of the long passage on the lower floor. You may open everything, you may go everywhere, but I forbid you to enter this little room. And I forbid you so seriously that if you were indeed to open the door, I should be so angry that I might do anything."

She promised to follow out these instructions exactly, and after embracing her, Blue Beard steps into his coach and is off upon his journey.

Her neighbours and friends did not wait to be invited before coming to call upon the young bride, so great was their eagerness to see the splendours of her house. They had not dared to venture while her husband was there, for his blue beard frightened them. But in less than no time there they were, running in and out of the rooms, the closets, and the wardrobes, each of which was finer than the last. Presently they went upstairs to the storerooms, and there they could not admire enough the profusion and magnificence of the tapestries, beds, sofas, cabinets, tables, and stands. There were mirrors in which they could view themselves from top to toe, some with frames of plate glass, others with frames of silver and gilt lacquer, that were the most superb and beautiful things that had ever been seen. They were loud and persistent in their envy of their friend's good fortune. She, on the other hand, derived little amusement from the sight of all these riches, the reason being that she was impatient to go and inspect the little room on the lower floor.

So overcome with curiosity was she that, without reflecting upon the discourtesy of leaving her guests, she ran down a private staircase, so precipitately that twice or thrice she nearly broke her neck, and so reached the door of the little room. There she paused for a while, thinking of the prohibition which her husband had made, and reflecting that harm might come to her as a result of disobedience. But the temptation was so great that she could not conquer it. Taking the little key, with a trembling hand she opened the door of the room.

At first she saw nothing, for the windows were closed, but after a few moments she perceived dimly that the floor was entirely covered with clotted blood, and that in this were reflected the dead bodies of several women that hung along the walls. These were all the wives of Blue Beard, whose throats he had cut, one after another.

She thought to die of terror, and the key of the room, which she had just withdrawn from the lock, fell from her hand.

When she had somewhat regained her senses, she picked up the key, closed the door, and went up to her chamber to compose herself a little. But this she could not do, for her nerves were too shaken. Noticing that the key of the little room was stained with blood, she wiped it two or three times. But the blood did not go. She washed it well, and even rubbed it with sand and grit. Always the blood remained. For the key was bewitched, and there was no means of cleaning it completely. When the blood was removed from one side, it reappeared on the other.

Blue Beard returned from his journey that very evening. He had received some letters on the way, he said, from which he learned that the business upon which he had set forth had just been concluded to his satisfaction. His wife did everything she could to make it appear that she was delighted by his speedy return.

On the morrow he demanded the keys. She gave them to him, but with so trembling a hand that he guessed at once what had happened.

"How comes it," he said to her, "that the key of the little room is not with the others?"

"I must have left it upstairs upon my table," she said.

"Do not fail to bring it to me presently," said Blue Beard.

After several delays the key had to be brought. Blue Beard examined it and addressed his wife.

"Why is there blood on this key?"

"I do not know at all," replied the poor woman, paler than death.

"You do not know at all?" exclaimed Blue Beard; "I know well enough. You wanted to enter the little room! Well, madam, enter it you shall—you shall go and take your place among the ladies you have seen there."

She threw herself at her husband's feet, asking his pardon with

tears, and with all the signs of a true repentance for her disobedience. She would have softened a rock, in her beauty and distress,
but Blue Beard had a heart harder than any stone.

"You must die, madam," he said; "and at once."

"Since I must die," she replied, gazing at him with eyes that
were wet with tears, "give me a little time to say my prayers."

"I give you one quarter of an hour," replied Blue Beard, "but
not a moment longer."

When the poor girl was alone, she called her sister to her and
said:

"Sister Anne"—for that was her name—"go up, I implore
you, to the top of the tower, and see if my brothers are not
approaching. They promised that they would come and visit me
to-day. If you see them, make signs to them to hasten."

Sister Anne went up to the top of the tower, and the poor
unhappy girl cried out to her from time to time:

"Anne, Sister Anne, do you see nothing coming?"

And Sister Anne replied:

"I see nought but dust in the sun and the green grass growing."
Presently Blue Beard, grasping a great cutlass, cried out at the top
of his voice:

"Come down quickly, or I shall come upstairs myself."

"Oh please, one moment more," called out his wife.

And at the same moment she cried in a whisper:

"Anne, Sister Anne, do you see nothing coming?"

"I see nought but dust in the sun and the green grass growing."

"Come down at once, I say," shouted Blue Beard, "or I will
come upstairs myself."

"I am coming," replied his wife.

Then she called:

"Anne, Sister Anne, do you see nothing coming?"

"I see," replied Sister Anne, "a great cloud of dust which comes
this way."

"Is it my brothers?"

"Alas, sister, no; it is but a flock of sheep."

"Do you refuse to come down?" roared Blue Beard.

"One little moment more," exclaimed his wife.

Once more she cried:

"Anne, Sister Anne, do you see nothing coming?"

"I see," replied her sister, "two horsemen who come this way, but they are as yet a long way off.... Heaven be praised," she exclaimed a moment later, "they are my brothers.... I am signalling to them all I can to hasten."

Blue Beard let forth so mighty a shout that the whole house shook. The poor wife went down and cast herself at his feet, all dishevelled and in tears.

"That avails you nothing," said Blue Beard; "you must die."

Seizing her by the hair with one hand, and with the other brandishing the cutlass aloft, he made as if to cut off her head.

The poor woman, turning towards him and fixing a dying gaze upon him, begged for a brief moment in which to collect her thoughts.

"No! no!" he cried; "commend your soul to Heaven." And ... raising his arm ———

At this very moment there came so loud a knocking at the gate that Blue Beard stopped short. The gate was opened, and two horsemen dashed in, who drew their swords and rode straight at Blue Beard. The latter recognised them as the brothers of his wife—one of them a dragoon, and the other a musketeer—and fled instantly in an effort to escape. But the two brothers were so close upon him that they caught him ere he could gain the first flight of steps. They plunged their swords through his body and left him dead. The poor woman was nearly as dead as her husband, and had not the strength to rise and embrace her brothers.

It was found that Blue Beard had no heirs, and that consequently his wife became mistress of all his wealth. She devoted a portion to arranging a marriage between her Sister Anne and a young gentleman with whom the latter had been for some time in love, while another portion purchased a captain's commission for each of her brothers. The rest formed a dowry for her own marriage with a very worthy man, who banished from her mind all memory of the evil days she had spent with Blue Beard.

Moral

Curiosity, in spite of its great charms,
Often brings with it serious regrets.
Every day a thousand examples appear.

In spite of a maiden's wishes, it's a fruitless pleasure,
For once satisfied, curiosity offers nothing,
And ever does it cost more dearly.

Another Moral

If one takes a sensible point of view
And studies this grim story,
He will recognize that this tale
Is one of days long past.
No longer is the husband so terrifying,
Demanding the impossible,
Being both dissatisfied and jealous;
In the presence of his wife he now is gracious enough,
And no matter what colour his beard may be
One does not have to guess who is master!

RUMPELSTILTSKIN

Jacob and Wilhelm Grimm

ONCE there was a miller who was poor but had a beautiful daughter. One day he happened to be talking with the king, and wanting to impress him he said: "I've got a daughter who can spin straw into gold." The king said to the miller: "That's just the kind of talent that appeals to me. If your daughter is as clever as you say, bring her to my palace tomorrow and I'll see what she can do." When the girl arrived, he took her to a room that was full of straw, gave her a spinning wheel, and said: "Now get to work. You have the whole night ahead of you, but if you haven't spun this straw into gold by tomorrow morning, you will die." Then he locked the room with his own hands and she was left all alone.

The poor miller's daughter sat there, and for the life of her she didn't know what to do. She hadn't the faintest idea how to spin straw into gold, and she was so frightened that in the end she began to cry. Then suddenly the door opened and in stepped a little man. "Good evening, Mistress Miller," he said. "Why are you crying so?" "Oh," she said. "I'm supposed to spin straw into gold,

and I don't know how." The little man asked: "What will you give
me if I spin it for you?" "My necklace," said the girl. The little
man took the necklace, sat down at the spinning wheel, and
whirr, whirr, whirr, three turns, and the spool was full. Then he
put on another, and whirr, whirr, whirr, three turns, and the second spool was full. All night he spun, and by sun-up all the straw
was spun and the spools were full of gold.

First thing in the morning the king stepped in. He was amazed
and delighted when he saw the gold, but the greed for gold grew
in his heart. He had the miller's daughter taken to a larger room
full of straw and told her to spin this too into gold if she valued
her life. She had no idea what to do and she was crying when the
door opened. Again the little man appeared and said: "What will
you give me if I spin this straw into gold for you?" "The ring off
my finger." The little man took the ring and started the wheel
whirring again, and by morning he had spun all the straw into
glittering gold. The king was overjoyed at the sight, but his
appetite for gold wasn't satisfied yet. He had the miller's daughter
taken into a still larger room full of straw and said: "You'll have to
spin this into gold tonight, but if you succeed, you shall be my
wife." "I know she's only a miller's daughter," he said to himself,
"but I'll never find a richer woman anywhere."

When the girl was alone, the little man came for the third time
and said: "What will you give me if I spin the straw into gold for
you this time?" "I have nothing more to give you," said the girl.
"Then promise to give me your first child if you get to be queen."
"Who knows what the future will bring?" thought the miller's
daughter. Besides, she had no choice. She gave the required
promise, and again the little man spun the straw into gold. When
the king arrived in the morning and found everything as he had
wished, he married her, and the beautiful miller's daughter
became a queen.

A year later she brought a beautiful child into the world. She
had forgotten all about the little man. Suddenly he stepped into
her room and said: "Now give me what you promised." The
queen was horrified; she promised him all the riches in the kingdom if only he let her keep her child, but the little man said: "No.
I'd sooner have a living thing than all the treasures in the world."
Then the queen began to weep and wail so heart-rendingly that

the little man took pity on her: "I'll give you three days' time," he said. "If by then you know my name, you can keep your child."

The queen racked her brains all night; she went over all the names she had ever heard, and she sent out a messenger to inquire all over the country what other names there might be. When the little man came next day, she started with Caspar, Melchior, and Balthazar, and reeled off all the names she knew, but at each one the little man said: "That is not my name." The second day she sent servants around the district to ask about names, and she tried the strangest and most unusual of them on the little man: "Could your name be Ribcage or Muttonchop or Lacelegs?" But each time he replied: "That is not my name."

The third day the messenger returned and said: "I haven't discovered a single new name, but as I was walking along the edge of the forest, I rounded a bend and found myself at the foot of a high hill, the kind of place where fox and hare bid each other good night. There I saw a hut, and outside the hut a fire was burning, and a ridiculous little man was dancing around the fire and hopping on one foot and bellowing:

> "Brew today, tomorrow bake,
> After that the child I'll take,
> And sad the queen will be to lose it.
> Rumpelstiltskin is my name
> But luckily nobody knows it."

You can imagine how happy the queen was to hear that name. It wasn't long before the little man turned up and asked her: "Well, Your Majesty, what's my name?" She started by asking: "Is it Tom?" "No." "Is it Dick?" "No." "Is it Harry?" "No."

"Could it be Rumpelstiltskin?"

"The Devil told you that! The Devil told you that!" the little man screamed, and in his rage he stamped his right foot so hard that it went into the ground up to his waist. Then in his fury he took his left foot in both hands and tore himself in two.

THE NINETEENTH CENTURY: FROM FOLK TALE TO LITERARY TALE

THE nineteenth century was truly the Golden Age of the literary folk and fairy tale: it began with the publication of the Grimms' tales in 1812-15, after which only two decades passed before the next major contributor appeared, in the shape of Hans Christian Andersen. In some ways, Andersen proved an ideal transitional figure in the evolution of the fairy tale, since he was both a recipient of oral folk tales and—later in his life—a writer of original fairy tales. His unique position is illustrated in the pair of tales with which we begin this section. The similarity of Hans Andersen's "The Tinderbox" to the Grimms' "The Blue Light" is unmistakable—and the differences are also revealing. The echoes of "The Story of Aladdin; or the Wonderful Lamp" must also have attracted Andersen; as a child, he had heard his father read stories from *The Arabian Nights*. We should also note that Andersen was barely a generation younger than the Grimm brothers and was well-acquainted with them. (Ironically, it appears that on at least one occasion the folk tale had a debt to Andersen: the Opies remind us that the Grimms published, in 1843, a tale that closely resembled "The Princess and the Pea.")

Hans Andersen was born in Odense, a town on the Danish island of Funen, the son of a poor cobbler and an illiterate washerwoman. His paternal grandmother appears to have been an important influence in his early life, in that she was both a pathological liar and a teller of tales (two sides of the same coin, some might say). Thus Andersen absorbed at first hand a living oral tradition, which he later drew upon and exploited as a writer. He was an awkward, unattractive child, which would be enough in itself to excite the mockery of other children; no doubt his aloof, dreamy nature only made his separation from his peers the more complete. Despite such unpropitious beginnings, Andersen was unshakable in his conviction that he was destined for greatness—and in this tension between the bitterness of rejection and the assumption of genius lies the key to his creativity. This is the dynamic that informs tale after tale, culminating in what is arguably his most famous, "The Ugly Duckling," which is surely a paradigm of autobiographical fantasy. In his hands, the fairy tale becomes a vehicle for all the frustration, disappointment, and resentment that he experienced in his own life, as well as a means of celebrating (even mythologizing) his progress from rags to occasional riches, from sordid obscurity to fame. In almost every Andersen tale, there is at least one central character that reflects some facet of Andersen himself; it is not coincidental that many of his tales end unhappily, or at least ambiguously, in contrast to the folk tale.

At the same time, there is no denying the skill with which Andersen recreates the flavor of the oral tale within the literary mode, although in the silent, solitary world of the older reader, this aspect of his tales is easily missed. Andersen is constantly inviting us to *hear* his story, to perceive it in the context of association between teller and listener. "Let me tell you a story," he says, at the beginning of "The Swineherd"; we are told in "The Nightingale" that "This story happened a long, long time ago; and that is just the reason why you should hear it now, before it is forgotten."

On a more consciously literary level, we may detect the influence of Romanticism, which again locates the tales within a specific time-frame. It may explain, for instance, their often melancholy mood; we may surmise that the Romantic stereotype of the passionate, lovelorn hero was one that had particular appeal to Andersen—he certainly appears with regularity in the tales. A close look at "The Nightingale" reveals a virtual primer in Romantic imagery and values, with the nightingale itself representing the artist in defiance of the complacent narrow-mindedness of society. Andersen reportedly wrote this tale as a tribute to the famous opera singer Jenny Lind (the "Swedish Nightingale"), but it is tempting to assume that he saw a good deal of himself in the nightingale.

The extent to which Andersen identified with certain of his characters is consistently revealed through a tell-tale intensity of feeling that is not always in accord with the story: the bitterness of the swineherd-prince's rejection of the princess, the ill-concealed vanity in the duckling's transformation into a swan ("Everyone agreed that the new swan was the most beautiful of them all"), and, in "The Nightingale," the extraordinary passage in which Death is literally and figuratively overcome by the Artist. One of the most remarkable of Andersen's self-projections is to be found in "The Little Mermaid," where he puts aside his reservations about the female sex, identifying with the mermaid as the embodiment of his own social inferiority and loneliness. Thus each tale becomes a re-creation of emotional experience, whether it be romantic yearning and personal misery on the one hand, or self-aggrandizement and revenge on the other. While there is no denying Andersen's considerable literary achievement in adapting the form and flavor of the folk tale to his personal preoccupations, there is also no escaping the neurotic obsessions that color his tales.

It is not surprising, given the nature of its creator, that the Andersen tale is often characterized by ambivalence. If we return to the ending of "The Swineherd," for instance, we can see how Andersen lulls us into expecting a happy ending—the Prince forgiving the Princess for her immaturity, having taught her a lesson—and then surprises us by ending the tale on a note of bitterness and contempt. Tale after tale reveals that Andersen's attitude toward women was rather complicated, to say the least. They figure largely in his work, yet, unless his intent is to depict the pathos of their innocent vulnerability (as in "The Little Mermaid"), their roles are generally characterized by dependence, passivity, and ignorance—to a much greater extent than the women of folk tale, in fact. Another manifestation of his ambivalence may be observed in his attitude toward royalty. The miserable deprivation of his early life remained a vivid and bitter memory, and as he grew older, Andersen naturally became aware of the enormous disparity between his own world and that of the aristocracy, surrounded by wealth and extravagance. Yet, he was so involved with his own fairy tale that his condemnation of royalty could hardly be unequivocal: after all, what is customarily the reward of the deserving poor youth, once he has shown his true mettle through honesty and perseverance? Thus he is torn between mockery and admiration, dismissiveness and envy — a conflict of feeling that is at the core of many of his tales.

Andersen's success inspired a wave of imitators, just as Perrault's tales had done in eighteenth-century France. One of the most interesting and original of those imitators was Oscar Wilde, whose tales were published toward the end of the century and reveal, at times, a fin-de-siècle sophistication that suggests he was speaking more to adults than to children.

We do not have to read very far into Wilde's tales before sensing Andersen's influence. Is it coincidence, for instance, that one of Wilde's tales is entitled "The Nightingale and the Rose" — those being the very gifts offered by Andersen's swineherd? Echoes abound, but it appears that Wilde's imitation was not intended as flattery. It is as if Wilde took elements of Andersen's tales to re-work them in a darker vein, being — one suspects — profoundly out of sympathy with the latter's vision of the world. The cynicism that is detectable in both men's work, for instance, can, in Andersen's case, be traced to a very personal source: it is generally the expression of his annoyance at not being accorded the admiration that he felt was his due. In Wilde's work, it is more the means by which he expresses his sardonic assessment of prevailing mores and values. What, for instance, are we to feel about the futility of the nightingale's sacrifice in "The Nightingale and the Rose"? Is Wilde deliberately imposing a worldly cynicism upon the fairy tale, thus achieving his effect by frustrating the reader's expectations? Or is he setting out to reject Andersen's vision, the more effectively by using the latter's own tools against him?

Although Wilde's family was as distinguished as Andersen's was obscure, there was perhaps some superficial similarity in these writers' exposure to folk tale, which in Wilde's case came about through his mother, who was an enthusiastic student of Irish folklore. Beyond that, however, the personalities and lives of these two men could hardly have been more different. Oscar Wilde is best remembered for his accomplishments as a wit and savant, and for his notoriety as a sophisticate and homosexual. The lighter and darker sides of his nature are well represented in his two best-known works, *The Importance of Being Earnest* and *The Picture of Dorian Grey*, which predictably have tended to overshadow his fairy tales, much as his gaudy reputation has obscured his humanity. It is, for example, a less familiar fact that Wilde enjoyed the role, for a time at least, of the loving father of two sons. Yet contrary to what we might expect, there is little justification for thinking that his published tales were domestically inspired, although it is clear from the reminiscences of his younger son that Wilde would tell them fairy stories on occasion, including his own. "Cyril [the older son] once asked him why he had tears in his eyes when he told us the story of the Selfish Giant, and he replied that 'really beautiful things always made him cry.'" (Vyvyan Holland, *Son of Oscar Wilde*).

That response may well be seen as crucial to understanding Wilde's attraction to the fairy tale. Throughout his life, Wilde was driven, both philosophically and experientially, by a horror of the ordinary, the mundane. We may suspect that he was drawn to use this ingenuous but exotic form of literature as a kind of spiritual release from the more contemporary preoccupations reflected in his life and his other writing and as an opportunity to revel in the aesthete's fascination with Beauty. While his tales may not be entirely free of self-indulgence, we must nevertheless acknowledge that his carefully cultivated public image of languor and excess is often belied by the passionate indignation that he directs at hypocrisy and self-righteousness. We may wonder if there was some prescient awareness on Wilde's part as he wrote these tales that he would in turn fall victim to such social prejudices. Whatever their origin, it is quickly apparent that the themes of compassion and self-sacrifice are central to many of his stories.

Wilde's cultivated brilliance as raconteur and man-of-the-world produces a self-conscious quality in his tales that gives them a very different feel from the tales of Perrault, Grimm, and even Andersen. These are the first tales in this anthology whose diction consistently draws attention to itself, to the extent that it becomes a major factor in our response to the story. Wilde is so meticulous in his choice of word and phrase, so attentive to rhythm and balance, that we should read these tales as prose-poems. Consequently, it is impossible to imagine a re-telling of any of his stories, in the manner of a folk tale: Wilde's language is so integral to the story that, like poetry, it resists paraphrase.

Thus, with Wilde's stories, we find ourselves unmistakably at the literary end of the fairy-tale continuum. As we have seen, his most obvious debt is to another writer of tales, and like his predecessor, he achieves many of his effects by deliberately contravening the traditional patterns of the fairy tale, whether by introducing a religious dimension, as in "The Selfish Giant," or by subverting its predictability. Wilde chose the fairy tale as the literary form that best suited his purposes and then developed it according to his needs. His work (and that of other fairy-tale writers to the present day) consequently demands the same critical sensitivity and sophistication as we would bring to his plays and poetry — or any other literary works.

The nineteenth century saw other significant developments of the literary fairy tale, such as John Ruskin's *The King of the Golden River* (1851), William Makepeace Thackeray's *The Rose and the Ring* (1854) and, later in the century, the longer, more ambitious works of George MacDonald. What is missing in this picture, however, is the substantial contribution made by women writers, whose work has been largely overshadowed by that of their male counterparts for reasons that have more to do with the profound gender bias that prevailed in the nineteenth century than with intrinsic literary merit. To explore even a selection of tales by writers such as Mary de Morgan, Frances Browne, Mrs. Molesworth, or Mrs. Mulock Craik is a task far beyond the confines of this book; however, if only to show that in the nineteenth century the fairy tale was being taken in directions quite distinct from those of Andersen and Wilde, we include a tale by Anne Thackeray Ritchie (daughter of William Makepeace Thackeray). Her version of "The Sleeping Beauty in the Wood" (1874), set in the world of the Victorian *bourgeoisie,* presents the tale in a radically different light. Ritchie's contention that "Fairy stories are everywhere and every day" makes clear her intention to locate the tale firmly in the here-and-now, thereby celebrating the magic that can be found even in the most prosaic of contexts. Mother Goose meets George Eliot — with illuminating results!

THE BLUE LIGHT

Jacob and Wilhelm Grimm

THERE once was a soldier who had served the king faithfully for many years, but when the war was over and he could serve no longer because of his many wounds, the king said to him: "You can go home. I don't need you any more. You won't be getting any more money, because when I pay wages I expect something in return." The soldier was very sad, for he couldn't see how he was going to keep body and soul together. With a heavy heart he left the king and walked all day until he came to a forest. As night was falling, he saw a light and headed for it. Soon he came to a house that belonged to a witch. "Give me a night's lodging and something to eat and drink," he said, "or I shall die." "Oho!" said she. "Who gives a runaway soldier anything? But I'll be merciful and take you in, if you'll do what I tell you." "And what may that be?" "To spade up my garden tomorrow." The soldier accepted her proposition and worked hard all the next day, but by the time he had finished, night was falling. "Hmm," said the witch, "I see that you can't start out today. I'll keep you another night, but in turn you must chop and split a cord of wood for me." And that took the soldier all day and at nightfall the witch asked him to stay the night. "I have only a little thing to ask of you tomorrow," she said. "There's an old dry well behind the house. My light has fallen into it. It burns blue and never goes out. I want you to go down and get it for me." Next day the old woman took him to the well and let him down in a basket. He found the blue light and gave the signal for her to pull him up. She pulled him up all right, but when he was just below the rim she held out her hand and wanted him to give her the blue light. "Oh no," he said, for he read her wicked thoughts. "I won't give you the light until I have both my feet on the ground." At that the witch flew into a rage, let him drop to the bottom, and went away.

The ground at the bottom was moist and the poor soldier's fall didn't hurt him. The blue light was still burning, but what was the good of that? He was doomed to die, and he knew it. For a while he just sat there, feeling very dejected. Then he happened to put his hand in his pocket and felt his pipe, which was still half full of tobacco. "My last pleasure on earth!" he said to himself, took out the pipe, lit it with the blue light and began to smoke. The smoke rose in a ring and suddenly a black dwarf stood before him. "Master," said the dwarf, "what do you command?" The soldier was amazed. "What am I supposed to command?" he asked. "I must do whatever you ask," said the dwarf. "That's fine," said the soldier. "Then first of all, help me out of this well." The dwarf took him by the hand and led him through an underground passage, and the soldier didn't forget to take the blue light with him. On the way the dwarf showed him all the treasures which the witch had amassed and hidden there, and the soldier took as much gold as he could carry. When he was back above ground, he said to the dwarf: "Now go and tie up the old witch and take her to jail." A second later bloodcurdling screams were heard. She rode past as quick as the wind on the back of a wildcat, and a short while later the dwarf came back. "Your orders have been carried out," he announced. "She's already hanging on the gallows. What else do you command, master?" "Nothing right now. You can go home, but be ready when I call you." "All you have to do," said the dwarf, "is light your pipe with the blue light. I'll be there before you know it." And at that he vanished.

The soldier went back to the town he had come from. He stopped at the best inn, had fine clothes made, and ordered the innkeeper to furnish his room as splendidly as possible. When the room was ready and the soldier moved in, he called the black dwarf and said: "I served the king faithfully, but he sent me away and let me go hungry. Now I'm going to get even." "What shall I do?" asked the dwarf. "Late tonight, when the king's daughter is asleep in her bed, bring her here without waking her. I'm going to make her work as my slavey." "That will be easy for me, but dangerous for you," said the dwarf. "If you're discovered, you'll be in hot water." At the stroke of twelve the door opened and the dwarf carried the king's daughter in. "Aha!" said the soldier. "So there you are. Well, get to work. Go get the broom and sweep the place out." When she had finished he called her over to where he was sitting, stretched out his legs, and said: "Pull my boots off." When she had pulled them off, he threw them in her face, and she had to pick them up, clean them, and polish them until they shone. Only half-opening her eyes, she obeyed his commands without a murmur. At first cockcrow the dwarf carried her back to her bed in the royal palace.

When the king's daughter got up in the morning, she went to her father and told him she had had a strange dream. "I was carried through the streets with the speed of lightning and taken to the room of a soldier. I had to be his slavey and do all the nasty work and sweep the room and clean his boots. It was only a dream, but I'm as tired as if I'd really done it all." "Your dream may have been true," said the king. "Here's my advice. Fill your pocket with peas and make a little hole in it. If they carry you off again, the peas will fall out and leave a trail on the street." When the king said this, the dwarf, who had made himself invisible, was standing right there and he heard it all. And that night when he carried the king's daughter through the streets, some peas did indeed fall out of her pocket, but they couldn't make a trail, because the crafty dwarf had strewn peas in all the streets beforehand. And again the king's daughter had to do slavey's work until cockcrow.

Next morning the king sent his men out to look for the trail, but they couldn't find it because in every street, all over town, children were picking up peas and saying: "Last night it rained peas." "We'll have to think of something else," said the king. "Keep your shoes on when you go to bed. And before you come back from that place, hide one of them. Never fear, I'll find it." The black dwarf heard the king's plan and that night when the soldier asked him once again to go and get the king's daughter, he advised against it. "I don't know of any way to thwart that scheme. If the shoe is found in your room, you'll really be in for it." "Do as you're told," said the soldier. And for the third time the king's daughter had to work as his slavey. But before the dwarf carried her back to the palace, she hid one of her shoes under the bed.

Next morning the king had the whole town searched for his daughter's shoe, and it was found in the soldier's room. The dwarf had implored the soldier to save himself, and he had left town in haste, but was soon caught and thrown into prison. In his hurry to escape he had forgotten his most precious possessions, the blue light and his gold, and all he had in his pocket was one ducat. As he was standing loaded with chains at the window of his prison cell, he saw an old friend passing, and tapped on the windowpane. When his friend came over to him, he said: "Do me a favor. Get me the little bundle I left at the inn. I'll give you a ducat." His friend ran to the inn and brought him his bundle. As soon as the soldier was alone, he lit his pipe with the light and the dwarf appeared. "Don't be afraid," said the dwarf. "Go where they take you, and let them do as they please. Just be sure to take the blue light with you." The next day the soldier was brought to trial and though he had done no evil the judge sentenced him to death. When he was led out to die, he asked the king for a last kindness. "What sort of kindness?" the king asked. "Let me smoke one last pipe on the way," said the soldier. "You can smoke three," said the king, "but don't expect me to spare your life." The soldier took out his pipe and lit it with the blue light. When a few rings of smoke had gone up, the dwarf appeared, holding a little cudgel. "What does my master command?" he asked. "Strike down those false judges and their henchmen, and don't spare the king who has treated me so badly." The dwarf raced back and forth like forked lightning and everybody his cudgel so much as touched fell to the ground and didn't dare to move. The king was so terrified that he begged for mercy and to preserve his bare life made over his kingdom to the soldier and gave him his daughter for his wife.

THE TINDERBOX

Hans Christian Andersen

A SOLDIER came marching down the road: Left ... right! Left ... right! He had a pack on his back and a sword at his side. He had been in the war and he was on his way home. Along the road he met a witch. She was a disgusting sight, with a lower lip that hung all the way down to her chest.

"Good evening, young soldier," she said. "What a handsome sword you have and what a big knapsack. I can see that you are a real soldier! I shall give you all the money that you want."

"Thank you, old witch," he said.

"Do you see that big tree?" asked the witch, and pointed to the one they were standing next to. "The trunk is hollow. You climb up to the top of the tree, crawl into the hole, and slide deep down inside it. I'll tie a rope around your waist, so I can pull you up again when you call me."

"What am I supposed to do down in the tree?" asked the soldier.

"Get money!" answered the witch and laughed. "Now listen to me. When you get down to the very bottom, you'll be in a great passageway where you'll be able to see because there are over a hundred lamps burning. You'll find three doors; and you can open them all because the keys are in the locks. Go into the first one; and there on a chest, in the middle of the room, you'll see a dog with eyes as big as teacups. Don't let that worry you. You will have my blue checked apron; just spread it out on the floor, put the dog down on top of it, and it won't do you any harm. Open the chest and take as many coins as you wish, they are all copper. If it's silver you're after, then go into the next room. There you'll find a dog with eyes as big as millstones; but don't let that worry you, put him on the apron and take the money. If you'd rather have gold, you can have that too; it's in the third room. Wait till you see that dog, he's got eyes as big as the Round Tower in Copenhagen; but don't let that worry you. Put him down on my apron and he won't hurt you; then you can take as much gold as you wish."

"That doesn't sound bad!" said the soldier. "But what am I to do for you, old witch? I can't help thinking that you must want something too."

"No," replied the witch. "I don't want one single coin. Just bring me the old tinderbox that my grandmother forgot the last time she was down there."

"I'm ready, tie the rope around my waist!" ordered the soldier.

"There you are, and here is my blue checked apron," said the witch.

The soldier climbed the tree, let himself fall into the hole, and found that he was in the passageway, where more than a hundred lights burned.

He opened the first door. Oh! There sat the dog with eyes as big as teacups glaring at him.

"You are a handsome fellow!" he exclaimed as he put the dog down on the witch's apron. He filled his pockets with copper coins, closed the chest, and put the dog back on top of it.

He went into the second room. Aha! There sat the dog with

eyes as big as millstones. "Don't keep looking at me like that," said the soldier good-naturedly. "It isn't polite and you'll spoil your eyes." He put the dog down on the witch's apron and opened the chest. When he saw all the silver coins, he emptied the copper out of his pockets and filled both them and his knapsack with silver.

Now he entered the third room. That dog was big enough to frighten anyone, even a soldier. His eyes were as large as the Round Tower in Copenhagen and they turned around like wheels.

"Good evening," said the soldier politely and saluted, for such a dog he had never seen before. For a while he just stood looking at it; but finally he said to himself, "Enough of this!" Then he put the dog down on the witch's apron and opened up the chest.

"God preserve me!" he cried. There was so much gold that there was enough to buy the whole city of Copenhagen, and all the gingerbread men, rocking horses, riding whips, and tin soldiers in the whole world. Quickly the soldier threw away all the silver coins that he had in his pockets and knapsack and put gold in them instead. He also filled his cap, and he stuffed so many coins in his boots he could hardly walk. Then he put the dog back on the chest, and slammed the door behind him.

"Pull me up, you old witch!" he shouted up through the hollow tree.

"Have you got the tinderbox?" she called back.

"Right you are, I have forgotten it," he replied honestly, and went back to get it. The witch hoisted him up and again he stood on the road; but now his pockets, knapsack, cap, and boots were filled with gold and he felt quite differently.

"Why do you want the tinderbox?" he asked.

"Mind your own business," answered the witch crossly. "You have got your money, just give me the tinderbox."

"Rubbish!" said the soldier. "Tell me what you are going to use it for, right now; or I'll draw my sword and cut off your head."

"No!" replied the witch firmly; so he chopped her head off. And when she lay there dead, he put all his gold in her apron, which he tied into a bundle, and threw over his shoulder. The tinderbox he dropped into his pocket; and off to town he went.

The town was nice, and the soldier went to the nicest inn, where he asked to be put up in the finest room and ordered all the things he liked to eat best for his supper, because now he had so much money that he was rich.

The servant who polished his boots thought it was very odd that a man so wealthy should have such worn-out boots. But the soldier hadn't had time to buy anything yet; the next day he bought boots and clothes that fitted his purse. And the soldier became a refined gentleman. People were eager to tell him all about their town and their king, and what a lovely princess his daughter was.

"I would like to see her," said the soldier.

"But no one sees her," explained the townfolk. "She lives in a copper castle, surrounded by walls, and towers, and a moat. The king doesn't dare allow anyone to visit her because it has been foretold that she will marry a common soldier, and the king doesn't want that to happen."

"If only I could see her," thought the soldier, though it was unthinkable.

The soldier lived merrily, went to the theatre, kept a carriage so he could drive in the king's park, and gave lots of money to the poor. He remembered well what it felt like not to have a penny in his purse.

He was rich and well dressed. He had many friends, and they all said that he was kind and a real cavalier; and such things he liked to hear. But since he used money every day and never received any, he soon had only two copper coins left.

He had to move out of the beautiful room downstairs, up to a tiny one in the garret, where he not only polished his boots himself but also mended them with a large needle. None of his friends came to see him, for they said there were too many stairs to climb.

It was a very dark evening and he could not even buy a candle. Suddenly he remembered that he had seen the stub of a candle in the tinderbox that he had brought up from the bottom of the hollow tree. He found the tinderbox and took out the candle. He struck the flint. There was a spark, and in through the door came the dog with eyes as big as teacups.

"What does my master command?" asked the dog.

"What's this all about?" exclaimed the soldier. "That certainly was an interesting tinderbox. Can I have whatever I want? Bring me some money," he ordered. In less time than it takes to say thank you, the dog was gone and back with a big sack of copper coins in his mouth.

Now the soldier understood why the witch had thought the tinderbox so valuable. If he struck it once, the dog appeared who sat on the chest full of copper coins; if he struck it twice, then the dog came who guarded the silver money; and if he struck it three times, then came the one who had the gold.

The soldier moved downstairs again, wore fine clothes again, and had fine friends, for now they all remembered him and cared for him as they had before.

One night, when he was sitting alone after his friends had gone, he thought, "It is a pity that no one can see that beautiful princess. What is the good of her beauty if she must always remain behind the high walls and towers of a copper castle? Will I never see her?... Where is my tinderbox?"

He made the sparks fly and the dog with eyes as big as teacups came. "I know it's very late at night," he said, "but I would so like to see the beautiful princess, if only for a minute."

Away went the dog; and faster than thought he returned with the sleeping princess on his back. She was so lovely that anyone would have known that she was a real princess. The soldier could not help kissing her, for he was a true soldier.

The dog brought the princess back to her copper castle; but in the morning while she was having tea with her father and mother, the king and queen, she told them that she had had a very strange dream that night. A large dog had come and carried her away to a soldier who kissed her.

"That's a nice story," said the queen, but she didn't mean it.

The next night one of the older ladies in waiting was sent to watch over the princess while she slept, to find out whether it had only been a dream, and not something worse.

The soldier longed to see the princess so much that he couldn't bear it, so at night he sent the dog to fetch her. The dog ran as fast as he could, but the lady in waiting had her boots on and she kept up with him all the way. When she saw which house he had entered, she took out a piece of chalk and made a big white cross on the door.

"Now we'll be able to find it in the morning," she thought, and went home to get some sleep.

When the dog returned the princess to the castle, he noticed the cross on the door of the house where his master lived; so he took a piece of white chalk and put crosses on all the doors of all the houses in the whole town. It was a very clever thing to do, for now the lady in waiting would never know which was the right door.

The next morning the king and queen, the old lady in waiting, and all the royal officers went out into town to find the house where the princess had been.

"Here it is!" exclaimed the king, when he saw the first door with a cross on it.

"No, my sweet husband, it is here," said his wife, who had seen the second door with a cross on it.

"Here's one!"

"There's one!"

Everyone shouted at once, for it didn't matter where anyone looked: there he would find a door with a cross on it; and so they all gave up.

Now the queen was so clever, she could do more than ride in a golden carriage. She took out her golden scissors and cut out a large piece of silk and sewed it into a pretty little bag. This she filled with the fine grain of buckwheat, and tied the bag around the princess' waist. When this was done, she cut a little hole in the bag just big enough for the little grains of buckwheat to fall out, one at a time, and show the way to the house where the princess was taken by the dog.

During the night the dog came to fetch the princess and carry her on his back to the soldier, who loved her so much that now he had only one desire, and that was to be a prince so that he could marry her.

The dog neither saw nor felt the grains of buckwheat that made a little trail all the way from the copper castle to the soldier's room at the inn. In the morning the king and queen had no difficulty in finding where the princess had been, and the soldier was thrown into jail.

There he sat in the dark with nothing to do; and what made matters worse was that everyone said, "Tomorrow you are going to be hanged!"

That was not amusing to hear. If only he had had his tinderbox, but he had forgotten it in his room. When the sun rose, he watched the people, through the bars of his window, as they hurried toward the gates of the city, for the hanging was to take place outside the walls. He heard the drums and the royal soldiers marching. Everyone was running. He saw a shoemaker's apprentice, who had not bothered to take off his leather apron and was wearing slippers. The boy lifted his legs so high, it looked as though he were galloping. One of his slippers flew off and landed near the window of the soldier's cell.

"Hey!" shouted the soldier. "Listen, shoemaker, wait a minute, nothing much will happen before I get there. But if you will run to the inn and get the tinderbox I left in my room, you can earn four copper coins. But you'd better use your legs or it will be too late."

The shoemaker's apprentice, who didn't have one copper coin, was eager to earn four; and he ran to get the tinderbox as fast as he could, and gave it to the soldier.

And now you shall hear what happened after that!

Outside the gates of the town, a gallows had been built; around it stood the royal soldiers and many hundreds of thousands of people. The king and the queen sat on their lovely throne, and opposite them sat the judge and the royal council.

The soldier was standing on the platform, but as the noose was put around his neck, he declared that it was an ancient custom to grant a condemned man his last innocent wish. The only thing he wanted was to be allowed to smoke a pipe of tobacco.

The king couldn't refuse; and the soldier took out his tinderbox and struck it: once, twice, three times! Instantly, the three dogs were before him: the one with eyes as big as teacups, the one with eyes as big as millstones, and the one with eyes as big as the Round Tower in Copenhagen.

"Help me! I don't want to be hanged!" cried the soldier.

The dogs ran toward the judge and the royal council. They took one man by the leg and another by the nose, and threw them up in the air, so high that when they hit the earth again they broke into little pieces.

"Not me!" screamed the king; but the biggest dog took both the king and the queen and sent them flying up as high as all the others had been.

The royal guards got frightened; and the people began to shout: "Little soldier, you shall be our king and marry the princess!"

The soldier rode in the king's golden carriage; and the three dogs danced in front of it and barked: "Hurrah!"

The little boys whistled and the royal guards presented arms. The princess came out of her copper castle and became queen, which she liked very much. The wedding feast lasted a week; and the three dogs sat at the table and made eyes at everyone.

THE UGLY DUCKLING

Hans Christian Andersen

IT was so beautiful out in the country. It was summer. The oats were still green, but the wheat was turning yellow. Down in the meadow the grass had been cut and made into haystacks; and there the storks walked on their long red legs talking Egyptian, because that was the language they had been taught by their mothers. The fields were enclosed by woods, and hidden among them were little lakes and pools. Yes, it certainly was lovely out there in the country!

The old castle, with its deep moat surrounding it, lay bathed in sunshine. Between the heavy walls and the edge of the moat there was a narrow strip of land covered by a whole forest of burdock plants. Their leaves were large and some of the stalks were so tall that a child could stand upright under them and imagine that he was in the middle of the wild and lonely woods. Here a duck had built her nest. While she sat waiting for the eggs to hatch, she felt a little sorry for herself because it was taking so long and hardly anybody came to visit her. The other ducks preferred swimming in the moat to sitting under a dock leaf and gossiping.

Finally the eggs began to crack. "Peep ... Peep," they said one after another. The egg yolks had become alive and were sticking out their heads.

"Quack ... Quack ..." said their mother. "Look around you." And the ducklings did; they glanced at the green world about them, and that was what their mother wanted them to do, for green was good for their eyes.

"How big the world is!" piped the little ones, for they had much more space to move around in now than they had had inside the egg.

"Do you think that this is the whole world?" quacked their mother. "The world is much larger than this. It stretches as far as the minister's wheat fields, though I have not been there.... Are you all here?" The duck got up and turned around to look at her nest. "Oh no, the biggest egg hasn't hatched yet; and I'm so tired of sitting here! I wonder how long it will take?" she wailed, and sat down again.

"What's new?" asked an old duck who had come visiting.

"One of the eggs is taking so long," complained the mother duck. "It won't crack. But take a look at the others. They are the sweetest little ducklings you have ever seen; and every one of them looks exactly like their father. That scoundrel hasn't come to visit me once."

"Let me look at the egg that won't hatch," demanded the old duck. "I am sure that it's a turkey egg! I was fooled that way once. You can't imagine what it's like. Turkeys are afraid of the water. I couldn't get them to go into it. I quacked and I nipped them, but nothing helped. Let me see that egg!... Yes, it's a turkey egg. Just let it lie there. You go and teach your young ones how to swim, that's my advice."

"I have sat on it so long that I suppose I can sit a little longer, at least until they get the hay in," replied the mother duck.

"Suit yourself," said the older duck, and went on.

At last the big egg cracked too. "Peep...Peep," said the young one, and tumbled out. He was big and very ugly.

The mother duck looked at him. "He's awfully big for his age," she said. "He doesn't look like any of the others. I wonder if he could be a turkey? Well, we shall soon see. Into the water he will go, even if I have to kick him to make him do it."

The next day the weather was gloriously beautiful. The sun

shone on the forest of burdock plants. The mother duck took her whole brood to the moat. "Quack ... Quack ..." she ordered.

One after another, the little ducklings plunged into the water. For a moment their heads disappeared, but then they popped up again and the little ones floated like so many corks. Their legs knew what to do without being told. All of the new brood swam very nicely, even the ugly one.

"He is no turkey," mumbled the mother. "See how beautifully he uses his legs and how straight he holds his neck. He is my own child and, when you look closely at him, he's quite handsome.... Quack! Quack! Follow me and I'll take you to the henyard and introduce you to everyone. But stay close to me, so that no one steps on you, and look out for the cat."

They heard an awful noise when they arrived at the henyard. Two families of ducks had got into a fight over the head of an eel. Neither of them got it, for it was swiped by the cat.

"That is the way of the world," said the mother duck, and licked her bill. She would have liked to have had the eel's head herself. "Walk nicely," she admonished them. "And remember to bow to the old duck over there. She has Spanish blood in her veins and is the most aristocratic fowl here. That is why she is so fat and has a red rag tied around one of her legs. That is the highest mark of distinction a duck can be given. It means so much that she will never be done away with; and all the other fowl and the human beings know who she is. Quack! Quack!... Don't walk, waddle like well-brought-up ducklings. Keep your legs far apart, just as your mother and father have always done. Bow your heads and say, 'Quack'!" And that was what the little ducklings did.

Other ducks gathered about them and said loudly, "What do we want that gang here for? Aren't there enough of us already? Pooh! Look how ugly one of them is! He's the last straw!" And one of the ducks flew over and bit the ugly duckling on the neck.

"Leave him alone!" shouted the mother. "He hasn't done anyone any harm."

"He's big and he doesn't look like everybody else!" replied the duck who had bitten him. "And that's reason enough to beat him."

"Very good-looking children you have," remarked the duck with the red rag around one of her legs. "All of them are beautiful except one. He didn't turn out very well. I wish you could make him over again."

"That's not possible, Your Grace," answered the mother duck. "He may not be handsome, but he has a good character and swims as well as the others, if not a little better. Perhaps he will grow handsomer as he grows older and becomes a bit smaller. He was in the egg too long, and that is why he doesn't have the right shape." She smoothed his neck for a moment and then added, "Besides, he's a drake; and it doesn't matter so much what he looks like. He is strong and I am sure he will be able to take care of himself."

"Well, the others are nice," said the old duck. "Make yourself at home, and if you should find an eel's head, you may bring it to me."

And they were "at home."

The poor little duckling, who had been the last to hatch and was so ugly, was bitten and pushed and made fun of both by the hens and by the other ducks. The turkey cock (who had been born with spurs on, and therefore thought he was an emperor) rustled his feathers as if he were a full-rigged ship under sail, and strutted up to the duckling. He gobbled so loudly at him that his own face got all red.

The poor little duckling did not know where to turn. How he grieved over his own ugliness, and how sad he was! The poor creature was mocked and laughed at by the whole henyard.

That was the first day; and each day that followed was worse than the one before. The poor duckling was chased and mistreated by everyone, even his own sisters and brothers, who quacked again and again, "If only the cat would get you, you ugly thing!"

Even his mother said, "I wish you were far away." The other ducks bit him and the hens pecked at him. The little girl who came to feed the fowls kicked him.

At last the duckling ran away. He flew over the tops of the bushes, frightening all the little birds so that they flew up into the air. "They, too, think I am ugly," thought the duckling, and closed his eyes—but he kept on running.

Finally he came to a great swamp where wild ducks lived; and here he stayed for the night, for he was too tired to go any farther.

In the morning he was discovered by the wild ducks. They

looked at him and one of them asked, "What kind of bird are you?"

The ugly duckling bowed in all directions, for he was trying to be as polite as he knew how.

"You are ugly," said the wild ducks, "but that is no concern of ours, as long as you don't try to marry into our family."

The poor duckling wasn't thinking of marriage. All he wanted was to be allowed to swim among the reeds and drink a little water when he was thirsty.

He spent two days in the swamp; then two wild geese came — or rather, two wild ganders, for they were males. They had been hatched not long ago; therefore they were both frank and bold.

"Listen, comrade," they said. "You are so ugly that we like you. Do you want to migrate with us? Not far from here there is a marsh where some beautiful wild geese live. They are all lovely maidens, and you are so ugly that you may seek your fortune among them. Come along."

"Bang! Bang!" Two shots were heard and both ganders fell down dead among the reeds, and the water turned red from their blood.

"Bang! Bang!" Again came the sound of shots, and a flock of wild geese flew up.

The whole swamp was surrounded by hunters; from every direction came the awful noise. Some of the hunters had hidden behind bushes or among the reeds but others, screened from sight by the leaves, sat on the long, low branches of the trees that stretched out over the swamp. The blue smoke from the guns lay like a fog over the water and along the trees. Dogs came splashing through the marsh, and they bent and broke the reeds.

The poor little duckling was terrified. He was about to tuck his head under his wing, in order to hide, when he saw a big dog peering at him through the reeds. The dog's tongue hung out of its mouth and its eyes glistened evilly. It bared its teeth. Splash! It turned away without touching the duckling.

"Oh, thank God!" he sighed. "I am so ugly that even the dog doesn't want to bite me."

The little duckling lay as still as he could while the shots whistled through the reeds. Not until the middle of the afternoon did the shooting stop; but the poor little duckling was still so frightened that he waited several hours longer before taking his head out from under his wing. Then he ran as quickly as he could out of the swamp. Across the fields and the meadows he went, but a wind had come up and he found it hard to make his way against it.

Towards evening he came upon a poor little hut. It was so wretchedly crooked that it looked as if it couldn't make up its mind which way to fall and that was why it was still standing. The wind was blowing so hard that the poor little duckling had to sit down in order not to be blown away. Suddenly he noticed that the door was off its hinges, making a crack; and he squeezed himself through it and was inside.

An old woman lived in the hut with her cat and her hen. The cat was called Sonny and could both arch his back and purr. Oh yes, it could also make sparks if you rubbed its fur the wrong way. The hen had very short legs and that was why she was called Cluck Lowlegs. But she was good at laying eggs, and the old woman loved her as if she were her own child.

In the morning the hen and the cat discovered the duckling. The cat meowed and the hen clucked.

"What is going on?" asked the old woman, and looked around. She couldn't see very well, and when she found the duckling she thought it was a fat, full-grown duck. "What a fine catch!" she exclaimed. "Now we shall have duck eggs, unless it's a drake. We'll give it a try."

So the duckling was allowed to stay for three weeks on probation, but he laid no eggs. The cat was the master of the house and the hen the mistress. They always referred to themselves as "we and the world," for they thought that they were half the world—and the better half at that. The duckling thought that he should be allowed to have a different opinion, but the hen did not agree.

"Can you lay eggs?" she demanded.

"No," answered the duckling.

"Then keep your mouth shut."

And the cat asked, "Can you arch your back? Can you purr? Can you make sparks?"

"No."

"Well, in that case, you have no right to have an opinion when sensible people are talking."

The duckling was sitting in a corner and was in a bad mood. Suddenly he recalled how lovely it could be outside in the fresh air when the sun shone: a great longing to be floating in the water came over the duckling, and he could not help talking about it.

"What is the matter with you?" asked the hen as soon as she had heard what he had to say. "You have nothing to do, that's why you get ideas like that. Lay eggs or purr, and such notions will disappear."

"You have no idea how delightful it is to float in the water, and to dive down to the bottom of a lake and get your head wet," said the duckling.

"Yes, that certainly does sound amusing," said the hen. "You must have gone mad. Ask the cat—he is the most intelligent being I know—ask him whether he likes to swim or dive down to the bottom of a lake. Don't take my word for anything.... Ask the old woman, who is the cleverest person in the world; ask her whether she likes to float and to get her head all wet."

"You don't understand me!" wailed the duckling.

"And if I don't understand you, who will? I hope you don't think that you are wiser than the cat or the old woman—not to mention myself. Don't give yourself airs! Thank your Creator for all He has done for you. Aren't you sitting in a warm room, where you can hear intelligent conversation that you could learn something from? While you, yourself, do nothing but say a lot of nonsense and aren't the least bit amusing! Believe me, that's the truth, and I am only telling it to you for your own good. That's how you recognize a true friend: it's someone who is willing to tell you the truth, no matter how unpleasant it is. Now get to work: lay some eggs, or learn to purr and arch your back."

"I think I'll go out into the wide world," replied the duckling.

"Go right ahead!" said the hen.

And the duckling left. He found a lake where he could float in the water and dive to the bottom. There were other ducks, but they ignored him because he was so ugly.

Autumn came and the leaves turned yellow and brown, then they fell from the trees. The wind caught them and made them dance. The clouds were heavy with hail and snow. A raven sat on a fence and screeched, "Ach! Ach!" because it was so cold. When just thinking of how cold it was is enough to make one shiver, what a terrible time the duckling must have had.

One evening just as the sun was setting gloriously, a flock of beautiful birds came out from among the rushes. Their feathers were so white that they glistened; and they had long, graceful necks. They were swans. They made a very loud cry, then they spread their powerful wings. They were flying south to a warmer climate, where the lakes were not frozen in the winter. Higher and higher they circled. The ugly duckling turned round and round in the water like a wheel and stretched his neck up toward the sky; he felt a strange longing. He screeched so piercingly that he frightened himself.

Oh, he would never forget those beautiful birds, those happy birds. When they were out of sight the duckling dived down under the water to the bottom of the lake; and when he came up again he was beside himself. He did not know the name of those birds or where they were going, and yet he felt he loved them as he had never loved any other creatures. He did not envy them. It did not even occur to him to wish that he were so handsome himself. He would have been happy if the other ducks had let him stay in the henyard: that poor, ugly bird!

The weather grew colder and colder. The duckling had to swim round and round in the water, to keep just a little space for himself that wasn't frozen. Each night his hole became smaller and smaller. On all sides of him the ice creaked and groaned. The little duckling had to keep his feet constantly in motion so that the last bit of open water wouldn't become ice. At last he was too tired to swim any more. He sat still. The ice closed in around him and he was frozen fast.

Early the next morning a farmer saw him and with his clogs broke the ice to free the duckling. The man put the bird under his arm and took it home to his wife, who brought the duckling back to life.

The children wanted to play with him. But the duckling was afraid that they were going to hurt him, so he flapped his wings and flew right into the milk pail. From there he flew into a big bowl of butter and then into a barrel of flour. What a sight he was!

The farmer's wife yelled and chased him with a poker. The children laughed and almost fell on top of each other, trying to catch him; and how they screamed! Luckily for the duckling, the door was open. He got out of the house and found a hiding place beneath some bushes, in the newly fallen snow; and there he lay so still, as though there was hardly any life left in him.

It would be too horrible to tell of all the hardship and suffering the duckling experienced that long winter. It is enough to know that he did survive. When again the sun shone warmly and the larks began to sing, the duckling was lying among the reeds in the swamp. Spring had come!

He spread out his wings to fly. How strong and powerful they were! Before he knew it, he was far from the swamp and flying above a beautiful garden. The apple trees were blooming and the lilac bushes stretched their flower-covered branches over the water of a winding canal. Everything was so beautiful: so fresh and green. Out of a forest of rushes came three swans. They ruffled their feathers and floated so lightly on the water. The ugly duckling recognized the birds and felt again that strange sadness come over him.

"I shall fly over to them, those royal birds! And they can hack me to death because I, who am so ugly, dare to approach them! What difference does it make? It is better to be killed by them than to be bitten by the other ducks, and pecked by the hens, and kicked by the girl who tends the henyard; or to suffer through the winter."

And he lighted on the water and swam towards the magnificent swans. When they saw him they ruffled their feathers and started to swim in his direction. They were coming to meet him.

"Kill me," whispered the poor creature, and bent his head humbly while he waited for death. But what was that he saw in the water? It was his own reflection; and he was no longer an awkward, clumsy, grey bird, so ungainly and so ugly. He was a swan!

It does not matter that one has been born in the henyard as long as one has lain in a swan's egg.

He was thankful that he had known so much want, and gone through so much suffering, for it made him appreciate his present happiness and the loveliness of everything about him all the more. The swans made a circle around him and caressed him with their beaks.

Some children came out into the garden. They had brought bread with them to feed the swans. The youngest child shouted, "Look, there's a new one!" All the children joyfully clapped their hands, and they ran to tell their parents.

Cake and bread were cast on the water for the swans. Everyone agreed that the new swan was the most beautiful of them all. The older swans bowed towards him.

He felt so shy that he hid his head beneath his wing. He was too happy, but not proud, for a kind heart can never be proud. He thought of the time when he had been mocked and persecuted. And now everyone said that he was the most beautiful of the most beautiful birds. And the lilac bushes stretched their branches right down to the water for him. The sun shone so warm and brightly. He ruffled his feathers and raised his slender neck, while out of the joy in his heart, he thought, "Such happiness I did not dream of when I was the ugly duckling."

THE NIGHTINGALE

Hans Christian Andersen

IN China, as you know, the emperor is Chinese, and so are his court and all his people. This story happened a long, long time ago; and that is just the reason why you should hear it now, before it is forgotten. The emperor's palace was the most beautiful in the whole world. It was made of porcelain and had been most costly to build. It was so fragile that you had to be careful not to touch anything and that can be difficult. The gardens were filled with the loveliest flowers; the most beautiful of them had little silver bells that tinkled so you wouldn't pass by without noticing them.

Everything in the emperor's garden was most cunningly arranged. The gardens were so large that even the head gardener did not know exactly how big they were. If you kept walking you finally came to the most beautiful forest, with tall trees that mirrored themselves in deep lakes. The forest stretched all the way to the sea, which was blue and so deep that even large boats could sail so close to the shore that they were shaded by the trees. Here lived a nightingale who sang so sweetly that even the fisherman, who came every night to set his nets, would stop to rest when he heard it, and say: "Blessed God, how beautifully it sings!" But he couldn't listen too long, for he had work to do, and soon he would forget the bird. Yet the next night when he heard it again, he would repeat what he had said the night before: "Blessed God, how beautifully it sings!"

From all over the world travellers came to the emperor's city to admire his palace and gardens; but when they heard the nightingale sing, they all declared that it was the loveliest of all. When they returned to their own countries, they would write long and learned books about the city, the palace, and the garden; but they didn't forget the nightingale. No, that was always mentioned in the very first chapter. Those who could write poetry wrote long odes about the nightingale who lived in the forest, on the shores of the deep blue sea.

These books were read the whole world over; and finally one was also sent to the emperor. He sat down in his golden chair and started to read it. Every once in a while he would nod his head because it pleased him to read how his own city and his own palace and gardens were praised; but then he came to the sentence: "But the song of the nightingale is the loveliest of all."

"What!" said the emperor. "The nightingale? I don't know it, I have never heard of it; and yet it lives not only in my empire but in my very garden. That is the sort of thing one can only find out by reading books."

He called his chief courtier, who was so very noble that if anyone of a rank lower than his own, either talked to him, or dared ask him a question, he only answered, "P." And that didn't mean anything at all.

"There is a strange and famous bird called the nightingale," began the emperor. "It is thought to be the most marvelous thing in my empire. Why have I never heard of it?"

"I have never heard of it," answered the courtier. "It has never been presented at court."

"I want it to come this evening and sing for me," demanded the emperor. "The whole world knows of it but I do not."

"I have never heard it mentioned before," said the courtier, and bowed. "But I shall search for it and find it."

But that was more easily said than done. The courtier ran all through the palace, up the stairs and down the stairs, and through the long corridors, but none of the people whom he asked had ever heard of the nightingale. He returned to the emperor and declared that the whole story was nothing but a fable, invented by those people who had written the books. "Your Imperial Majesty should not believe everything that is written. A discovery is one thing and artistic imagination something quite different; it is fiction."

"The book I have just read," replied the emperor, "was sent to me by the great Emperor of Japan; and therefore, every word in it must be the truth. I want to hear the nightingale! And that tonight! If it does not come, then the whole court shall have their stomachs thumped, and that right after they have eaten."

"*Tsing-pe!*" said the courtier. He ran again up and down the stairs and through the corridors; and half the court ran with him, because they didn't want their stomachs thumped! Everywhere they asked about the nightingale that the whole world knew about, and yet no one at court had heard of.

At last they came to the kitchen, where a poor little girl worked, scrubbing the pots and pans. "Oh, I know the nightingale," she said, "I know it well, it sings so beautifully. Every evening I am allowed to bring some leftovers to my poor sick mother who lives down by the sea. Now it is far away, and as I return I often rest in the forest and listen to the nightingale. I get tears in my eyes from it, as though my mother were kissing me."

"Little kitchenmaid," said the courtier, "I will arrange for a permanent position in the kitchen for you, and permission to see the emperor eat, if you will take us to the nightingale; it is summoned to court tonight."

Half the court went to the forest to find the nightingale. As they were walking along a cow began to bellow.

"Oh!" shouted all the courtiers. "There it is. What a marvelously powerful voice the little animal has; we have heard it before."

"That is only a cow," said the little kitchenmaid. "We are still far from where the nightingale lives."

They passed a little pond; the frogs were croaking.

"Lovely," sighed the Chinese imperial dean. "I can hear her, she sounds like little church bells ringing."

"No, that is only the frogs," said the little kitchenmaid, "but any time now we may hear it."

Just then the nightingale began singing.

"There it is!" said the little girl. "Listen. Listen. It is up there on that branch." And she pointed to a little grey bird sitting amid the greenery.

"Is that possible?" exclaimed the chief courtier. "I had not imagined it would look like that. It looks so common! I think it has lost its colour from shyness and out of embarrassment at seeing so many noble people at one time."

"Little nightingale," called the kitchenmaid, "our emperor wants you to sing for him."

"With pleasure," replied the nightingale, and sang as beautifully as he could.

"It sounds like little glass bells," sighed the chief courtier. "Look at its little throat, how it throbs. It is strange that we have never heard of it before; it will be a great success at court."

"Shall I sing another song for the emperor?" asked the nightingale, who thought that the emperor was there.

"Most excellent little nightingale," began the chief courtier, "I have the pleasure to invite you to attend the court tonight, where His Imperial Majesty, the Emperor of China, wishes you to enchant him with your most charming art."

"It sounds best in the green woods," said the nightingale; but when he heard that the emperor insisted, he followed them readily back to the palace.

There every room had been polished and thousands of little golden lamps reflected themselves in the shiny porcelain walls and floors. In the corridors stood all the most beautiful flowers, the ones with silver bells on them, and there was such a draught from all the servants running in and out, and opening and closing doors, that all the bells were tinkling and you couldn't hear what anyone said.

In the grand banquet hall, where the emperor's throne stood, a little golden perch had been hung for the nightingale to sit on. The whole court was there and the little kitchenmaid, who now had the title of Imperial Kitchenmaid, was allowed to stand behind one of the doors and listen. Everyone was dressed in their finest clothes and they all were looking at the little grey bird, towards which the emperor nodded very kindly.

The nightingale's song was so sweet that tears came into the emperor's eyes; and when they ran down his cheeks, the little nightingale sang even more beautifully than it had before. His song spoke to one's heart, and the emperor was so pleased that he ordered his golden slipper to be hung around the little bird's neck. There was no higher honour. But the nightingale thanked him and said that he had been honored enough already.

"I have seen tears in the eyes of an emperor, and that is a great enough treasure for me. There is a strange power in an emperor's tears and God knows that is reward enough." Then he sang yet another song.

"That was the most charming and elegant song we have ever heard," said all the ladies of the court. And from that time onward they filled their mouths with water, so they could make a clucking noise, whenever anyone spoke to them, because they thought that then they sounded like the nightingale. Even the chambermaids and the lackeys were satisfied; and that really meant something, for servants are the most difficult to please. Yes, the nightingale was a success.

He was to have his own cage at court, and permission to take a walk twice a day and once during the night. Twelve servants were to accompany him; each held on tightly to a silk ribbon that was attached to the poor bird's legs. There wasn't any pleasure in such an outing.

The whole town talked about the marvelous bird. Whenever two people met in the street they would sigh; one would say, "night," and the other, "gale"; and then they would understand each other perfectly. Twelve delicatessen shop owners named their children "Nightingale," but not one of them could sing.

One day a package arrived for the emperor; on it was written: "Nightingale."

"It is probably another book about our famous bird," said the emperor. But he was wrong; it was a mechanical nightingale. It lay in a little box and was supposed to look like the real one, though it was made of silver and gold and studded with sapphires, diamonds, and rubies. When you wound it up, it could sing one of the songs the real nightingale sang; and while it performed its little silver tail would go up and down. Around its neck hung a ribbon on which was written: "The Emperor of Japan's nightingale is inferior to the Emperor of China's."

"It is beautiful!" exclaimed the whole court. And the messenger who had brought it had the title of Supreme Imperial Nightingale Deliverer bestowed upon him at once.

"They ought to sing together, it will be a duet," said everyone, and they did. But that didn't work out well at all; for the real bird sang in his own manner and the mechanical one had a cylinder inside its chest instead of a heart. "It is not its fault," said the imperial music master. "It keeps perfect time, it belongs to my school of music." Then the mechanical nightingale had to sing solo. Everyone agreed that its song was just as beautiful as the real nightingale's; and besides, the artificial bird was much pleasanter to look at, with its sapphires, rubies, and diamonds that glittered like bracelets and brooches.

The mechanical nightingale sang its song thirty-three times and did not grow tired. The court would have liked to hear it the thirty-fourth time, but the emperor thought that the real nightingale ought to sing now. But where was it? Nobody had noticed that he had flown out through an open window, to his beloved green forest.

"What is the meaning of this!" said the emperor angrily, and the whole court blamed the nightingale and called him an ungrateful creature.

"But the best bird remains," they said, and the mechanical bird sang its song once more. It was the same song, for it knew no other; but it was very intricate, so the courtiers didn't know it by heart yet. The Imperial Music Master praised the bird and declared that it was better than the real nightingale, not only on the outside where the diamonds were, but also inside.

"Your Imperial Majesty and gentlemen: you understand that the real nightingale cannot be depended upon. One never knows what he will sing; whereas, in the mechanical bird, everything is determined. There is one song and no other! One can explain everything. We can open it up to examine and appreciate how human thought has fashioned the wheels and the cylinder, and put them where they are, to turn just as they should."

"Precisely what I was thinking!" said the whole court in a chorus. And the Imperial Music Master was given permission to show the new nightingale to the people on the following Sunday.

The emperor thought that they, too, should hear the bird. They did and they were as delighted as if they had got drunk on too much tea. It was all very Chinese. They pointed with their licking fingers toward heaven, nodded, and said: "Oh!"

But the poor fisherman, who had heard the real nightingale, mumbled, "It sounds beautiful and like the bird's song, but something is missing, though I don't know what it is."

The real nightingale was banished from the empire.

The mechanical bird was given a silk pillow to rest upon, close to the emperor's bed; and all the presents it had received were piled around it. Among them were both gold and precious stones. Its title was Supreme Imperial Night-table Singer and its rank was Number One to the Left—the emperor thought the left side was more distinguished because that is the side where the heart is, even in an emperor.

The Imperial Music Master wrote a work in twenty-five volumes about the mechanical nightingale. It was not only long and learned but filled with the most difficult Chinese words, so everyone bought it and said they had read and understood it, for otherwise they would have been considered stupid and had to have their stomachs poked.

A whole year went by. The emperor, the court, and all the Chinese in China knew every note of the Supreme Imperial Night-table Singer's song by heart; but that was the very reason why they liked it so much: they could sing it themselves, and they did. The street urchins sang: "Zi-zi-zizzi, cluck-cluck-cluck-cluck." And so did the emperor. Oh, it was delightful!

But one evening, when the bird was singing its very best and the emperor was lying in bed listening to it, something said "Clang," inside it. It was broken! All the wheels whirred around and then the bird was still.

The emperor jumped out of bed and called his physician but he couldn't do anything, so the imperial watchmaker was fetched. After a great deal of talking and tinkering he repaired the bird, but he declared that the cylinders were worn and new ones could not be fitted. The bird would have to be spared; it could not be played so often.

It was a catastrophe. Only once a year was the mechanical bird allowed to sing, and then it had difficulty finishing its song. But the imperial music master made a speech wherein he explained, using the most difficult words, that the bird was as good as ever; and then it was.

Five years passed and a great misfortune happened. Although everyone loved the old emperor, he had fallen ill; and they all agreed that he would not get well again. It was said that a new emperor had already been chosen; and when people in the street asked the chief courtier how the emperor was, he would shake his head and say: "P."

Pale and cold, the emperor lay in his golden bed. The whole court believed him to be already dead and they were busy visiting and paying their respects to the new emperor. The lackeys were all out in the street gossiping, and the chambermaids were drinking coffee. All the floors in the whole palace were covered with black carpets so that no one's steps would disturb the dying emperor; and that's why it was as quiet as quiet could be in the whole palace.

But the emperor was not dead yet. Pale and motionless he lay in his great golden bed; the long velvet curtains were drawn, and the golden tassels moved slowly in the wind, for one of the windows was open. The moon shone down upon the emperor, and its light was reflected in the diamonds of the mechanical bird.

The emperor could hardly breathe; he felt as though someone were sitting on his chest. He opened his eyes. Death was sitting there. He was wearing the emperor's golden crown and held his gold saber in one hand and his imperial banner in the other. From the folds of the curtains that hung around his bed, strange faces looked down at the emperor. Some of them were frighteningly ugly, and others mild and kind. They were the evil and good deeds that the emperor had done. Now, while Death was sitting on his heart, they were looking down at him.

"Do you remember?" whispered first one and then another. And they told him things that made the cold sweat of fear appear on his forehead.

"No, no, I don't remember! It is not true!" shouted the emperor. "Music, music, play the great Chinese gong," he begged, "so that I will not be able to hear what they are saying."

But the faces kept talking and Death, like a real Chinese, nodded his head to every word that was said.

"Little golden nightingale, sing!" demanded the emperor. "I have given you gold and precious jewels and with my own hands have I hung my golden slipper around your neck. Sing! Please sing!"

But the mechanical nightingale stood as still as ever, for there was no one to wind it up; and then, it couldn't sing.

Death kept staring at the emperor out of the empty sockets in his skull; and the palace was still, so terrifyingly still.

All at once the most beautiful song broke the silence. It was the nightingale, who had heard of the emperor's illness and torment. He sat on a branch outside his window and sang to bring him comfort and hope. As he sang, the faces in the folds of the curtains faded and the blood pulsed with greater force through the emperor's weak body. Death himself listened and said, "Please, little nightingale, sing on!"

"Will you give me the golden saber? Will you give me the imperial banner? Will you give me the golden crown?"

Death gave each of his trophies for a song; and then the nightingale sang about the quiet churchyard, where white roses grow, where fragrant elderberry trees are, and where the grass is green from the tears of those who come to mourn. Death longed so much for his garden that he flew out of the window, like a white cold mist.

"Thank you, thank you," whispered the emperor, "you heavenly little bird, I remember you. You have I banished from my empire and yet you came to sing for me; and when you sang the evil phantoms that taunted me disappeared, and Death himself left my heart. How shall I reward you?"

"You have rewarded me already," said the nightingale. "I shall never forget that, the first time I sang for you, you gave me the tears from your eyes; and to a poet's heart, those are jewels. But sleep so you can become well and strong; I shall sing for you."

The little grey bird sang; and the emperor slept, so blessedly, so peacefully.

The sun was shining in through the window when he woke; he did not feel ill any more. None of his servants had come, for they thought that he was already dead; but the nightingale was still there and he was singing.

"You must come always," declared the emperor. "I shall only ask you to sing when you want to. And the mechanical bird I shall break in a thousand pieces."

"Don't do that," replied the nightingale. "The mechanical bird sang as well as it could, keep it. I can't build my nest in the palace; let me come to visit you when I want to, and I shall sit on the branch outside your window and sing for you. And my song shall make you happy and make you thoughtful. I shall sing not only of those who are happy but also of those who suffer. I shall sing of the good and of the evil that happen around you, and yet are hidden from you. For a little songbird flies far. I visit the poor fisherman's cottage and the peasant's hut, far away from your palace and your court. I love your heart more than your crown, and yet I feel that the crown has a fragrance of something holy about it. I will come! I will sing for you! Only one thing must you promise me."

"I will promise you anything," said the emperor, who had dressed himself in his imperial clothes and was holding his golden saber, pressing it against his heart.

"I beg of you never tell anyone that you have a little bird that tells you everything, for then you will fare even better." And with those words the nightingale flew away.

The servants entered the room to look at their dead master. There they stood gaping when the emperor said: "Good morning."

THE LITTLE MERMAID

Hans Christian Andersen

FAR, far from land, where the waters are as blue as the petals of the cornflower and as clear as glass, there, where no anchor can reach the bottom, live the mer-people. So deep is this part of the sea that you would have to pile many church towers on top of each other before one of them emerged above the surface.

Now you must not think that at the bottom of the sea there is only white sand. No, here grow the strangest plants and trees; their stems and leaves are so subtle that the slightest current in the water makes them move, as if they were alive. Big and small fishes flit in and out among their branches, just as the birds do up on earth. At the very deepest place, the mer-king has built his castle. Its walls are made of coral and its long pointed windows of amber. The roof is oyster shells that are continually opening and closing. It looks very beautiful, for in each shell lies a pearl, so lustrous that it would be fit for a queen's crown.

The mer-king had been a widower for many years; his mother kept house for him. She was a very intelligent woman but a little too proud of her rank: she wore twelve oysters on her tail; the nobility were only allowed six. Otherwise, she was a most praise-worthy woman, and she took excellent care of her grandchildren, the little princesses. They were six lovely mermaids; the youngest was the most beautiful. Her complexion was as fine as the petal of a rose and her eyes as blue as the deepest lake but, just like every-one else down there, she had no feet; her body ended in a fishtail.

The mermaids were allowed to play all day in the great hall of the castle, where flowers grew on the walls. The big amber windows were kept open and the fishes swam in and out, just as the swallows up on earth fly in through our windows if they are open. But unlike the birds of the air, the fishes were not fright-ened, they swam right up to the little princesses and ate out of their hands and let themselves be petted.

Around the castle was a great park where there grew fiery-red and deep-blue trees. Their fruits shone as though they were the purest gold, their flowers were like flames, and their branches and leaves were ever in motion. The earth was the finest sand, not white but blue, the colour of burning sulphur. There was a blue tinge to everything, down on the bottom of the sea. You could almost believe that you were suspended in mid-air and had the blue sky both above and below you. When the sea was calm, the sun appeared like a crimson flower, from which all light flowed.

Each little princess had her own garden, where she could plant the flowers she liked. One of them had shaped her flower bed so it resembled a whale; and another, as a mermaid. The youngest had planted red flowers in hers; she wanted it to look like the sun; it was round and the crimson flowers did glow as though they were so many little suns. She was a strange little child; quiet and thoughtful. Her sisters' gardens were filled with all sorts of things that they had collected from shipwrecks, but she had only a marble statue of a boy in hers. It had been cut out of stone that was almost transparently clear and had sunk to the bottom of the sea when the ship that had carried it was lost. Close to the statue she had planted a pink tree it looked like a weeping willow. The tree was taller than sculpture. Its long soft branches bent towards the sand; it looked as if the top of the tree and its roots wanted to kiss each other.

The princesses liked nothing better than to listen to their old grandmother tell about the world above. She had to recount countless times all she knew about ships, towns, human beings, and the animals that lived up on land. The youngest of the mermaids thought it particularly wonderful that the flowers up there had fragrance, for that they did not have on the bottom of the sea. She also liked to hear about the green forest, where the fishes that swam among the branches could sing most beautifully. Grandmother called the birds "fishes"; otherwise, her little grandchildren would not have understood her, since they had never seen a bird.

"But when you are fifteen, then you will be allowed to swim to the surface," she promised. "Then you can climb up on a rock and sit and watch the big ships sail by. If you dare, you can swim close enough to the shore to see the towns and the forest."

The following year, the oldest of the princesses would be fifteen. From one sister to the next, there was a difference in age of about a year, which meant that the youngest would have to wait more than five whole years before she would be allowed to swim up from the bottom of the sea and take a look at us. But each promised the others that she would return after her first day above, and tell about the things she had seen and describe what she thought was loveliest of all. For the old grandmother could not satisfy their curiosity.

None of the sisters longed so much to see the world above as the youngest, the one who had to wait the longest before she could leave her home. Many a night this quiet, thoughtful little mermaid would stand by the open window, looking up through the dark blue waters where the fishes swam. She could see the moon and the stars; they looked paler but larger down here under the sea. Sometimes a great shadow passed by like a cloud and then she knew that it was either a whale or a ship, with its crew and passengers, that was sailing high above her. None on board could have imagined that a little beautiful mermaid stood in the depths below them and stretched her little white hands up towards the keel of their ship.

The oldest of the sisters had her fifteenth birthday and swam up to the surface of the sea. When she returned she had hundreds of things to tell. But of everything that had happened to her, the loveliest experience by far, she claimed, had been to lie on a sand-bank, when the sea was calm and the moon was out, and look at a great city. The lights from the windows and streets had shone like hundreds of stars; and she had been able to hear the rumbling of the carriages and the voices of human beings and, best of all, the sound of music. She had seen all the church towers and steeples and heard their bells ring. And just because she would never be able to enter the city, she longed to do that more than anything else.

How carefully her youngest sister listened to every word and remembered everything that she had been told. When, late in the evening, the little mermaid would stand dreaming by the window and look up through the blue water, then she imagined that she could see the city and hear the bells of the churches ringing.

The next year the second of the sisters was allowed to swim away from home. Her little head had emerged above the water just at the moment when the sun was setting. This sight had been so beautiful that she could hardly describe it. The whole heaven had been covered in gold and the clouds that had sailed above her had been purple and crimson. A flight of wild swans, like a white veil just above the water, had flown by. She had swum toward the sun, but it had set, taking the colors of the clouds, sea, and sky with it.

The third of the sisters, who came of age the following year, was the most daring among them. She had swum way up a broad river! There she had seen green hills covered with vineyards, castles, and farms that peeped out through the great forests. She had heard the birds sing and the sun had been so hot that she had had to swim under the water, some of the time, just to cool off. In a little bay, she had come upon some naked children who were playing and splashing in the water. She had wanted to join them, but when they saw her they got frightened and ran away. A little black animal had come: it was a dog. But she had never seen one before. It had barked so loudly and fiercely that she became terrified and swam right back to the sea. What she never would forget as long as she lived were the beautiful forest, the green hills, and the sweet little children who had been able to swim even though they had no fishtails as she had.

The fourth of the sisters was timid. She stayed far away from shore, out in the middle of the ocean. But that was the most beautiful place of all, she asserted. You could see ever so far and the sky above was like a clear glass bell. The ships she had seen had been so far away that they had looked no bigger than gulls. But the little dolphins had turned somersaults for her and the great whales had sprayed water high up into the air, so that it looked as though there were more than a hundred fountains.

The fifth sister's birthday was in the winter and, therefore, she saw something none of her sisters had seen. The ocean had been green, and huge icebergs had been floating on it. Each of them had been as lovely as a pearl and yet larger than the church towers that human beings built. They had the most fantastic shapes and their surface glittered like diamonds. She had climbed up on the largest one of them all; the wind had played with her long hair, and all the ships had fearfully kept away. Toward evening a storm had begun to blow; dark clouds had gathered and bolts of lightning had flashed while the thunder rolled. The waves had lifted the iceberg high up on their shoulders, and the lightning had colored the ice red. The ships had taken down their sails; and on board, fear and terror had reigned. But the mermaid had just sat on her iceberg and watched the bolts of lightning zigzag across the sky.

The first time that any of the sisters had been allowed to swim to the surface, each had been delighted with her freedom and all she had seen. But now that they were grownups and could swim anywhere they wished, they lost interest in wandering far away; after a month or two the world above lost its attraction. When they were away, they longed for their father's castle, declaring it the most beautiful place of all and the only spot where one really felt at home.

Still, many evenings the five sisters would take each other's hands and rise up through the waters. They had voices far lovelier than any human being. When a storm began to rage and a ship was in danger of being wrecked, then the five sisters would swim in front of it and sing about how beautiful it was down at the bottom of the sea. They begged the sailors not to be frightened but to come down to them. The men could not understand the mermaids' songs; they thought it was the wind that was singing. Besides, they would never see the beauty of the world below them, for if a ship sinks the seamen drown, and when they arrive at the mer-king's castle they are dead.

On such evenings, while her sisters swam, hand in hand, up through the water, the youngest princess had to stay below. She would look sadly up after them and feel like crying; but mermaids can't weep and that makes their suffering even deeper and greater.

"Oh, if only I were fifteen," she would sigh. "I know that I shall love the world above, and the human beings who live up there!"

At last she, too, was fifteen!

"Now you are off our hands," said the old dowager queen. "Let me dress you, just as I dressed your sisters." She put a wreath of white lilies around her hair; each of the petals of every flower was half a pearl. She let eight oysters clip themselves onto the little mermaid's tail, so that everyone could see that she was a princess.

"It hurts," said the little mermaid.

"One has to suffer for position," said her old grandmother. The little mermaid would gladly have exchanged her heavy pearl wreath for one of the red flowers from her garden (she thought they suited her much better) but she didn't dare.

"Farewell," she said and rose, light as a bubble, up through the water.

The sun had just set when she lifted her head above the surface. The clouds still had the color of roses and in the horizon was a fine line of gold; in the pale pink sky the first star of evening sparkled, clearly and beautifully. The air was warm and the sea was calm. She saw a three-masted ship; only one of its sails was unfurled, and it hung motionless in the still air. Up on the yards the sailors sat, looking down upon the deck from which music could be heard. As the evening grew darker, hundreds of little colored lamps were hung from the rigging; they looked like the flags of all the nations of the world. The little mermaid swam close to a porthole and the swells lifted her gently so that she could look in through it. The great cabin was filled with gaily dressed people; the handsomest among them was a young prince with large, dark eyes. He looked no older than sixteen, and that was, in truth, his age; that very day was his birthday. All the festivities were for him. The sailors danced on the deck, and as the young prince came up to watch them, a hundred rockets flew into the sky.

The night became as bright as day and the little mermaid got so frightened that she ducked down under the water. But she soon stuck her head up again; and then it looked as if all the stars of the heavens were falling down on top of her. She had never seen fireworks before. Pinwheels turned; rockets shot into the air, and their lights reflected in the dark mirror of the sea. The deck of the ship was so illuminated that every rope could clearly be seen. Oh, how handsome the young prince was! He laughed and smiled and shook hands with everyone, while music was played in the still night.

It grew late, but the little mermaid could not turn her eyes away from the ship and the handsome prince. The colored lamps were put out. No more rockets shot into the air and no more cannons were fired. From the depth of the ocean came a rumbling noise. The little mermaid let the waves be her rocking horse, and they lifted her so that she could look in through the porthole. The ship started to sail faster and faster, as one sail after another was unfurled. Now the waves grew in size and black clouds could be seen on the horizon and far away lightning flashed.

A storm was brewing. The sailors took down the sails. The great ship tossed and rolled in the huge waves that rose as though they were mountains that wanted to bury the ship and break its proud mast. But the ship, like a swan, rode on top of the waves and let them lift her high into the sky. The little mermaid thought it was very amusing to watch the ship sailing so fast, but the sailors didn't. The ship creaked and groaned; the great planks seemed to bulge as the waves hit them. Suddenly the mast snapped as if it were a reed. It tumbled into the water. The ship heeled over, and the sea broke over it.

Only now did the little mermaid understand that the ship was in danger. She had to be careful herself and keep away from the spars and broken pieces of timber that were being flung by the waves. For a moment it grew so dark that she could see nothing, then a bolt of lightning illuminated the sinking ship. She looked for the young prince among the terrified men on board who were trying to save themselves, but not until that very moment, when the ship finally sank, did she see him.

At first, she thought joyfully, "Now he will come down to me!" But then she remembered that man could not live in the sea and the young prince would be dead when he came to her father's castle.

"He must not die," she thought, and dived in among the wreckage, forgetting the danger that she herself was in, for any one of the great beams that were floating in the turbulent sea could have crushed her.

She found him! He was too tired to swim any farther; he had no more strength in his arms and legs to fight the storm-whipped waves. He closed his eyes, waiting for death, and he would have drowned, had the little mermaid not saved him. She held his head above water and let the waves carry them where they would.

By morning the storm was over. Of the wrecked ship not a splinter was to be found. The sun rose, glowing red, and its rays gave color to the young prince's cheeks but his eyes remained closed. The little mermaid kissed his forehead and stroked his wet hair. She thought that he looked like the statue in her garden. She kissed him again and wished passionately that he would live.

In the far distance she saw land; the mountains rose blue in the morning air. The snow on their peaks was as glittering white as swan's feathers. At the shore there was a green forest, and in its midst lay a cloister or a church, the little mermaid did not know which. Lemon and orange trees grew in the garden, and by the entrance gate stood a tall palm tree. There was a little bay nearby, where the water was calm and deep. The mermaid swam with her prince toward the beach. She laid him in the fine white sand, taking care to place his head in the warm sunshine far from the water.

In the big white buildings bells were ringing and a group of young girls was coming out to walk in the garden. The little mermaid swam out to some rocks and hid behind them. She covered her head with seaweed so that she could not be seen and then peeped toward land, to see who would find the poor prince.

Soon one of the young girls discovered him. At first she seemed frightened, and she called the others. A lot of people came. The prince opened his eyes and smiled up at those who stood around him—not out at the sea, where the little mermaid was hiding. But then he could not possibly have known that she was there and that it was she who had saved him. The little mermaid felt so terribly sad; the prince was carried into the big white building, and the little mermaid dived sorrowfully down into the sea and swam home to her father's castle.

She had always been quiet and thoughtful. Now she grew even more silent. Her sisters asked her what she had seen on her first visit up above, but she did not answer.

Many mornings and evenings she would swim back to the place where she had last seen the prince. She watched the fruits in the orchard ripen and be picked, and saw the snow on the high mountains melt, but she never saw the prince. She would return from each of these visits a little sadder. She would seek comfort by embracing the statue in her garden, which looked like the prince. She no longer tended her flowers, and they grew into a wilderness, covering the paths and weaving their long stalks and leaves into the branches of the trees, so that it became quite dark down in her garden.

At last she could bear her sorrow no longer and told one of her sisters about it; and almost at once the others knew as well. But no one else was told; that is, except for a couple of other mermaids, but they didn't tell it to anyone except their nearest and dearest friends. It was one of these friends who knew who the prince was. She, too, had seen the birthday party on the ship, and she could tell where he came from and where his kingdom was.

"Come, little sister," the other princesses called, and with their arms around each other's shoulders they swam.

All in a row they rose to the surface when they came to the shore where the prince's castle stood. It was built of glazed yellow stones and had many flights of marble stairs leading up to it. The steps of one of them went all the way down to the sea. Golden domes rose above the roofs, and pillars bore an arcade that went all

the way around the palace. Between the pillars stood marble statues; they looked almost as if they were alive. Through the clear
glass of the tall windows, one could look into the most beautiful
chambers and halls, where silken curtains and tapestries hung on
the walls; and there were large paintings that were a real pleasure
to look at. In the largest hall was a fountain. The water shot high
up toward the glass cupola in the roof, through which the sunbeams fell on the water and the beautiful flowers that grew in the
basin of the fountain.

Now that she knew where the prince lived, the little mermaid
spent many evenings and nights looking at the splendid palace.
She swam nearer to the land than any of her sisters had ever
dared. There was a marble balcony that cast its shadow across a
narrow canal, and beneath it she hid and watched the young
prince, who thought that he was all alone in the moonlight.

Many an evening she saw the prince sail with his musicians in
his beautiful boat. She peeped from behind the tall reeds; and if
someone noticed her silver-white veil, they probably thought that
they had only seen a swan stretching its wings.

Many a night she heard the fishermen talking to each other
and telling about how kind and good the prince was; and she was
so glad that she had saved his life when she had found him, half
dead, drifting on the waves. She remembered how his head had
rested on her chest and with what passion she had kissed him.
But he knew nothing about his rescue; he could not even dream
about her.

More and more she grew to love human beings and wished
that she could leave the sea and live among them. It seemed to
her that their world was far larger than hers; on ships, they could
sail across the oceans and they could climb the mountains high up
above the clouds. Their countries seemed ever so large, covered
with fields and forests; she knew that they stretched much farther
than she could see. There was so much that she wanted to know;
there were many questions that her sisters could not answer.
Therefore she asked her old grandmother, since she knew much
about the "higher world," as she called the lands above the sea.

"If men are not so unlucky as to drown," asked the little mermaid, "then do they live forever? Don't they die as we do, down
here in the sea?"

"Yes, they do," answered her grandmother. "Men must also die and their life span is shorter than ours. We can live until we are three hundred years old; but when we die, we become the foam on the ocean. We cannot even bury our loved ones. We do not have immortal souls. When we die, we shall never rise again. We are like the green reeds: once they are cut they will never be green again. But men have souls that live eternally, even after their bodies have become dust. They rise high up into the clear sky where the stars are. As we rise up through the water to look at the world of man, they rise up to the unknown, the beautiful world, that we shall never see."

"Why do I not have an immortal soul!" sighed the little mermaid unhappily. "I would give all my three hundred years of life for only one day as a human being if, afterward, I should be allowed to live in the heavenly world."

"You shouldn't think about things like that," said her old grandmother. "We live far happier down here than man does up there."

"I am going to die, become foam on the ocean, and never again hear the music of the waves or see the flowers and the burning red sun. Can't I do anything to win an immortal soul?"

"No," said the old merwoman. "Only if a man should fall so much in love with you that you were dearer to him than his mother and father; and he cared so much for you that all his thoughts were of his love for you; and he let a priest take his right hand and put it in yours, while he promised to be eternally true to you, then his soul would flow into your body and you would be able to partake of human happiness. He can give you a soul and yet keep his own. But it will never happen. For that which we consider beautiful down here in the ocean, your fishtail, they find ugly up above, on earth. They have no sense; up there, you have to have two clumsy props, which they call legs, in order to be called beautiful."

The little mermaid sighed and glanced sadly down at her fishtail.

"Let us be happy," said her old grandmother. "We can swim and jump through the waves for three hundred years, that is time enough. Tonight we are going to give a court ball in the castle."

Such a splendor did not exist up above on the earth. The walls and the ceilings of the great hall were made of clear glass; four hundred giant green and pink oyster shells stood in rows along the walls. Blue flames rose from them and not only lighted the hall but also illuminated the sea outside. Numberless fishes — both big and small — swam close to the glass walls; some of them had purple scales, others seemed to be of silver and gold. Through the great hall flowed a swiftly moving current, and on that the mermen and mermaids danced, while they sang their own beautiful songs. Such lovely voices are never heard up on earth; and the little mermaid sang most beautifully of them all. The others clapped their hands when she had finished, and for a moment she felt happy, knowing that she had the most beautiful voice both on earth and in the sea.

But soon she started thinking again of the world above. She could not forget the handsome prince, and mourned because she did not have an immortal soul like his. She sneaked out of her father's palace, away from the ball, from the gaiety, down into her little garden.

From afar the sound of music, of horns being played, came down to her through the water; and she thought: "Now he is sailing up there, the prince whom I love more than I love my father and mother: he who is ever in my thoughts and in whose hands I would gladly place all my hope of happiness. I would dare to do anything to win him and an immortal soul! While my sisters are dancing in the palace, I will go to the sea witch, though I have always feared her, and ask her to help me."

The little mermaid swam toward the turbulent maelstrom; beyond it the sea witch lived. In this part of the great ocean the little mermaid had never been before; here no flowers or seaweeds grew, only the gray naked sea bed stretched toward the center of the maelstrom, that great whirlpool where the water, as if it had been set in motion by gigantic mill wheels, twisted and turned: grinding, tearing, and sucking anything that came within its reach down into its depths. Through this turbulence the little mermaid had to swim, for beyond it lay the bubbling mud flats that the sea witch called her bog and that had to be crossed to come to the place where she lived.

The sea witch's house was in the midst of the strangest forest. The bushes and trees were gigantic polyps that were half plant and half animal. They looked like snakes with hundreds of heads, but they grew out of the ground. Their branches were long slimy arms, and they had fingers as supple as worms; every limb was in constant motion from the root to the utmost point. Everything they could reach they grasped, and never let go of it again. With dread the little mermaid stood at the entrance to the forest; her heart was beating with fear, she almost turned back. But then she remembered her prince and the soul she wanted to gain and her courage returned.

She braided her long hair and bound it around her head, so the polyps could not catch her by it. She held her arms folded tightly across her breast and then she flew through the water as fast as the swiftest fish. The ugly polyps stretched out their arms and their fingers tried to grasp her. She noticed that every one of them was holding, as tightly as iron bands, onto something it had caught. Drowned human beings peeped out as white skeletons among the polyps' arms. There were sea chests, rudders of ships, skeletons of land animals; and then she saw a poor little mermaid who had been caught and strangled; and this sight was to her the most horrible.

At last she came to a great, slimy, open place in the middle of the forest. Big fat eels played in the mud, showing their ugly yellow stomachs. Here the witch had built her house out of the bones of drowned sailors, and there she sat letting a big ugly toad eat out of her mouth, as human beings sometimes let a canary eat sugar candy out of theirs. The ugly eels she called her little chickens, and held them close to her spongy chest.

"I know what you want," she cackled. "And it is stupid of you. But you shall have your wish, for it will bring you misery, little princess. You want to get rid of your fishtail, and instead have two stumps to walk on as human beings have, so that the prince will fall in love with you; and you will gain both him and an immortal soul." The witch laughed so loudly and evilly that the toad and eels she had had on her lap jumped down into the mud.

"You came at the right time," she said. "Tomorrow I could not have helped you; you would have had to wait a year. I will mix you a potion. Drink it tomorrow morning before the sun rises, while you are sitting on the beach. Your tail will divide and shrink, until it becomes what human beings call 'pretty legs.' It will hurt; it will feel as if a sword were going through your body. All who see you will say that you are the most beautiful human child they have ever seen. You will walk more gracefully than any dancer; but every time your foot touches the ground it will feel as though you were walking on knives so sharp that your blood must flow. If you are willing to suffer all this, then I can help you."

"I will," whispered the little mermaid, and thought of her prince and how she would win an immortal soul.

"But remember," screeched the witch, "that once you have a human body you can never become a mermaid again. Never again shall you swim through the waters with your sisters to your father's castle. If you cannot make the prince fall so much in love with you that he forgets both his father and mother, because his every thought concerns only you, and he orders the priest to take his right hand and place it in yours, so that you become man and wife; then, the first morning after he has married another, your heart will break and you will become foam on the ocean."

"I still want to try," said the little mermaid, and her face was as white as a corpse.

"But you will have to pay me, too," grinned the witch. "And I want no small payment. You have the most beautiful voice of all those who live in the ocean. I suppose you have thought of using that to charm your prince; but that voice you will have to give to me. I want the most precious thing you have to pay for my potion. It contains my own blood, so that it can be as sharp as a double-edged sword."

"But if you take my voice," said the little mermaid, "what will I have left?"

"Your beautiful body," said the witch. "Your graceful walk and your lovely eyes. Speak with them and you will be able to capture a human heart. Have you lost your courage? Stick out your little tongue, and let me cut it off in payment, and you shall have the potion."

"Let it happen," whispered the little mermaid.

The witch took out a caldron in which to make the magic potion. "Cleanliness is a virtue," she said. And before she put the pot over the fire, she scrubbed it with eels, which she had made into a whisk.

She cut her chest and let her blood drip into the vessel. The steam that rose became strange figures that were terrifying to see. Every minute, the witch put something different into the caldron. When the brew reached a rolling boil, it sounded as though a crocodile were crying. At last the potion was finished. It looked as clear and pure as water.

"Here it is," said the witch, and cut out the little mermaid's tongue. Now she was mute, she could neither speak nor sing.

"If any of the polyps should try to grab you, on your way back through my forest," said the witch, "you need only spill one drop of the potion on it and its arms and fingers will splinter into a thousand pieces."

But the little mermaid didn't have to do that. Fearfully, the polyps drew away when they saw what she was carrying in her hands; the potion sparkled as though it were a star. Safely, she returned through the forest, the bog, and the maelstrom.

She could see her father's palace. The lights were extinguished in the great hall. Everyone was asleep; and yet she did not dare to seek out her sisters; now that she was mute and was going away from them forever. She felt as if her heart would break with sorrow. She sneaked down into the garden and picked a flower from each of her sisters' gardens; then she threw a thousand finger kisses toward the palace and swam upward through the deep blue sea.

The sun had not yet risen when she reached the prince's castle and sat down on the lowest step of the great marble stairs. The moon was still shining clearly. The little mermaid drank the potion and it felt as if a sword were piercing her little body. She fainted and lay as though she were dead.

When the sun's rays touched the sea she woke and felt a burning pain; but the young prince stood in front of her and looked at her with his coal-black eyes. She looked downward and saw then that she no longer had a fishtail but the most beautiful, little, slender legs that any girl could wish for. She was naked; and therefore she took her long hair and covered herself with it.

The prince asked her who she was and how she had got there. She looked gently and yet ever so sadly up at him with her deep blue eyes, for she could not speak. He took her by the hand and led her up to his castle. And just as the witch had warned, every step felt as though she were walking on sharp knives. But she suffered it gladly. Gracefully as a bubble rising in the water, she walked beside the prince; and everyone who saw her wondered how she could walk so lightly.

In the castle, she was clad in royal clothes of silk and muslin. She was the most beautiful of all, but she was mute and could neither sing nor speak. Beautiful slave girls, clad in silken clothes embroidered with gold, sang for the prince and his royal parents. One sang more beautifully than the rest, and the prince clapped his hands and smiled to her; then the little mermaid was filled with sorrow, for she knew that she had once sung far more beautifully. And she thought, "Oh, if he only knew that to be with him I have given away my voice for all eternity."

Now the slave girls danced, gracefully they moved to the beautiful music. Suddenly the little mermaid lifted her hands and rose on the tips of her toes. She floated more than danced across the floor. No one had ever seen anyone dance as she did. Her every movement revealed her loveliness and her eyes spoke far more eloquently than the slave's song.

Everyone was delighted, especially the prince. He called her his little foundling. She danced again and again, even though each time her little foot touched the floor she felt as if she had stepped on a knife. The prince declared that she should never leave him, and she was given permission to sleep in front of his door on a velvet pillow.

The prince had men's clothes made for her, so that she could accompany him when he went horseback riding. Through the sweet-smelling forest they rode, where green branches touched their shoulders and little birds sang among the leaves. Together they climbed the high mountains and her feet bled so much that others noticed it; but she smiled and followed her prince up ever higher until they could see the clouds sail below them, like flocks of birds migrating to foreign lands.

At night in the castle, while the others slept, she would walk down the broad marble stairs to the sea and cool her poor burning feet in the cold water. Then she would think of her sisters, down in the deep sea.

One night they came; arm in arm they rose above the surface of the water, singing ever so sadly. She waved to them, and they recognized her, and they told her how much sorrow she had brought them. After that they visited her every night; and once she saw, far out to sea, her old grandmother. It had been years since she had stuck her head up into the air; and there, too, was her father the mer-king with his crown on his head. They stretched their hands toward her but did not dare come as near to the land as her sisters.

Day by day the prince grew fonder and fonder of her; but he loved her as he would have loved a good child, and had no thought of making her his queen. And she had to become his wife or she would never have an immortal soul, but on the morning after his marriage would become foam on the great ocean.

"Don't you love me more than you do all others?" was the message in the little mermaid's eyes when the prince kissed her lovely forehead.

"Yes, you are the dearest to me," said the prince, "for you have the kindest heart of them all. You are devoted to me and you look like a young girl I once saw, and will probably never see again. I was in a shipwreck. The waves carried me ashore, where a holy temple lay. Many young girls were in service there; one of them, the youngest of them all, found me on the beach and saved my life. I saw her only twice, but she is the only one I can love in this world; and you look like her. You almost make her picture disappear from my soul. She belongs to the holy temple and, therefore, good fortune has sent you to me instead, and we shall never part."

"Oh, he does not know that it was I who saved his life," thought the little mermaid. "I carried him across the sea to the forest where the temple stood. I hid behind the rocks and watched over him until he was found. I saw that beautiful girl whom he loves more than me!" And the little mermaid sighed deeply, for cry she couldn't. "He has said that the girl belongs to the holy temple and will never come out into the world, and they will never meet again. But I am with him and see him every day. I will take care of him, love him, and devote my life to him."

Everyone said that the young prince was to be married; he was to have the neighboring king's daughter, a beautiful princess. A magnificent ship was built and made ready. It was announced that the prince was traveling to see the neighboring kingdom, but that no one believed. "It is not the country but the princess he is to inspect," they all agreed.

The little mermaid shook her head and smiled; she knew what the prince thought, and they didn't.

"I must go," he had told her, "I must look at the beautiful princess, my parents demand it. But they won't force me to carry her home as my bride. I can't love her. She does not look like the girl from the temple as you do. If I ever marry, I shall most likely choose you, my little foundling with the eloquent eyes." And he kissed her on her red lips and played with her long hair, and let his head rest so near her heart that it dreamed of human happiness and an immortal soul.

"Are you afraid of the ocean, my little silent child?" asked the prince as they stood on the deck of the splendid ship that was to sail them to the neighboring kingdom. He told the little mermaid how the sea can be still or stormy, and about the fishes that live in it, and what the divers had seen underneath the water. She smiled as he talked, for who knew better than she about the world on the bottom of the ocean?

In the moonlit night, when everyone slept but the sailor at the rudder and the lookout in the bow, she sat on the bulwark and looked down into the clear water. She thought she saw her father's palace; and on the top of its tower her old grandmother was standing with her silver crown on her head, looking up through the currents of the sea, toward the keel of the ship. Her sisters came; they looked at her so sorrowfully and wrung their white hands in despair; she waved to them and smiled. She wanted them to know that she was happy, but just at that moment the little cabin boy came and her sisters dived down under the water; he saw nothing but some white foam on the ocean.

The next morning the ship sailed into the harbor of the great town that belonged to the neighboring king. All the church bells were ringing, and from the tall towers trumpets blew, while the soldiers stood at attention, with banners flying and bayonets on their rifles.

Every day another banquet was held, and balls and parties followed one after the other. But the princess attended none of them, for she did not live in the palace; she was being educated in the holy temple, where she was to learn all the royal virtues. But at last she came.

The little mermaid wanted ever so much to see her; and when

she finally did, she had to admit that a more beautiful girl she had never seen before. Her skin was so delicate and fine, and beneath her long dark lashes smiled a pair of faithful, dark blue eyes.

"It is you!" exclaimed the prince. "You are the one who saved me, when I lay half dead on the beach!" And he embraced his blushing bride.

"Oh, now I am too happy," he said to the little mermaid. "That which I never dared hope has now happened! You will share my joy, for I know that you love me more than any of the others do."

The little mermaid kissed his hand; she felt as if her heart were breaking. His wedding morning would bring her death and she would be changed into foam of the ocean.

All the churchbells rang and heralds rode through the streets and announced the wedding to the people. On all the altars costly silver lamps burned with fragrant oils. The priests swung censers with burning incense in them, while the prince and the princess gave each other their hands, and the bishop blessed them. The little mermaid, dressed in silk and gold, held the train of the bride's dress, but her ears did not hear the music, nor did her eyes see the holy ceremony, for this night would bring her death, and she was thinking of all she had lost in this world.

The bride and bridegroom embarked upon the prince's ship; cannons saluted and banners flew. On the main deck, a tent of gold and scarlet cloth had been raised; there on the softest of pillows the bridal couple would sleep.

The sails were unfurled, and they swelled in the wind and the ship glided across the transparent sea.

When it darkened and evening came, colored lamps were lit and the sailors danced on the deck. The little mermaid could not help remembering the first time she had emerged above the waves, when she had seen the almost identical sight. She whirled in the dance, glided as the swallow does in the air when it is pursued. Everyone cheered and applauded her. Never had she danced so beautifully; the sharp knives cut her feet, but she did not feel it, for the pain in her heart was far greater. She knew that this was the last evening that she would see him for whose sake she had given away her lovely voice and left her home and her family; and he would never know of her sacrifice. It was the last night that she would breathe the same air as he, or look out over the deep sea

and up into the star-blue heaven. A dreamless, eternal night awaited her, for she had no soul and had not been able to win one.

Until midnight all was gaiety aboard the ship, and the mermaid
danced and laughed with the thought of death in her heart. Then
the prince kissed his bride and she fondled his long black hair and,
arm in arm, they walked into their splendorous tent, to sleep.

The ship grew quiet. Only the sailor at the helm and the little
mermaid were awake. She stood with her white arms resting on
the railing and looked toward the east. She searched the horizon
for the pink of dawn; she knew that the first sunbeams would kill
her.

Out of the sea rose her sisters, but the wind could no longer
play with their long beautiful hair, for their heads had been shorn.

"We have given our hair to the sea witch, so that she would
help you and you would not have to die this night. Here is a knife
that the witch has given us. Look how sharp it is! Before the sun
rises, you must plunge it into the heart of the prince; when his
warm blood sprays on your feet, they will turn into a fishtail and
you will be a mermaid again. You will be able to live your three
hundred years down in the sea with us, before you die and
become foam on the ocean. Hurry! He or you must die before
the sun rises. Our grandmother mourns; she, too, has no hair; hers
has fallen out from grief. Kill the prince and come back to us!
Hurry! See, there is a pink haze on the horizon. Soon the sun will
rise and you will die."

The little mermaid heard the sound of her sisters' deep and
strange sighing before they disappeared beneath the waves.

She pulled aside the crimson cloth of the tent and saw the
beautiful bride sleeping peacefully, with her head resting on the
prince's chest. The little mermaid bent down and kissed his handsome forehead. She turned and looked at the sky; more and more,
it was turning red. She glanced at the sharp knife; and once more
she looked down at the prince. He moved a little in his sleep and
whispered the name of his bride. Only she was in his thoughts, in
his dreams! The little mermaid's hand trembled as it squeezed the
handle of the knife, then she threw the weapon out into the sea.
The waves turned red where it fell, as if drops of blood were seep-
ing up through the water.

Again she looked at the prince; her eyes were already glazed in death. She threw herself into the sea and felt her body changing into foam.

The sun rose out of the sea, its rays felt warm and soft on the deathly cold foam. But the little mermaid did not feel death, she saw the sun, and up above her floated hundreds of airy, transparent forms. She could see right through them, see the sails of the ship and the blood-red clouds. Their voices were melodious, so spiritual and tender that no human ear could hear them, just as their forms were so fragile and fine that no human eye could see them. So light were they that they glided through the air, though they had no wings. The little mermaid looked down and saw that she had an ethereal body like theirs.

"Where am I?" she asked; and her voice sounded like theirs — so lovely and so melodious that no human music could reproduce it.

"We are the daughters of the air," they answered. "Mermaids have no immortal soul and can never have one, unless they can obtain the love of a human being. Their chance of obtaining eternal life depends upon others. We, daughters of the air, have not received an eternal soul either; but we can win one by good deeds. We fly to the warm countries, where the heavy air of the plague rests, and blow cool winds to spread it. We carry the smell of flowers that refresh and heal the sick. If for three hundred years we earnestly try to do what is good, we obtain an immortal soul and can take part in the eternal happiness of man. You, little mermaid, have tried with all your heart to do the same. You have suffered and borne your suffering bravely; and that is why you are now among us, the spirits of the air. Do your good deeds and in three hundred years an immortal soul will be yours."

The little mermaid lifted her arms up toward God's sun, and for the first time she felt a tear.

She heard noise coming from the ship. She saw the prince and the princess searching for her. Sadly they looked at the sea, as if they knew that she had thrown herself into the waves. Without being seen, she kissed the bride's forehead and smiled at the prince; then she rose together with the other children of the air, up into a pink cloud that was sailing by.

"In three hundred years I shall rise like this into God's kingdom," she said.

"You may be able to go there before that," whispered one of the others to her. "Invisibly, we fly through the homes of human beings. They can't see us, so they don't know when we are there; but if we find a good child, who makes his parents happy and deserves their love, we smile and God takes a year away from the time of our trial. But if there is a naughty and mean child in the house we come to, we cry; and for every tear we shed, God adds a day to the three hundred years we already must serve."

THE SWINEHERD

Hans Christian Andersen

THERE once was a poor prince. He had a kingdom and, though it wasn't very big, it was large enough to marry on, and married he wanted to be.

Now it was rather bold of him to say to the emperor's daughter: "Do you want me?" But he was a young man of spirit who was quite famous, and there were at least a hundred princesses who would have said thank you very much to his proposal. But the emperor's daughter didn't. Let me tell you the story.

On the grave of the prince's father there grew a rose tree. It was a beautiful tree that only flowered every fifth year; and then it bore only one rose. That rose had such a sweet fragrance that anyone who smelled it forgot immediately all his sorrow and troubles. The prince also owned a nightingale which sang as though all the melodies ever composed lived in its throat — so beautiful was its song. The prince decided to send the rose and the nightingale to the emperor's daughter, and had two little silver chests made to put them in.

The emperor ordered the gifts to be carried into the grand assembly room where the princess was playing house with her ladies in waiting. That was their favorite game and they never played any other. When the princess saw the pretty little silver chests she clapped her hands and jumped for joy.

"Oh, I hope one of them contains a pretty little kitten," she said, but when she opened the chest, she found a rose.

"It is very prettily made," said one of the ladies in waiting.

"It is more than pretty; it is nice," remarked the emperor. Then the princess touched the rose and she almost wept with disappointment.

"Oh, Papa," she shrieked. "It is not glass, it's real!"

"Oh, oh!" shrieked all the ladies in waiting. "How revolting! It is real!"

"Let's see what is in the other chest first, before we get angry," admonished the emperor. There was the nightingale, who sang so beautifully that it was difficult to find anything wrong with it.

"*Superbe! Charmant!*" said the ladies in waiting. They all spoke French, one worse than the other.

"That bird reminds me of the late empress' music box," said an old courtier. "It has the same tone, the same sense of rhythm."

"You are right," said the emperor, and cried like a baby.

"I would like to know if that is real too," demanded the princess.

"Oh yes, it is a real bird," said one of the pages who had brought the gifts.

"In that case we will let the bird fly away," said the princess; and she sent a messenger to say that she would not even permit the prince to come inside her father's kingdom.

But the prince was not easily discouraged. He smeared his face with both black and brown shoe polish, put a cap on his head, then he walked up to the emperor's castle and knocked.

"Good morning, Emperor," said the young man, for it was the emperor himself who had opened the door. "Can I get a job in the castle?"

"Oh there are so many people who want to work here," answered the emperor, and shook his head. "But I do need someone to tend the pigs, we have such an awful lot of them."

And so the prince was hired as the emperor's swineherd. There was a tiny, dirty room next to the pigpen, and that was where he was expected to live.

The young man spent the rest of the day making a very pretty little pot. By evening it was finished. The pot had little bells all around it, and when it boiled, they played that old song:

Ach, du lieber Augustin,
Alles ist weg, weg, weg.

But the strangest and most wonderful thing about the pot was that, if you held your finger in the steam above it, then you could smell what was cooking on any stove in town. Now there was something a little different from the rose.

The princess was out walking with her ladies in waiting, and when she heard the musical pot she stopped immediately. She listened and smiled, for "Ach, du lieber Augustin" she knew. She could play the melody herself on the piano with one finger.

"It is a song I know!" she exclaimed. "That swineherd must be cultured. Please go in and ask him what the instrument costs."

One of the ladies in waiting was ordered to run over to the pigpen, but she put wooden shoes on first.

"What do you want for the pot?" she asked.

"Ten kisses from the princess," said the swineherd.

"God save us!" cried the lady in waiting.

"I won't settle for less," said the swineherd.

"Well, what did he want?" asked the princess.

"I can't say it," blushed the lady in waiting.

"Then you can whisper it," said the princess, and the lady in waiting whispered.

"He is very naughty," said the princess, and walked on. But she had gone only a few steps when she heard the little bells play again, and they sounded even sweeter to her than they had before.

Ach, du lieber Augustin,
Alles ist weg, weg, weg.

"Listen," she said, "ask him if he will be satisfied with ten kisses from one of my ladies in waiting."

"No, thank you!" replied the swineherd to that proposal. "Ten kisses from the princess or I keep my pot."

"This is most embarrassing," declared the princess. "You will all have to stand around me so no one can see it."

And the ladies in waiting formed a circle and held out their skirts so no one could peep. The swineherd got his kisses and the princess the pot.

Oh, what a grand time they had! All day and all evening they made the little pot boil. There wasn't a stove in the whole town that had anything cooking on it that they didn't know about.

They knew what was served for dinner on every table: both the count's and the cowherd's. The ladies in waiting were so delighted that they clapped their little hands.

"We know who is going to have soup and pancakes and who is eating porridge and rib roast! Oh, it is most interesting."

"Very!" said the imperial housekeeper.

"Keep your mouth shut. Remember, I am the princess," said the emperor's daughter.

And all the ladies in waiting and the imperial housekeeper said: "God preserve us, we won't say a word."

The swineherd—that is to say, the prince whom everyone thought was a swineherd—did not like to waste his time, so he constructed a rattle which was so ingenious that, when you swung it around, it played all the waltzes, polkas, and dance melodies ever composed since the creation of the world.

"It is superb!" exclaimed the princess as she was walking past the pigsty. "I have never heard a more exquisite composition. Do go in and ask what he wants for the instrument, but I won't kiss him!"

"He wants a hundred kisses from the princess," said the lady in waiting who had been sent to speak to the swineherd.

"He must be mad," declared the princess. She walked on a few steps and then she stood still. "One ought to encourage art," she said. "I am the emperor's daughter. Tell him he can have ten kisses from me just as he got yesterday. The rest he can get from my ladies in waiting."

"But we don't want to kiss him," they all cried.

"Stuff and nonsense!" replied the princess, for she was angry. "If I can kiss him, you can too. Besides, what do you think I give you room and board for?"

And one of the ladies in waiting went to talk with the swineherd. "One hundred kisses from the princess or I keep the rattle," was the message she came back with.

"Then gather around me!" commanded the princess. The ladies in waiting took their positions and the kissing began.

"I wonder what is going on down there by the pigsty," said the emperor, who was standing out on the balcony. He rubbed his eyes and put his glasses on. "It is the ladies in waiting. What devilment are they up to? I'd better go down and see." Then he pulled up the backs of his slippers, for they were really only a comfortable old pair of shoes with broken backs. Oh, how he ran! But as soon as he came near the pigsty he walked on tiptoe.

The ladies in waiting were so busy counting kisses — to make sure that the bargain was justly carried out and that the swineherd did not get one kiss too many or one too few — that they didn't hear or see the emperor, who was standing on tiptoe outside the circle.

"What's going on here?" he shouted. When he saw the kissing he took off one of his slippers and started hitting the ladies in waiting on the tops of their heads, just as the swineherd was getting his eighty-sixth kiss.

"*Heraus!* Get out!" he screamed, for he was really angry; and both the swineherd and the princess were thrown out of his empire.

There they stood: the princess was crying, the swineherd was grumbling, and the rain was streaming down.

"Oh, poor me!" wailed the princess. "If only I had married the prince. Oh, I am so unhappy!"

The swineherd stepped behind a tree, rubbed all the black and brown shoe polish off his face, and put on his splendid royal robes. He looked so impressive that the princess curtsied when she saw him.

"I have come to despise you," said the prince. "You did not want an honest prince. You did not appreciate the rose or the nightingale, but you could kiss a swineherd for the sake of a toy. Farewell!"

The prince entered his own kingdom and locked the door behind him; and there the princess could stand and sing:

> *Ach, du lieber Augustin,*
> *Alles ist weg, weg, weg.*

For, indeed, everything was "all gone!"

THE NIGHTINGALE AND THE ROSE

Oscar Wilde

"She said that she would dance with me if I brought her red roses," cried the young Student, "but in all my garden there is no red rose."

From her nest in the holm-oak tree the Nightingale heard him, and she looked out through the leaves and wondered.

"No red rose in all my garden!" he cried, and his beautiful eyes filled with tears. "Ah, on what little things does happiness depend! I have read all that the wise men have written, and all the secrets of philosophy are mine, yet for want of a red rose my life is made wretched."

"Here at last is a true lover," said the Nightingale. "Night after night have I sung of him though I knew him not: night after night have I told his story to the stars and now I see him. His hair is dark as the hyacinth-blossom, and his lips are red as the rose of his desire, but passion has made his face like pale ivory and sorrow has set her seal upon his brow."

"The Prince gives a ball tomorrow night," murmured the young Student, "and my love will be of the company. If I bring her a red rose she will dance with me till dawn. If I bring her a red rose, I shall hold her in my arms, and she will lean her head upon my shoulder and her hand will be clasped in mine. But there is no red rose in my garden, so I shall sit lonely and she will pass me by. She will have no heed of me, and my heart will break."

"Here, indeed, is the true lover," said the Nightingale. "What I sing of, he suffers: what is joy to me, to him is pain. Surely love is a wonderful thing. It is more precious than emeralds and dearer than fine opals. Pearls and pomegranates cannot buy it, nor is it set forth in the market-place. It may not be purchased of the merchants, nor can it be weighed out in the balance for gold."

"The musicians will sit in their gallery," said the young Student, "and play upon their stringed instruments, and my love will dance to the sound of the harp and the violin. She will dance so lightly that her feet will not touch the floor, and the courtiers in their gay dresses will throng round her. But with me she will not dance, for

I have no red rose to give her"; and he flung himself down on the grass, and buried his face in his hands, and wept.

"Why is he weeping?" asked a little Green Lizard, as he ran past him with his tail in the air.

"Why, indeed?" said a Butterfly, who was fluttering about after a sunbeam.

"Why, indeed?" whispered a Daisy to his neighbor, in a soft, low voice.

"He is weeping for a red rose," said the Nightingale.

"For a red rose?" they cried; "how very ridiculous!" and the little Lizard, who was something of a cynic, laughed outright.

But the Nightingale understood the secret of the Student's sorrow, and she sat silent in the oak-tree, and thought about the mystery of Love.

Suddenly she spread her brown wings for flight, and soared into the air. She passed through the grove like a shadow and like a shadow she sailed across the garden.

In the centre of the grass-plot was standing a beautiful rose-tree, and when she saw it she flew over to it, and lit upon a spray.

"Give me a red rose," she cried, "and I will sing you my sweetest song."

But the Tree shook its head.

"My roses are white," it answered; "as white as the foam of the sea, and whiter than the snow on the mountain. But go to my brother who grows round the old sun-dial, and perhaps he will give you what you want."

So the Nightingale flew over to the Rose-tree that was growing round the old sun-dial.

"Give me a red rose," she cried, "and I will sing you my sweetest song."

But the Tree shook its head.

"My roses are yellow," it answered; "as yellow as the hair of the mermaiden who sits upon an amber throne, and yellower than the daffodil that blooms in the meadow before the mower comes with his scythe. But go to my brother who grows beneath the Student's window, and perhaps he will give you what you want."

So the Nightingale flew over to the Rose-tree that was growing beneath the Student's window.

"Give me a red rose," she cried, "and I will sing you my sweet-est song."

But the Tree shook its head.

"My roses are red," it answered; "as red as the feet of the dove, and redder than the great fans of coral that wave and wave in the ocean-cavern. But the winter has chilled my veins, and the frost has nipped my buds, and the storm has broken my branches, and I shall have no roses at all this year."

"One red rose is all I want," cried the Nightingale, "only one red rose! Is there no way by which I can get it?"

"There is a way," answered the Tree; "but it is so terrible that I dare not tell it to you."

"Tell it to me," said the Nightingale, "I am not afraid."

"If you want a red rose," said the Tree, "you must build it out of music by moonlight, and stain it with your own heart's-blood. You must sing to me with your breast against a thorn. All night long you must sing to me, and the thorn must pierce your heart, and your life-blood must flow into my veins, and become mine."

"Death is a great price to pay for a red rose," cried the Nightin-gale, "and Life is very dear to all. It is pleasant to sit in the green wood, and to watch the Sun in his chariot of gold, and the Moon in her chariot of pearl. Sweet is the scent of the hawthorn, and sweet are the bluebells that hide in the valley, and the heather that blows on the hill. Yet Love is better than Life, and what is the heart of a bird compared to the heart of a man?"

So she spread her brown wings for flight, and soared into the air. She swept over the garden like a shadow, and like a shadow she sailed through the grove.

The young Student was still lying on the grass, where she had left him, and the tears were not yet dry in his beautiful eyes.

"Be happy," cried the Nightingale, "be happy; you shall have your red rose. I will build it out of music by moonlight, and stain it with my own heart's-blood. All that I ask of you in return is that you will be a true lover, for Love is wiser than Philosophy, though he is wise, and mightier than Power, though he is mighty. flame-coloured are his wings, and coloured like flame is his body. His lips are sweet as honey, and his breath is like frankincense."

The Student looked up from the grass, and listened, but he

could not understand what the Nightingale was saying to him, for he only knew the things that are written down in books.

But the Oak-tree understood, and felt sad, for he was very fond of the little Nightingale who had built her nest in his branches.

"Sing me one last song," he whispered; "I shall feel lonely when you are gone."

So the Nightingale sang to the Oak-tree, and her voice was like water bubbling from a silver jar.

When she had finished her song, the Student got up, and pulled a note-book and a lead-pencil out of his pocket.

"She has form," he said to himself, as he walked away through the grove — "that cannot be denied to her; but has she got feeling? I am afraid not. In fact, she is like most artists; she is all style without any sincerity. She would not sacrifice herself for others. She thinks merely of music, and everybody knows that the arts are selfish. Still, it must be admitted that she has some beautiful notes in her voice. What a pity it is that they do not mean anything, or do any practical good!" And he went into his room, and lay down on his little pallet-bed, and began to think of his love; and, after a time, he fell asleep.

And when the moon shone in the heavens the Nightingale flew to the Rose-tree, and set her breast against the thorn. All night long she sang, with her breast against the thorn, and the cold crystal Moon leaned down and listened. All night long she sang, and the thorn went deeper and deeper into her breast, and her life-blood ebbed away from her.

She sang first of the birth of love in the heart of a boy and a girl. And on the topmost spray of the Rose-tree there blossomed a marvelous rose, petal following petal, as song followed song. Pale was it, at first, as the mist that hangs over the river — pale as the feet of the morning, and silver as the wings of the dawn. As the shadow of a rose in a mirror of silver, as the shadow of a rose in a water-pool, so was the rose that blossomed on the topmost spray of the Tree.

But the Tree cried to the Nightingale to press closer against the thorn. "Press closer, little Nightingale," cried the Tree, "or the Day will come before the rose is finished."

So the Nightingale pressed closer against the thorn, and louder and louder grew her song, for she sang of the birth of passion in the soul of a man and a maid.

And a delicate flush of pink came into the leaves of the rose, like the flush in the face of the bridegroom when he kisses the lips of the bride. But the thorn had not yet reached her heart, so the rose's heart remained white, for only a Nightingale's heart's-blood can crimson the heart of a rose.

And the Tree cried to the Nightingale to press closer against the thorn. "Press closer, little Nightingale," cried the Tree, "or the Day will come before the rose is finished."

So the Nightingale pressed closer against the thorn, and the thorn touched her heart, and a fierce pang of pain shot through her. Bitter, bitter was the pain, and wilder and wilder grew her song, for she sang of the Love that is perfected by Death, of the Love that dies not in the tomb.

And the marvelous rose became crimson, like the rose of the eastern sky. Crimson was the girdle of petals, and crimson as a ruby was the heart.

But the Nightingale's voice grew fainter, and her little wings began to beat, and a film came over her eyes. Fainter and fainter grew her song, and she felt something choking in her throat.

Then she gave one last burst of music. The white Moon heard it, and she forgot the dawn, and lingered on in the sky. The red rose heard it, and it trembled all over with ecstasy, and opened its petals to the cold morning air. Echo bore it to her purple cavern in the hills, and woke the sleeping shepherds from their dreams. It floated through the reeds of the river, and they carried its message to the sea.

"Look, look!" cried the Tree, "the rose is finished now"; but the Nightingale made no answer, for she was lying dead in the long grass, with the thorn in her heart.

And at noon the Student opened his window and looked out.

"Why, what a wonderful piece of luck!" he cried; "here is a red rose! I have never seen any rose like it in all my life. It is so beautiful that I am sure it has a long Latin name"; and he leaned down and plucked it.

Then he put on his hat, and ran up to the Professor's house with the rose in his hand.

The daughter of the Professor was sitting in the doorway winding blue silk on a reel, and her little dog was lying at her feet.

"You said that you would dance with me if I brought you a red rose," cried the Student. "Here is the reddest rose in all the world. You will wear it tonight next your heart, and as we dance together it will tell you how I love you."

But the girl frowned.

"I am afraid it will not go with my dress," she answered; "and, besides, the Chamberlain's nephew has sent me some real jewels, and everybody knows that jewels cost far more than flowers."

"Well, upon my word, you are very ungrateful," said the Student angrily, and he threw the rose into the street, where it fell into the gutter, and a cart-wheel went over it.

"Ungrateful!" said the girl. "I tell you what, you are very rude; and, after all, who are you? Only a Student. Why, I don't believe you have even got silver buckles to your shoes as the Chamberlain's nephew has"; and she got up from her chair and went into the house.

"What a silly thing Love is!" said the Student as he walked away. "It is not half as useful as Logic, for it does not prove anything, and it is always telling one of things that are not going to happen, and making one believe things that are not true. In fact, it is quite unpractical, and, as in this age to be practical is everything, I shall go back to Philosophy and study Metaphysics."

So he returned to his room and pulled out a great dusty book, and began to read.

THE HAPPY PRINCE

Oscar Wilde

HIGH above the city, on a tall column, stood the statue of the Happy Prince. He was gilded all over with thin leaves of fine gold, for eyes he had two bright sapphires, and a large red ruby glowed on his sword-hilt.

He was very much admired indeed. "He is as beautiful as a weathercock," remarked one of the Town Councilors who wished to gain a reputation for having artistic tastes; "only not quite so useful," he added, fearing lest people should think him unpractical, which he really was not.

"Why can't you be like the Happy Prince?" asked a sensible mother of her little boy who was crying for the moon. "The Happy Prince never dreams of crying for anything."

"I am glad there is someone in the world who is quite happy," muttered a disappointed man as he gazed at the wonderful statue.

"He looks just like an angel," said the Charity Children as they came out of the cathedral in their bright scarlet cloaks and their clean white pinafores.

"How do you know?" said the Mathematical Master, "you have never seen one."

"Ah! but we have, in our dreams," answered the children, and the Mathematical Master frowned and looked very severe, for he did not approve of children dreaming.

One night there flew over the city a little Swallow. His friends had gone away to Egypt six weeks before, but be had stayed behind, for he was in love with the most beautiful Reed. He had met her early in the spring as he was flying down the river after a big yellow moth, and had been so attracted by her slender waist that he had stopped to talk to her.

"Shall I love you?" said the Swallow, who liked to come to the point at once, and the Reed made him a low bow. So he flew round and round her, touching the water with his wings, and making silver ripples. This was his courtship, and it lasted all through the summer.

"It is a ridiculous attachment," twittered the other Swallows; "she has no money, and far too many relations"; and indeed the river was quite full of Reeds. Then, when the autumn came they all flew away.

After they had gone he felt lonely, and began to tire of his lady-love. "She has no conversation," he said, "and I am afraid that she is a coquette, for she is always flirting with the wind." And certainly, whenever the wind blew, the Reed made the most graceful curtsies. "I admit that she is domestic," he continued, "but I love travelling, and my wife, consequently, should love travelling also."

"Will you come away with me?" he said finally to her, but the Reed shook her head, she was so attached to her home.

"You have been trifling with me," he cried. "I am off to the Pyramids. Good-bye!" and he flew away.

All day long he flew, and at night-time he arrived at the city. "Where shall I put up?" he said; "I hope the town has made preparations."

Then he saw the statue on the tall column.

"I will put up there," he cried; "it is a fine position, with plenty of fresh air." So he alighted just between the feet of the Happy Prince.

"I have a golden bedroom," he said softly to himself as he looked round, and he prepared to go to sleep; but just as he was putting his head under his wing a large drop of water fell on him. "What a curious thing!" he cried; "there is not a single cloud in the sky, the stars are quite clear and bright, and yet it is raining. The climate in the north of Europe is really dreadful. The Reed used to like the rain, but that was merely her selfishness."

Then another drop fell.

"What is the use of a statue if it cannot keep the rain off?" he said; "I must look for a good chimney-pot," and he determined to fly away.

But before he had opened his wings, a third drop fell, and he looked up, and saw — Ah! what did he see?

The eyes of the Happy Prince were filled with tears, and tears were running down his golden cheeks. His face was so beautiful in the moonlight that the little Swallow was filled with pity.

"Who are you?" he said.

"I am the Happy Prince."

"Why are you weeping then?" asked the Swallow; "you have quite drenched me."

"When I was alive and had a human heart," answered the statue, "I did not know what tears were, for I lived in the Palace of Sans-Souci, where sorrow is not allowed to enter. In the daytime I played with my companions in the garden, and in the evening I led the dance in the Great Hall. Round the garden ran a very lofty wall, but I never cared to ask what lay beyond it, everything about me was so beautiful. My courtiers called me the Happy Prince, and happy indeed I was, if pleasure be happiness. So I lived, and so I died. And now that I am dead they have set me up here so high that I can see all the ugliness and all the misery of my city, and though my heart is made of lead yet I cannot choose but weep."

"What! Is he not solid gold?" said the Swallow to himself. He was too polite to make any personal remarks out loud.

"Far away," continued the statue in a low musical voice, "far away in a little street there is a poor house. One of the windows is open, and through it I can see a woman seated at a table. Her face is thin and worn, and she has coarse, red hands, all pricked by the needle, for she is a seamstress. She is embroidering passion-flowers on a satin gown for the loveliest of the Queen's maids-of-honour to wear at the next Court ball. In a bed in the corner of the room her little boy is lying ill. He has a fever, and is asking for oranges. His mother has nothing to give him but river water, so he is crying. Swallow, Swallow, little Swallow, will you not bring her the ruby out of my sword-hilt? My feet are fastened to this pedestal and I cannot move."

"I am waited for in Egypt," said the Swallow. "My friends are flying up and down the Nile, and talking to the large lotus-flowers. Soon they will go to sleep in the tomb of the great King. The King is there himself in his painted coffin. He is wrapped in yellow linen, and embalmed with spices. Round his neck is a chain of pale green jade, and his hands are like withered leaves."

"Swallow, Swallow, little Swallow," said the Prince, "will you not stay with me for one night, and be my messenger? The boy is so thirsty, and the mother so sad."

"I don't think I like boys," answered the Swallow. "Last summer, when I was staying on the river, there were two rude boys, the miller's sons, who were always throwing stones at me. They never hit me, of course; we swallows fly far too well for that, and besides I come of a family famous for its agility; but still, it was a mark of disrespect."

But the Happy Prince looked so sad that the little Swallow was sorry. "It is very cold here," he said; "but I will stay with you for one night, and be your messenger."

"Thank you, little Swallow," said the Prince.

So the Swallow picked out the great ruby from the Prince's sword, and flew away with it in his beak over the roofs of the town.

He passed by the cathedral tower, where the white marble

angels were sculptured. He passed by the palace and heard the sound of dancing. A beautiful girl came out on the balcony with her lover. "How wonderful the stars are," he said to her, "and how wonderful is the power of love!"

"I hope my dress will be ready in time for the State ball," she answered; "I have ordered passion-flowers to be embroidered on it; but the seamstresses are so lazy."

He passed over the river, and saw the lanterns hanging to the masts of the ships. He passed over the Ghetto, and saw the old Jews bargaining with each other, and weighing out money in copper scales. At last he came to the poor house and looked in. The boy was tossing feverishly on his bed, and the mother had fallen asleep, she was so tired. In he hopped, and laid the great ruby on the table beside the woman's thimble. Then he flew gently round the bed, fanning the boy's forehead with his wings. "How cool I feel!" said the boy, "I must be getting better"; and he sank into a delicious slumber.

Then the Swallow flew back to the Happy Prince, and told him what he had done. "It is curious," he remarked, "but I feel quite warm now, although it is so cold."

"That is because you have done a good action," said the Prince. And the little Swallow began to think, and then he fell asleep. Thinking always made him sleepy.

When day broke he flew down to the river and had a bath. "What a remarkable phenomenon!" said the Professor of Ornithology as he was passing over the bridge. "A swallow in winter!" And he wrote a long letter about it to the local newspaper. Everyone quoted it, it was full of so many words that they could not understand.

"Tonight I go to Egypt," said the Swallow, and he was in high spirits at the prospect. He visited all the public monuments, and sat a long time on top of the church steeple. Wherever he went the Sparrows chirruped, and said to each other, "What a distinguished stranger!" so he enjoyed himself very much.

When the moon rose he flew back to the Happy Prince. "Have you any commissions for Egypt?" he cried; "I am just starting."

"Swallow, Swallow, little Swallow," said the Prince, "will you not stay with me one night longer?"

"I am waited for in Egypt," answered the Swallow. "Tomorrow

my friends will fly up to the Second Cataract. The river-horse couches there among the bulrushes, and on a great granite throne sits the God Memnon. All night long he watches the stars, and when the morning star shines he utters one cry of joy, and then he is silent. At noon the yellow lions come down to the water's edge to drink. They have eyes like green beryls, and their roar is louder than the roar of the cataract."

"Swallow, Swallow, little Swallow," said the Prince, "far away across the city I see a young man in a garret. He is leaning over a desk covered with papers, and in a tumbler by his side there is a bunch of withered violets. His hair is brown and crisp, and his lips are red as a pomegranate, and he has large and dreamy eyes. He is trying to finish a play for the Director of the Theatre, but he is too cold to write any more. There is no fire in the grate, and hunger has made him faint."

"I will wait with you one night longer," said the Swallow, who really had a good heart. "Shall I take him another ruby?"

"Alas! I have no ruby now," said the Prince: "my eyes are all that I have left. They are made of rare sapphires, which were brought out of India a thousand years ago. Pluck out one of them and take it to him. He will sell it to the jeweller, and buy firewood, and finish his play."

"Dear Prince," said the Swallow, "I cannot do that"; and he began to weep.

"Swallow, Swallow, little Swallow," said the Prince, "do as I command you."

So the Swallow plucked out the Prince's eye, and flew away to the student's garret. It was easy enough to get in, as there was a hole in the roof. Through this he darted, and came into the room. The young man had his head buried in his hands, so he did not hear the flutter of the bird's wings, and when he looked up he found the beautiful sapphire lying on the withered violets.

"I am beginning to be appreciated," he cried; "this is from some great admirer. Now I can finish my play," and he looked quite happy.

The next day the Swallow flew down to the harbour. He sat on the mast of a large vessel and watched the sailors hauling big chests out of the hold with ropes. "Heave a-hoy!" they shouted as each chest came up. "I am going to Egypt!" cried the Swallow, but nobody minded, and when the moon rose he flew back to the Happy Prince.

"I am come to bid you good-bye," he cried.

"Swallow, Swallow, little Swallow," said the Prince, "will you not stay with me one night longer?"

"It is winter," answered the Swallow, "and the chill snow will soon be here. In Egypt the sun is warm on the green palm-trees, and the crocodiles lie in the mud and look lazily about them. My companions are building a nest in the Temple of Baalbek, and the pink and white doves are watching them, and cooing to each other. Dear Prince, I must leave you, but I will never forget you, and next spring I will bring you back two beautiful jewels in place of those you have given away. The ruby shall be redder than a red rose, and the sapphire shall be as blue as the great sea."

"In the square below," said the Happy Prince, "there stands a little match-girl. She has let her matches fall in the gutter, and they are all spoiled. Her father will beat her if she does not bring home some money, and she is crying. She has no shoes or stock-ings, and her little head is bare. Pluck out my other eye, and give it to her, and her father will not beat her."

"I will stay with you one night longer," said the Swallow, "but I cannot pluck out your eye. You would be quite blind then."

"Swallow, Swallow, little Swallow," said the Prince, "do as I command you."

So he plucked out the Prince's other eye, and darted down with it. He swooped past the match-girl, and slipped the jewel into the palm of her hand. "What a lovely bit of glass!" cried the little girl; and she ran home, laughing.

Then the Swallow came back to the Prince. "You are blind now," he said, "so I will stay with you always."

"No little Swallow," said the poor Prince, "you must go away to Egypt."

"I will stay with you always," said the Swallow, and he slept at the Prince's feet.

All the next day he sat on the Prince's shoulder, and told him stories of what he had seen in strange lands. He told him of the red ibises, who stand in long rows on the banks of the Nile, and catch goldfish in their beaks; of the Sphinx, who is as old as the world itself and lives in the desert, and knows everything; of the merchants, who walk slowly by the side of their camels and carry amber beads in their hands; of the King of the Mountains of the Moon, who is as black as ebony, and worships a large crystal; of the great green snake that sleeps in a palm-tree, and has twenty priests to feed it with honey-cakes; and of the pygmies who sail over a big lake on large flat leaves, and are always at war with the butterflies.

"Dear little Swallow," said the Prince, "you tell me of marvelous things, but more marvelous than anything is the suffering of men and of women. There is no Mystery so great as Misery. fly over my city, little Swallow, and tell me what you see there."

So the Swallow flew over the great city, and saw the rich making merry in their beautiful houses, while the beggars were sitting at the gates. He flew into dark lanes, and saw the white faces of starving children looking out listlessly at the black streets. Under the archway of a bridge two little boys were lying in one another's arms to try and keep themselves warm. "How hungry we are!" they said. "You must not lie here," shouted the watchman, and they wandered out into the rain.

Then he flew back and told the Prince what he had seen.

"I am covered with fine gold," said the Prince, "you must take it off, leaf by leaf, and give it to my poor; the living always think that gold can make them happy."

Leaf after leaf of the fine gold the Swallow picked off, till the Happy Prince looked quite dull and grey. Leaf after leaf of the fine gold he brought to the poor, and the children's faces grew rosier, and they laughed and played games in the street. "We have bread now!" they cried.

Then the snow came, and after the snow came the frost. The streets looked as if they were made of silver, they were so bright and glistening; long icicles like crystal daggers hung down from the eaves of the houses, everybody went about in furs, and the little boys wore scarlet caps and skated on the ice.

The poor little Swallow grew colder and colder, but he would not leave the Prince, he loved him too well. He picked up crumbs outside the baker's door when the baker was not looking, and tried to keep himself warm by flapping his wings.

But at last he knew that he was going to die. He had just enough strength to fly up to the Prince's shoulder once more. "Good-bye, dear Prince!" he murmured, "will you let me kiss your hand?"

"I am glad that you are going to Egypt at last, little Swallow," said the Prince, "you have stayed too long here; but you must kiss me on the lips, for I love you."

"It is not to Egypt that I am going," said the Swallow. "I am going to the House of Death. Death is the brother of Sleep, is he not?"

And he kissed the Happy Prince on the lips, and fell down dead at his feet.

At that moment a curious crack sounded inside the statue, as if something had broken. The fact is that the leaden heart had snapped right in two. It certainly was a dreadfully hard frost.

Early the next morning the Mayor was walking in the square below in company with the Town Councilors. As they passed the column he looked up at the statue: "Dear me! How shabby the Happy Prince looks!" he said.

"How shabby, indeed!" cried the Town Councilors, who always agreed with the Mayor: and they went up to look at it.

"The ruby has fallen out of his sword, his eyes are gone, and he is golden no longer," said the Mayor; "in fact, he is little better than a beggar!"

"Little better than a beggar," said the Town Councilors.

"And here is actually a dead bird at his feet!" continued the Mayor. "We must really issue a proclamation that birds are not to be allowed to die here." And the Town Clerk made a note of the suggestion.

So they pulled down the statue of the Happy Prince. "As he is no longer beautiful he is no longer useful," said the Art Professor at the University.

Then they melted the statue in a furnace, and the Mayor held a meeting of the Corporation to decide what was to be done with the metal. "We must have another statue, of course," he said, "and it shall be a statue of myself."

"Of myself," said each of the Town Councilors, and they quarrelled. When I last heard of them they were quarrelling still.

"What a strange thing!" said the overseer of the workmen at

the foundry. "This broken lead heart will not melt in the furnace. We must throw it away." So they threw it on a dust-heap where the dead Swallow was also lying.

"Bring me the two most precious things in the city," said God to one of His Angels; and the Angel brought Him the leaden heart and the dead bird.

"You have rightly chosen," said God, "for in my garden of Paradise this little bird shall sing for evermore, and in my city of gold the Happy Prince shall praise me."

THE SELFISH GIANT

Oscar Wilde

EVERY afternoon, as they were coming from school, the children used to go and play in the Giant's garden.

It was a large lovely garden, with soft green grass. Here and there over the grass stood beautiful flowers like stars, and there were twelve peach-trees that in the spring-time broke out into delicate blossoms of pink and pearl, and in the autumn bore rich fruit. The birds sat on the trees and sang so sweetly that the children used to stop their games in order to listen to them. "How happy we are here!" they cried to each other.

One day the Giant came back. He had been to visit his friend the Cornish ogre, and had stayed with him for seven years. After the seven years were over he had said all that he had to say, for his conversation was limited, and he determined to return to his own castle. When he arrived he saw the children playing in the garden.

"What are you doing here?" he cried in a very gruff voice, and the children ran away.

"My own garden is my own garden," said the Giant; "anyone can understand that, and I will allow nobody to play in it but myself." So he built a high wall all round it, and put up a notice-board.

TRESSPASSERS WILL BE PROSECUTED

He was a very selfish Giant.

The poor children had now nowhere to play. They tried to play on the road, but the road was very dusty and full of hard stones, and they did not like it. They used to wander round the high walls when their lessons were over, and talk about the beautiful garden inside. "How happy we were there!" they said to each other.

Then the Spring came, and all over the country there were little blossoms and little birds. Only in the garden of the Selfish Giant it was still winter. The birds did not care to sing in it as there were no children, and the trees forgot to blossom. Once a beautiful flower put its head out from the grass, but when it saw the notice-board it was so sorry for the children that it slipped back into the ground again, and went off to sleep. The only people who were pleased were the Snow and the Frost. "Spring has forgotten this garden," they cried, "so we will live here all the year round." The Snow covered up the grass with her great white cloak, and the Frost painted all the trees silver. Then they invited the North Wind to stay with them, and he came. He was wrapped in furs, and he roared all day about the garden, and blew the chimney pots down. "This is a delightful spot," he said, "we must ask the Hail on a visit." So the Hail came. Every day for three hours he rattled on the roof of the castle till he broke most of the slates, and then he ran round and round the garden as fast as he could go. He was dressed in grey, and his breath was like ice.

"I cannot understand why the Spring is so late in coming," said the Selfish Giant, as he sat at the window and looked out at his cold, white garden; "I hope there will be a change in the weather."

But the Spring never came, nor the summer. The Autumn gave golden fruit to every garden, but to the Giant's garden she gave none. "He is too selfish," she said. So it was always winter there, and the North Wind and the Hail, and the Frost, and the Snow danced about through the trees.

One morning the Giant was lying awake in bed when he heard some lovely music. It sounded so sweet to his ears that he thought it must be the King's musicians passing by. It was really only a little linnet singing outside his window, but it was so long since he had heard a bird sing in his garden that it seemed to him to be the most beautiful music in the world. Then the Hail stopped dancing over his head, and the North Wind ceased roaring, and a delicious perfume came to him through the open casement. "I believe the Spring has come at last," said the Giant; and he jumped out of bed and looked out.

What did he see?

He saw a most wonderful sight. Through a little hole in the wall the children had crept in, and they were sitting in the branches of the trees. In every tree that he could see there was a little child. And the trees were so glad to have the children back again that they had covered themselves with blossoms, and were waving their arms gently above the children's heads. The birds were flying about and twittering with delight, and the flowers were looking up through the green grass and laughing. It was a lovely scene, only in one corner it was still winter. It was the farthest corner of the garden, and in it was standing a little boy. He was so small that he could not reach up to the branches of the tree, and he was wandering all round it, crying bitterly. The poor tree was still covered with frost and snow, and the North Wind was blowing and roaring above it. "Climb up! Little boy," said the Tree, and it bent its branches down as low as it could; but the boy was too tiny.

And the Giant's heart melted as he looked out. "How selfish I have been!" he said: "now I know why the Spring would not come here. I will put that poor little boy on the top of the tree, and then I will knock down the wall, and my garden shall be the children's playground for ever and ever." He was really very sorry for what he had done.

So he crept downstairs and opened the front door quite softly, and went out into the garden. But when the children saw him they were so frightened that they all ran away, and the garden became winter again. Only the little boy did not run for his eyes were so full of tears that he did not see the Giant coming. And the Giant stole up behind him and took him gently in his hand, and put him up into the tree. And the tree broke at once into blossom, and the birds came and sang on it, and the little boy stretched out his two arms and flung them round the Giant's neck, and kissed him. And the other children when they saw that the Giant was not wicked any longer, came running back, and

with them came the Spring. "It is your garden now, little children," said the Giant, and he took a great axe and knocked down
the wall. And when the people were going to market at twelve
o'clock they found the Giant playing with the children in the
most beautiful garden they had ever seen.

All day long they played, and in the evening they came to the
Giant to bid him good-bye.

"But where is your little companion?" he said: "the boy I put
into the tree." The Giant loved him the best because he had kissed
him.

"We don't know," answered the children. "He has gone away."

"You must tell him to be sure and come tomorrow," said the
Giant. But the children said that they did not know where he
lived and had never seen him before; and the Giant felt very sad.

Every afternoon, when school was over, the children came and
played with the Giant. But the little boy whom the Giant loved
was never seen again. The Giant was very kind to all the children,
yet he longed for his first little friend, and often spoke of him.
"How I would like to see him!" he used to say.

Years went over, and the Giant grew very old and feeble. He
could not play about any more, so he sat in a huge armchair, and
watched the children at their games, and admired his garden. "I
have many beautiful flowers," he said; "but the children are the
most beautiful flowers of all."

One winter morning he looked out of his window as he was
dressing. He did not hate the Winter now, for he knew that it was
merely the Spring asleep, and that the flowers were resting.

Suddenly he rubbed his eyes in wonder and looked and
looked. It certainly was a marvelous sight. In the farthest corner
of the garden was a tree quite covered with lovely white blossoms.
Its branches were golden, and silver fruit hung down from them,
and underneath it stood the little boy he had loved.

Downstairs ran the Giant in great joy, and out into the garden.
He hastened across the grass, and came near to the child. And
when he came quite close his face grew red with anger, and he
said, "Who hath dared to wound thee?" For on the palms of the
child's hands were the prints of two nails, and the prints of two
nails were on the little feet.

"Who hath dared to wound thee?" cried the Giant, "tell me,

that I may take my big sword and slay him."

"Nay," answered the child: "but these are the wounds of Love."

"Who are thou?" said the Giant, and a strange awe fell on him, and he knelt before the little child.

And the child smiled on the Giant, and said to him, "You let me play once in your garden, today you shall come with me to my garden, which is Paradise."

And when the children ran in that afternoon, they found the Giant lying dead under the tree, all covered with white blossoms.

THE SLEEPING BEAUTY
IN THE WOOD

Anne Thackeray Ritchie

A KIND enchantress one day put into my hand a mystic volume prettily lettered and bound in green, saying, "I am so fond of this book. It has all the dear old fairy tales in it; one never tires of them. Do take it."

I carried the little book away with me, and spent a very pleasant, quiet evening at home by the fire, with H. at the opposite corner, and other old friends, whom I felt I had somewhat neglected of late. Jack and the Beanstalk, Puss in Boots, the gallant and quixotic Giant-killer, and dearest Cinderella, whom we every one of us must have loved, I should think, ever since we first knew her in her little brown pinafore: I wondered, as I shut them all up for the night between their green boards, what it was that made these stories so fresh and so vivid. Why did not they fall to pieces, vanish, explode, disappear, like so many of their contemporaries and descendants? And yet, far from being forgotten and passing away, it would seem as if each generation in turn, as it came into the world, looks to be delighted still by the brilliant pageant, and never tires or wearies of it. And on their side princes and princesses never seem to grow any older; the castles and the lovely gardens flourish without need of repair or whitewash, or plumbers or glaziers. The princesses' gowns, too,—sun, moon, and star color,—do not wear out or pass out of fashion or require altering. Even the seven-leagued boots do not appear to be the worse for

wear. Numbers of realistic stories for children have passed away.
Little Henry and his Bearer, Poor Harry and Lucy,[1] have very
nearly given up their little artless ghosts and prattle, and ceased
making their own beds for the instruction of less excellently
brought up little boys and girls; and, notwithstanding a very interesting article in the *Saturday Review*, it must be owned that Harry
Sandford and Tommy Merton[2] are not familiar playfellows in our
nurseries and school-rooms, and have passed somewhat out of
date. But not so all these centenarians,—Prince Riquet,[3]
Carabas,[4] Little Red Riding-hood, Bluebeard, and others. They
seem as if they would never grow old. They play with the children, they amuse the elders, there seems no end to their fund of
spirits and perennial youth.

H., to whom I made this remark, said, from the opposite
chimney-corner, "No wonder; the stories are only histories of
real, living persons turned into fairy princes and princesses. Fairy
stories are everywhere and every day. We are all princes and
princesses in disguise, or ogres or wicked dwarfs. All these histories are the histories of human nature, which does not seem to
change very much in a thousand years or so, and we don't get tired
of the fairies because they are so true to it."

After this little speech of H.'s, we spent an unprofitable half-
hour reviewing our acquaintance, and classing them under their
real characters and qualities. We had dined with Lord Carabas
only the day before, and met Puss in Boots; Beauty and the Beast
were also there. We uncharitably counted up, I am ashamed to say,
no less than six Bluebeards. Jack and the Beanstalk we had met
just starting on his climb. A Red Riding-hood; a girl with toads
dropping from her mouth: we knew three or four of each. Cin-

---

1. *Little Henry and his Bearer* (1814), by Mary Martha Sherwood; *Harry and Lucy*
   (1801), by Maria Edgeworth. Both these women, the former a Sunday-school
   moralist and the latter a Rational moralist, wrote for the spiritual and moral
   improvement (rather than the entertainment) of their child-readers.

2. *The History of Sandford and Merton* (1783-89), by Thomas Day. Another classic
   of the Rational-moralist school of writing.

3. Prince Riquet: character in Charles Perrault's fairy tale, "Riquet of the Tuft."

4. Carabas: "Marquis of Carabas" is the title that Puss in Boots invents for his
   master (p.155).

derellas—alas! who does not know more than one dear, poor, pretty Cinderella; and as for sleeping princesses in the woods, how many one can reckon up! Young, old, ugly, pretty, awakening, sleeping still.

"Do you remember Cecilia Lulworth," said H., "and Dorlicote? Poor Cecilia!"

Some lives are *couleur de rose*, people say; others seem to be, if not *couleur de rose* all through, yet full of bright, beautiful tints, blues, pinks, little bits of harmonious cheerfulness. Other lives, if not so brilliant, and seeming more or less gray at times, are very sweet and gentle in tone, with faint gleams of gold or lilac to brighten them. And then again others, alas! are black and hopeless from the beginning. Besides these, there are some which have always appeared to me as if they were of a dark, dull hue; a dingy, heavy brown, which no happiness, or interest, or bright color could never enliven. Blues turn sickly, roses seem faded, and yellow lilacs look red and ugly upon these heavy backgrounds. Poor Cecilia,—as H. called her,—hers had always seemed to me one of these latter existences, unutterably dull, commonplace, respectable, stinted, ugly, and useless.

Lulworth Hall, with the great, dark park bounded by limestone walls, with iron gates here and there, looked like a blot upon the bright and lovely landscape. The place from a distance, compared with the surrounding country, was a blur and a blemish as it were,—sad, silent, solitary.

Travellers passing by sometimes asked if the place was uninhabited, and were told, "No, shure,—fam'ly lives thear all the yeaurr round." Some charitable souls might wonder what life could be like behind those dull gates. One day a young fellow riding by saw rather a sweet woman's face gazing for an instant through the bars, and he went on his way with a momentary thrill of pity. Need I say that it was poor Cecilia who looked out vacantly to see who was passing along the high-road. She was surrounded by hideous moreen, oil-cloth, punctuality, narrow-mindedness, horsehair, and mahogany. Loud bells rang at intervals, regular, monotonous. Surly but devoted attendants waited upon her. She was rarely alone; her mother did not think it right that a girl in Cecilia's position should "race" about the grounds unattended; as for going outside the walls it was not to be thought of. When

Cecilia went out with her gloves on, and her goloshes, her mother's companion, Miss Bowley, walked beside her up and down the dark laurel walk at the back of the house,—up and down, down and up, up and down. "I think I am getting tired, Maria," Miss Lulworth would say at last. "If so we had better return to the hall," Maria would reply, "although it is before our time." And then they would walk home in silence, between the iron railings and laurel-bushes.

As Cecilia walked erectly by Miss Bowley's side, the rooks went whirling over their heads, the slugs crept sleepily along the path under the shadow of the grass and the weeds; they heard no sounds except the cawing of the birds, and the distant monotonous, hacking noise of the gardener and his boy digging in the kitchen-garden.

Cecilia, peeping into the long drab drawing-room on her return, might, perhaps, see her mother, erect and dignified, at her open desk, composing, writing, crossing, re-reading, an endless letter to an indifferent cousin in Ireland, with a single candle and a small piece of blotting-paper, and a pen-wiper made of ravellings, all spread out before her.

"You have come home early, Cecil," says the lady, without looking up. "You had better make the most of your time, and practise till the dressing-bell rings. Maria will kindly take up your things."

And then in the chill twilight Cecilia sits down to the jangling instrument, with the worn silk flutings. A faded rack it is upon which her fingers had been distended ever since she can remember. A great many people think, there is nothing in the world so good for children as scoldings, whippings, dark cupboards, and dry bread and water, upon which they expect them to grow up into tall, fat, cheerful, amiable men and women; and a great many people think that for grown-up young people the silence, the chillness, the monotony and sadness of their own fading twilight days is all that is required. Mrs. Lulworth and Maria Bowley, her companion, Cecilia's late governess, were quite of this opinion. They themselves, when they were little girls, had been slapped, snubbed, locked up in closets, thrust into bed at all sorts of hours, flattened out on backboards, set on high stools to play the piano for days together, made to hem frills five or six weeks long, and to learn immense pieces of poetry, so that they had to stop at home all the afternoon. And though Mrs. Lulworth had grown up stupid, suspicious, narrow-minded, soured, and overbearing, and had married for an establishment, and Miss Bowley, her governess's daughter, had turned out nervous, undecided, melancholy, and anxious, and had never married at all, yet they determined to bring up Cecilia as they themselves had been brought up, and sincerely thought they could not do better.

When Mrs. Lulworth married, she said to Maria, "You must come and live with me, and help to educate my children some day, Maria. For the present I shall not have a home of my own; we are going to reside with my husband's aunt, Mrs. Dormer. She is a very wealthy person, far advanced in years. She is greatly annoyed with Mr. and Mrs. John Lulworth's vagaries, and she has asked me and my husband to take their places at Dorlicote Hall." At the end of ten years Mrs. Lulworth wrote again: "We are now permanently established in our aunt's house. I hear you are in want of a situation; pray come and superintend the education of my only child, Cecilia (she is named after her godmother, Mrs. Dormer). She is now nearly three years old, and I feel that she begins to require some discipline."

This letter was written at that same desk twenty-two years before Cecilia began her practising that autumn evening. She was twenty-five years old now, but like a child in inexperience, in ignorance, in placidity; a fortunate stolidity and slowness of temperament had saved her from being crushed and nipped in the bud, as it were. She was not bored because she had never known any other life. It seemed to her only natural that all days should be alike, rung in and out by the jangling breakfast, lunch, dinner, and prayer-bells. Mr. Dormer—a little chip of a man—read prayers suitable for every day in the week; the servants filed in, maids first, then the men. Once Cecilia saw one of the maids blush and look down smiling as she marched out after the others. Miss Dormer wondered a little, and thought she would ask Susan why she looked so strangely; but Susan married the groom soon after, and went away, and Cecilia never had an opportunity of speaking to her.

Night after night Mr. Dormer replaced his spectacles with a click, and pulled up his shirt-collar when the service was ended.

Night after night old Mrs. Dormer coughed a little moaning cough. If she spoke, it was generally to make some little, bitter remark. Every night she shook hands with her nephew and niece, kissed Cecilia's blooming cheek, and patted out of the room. She was a little woman with starling eyes. She had never got over her husband's death. She did not always know when she moaned. She dressed in black, and lived alone in her turret, where she had various old-fashioned occupations,—tatting, camphor-boxes to sort, a real old spinning-wheel and distaff among other things, at which Cecilia, when she was a child, had pricked her fingers trying to make it whirr as her aunt did. Spinning-wheels have quite gone out, but I know of one or two old ladies who still use them. Mrs. Dormer would go nowhere, and would see no one. So at least her niece, the master-spirit, declared, and the old lady got to believe it at last. I don't know how much the fear of the obnoxious John and his wife and children may have had to do with this arrangement.

When her great aunt was gone it was Cecilia's turn to gather her work together at a warning sign from her mother, and walk away through the long, chilly passages to her slumbers in the great green four-post bed. And so time passed. Cecilia grew up. She had neither friends nor lovers. She was not happy nor unhappy. She could read, but she never cared to open a book. She was quite contented; for she thought Lulworth Hall the finest place, and its inmates the most important people in the world. She worked a great deal, embroidering interminable quilts and braided toilet-covers and fish-napkins. She never thought of anything but the utterest commonplaces and platitudes. She considered that being respectable and decorous, and a little pompous and overbearing, was the duty of every well-brought-up lady and gentleman. To-night she banged away very placidly at Rhodes' air,[1] for the twentieth time breaking down in the same passage and making the same mistake, until the dressing-bell rang, and Cecilia, feeling she had done her duty, then extinguished her candle, and went upstairs across the great, chill hall, up the bare oil-cloth gallery, to her room.

---

1. Rhodes' air: Hugh Rhodes was similarly concerned about childhood morality; see his *Boke of Nurture* (1545).

Most young women have some pleasure, whatever their troubles may be, in dressing, and pretty trinkets and beads and ribbons and necklaces. An unconscious love of art and intuition leads some of them, even plain ones, to adorn themselves. The colors and ribbon ends brighten bright faces, enliven dull ones, deck what is already lovable, or, at all events, make the most of what materials there are. Even a Maypole, crowned and flowered and tastily ribboned, is a pleasing object. And, indeed, the art of decoration—seems to me a charming natural instinct, and one which is not nearly enough encouraged, and a gift which every woman should try to acquire. Some girls, like birds, know how to weave, out of ends of rags, of threads and morsels and straws, a beautiful whole, a work of real genius for their habitation. Frivolities, say some; waste of time, say others,—expense, vanity. The strong-minded dowagers shake their heads at it all,—Mrs. Lulworth among them; only why had Nature painted Cecilia's cheeks of brightest pink, instead of bilious orange, like poor Maria Bowley's? why was her hair all crisp and curly? and were her white, even teeth, and her clear, gray eyes, vanity and frivolity too? Cecilia was rather too stout for her age; she had not much expression in her face. And no wonder. There was not much to be expressive about in her poor little stinted life. She could not go into raptures over the mahogany sideboard, the camphene lamp in the drawing-room, the four-post beds indoors, the laurel-bushes without, the Moorish temple with yellow glass windows, or the wigwam summer-house, which were the alternate boundaries of her daily walks.

Cecilia was not allowed a fire to dress herself by; a grim maid, however, attended, and I suppose she was surrounded, as people say, by every comfort. There was a horsehair sofa, everything was large, solid, brown as I have said, grim, and in its place. The rooms at Lulworth Hall did not take the impression of their inmate; the inmate was moulded by the room. There were in Cecilia's no young lady-like trifles lying here and there; upon the chest of drawers there stood a mahogany workbox, square, with a key,— that was the only attempt at feminine elegance,—a little faded chenille, I believe, was to be seen round the clock on the chimney-piece, and a black and white check dressing-gown and an ugly little pair of slippers were set out before the toilet-table. On the bed,

Cecilia's dinner-costume was lying,—a sickly green dress, trimmed with black,—and a white flower for her hair. On the toilet-table an old-fashioned jasper serpent-necklace and a set of amethysts were displayed for her to choose from, also mittens and a couple of hair-bracelets. The girl was quite content, and she would go down gravely to dinner, smoothing out her hideous toggery.

Mrs. Dormer never came down before dinner. All day long she stayed up in her room, dozing and trying remedies, and occasionally looking over old journals and letters until it was time to come downstairs. She liked to see Cecilia's pretty face at one side of the table, while her nephew carved, and Mrs. Lulworth recounted any of the stirring events of the day. She was used to the life,—she was sixty when they came to her, she was long past eighty now,—the last twenty years had been like a long sleep, with the dream of what happened when she was alive and in the world continually passing before her.

When the Lulworths first came to her she had been in a low and nervous state, only stipulated for quiet and peace, and that no one was to come to her house of mourning. The John Lulworths, a cheery couple, broke down at the end of a month or two, and preferred giving up all chance of their aunt's great inheritance to living in such utter silence and seclusion. Upon Charles, the younger brother and his wife, the habit had grown, until now anything else would have been toil and misery to them. Except the old rector from the village, the doctor now and then, no other human creature ever crossed the threshold. For Cecilia's sake Miss Bowley once ventured to hint,—

"Cecilia with her expectations has the whole world before her."

"Maria!" said Mrs. Lulworth, severely; and, indeed, to this foolish woman it seemed as if money would add more to her daughter's happiness than the delights, the wonders, the interests, the glamours of youth. Charles Lulworth, shrivelled, selfish, dull, worn-out, did not trouble his head about Cecilia's happiness, and let his wife do as she liked with the girl.

This especial night when Cecilia came down in her ugly green dress, it seemed to her as if something unusual had been going on.

The old lady's eyes looked bright and glittering, her father seemed more animated than usual, her mother looked mysterious and put out. It might have been fancy, but Cecilia thought they all stopped talking as she came into the room; but then dinner was announced, and her father offered Mrs. Dormer his arm immediately, and they went into the dining-room.

It must have been fancy. Everything was as usual. "They have put up a few hurdles in Dalron's field, I see," said Mrs. Lulworth. "Charles, you ought to give orders for repairing the lock of the harness-room."

"Have they seen to the pump-handle?" said Mr. Lulworth.

"I think not." And then there was a dead silence.

"Potatoes," said Cecilia, to the footman. "Mamma, we saw ever so many slugs in the laurel walk, Maria and I,—didn't we, Maria? I think there are a great many slugs in our place."

Old Mrs. Dormer looked up while Cecilia was speaking, and suddenly interrupted her in the middle of her sentence. "How old are you, child?" she said; "are you seventeen or eighteen?"

"Eighteen! Aunt Cecilia. I am five-and-twenty," said Cecilia, staring.

"Good gracious! is it possible?" said her father, surprised.

"Cecil is a woman now, " said her mother.

"Five-and-twenty!" said the old lady, quite crossly. "I had no idea time went so fast. She ought to have been married long ago; that is, if she means to marry at all."

"Pray, my dear aunt, do not put such ideas—" Mrs. Lulworth began.

"I don't intend to marry," said Cecilia, peeling an orange, and quite unmoved, and she slowly curled the rind of her orange in the air. "I think people are very stupid to marry. Look at poor Jane Simmonds; her husband beats her; Jones saw her."

"So you don't intend to marry?" said the old lady, with an odd inflection in her voice. "Young ladies were not so wisely brought up in my early days," and she gave a great sigh. "I was reading an old letter this morning from your poor father, Charles,—all about happiness, and love in a cot, and two little curly-headed boys,— Jack, you know, and yourself. I should rather like to see John again."

"What, my dear aunt, after his unparalleled audacity? I declare the thought of his impudent letter makes my blood boil," exclaimed Mrs. Lulworth.

"Does it?" said the old lady. "Cecilia, my dear, you must know that your uncle has discovered that the entail was not cut off from a certain property which my father left me, and which I brought to my husband. He has therefore written me a very business-like letter, in which he says he wishes for no alteration at present, but begs that, in the event of my making my will, I should remember this, and not complicate matters by leaving it to yourself, as had been my intention. I see nothing to offend in the request. Your mother thinks differently."

Cecilia was so amazed at being told anything that she only stared again, and, opening a wide mouth, popped into it such a great piece of orange that she could not speak for some minutes.

"Cecilia has certainly attained years of discretion," said her great-aunt; "she does not compromise herself by giving any opinion on matters she does not understand."

Notwithstanding her outward imperturbability, Cecilia was a little stirred and interested by this history, and by the little conversation which had preceded it. Her mother was sitting upright in her chair as usual, netting with vigorous action; her large foot outstretched, her stiff, bony hands working and jerking monotonously. Her father was dozing in his arm-chair. Old Mrs. Dormer, too, was nodding in her corner. The monotonous Maria was stitching in the lamplight. Gray and black shadows loomed all round her. The far end of the room was quite dark; the great curtains swept from their ancient cornices. Cecilia, for the first time in all her life, wondered whether she should ever live all her life in this spot,—ever go away? It seemed impossible, unnatural, that she should ever do so. Silent, dull as it was, she was used to it, and did not know what was amiss ...

Young Frank Lulworth, the lawyer of the family—John Lulworth's eldest son—it was who had found it all out. His father wrote that with Mrs. Dormer's permission he proposed coming down in a day or two to show her the papers, and to explain to her personally how the matter stood. "My son and I," said John Lulworth, "both feel that this would be far more agreeable to our feelings, and perhaps to yours, than having recourse to the usual professional intervention; for we have no desire to press our claims for the present; and we only wish that in the ultimate disposal of your property you should be aware how the matter really stands. We have always been led to suppose that the estate actually in question has been long destined by you for your grand-niece, Cecilia Lulworth. I hear from our old friend, Dr. Hicks, that she is remarkably pretty and very amiable. Perhaps such vague possibilities are best unmentioned; but it has occurred to me that in the event of a mutual understanding springing up between the young folks,—my son and your grand-niece,—the connection might be agreeable to us all, and lead to a renewal of that family intercourse which has been, to my great regret, suspended for some time past."

Old Mrs. Dormer, in her shaky Italian handwriting, answered her nephew's letter by return of post:—

> "MY DEAR NEPHEW,—I must acknowledge the receipt of your epistle of the 13th instant. By all means invite your son to pay us his proposed visit. We can then talk over business matters at our leisure, and young Francis can be introduced to his relatives. Although a long time has elapsed since we last met, believe me, my dear nephew, not unmindful of by-gone associations, and yours, very truly, always,
>
> "C. DORMER."

The letter was in the postman's bag when old Mrs. Dormer informed Mrs. Charles of what she had done.

Frank Lulworth thought that in all his life he had never seen anything so dismal, so silent, so neglected, as Dorlicote Park, when he drove up, a few days after, through the iron gates and along the black laurel wilderness which led to the house. The laurel branches, all unpruned, untrained, were twisting savagely in and out, wreathing and interlacing one another, clutching tender shootings, wrestling with the young oak-trees and the limes. He passed by black and sombre avenues leading to mouldy temples, to crumbling summer-houses; he saw what had once been a flower-garden, now all run to seed,— wild, straggling, forlorn; a broken-down bench, a heap of hurdles lying on the ground, a field-mouse darting across the road, a desolate autumn sun shining upon all this mouldering ornament and confusion. It seemed more forlorn and melancholy by contrast, somehow, coming as he did out of the loveliest country and natural sweetness into the dark and tangled wilderness within these limestone walls of Dorlicote.

The parish of Dorlicote-cum-Rockington looks prettier in the autumn than at any other time. A hundred crisp tints, jewelled rays,—grays, browns, purples, glinting golds, and silvers,—rustle and sparkle upon the branches of the nut-trees, of the bushes and thickets. Soft blue mists and purple tints rest upon the distant hills; scarlet berries glow among the brown leaves of the hedges; lovely mists fall and vanish suddenly, revealing bright and sweet autumnal sights; blackberries, stacks of corn, brown leaves crisping upon the turf, great pears hanging sweetening in the sun over the cottage lintels, cows grazing and whisking their tails, blue smoke curling from the tall farm chimneys; all is peaceful, prosperous, golden. You can see the sea on clear days from certain knolls and hillocks …

Out of all these pleasant sights young Lulworth came into this dreary splendor. He heard no sounds of life,—he saw no one. His coachman had opened the iron gate. "They doan't keep no one to moind the gate," said the driver; "only tradesmen cooms to th'ouse." Even the gardener and his boy were out of the way; and when they got sight of the house at last, many of the blinds were down and shutters shut, and only two chimneys were smoking. There was some one living in the place, however, for a watch-dog who was lying asleep in his kennel woke up and gave a heart-rending howl when Frank got out and rang at the bell.

He had to wait an immense time before anybody answered, although a little page in buttons came and stared at him in blank amazement from one of the basement windows, and never moved. Through the same window Frank could see into the kitchen, and he was amused when a sleepy, fat cook came up behind the little page and languidly boxed his ears, and seemed to order him off the premises.

The butler, who at last answered the door, seemed utterly taken aback,—nobody had called for months past, and here was a perfect stranger taking out his card, and asking for Mrs. Dormer, as if it was the most natural thing in the world. The under-butler was half-asleep in his pantry, and had not heard the door-bell. The page—the very same whose ears had been boxed—came wondering to the door, and went to ascertain whether Mrs. Dormer would see the gentleman or not.

"What a vault, what a catacomb, what an ugly old place!" thought Frank, as he waited. He heard steps far, far away; then came a long silence, and then a heavy tread slowly approaching, and the old butler beckoned to him to follow,—through a cobweb-color room, through a brown room, through a gray room, into a great, dim, drab drawing-room, where the old lady was sitting alone. She had come down her back stairs to receive him; it was years since she had left her room before dinner.

Even old ladies look kindly upon a tall, well-built, good-looking, good-humored young man. Frank's nose was a little too long, his mouth a little too straight; but he was a handsome young fellow, with a charming manner. Only, as he came up, he was somewhat shy and undecided,—he did not know exactly how to address the old lady. This was his great-aunt. He knew nothing whatever about her, but she was very rich; she had invited him to come, and she had a kind face, he thought; should he,—ought he to embrace her? Perhaps he ought, and he made the slightest possible movement in this direction. Mrs. Dormer, divining his object, pushed him weakly away. "How do you do? No embraces, thank you. I don't care for kissing at my age. Sit down,—there, in that chair opposite,—and now tell me about your father, and all the family, and about this ridiculous discovery of yours. I don't believe a word of it."

The interview between them was long and satisfactory on the whole. The unconscious Cecilia and Miss Bowley returned that afternoon from their usual airing, and, as it happened, Cecilia said, "O Maria! I left my mittens in the drawing-room last night. I will go and fetch them." And, little thinking of what was awaiting her, she flung open the door and marched in through the ante-room,—mushroom hat and brown veil, goloshes and dowdy gown, as usual. "What is this?" thought young Lulworth; "why, who would have supposed it was such a pretty girl?" for suddenly the figure stopped short, and a lovely, fresh face looked up in utter amazement out of the hideous disguise.

"There, don't stare, child," said the old lady. "This is Francis

Lulworth, a very intelligent young man, who has got hold of your fortune and ruined all your chances, my dear. He wanted to embrace me just now. Francis, you may as well salute your cousin instead: she is much more of an age for such compliments," said Mrs. Dormer, waving her hand.

The impassive Cecilia, perfectly bewildered, and not in the least understanding, only turned her great, sleepy, astonished eyes upon her cousin, and stood perfectly still as if she was one of those beautiful wax-dolls one sees stuck up to be stared at. If she had been surprised before, utter consternation can scarcely convey her state of mind when young Lulworth stepped up and obeyed her aunt's behest. And, indeed, a stronger-minded person than Cecilia might have been taken aback, who had come into the drawing-room to fetch her mittens, and was met in such an astounding fashion. Frank, half laughing, half kindly, seeing that Cecilia stood quite still and stared at him, supposed it was expected, and did as he was told.

The poor girl gave one gasp of horror, and blushed for the first time, I believe, in the course of her whole existence. Bowley, fixed and open-mouthed from the inner room, suddenly fled with a scream, which recalled Cecilia to a sense of outraged propriety; for, blushing and blinking more deeply, she at last gave three little sobs, and then, O horror! burst into tears!

"Highty-tighty! what a much ado about nothing!" said the old lady, losing her temper and feeling not a little guilty, and much alarmed as to what her niece Mrs. Lulworth might say were she to come on the scene.

"I beg your pardon. I am so very, very sorry, " said the young man, quite confused and puzzled. "I ought to have known better. I frightened you. I am your cousin, you know, and really,—pray, pray excuse my stupidity," he said, looking anxiously into the fair, placid face along which the tears were coursing in two streams, like a child's.

"Such a thing never happened in all my life before," said Cecilia. "I know it is wrong to cry, but really — really —"

"Leave off crying directly, miss," said her aunt, testily, "and let us have no more of this nonsense." The old lady dreaded the mother's arrival every instant. Frank, half laughing, but quite unhappy at the poor girl's distress, had taken up his hat to go that minute, not knowing what else to do.

"Ah! you're going," says old Mrs. Dormer; "no wonder. Cecilia, you have driven your cousin away by your rudeness."

"I'm not rude," sobbed Cecilia. "I can't help crying."

"The girl is a greater idiot than I took her for," cried the old lady. "She has been kept here locked up until she has not a single idea left in her silly noddle. No man of sense could endure her for five minutes. You wish to leave the place, I see, and no wonder!"

"I really think," said Frank, "that under the circumstances it is the best thing I can do. Miss Lulworth, I am sure, would wish me to go."

"Certainly," said Cecilia. "Go away, pray go away. Oh, how silly I am!"

Here was a catastrophe!

The poor old fairy was all puzzled and bewildered: her arts were powerless in this emergency. The princess had awakened, but in tears. The prince still stood by, distressed and concerned, feeling horribly guilty, and yet scarcely able to help laughing. Poor Cecilia! her aunt's reproaches had only bewildered her more and more; and for the first time in her life she was bewildered, discomposed, forgetful of hours. It was the hour of calisthenics; but Miss Lulworth forgot everything that might have been expected from a young lady of her admirable bringing-up.

Fairy tales are never very long, and this one ought to come to an end. The princess was awake now; her simplicity and beauty touched the young prince, who did not, I think, really intend to go, though he took up his hat.

Certainly the story would not be worth the telling if they had not been married soon after, and lived happily all the rest of their lives.

★ ★ ★

It is not in fairy tales only that things fall out as one could wish, and indeed, H. and T. agreed the other night that fairies, although invisible, had not entirely vanished out of the land.

It is certainly like a fairy transformation to see Cecilia nowadays in her own home with her children and husband about her. Bright, merry, full of sympathy and interest, she seems to grow prettier every minute.

When Frank fell in love with her and proposed, old Mrs. Dormer insisted upon instantly giving up the Dorlicote Farm for the young people to live in. Mr. and Mrs. Frank Lulworth are obliged to live in London, but they go there every summer with their children; and for some years after her marriage, Cecilia's godmother, who took the opportunity of the wedding to break through many of her recluse habits, used to come and see her every day in a magnificent yellow chariot.

Some day I may perhaps tell you more about the fairies and enchanting princesses of my acquaintance.

THE TWENTIETH CENTURY:
DEALING WITH THE DARK SIDE

FROM the beginning, the oral tale has been subject to a version of the Darwinian law of survival of the fittest. The few tales containing that magic seed of memorability were those that were passed down through the generations, to be finally recorded in print. Today, however, the *permanence* of print has altered the situation in that, while modern re-tellings of well-known fairy tales are abundant, the reader must be ready to distinguish the mediocre from the memorable. Many writers have been seduced by the apparent simplicity of the fairy tale to try their hand at the form; surprisingly few have managed better than a pale imitation.

There can be little doubt that the strongest influence on fairy tales in recent years has been feminism, which partly explains why three of the four tales in this section are by women writers. As women have struggled to assert their position in the social and political worlds, some have identified the fairy tale as an early contributor to sexual inequality, noting that the female is often depicted as passive and subservient, the beautiful appendage to the superior male. While many memorable *original* stories have been woven on a fairy-tale framework in recent decades, we have selected four that are re-workings of classic tales found earlier in this anthology, the better to illustrate the literary evolution that has replaced the oral development of earlier times.

It is quickly apparent that Angela Carter is not writing for the child-reader: her diction is too sophisticated, her interpretation of the tale too complex and disturbing for the younger mind. It is as if Carter is returning the tale to something resembling its original condition, while recognizing that modern literate adults represent a very different audience from their ancestors who first *heard* them in a very different world. It is clearly the *real* world behind the folk tale that particularly fascinated Carter. In addition to "The Company of Wolves," she wrote two other variations on the theme of Little Red Riding Hood (entitled "The Werewolf" and "Wolf Alice"), all of which explore the potent cocktail that super-stition, fear, and primitive religion stir up in the human imagina-tion. Thus, the first part of her tale is devoted to creating a histor-ical context that is a far cry from the romantic dream-world which has become the customary backdrop to modern retellings of folk tales. Consequently, this heroine has a flesh-and-blood materiality that is just one among several reminders of the early "Story of Grandmother." Carter's most significant revision of the tale comes at the end, however, when she startles us by refusing to condemn the "wolf." If he is to be perceived in human terms, she seems to be saying, then we must confront those disturbing aspects of masculinity rather than simply rejecting them; perhaps such a liberated response would result in a very different outcome....

Tanith Lee's tale "When the Clock Strikes" provides an equally radical departure from the familiar "Cinderella," although on clos-er examination we may discover that Lee's re-working in fact retains a good deal in common with the Grimm Brothers' version of this story and with the traditional folk tale in general. Like the Grimms, Lee focuses on the themes of identity and recognition, justice and revenge, power and its sources. Like Ashputtle, Ashella has been cheated of her rightful place in society and must rely on the mysterious forces associated with her mother to regain it. But where the earlier heroine is the epitome of submissive patience and longsuffering, her successor here is a study in cold, implacable evil: she is sister to the driven revenge-seekers of Jacobean tragedy. At the same time, we may question whether the ferocity in Lee's depiction indicates her emphatic rejection of the female stereo-type that has, for better or worse, made Cinderella the ultimate romantic heroine of our times. It is telling that as we are drawn deeper into the horror of Lee's story, we find ourselves from sheer force of habit wondering from whence reconciliation will come. We are reluctant to accept what Lee makes quite obvious from the beginning: so passionate is the hatred passed on from mother to daughter that the prince's love is a mere feather in the wind. His death at the hands of "intriguers" as he is desperately seeking the owner of the glass slipper comes, one feels, as a blessing. Like Carter before her, Lee uses the fairy tale to explore the primitive, visceral side of human nature, which results in imagery that contrasts powerfully with the cotton-candy commercialism of Disney. The dark intensity of this re-telling highlights a pattern that can be detected in a surprising number of tales: the young protagonist must overcome some burden or challenge that has been inherited from a parent—perhaps the consequence of omission (as in "Sleeping Beauty" and "Little Red Riding Hood") or of commission (as in "Rapunzel" and "Snow White").

Although "When the Clock Strikes" is in many respects an "anti-tale," it is interesting to note that Lee nevertheless creates the illusion of the tale being narrated—to an increasingly discomfited listener who is familiar with the "original" tale—by a mysterious individual whose motivation remains in question to the tale's unsettling end. Like Carter, Lee approaches the folk tale much as a restorer might work on an old painting which has had much of its vitality obscured by layers of dirt and varnish and by lesser artists "improving" it.

Emma Donoghue is far from the first to re-tell well-known fairy tales from a first-person perspective, but she is certainly one of the most insightful. Her version of "The Goose Girl" is narrated not by the princess but by the servant-girl, who even in the Grimm Brothers' version is arguably the more intriguing and complex character. What Donoghue explores in this tale is the nature of social rather than sexual inequality, as the dark, bitter servant-girl imposes her will upon the fair, compliant princess. As in the two previous tales, the revisionist perspective achieves its effect by frustrating our expectations at the moment of crisis, when we anticipate the exposure of the servant-girl as an impostor. Instead, Donoghue's goose-girl princess acknowledges that temperament is destiny by willingly ceding her royal position to her bold and assertive servant.

Finally, there is no escaping the fact that the ingenuous charm of the fairy tale makes it, in our sceptical and sophisticated world, a prime target for parody. Yet, even in the garish colors of burlesque, the tale continues to show us to ourselves, albeit more sharply since it now has a satiric edge. The success of James Finn Garner's *Politically Correct Bedtime Stories* is one more indication that the fairy tale's versatility and appeal are as strong as ever.

THE COMPANY OF WOLVES

Angela Carter

ONE beast and only one howls in the woods by night.

The wolf is carnivore incarnate and he's as cunning as he is ferocious; once he's had a taste of flesh, then nothing else will do.

At night, the eyes of wolves shine like candle flames, yellowish, reddish, but that is because the pupils of their eyes fatten on darkness and catch the light from your lantern to flash it back to you—red for danger; if a wolf's eyes reflect only moonlight, then they gleam a cold and unnatural green, a mineral, a piercing color. If the benighted traveler spies those luminous, terrible sequins stitched suddenly on the black thickets, then he knows he must run, if fear has not struck him stock-still.

But those eyes are all you will be able to glimpse of the forest assassins as they cluster invisibly round your smell of meat as you go through the wood unwisely late. They will be like shadows, they will be like wraiths, gray members of a congregation of nightmare. Hark! his long, wavering howl ... an aria of fear made audible.

The wolfsong is the sound of the rendering you will suffer, in itself a murdering.

It is winter and cold weather. In this region of mountain and forest, there is now nothing for the wolves to eat. Goats and sheep are locked up in the byre, the deer departed for the remaining pasturage on the southern slopes—wolves grow lean and famished. There is so little flesh on them that you could count the starveling ribs through their pelts, if they gave you time before they pounced. Those slavering jaws; the lolling tongue; the rime of saliva on the grizzled chops—of all the teeming perils of the night and the forest, ghosts, hobgoblins, ogres that grill babies upon gridirons, witches that fatten their captives in cages for cannibal tables, the wolf is worst, for he cannot listen to reason.

You are always in danger in the forest, where no people are. Step between the portals of the great pines where the shaggy branches tangle about you, trapping the unwary traveler in nets as if the vegetation itself were in a plot with the wolves who live there, as though the wicked trees go fishing on behalf of their friends — step between the gateposts of the forest with the greatest trepidation and infinite precautions, for if you stray from the path for one instant, the wolves will eat you. They are gray as famine, they are as unkind as plague.

The grave-eyed children of the sparse villages always carry knives with them when they go out to tend the little flocks of goats that provide the homesteads with acrid milk and rank, maggoty cheeses. Their knives are half as big as they are; the blades are sharpened daily.

But the wolves have ways of arriving at your own hearthside. We try and try but sometimes we cannot keep them out. There is no winter's night the cottager does not fear to see a lean, gray, famished snout questing under the door, and there was a woman once bitten in her own kitchen as she was straining the macaroni.

Fear and flee the wolf; for worst of all, the wolf may be more than he seems.

There was a hunter once, near here, that trapped a wolf in a pit. This wolf had massacred the sheep and goats; eaten up a mad old man who used to live by himself in a hut halfway up the mountain and sing to Jesus all day; pounced on a girl looking after the sheep, but she made such a commotion that men came with rifles and scared him away and tried to track him into the forest but he was cunning and easily gave them the slip. So this hunter dug a pit and put a duck in it, for bait, all alive-oh; and he covered the pit with straw smeared with wolf dung. Quack, quack! went the duck, and a wolf came slinking out of the forest, a big one, a heavy one, he weighed as much as a grown man and the straw gave way beneath him — into the pit he tumbled. The hunter jumped down after him, slit his throat, cut off all his paws for a trophy.

And then no wolf at all lay in front of the hunter, but the bloody trunk of a man, headless, footless, dying, dead.

related to
pg 288?

A witch from up the valley once turned an entire wedding party into wolves because the groom had settled on another girl. She used to order them to visit her, at night, from spite, and they would sit and howl around her cottage for her, serenading her with their misery.

Not so very long ago, a young woman in our village married a man who vanished clean away on her wedding night. The bed was made with new sheets and the bride lay down in it; the groom said he was going out to relieve himself, insisted on it, for the sake of decency, and she drew the coverlet up to her chin and lay there. And she waited and she waited and then she waited again — surely he's been gone a long time? Until she jumps up in bed and shrieks to hear a howling, coming on the wind from the forest.

That long-drawn, wavering howl has, for all its fearful resonance, some inherent sadness in it, as if the beasts would love to be less beastly if only they knew how and never cease to mourn their own condition. There is a vast melancholy in the canticles of the wolves, melancholy infinite as the forest, endless as these long nights of winter, and yet that ghastly sadness, that mourning for their own, irremediable appetites, can never move the heart, for not one phrase in it hints at the possibility of redemption; grace could not come to the wolf from its own despair, only through some external mediator, so that, sometimes, the beast will look as if he half welcomes the knife that dispatches him.

That young woman's brothers searched the outhouses and the haystacks but never found any remains, so the sensible girl dried her eyes and found herself another husband, not too shy to piss in a pot, who spent the nights indoors. She gave him a pair of bonny babies and all went right as a trivet until, one freezing night, the night of the solstice, the hinge of the year when things do not fit together as well as they should, the longest night, her first good man came home again.

A great thump on the door announced him as she was stirring the soup for the father of her children and she knew him the moment she lifted the latch to him although it was years since she's worn black for him and now he was in rags and his hair hung down his back and never saw a comb, alive with lice.

"Here I am again, missis," he said. "Get me my bowl of cabbage and be quick about it."

Then her second husband came in with wood for the fire and when the first one saw she'd slept with another man and, worse, clapped his red eyes on her little children, who'd crept into the kitchen to see what all the din was about, he shouted: "I wish I were a wolf again, to teach this whore a lesson!" So a wolf he instantly became and tore off the eldest boy's left foot before he was chopped up with a hatchet they used for chopping logs. But when the wolf lay bleeding and gasping its last, the pelt peeled off again and he was just as he had been, years ago, when he ran away from his marriage bed, so that she wept and her second husband beat her.

They say there's an ointment the Devil gives you that turns you into a wolf the minute you rub it on. Or that he was born feet first and had a wolf for his father and his torso is a man's but his legs and genitals are a wolf's. And he has a wolf's heart.

Seven years is a werewolf's natural span, but if you burn his human clothing you condemn him to wolfishness for the rest of his life, so old wives hereabouts think it some protection to throw a hat or an apron at the werewolf, as if clothes made the man. Yet by the eyes, those phosphorescent eyes, you know him in all his shapes; the eyes alone unchanged by metamorphosis.

Before he can become a wolf, the lycanthrope strips stark naked. If you spy a naked man among the pines, you must run as if the Devil were after you.

It is midwinter and the robin, friend of man, sits on the handle of the gardener's spade and sings. It is the worst time in all the year for wolves, but this strong-minded child insists she will go off through the wood. She is quite sure the wild beasts cannot harm her although, well-warned, she lays a carving knife in the basket her mother has packed with cheeses. There is a bottle of harsh liquor distilled from brambles; a batch of flat oat cakes baked on the hearthstone; a pot or two of jam. The flaxen-haired girl will take these delicious gifts to a reclusive grandmother so old the burden of her years is crushing her to death. Granny lives two hours' trudge through the winter woods; the child wraps herself up in her thick shawl, draws it over her head. She steps into her stout wooden shoes; she is dressed and ready and it is Christmas Eve. The malign door of the solstice still swings upon its hinges, but she has been too much loved ever to feel scared.

Children do not stay young for long in this savage country. There are no toys for them to play with, so they work hard and grow wise, but this one, so pretty and the youngest of her family, a little latecomer, had been indulged by her mother and the grandmother who'd knitted the red shawl that, today, has the ominous if brilliant look of blood on snow. Her breasts have just begun to swell; her hair is like lint, so fair it hardly makes a shadow on her pale forehead; her cheeks are an emblematic scarlet and white and she has just started her woman's bleeding, the clock inside her that will strike, henceforward, once a month.

She stands and moves within the invisible pentacle of her own virginity. She is an unbroken egg; she is a sealed vessel; she has inside her a magic space the entrance to which is shut tight with a plug of membrane; she is a closed system; she does not know how to shiver. She has her knife and she is afraid of nothing.

Her father might forbid her, if he were home, but he is away in the forest, gathering wood, and her mother cannot deny her.

The forest closed upon her like a pair of jaws.

There is always something to look at in the forest, even in the middle of winter—the huddled mounds of birds, succumbed to the lethargy of the season, heaped on the creaking boughs and too forlorn to sing; the bright frills of the winter fungi on the blotched trunks of the trees; the cuneiform slots of rabbits and deer, the herringbone tracks of the birds, a hare as lean as a rasher of bacon streaking across the path where the thin sunlight dapples the russet brakes of last year's bracken.

When she heard the freezing howl of a distant wolf, her practiced hand sprang to the handle of her knife, but she saw no sign of a wolf at all, nor of a naked man, neither, but then she heard a clattering among the brushwood and there sprang onto the path a fully clothed one, a very handsome young one, in the green coat and wide-awake hat of a hunter, laden with carcasses of game birds. She had her hand on her knife at the first rustle of twigs, but he laughed with a flash of white teeth when he saw her and made her a comic yet flattering little bow; she'd never seen such a fine fellow before, not among the rustic clowns of her native village. So on they went together, through the thickening light of the afternoon.

Soon they were laughing and joking like old friends. When he offered to carry her basket, she gave it to him although her knife was in it because he told her his rifle would protect them. As the day darkened, it began to snow again; she felt the first flakes settle on her eyelashes, but now there was only half a mile to go and there would be a fire, and hot tea, and a welcome, a warm one, surely, for the dashing huntsman as well as for herself.

This young man had a remarkable object in his pocket. It was a compass. She looked at the little round glass face in the palm of his hand and watched the wavering needle with a vague wonder. He assured her this compass had taken him safely through the wood on his hunting trip because the needle always told him with perfect accuracy where the north was. She did not believe it; she knew she should never leave the path on the way through the wood or else she would be lost instantly. He laughed at her again; gleaming trails of spittle clung to his teeth. He said if he plunged off the path into the forest that surrounded them, he could guarantee to arrive at her grandmother's house a good quarter of an hour before she did, plotting his way through the undergrowth with his compass, while she trudged the long way, along the winding path.

I don't believe you. Besides, aren't you afraid of the wolves?

He only tapped the gleaming butt of his rifle and grinned.

Is it a bet? he asked her. Shall we make a game of it? What will you give me if I get to your grandmother's house before you?

What would you like? she asked disingenuously.

A kiss.

Commonplaces of a rustic seduction; she lowered her eyes and blushed.

He went through the undergrowth and took her basket with him, but she forgot to be afraid of the beasts, although now the moon was rising, for she wanted to dawdle on her way to make sure the handsome gentleman would win his wager.

Grandmother's house stood by itself a little way out of the village. The freshly falling snow blew in eddies about the kitchen garden and the young man stepped delicately up the snowy path to the door as if he were reluctant to get his feet wet, swinging his bundle of game and the girl's basket and humming a little tune to himself.

There is a faint trace of blood on his chin; he has been snacking on his catch.

Aged and frail, granny is three-quarters succumbed to the mortality the ache in her bones promises her and almost ready to give in entirely. A boy came out from the village to build up her hearth for the night an hour ago and the kitchen crackles with busy firelight. She has her Bible for company; she is a pious old woman. She is propped up on several pillows in the bed set into the wall peasant fashion, wrapped up in the patchwork quilt she made before she was married, more years ago than she cares to remember. Two china spaniels with liver-colored blotches on their coats and black noses sit on either side of the fireplace. There is a bright rug of woven rags on the pantiles. The grandfather clock ticks away her eroding time.

We keep the wolves out by living well.

He rapped upon the panels with his hairy knuckles.

It is your granddaughter, he mimicked in a high soprano.

Lift up the latch and walk in, my darling.

You can tell them by their eyes, eyes of a beast of prey, nocturnal, devastating eyes as red as a wound; you can hurl your Bible at him and your apron after, granny; you thought that was a sure prophylactic against these infernal vermin ... Now call on Christ and his mother and all the angels in heaven to protect you, but it won't do you any good.

His feral muzzle is sharp as a knife; he drops his golden burden of gnawed pheasant on the table and puts down your dear girl's basket, too. Oh, my God, what have you done with her?

Off with his disguise, that coat of forest-colored cloth, the hat with the feather tucked into the ribbon; his matted hair streams down his white shirt and she can see the lice moving in it. The sticks in the hearth shift and hiss; night and the forest has come into the kitchen with darkness tangled in its hair.

He strips off his shirt. His skin is the color and texture of vellum. A crisp stripe of hair runs down his belly, his nipples are ripe and dark as poison fruit, but he's so thin you could count the ribs under his skin if only he gave you the time. He strips off his

286

trousers and she can see how hairy his legs are. His genitals, huge. Ah! huge.

The last thing the old lady saw in all this world was a young man, eyes like cinders, naked as a stone, approaching her bed.

The wolf is carnivore incarnate.

When he had finished with her, he licked his chops and quickly dressed himself again, until he was just as he had been when he came through her door. He burned the inedible hair in the fireplace and wrapped the bones up in a napkin that he hid away under the bed in the wooden chest in which he found a clean pair of sheets. These he carefully put on the bed instead of the telltale stained ones he stowed away in the laundry basket. He plumped up the pillows and shook out the patchwork quilt, he picked up the Bible from the floor, closed it and laid it on the table. All was as it had been before except that grandmother was gone. The sticks twitched in the grate, the clock ticked and the young man sat patiently, deceitfully beside the bed in granny's nightcap.

Rat-a-tap-tap.

Who's there, he quavers in granny's antique falsetto.

Only your granddaughter.

So she came in, bringing with her a flurry of snow that melted in tears on the tiles, and perhaps she was a little disappointed to see only her grandmother sitting beside the fire. But then he flung off the blanket and sprang to the door, pressing his back against it so that she could not get out again.

The girl looked round the room and saw there was not even the indentation of a head on the smooth cheek of the pillow and how, for the first time she's seen it so, the Bible lay closed on the table. The tick of the clock cracked like a whip. She wanted her knife from her basket but she did not dare reach for it because his eyes were fixed upon her—huge eyes that now seemed to shine with a unique, interior light, eyes the size of saucers, saucers full of Greek fire, diabolic phosphorescence.

What big eyes you have.

All the better to see you with.

No trace at all of the old woman except for a tuft of white hair that had caught in the bark of an unburned log. When the girl saw that, she knew she was in danger of death.

Where is my grandmother?

There's nobody here but we two, my darling.

Now a great howling rose up all around them, near, very near, as close as the kitchen garden, the howling of a multitude of wolves; she knew the worst wolves are hairy on the inside and she shivered, in spite of the scarlet shawl she pulled more closely round herself as if it could protect her, although it was as red as the blood she must spill.

Who has come to sing us carols? she said.

Those are the voices of my brothers, darling; I love the company of wolves. Look out of the window and you'll see them.

Snow half-caked the lattice and she opened it to look into the garden. It was a white night of moon and snow; the blizzard whirled round the gaunt, gray beasts who squatted on their haunches among the rows of winter cabbage, pointing their sharp snouts to the moon and howling as if their hearts would break. Ten wolves; twenty wolves — so many wolves she could not count them, howling in concert as if demented or deranged. Their eyes reflected the light from the kitchen and shone like a hundred candles.

It is very cold, poor things, she said; no wonder they howl so.

She closed the window on the wolves' threnody and took off her scarlet shawl, the color of poppies, the color of sacrifices, the color of her menses, and since her fear did her no good, she ceased to be afraid.

What shall I do with my shawl?

Throw it on the fire, dear one. You won't need it again.

She bundled up her shawl and threw it on the blaze, which instantly consumed it. Then she drew her blouse over her head; her small breasts gleamed as if the snow had invaded the room.

What shall I do with my blouse?

Into the fire with it, too, my pet.

The thin muslin went flaring up the chimney like a magic bird and now off came her skirt, her woolen stockings, her shoes, and onto the fire they went, too, and were gone for good. The firelight shone through the edges of her skin; now she was clothed only in her untouched integument of flesh. Thus dazzling, naked, she combed out her hair with her fingers; her hair looked white as the snow outside. Then went directly to the man with red eyes in whose unkempt mane the lice moved; she stood up on tiptoe and

288

unbuttoned the collar of his shirt.

What big arms you have.

All the better to hug you with.

Every wolf in the world now howled a prothalamion outside the window as she freely gave the kiss she owed him.

What big teeth you have!

She saw how his jaw began to slaver and the room was full of the clamour of the forest's *Liebestod*, but the wise child never flinched, even when he answered:

All the better to eat you with.

The girl burst out laughing; she knew she was nobody's meat. She laughed at him full in the face, she ripped off his shirt for him and flung it into the fire, in the fiery wake of her own discarded clothing. The flames danced like dead souls on Walpurgisnacht and the old bones under the bed set up a terrible clattering, but she did not pay them any heed.

Carnivore incarnate, only immaculate flesh appeases him. *he is possible.*

She will lay his fearful head on her lap and she will pick out the lice from his pelt and perhaps she will put the lice into her own mouth and eat them, as he will bid her, as she would do in a savage marriage ceremony.

The blizzard will die down.

The blizzard died down, leaving the mountains as randomly covered with snow as if a blind woman had thrown a sheet over them, the upper branches of the forest pines limed, creaking, swollen with the fall.

Snowlight, moonlight, a confusion of pawprints.

All silent, all still.

Midnight; and the clock strikes. It is Christmas Day, the werewolves' birthday; the door of the solstice stands wide open; let them all sink through.

See! Sweet and sound she sleeps in granny's bed, between the paws of the tender wolf.

WHEN THE CLOCK STRIKES

Tanith Lee

YES, the great ballroom is filled only with dust now. The slender columns of white marble and the slender columns of rose-red marble are woven together by cobwebs. The vivid frescoes, on which the duke's treasury spent so much, are dimmed by the dust; the faces of the painted goddesses look gray. And the velvet curtains — touch them, they will crumble. Two hundred years, now, since anyone danced in this place on the sea-green floor in the candle gleam. Two hundred years since the wonderful clock struck for the very last time.

I thought you might care to examine the clock. It was considered exceptional in its day. The pedestal is ebony and the face fine porcelain. And these figures, which are of silver, would pass slowly about the circlet of the face. Each figure represents, you understand, an hour. And as the appropriate hours came level with this golden bell, they would strike it the correct number of times. All the figures are unique, you see. Beginning at the first hour, they are, in this order, a girl-child, a dwarf, a maiden, a youth, a lady and a knight. And here, notice, the figures grow older as the day declines: a queen and king for the seventh and eighth hours, and after these, an abbess and a magician and next to last, a hag. But the very last is strangest of all. The twelfth figure: do you recognize him? It is Death. Yes, a most curious clock. It was reckoned a marvelous thing then. But it has not struck for two hundred years. Possibly you have been told the story? No? Oh, but I am certain that you have heard it, in another form, perhaps.

However, as you have some while to wait for your carriage, I will recount the tale, if you wish.

I will start with what is said of the clock. In those years, this city was prosperous, a stronghold — not as you see it today. Much was made in the city that was ornamental and unusual. But the clock, on which the twelfth hour was Death, caused something of a stir. It was thought unlucky, foolhardy, to have such a clock. It began to be murmured, jokingly by some, by others in earnest, that one night when the clock struck the twelfth hour, Death would truly strike with it.

Now life has always been a chancy business, and it was more so then. The Great Plague had come but twenty years before and was not yet forgotten. Besides, in the duke's court there was much intrigue, while enemies might be supposed to plot beyond the city walls, as happens even in our present age. But there was another thing.

It was rumored that the duke had obtained both his title and the city treacherously. Rumor declared that he had systematically destroyed those who had stood in line before him, the members of the princely house that formerly ruled here. He had accomplished the task slyly, hiring assassins talented with poisons and daggers. But rumor also declared that the duke had not been sufficiently thorough. For though he had meant to rid himself of all that rival house, a single descendant remained, so obscure he had not traced her—for it was a woman.

women not important.

Of course, such matters were not spoken of openly. Like the prophecy of the clock, it was a subject for the dark.

Nevertheless, I will tell you at once, there was such a descendant he had missed in his bloody work. And she was a woman. Royal and proud she was, and seething with bitter spite and a hunger for vengeance, and as bloody as the duke, had he known it, in her own way.

For her safety and disguise, she had long ago wed a wealthy merchant in the city, and presently bore the man a daughter. The merchant, a dealer in silks, was respected, a good fellow but not wise. He rejoiced in his handsome and aristocratic wife. He never dreamed what she might be about when he was not with her. In fact, she had sworn allegiance to Satanas. In the dead of night she would go up into an old tower adjoining the merchant's house, and there she would say portions of the Black Mass, offer sacrifice, and thereafter practice witchcraft against the duke. This witchery took a common form, the creation of a wax image and the maiming of the image that, by sympathy, the injuries inflicted on the wax be passed on to the living body of the victim. The woman was capable in what she did. The duke fell sick. He lost the use of his limbs and was racked by excruciating pains from which he could get no relief. Thinking himself on the brink of death, the duke named his sixteen-year-old son his heir. This son was dear to the duke, as everyone knew, and be sure the woman knew it too.

She intended sorcerously to murder the young man in his turn, preferably in his father's sight. Thus she let the duke linger in his agony and commenced planning the fate of the prince.

Now all this while she had not been toiling alone. She had one helper. It was her own daughter, a maid of fourteen, that she had recruited to her service nearly as soon as the infant could walk. At six or seven, the child had been lisping the satanic rite along with her mother. At fourteen, you may imagine, the girl was well versed in the black arts, though she did not have her mother's natural genius for them.

Perhaps you would like me to describe the daughter at this point. It has a bearing on the story, for the girl was astonishingly beautiful. Her hair was the rich dark red of antique burnished copper, her eyes were the hue of the reddish-golden amber that traders bring from the East. When she walked, you would say she was dancing. But when she danced, a gate seemed to open in the world, and bright fire spangled inside it, but she was the fire.

The girl and her mother were close as gloves in a box. Their games in the old tower bound them closer. No doubt the woman believed herself clever to have got such a helpmate, but it proved her undoing.

It was in this manner. The silk merchant, who had never suspected his wife for an instant of anything, began to mistrust the daughter. She was not like other girls. Despite her great beauty, she professed no interest in marriage and none in clothes or jewels. She preferred to read in the garden at the foot of the tower. Her mother had taught the girl her letters, though the merchant himself could read but poorly. And often the father peered at the books his daughter read, unable to make head nor tail of them, yet somehow not liking them. One night very late, the silk merchant came home from a guild dinner in the city, and he saw a slim pale shadow gliding up the steps of the old tower, and he knew it for his child. On impulse, he followed her, but quietly. He had not considered any evil so far and did not want to alarm her. At an angle of the stair, the lighted room above, he paused to spy and listen. He had something of a shock when he heard his wife's voice rise up in glad welcome. But what came next drained the blood from his heart. He crept away and went to his cellar for wine to stay himself. After the third glass he ran for neighbors and for the watch.

The woman and her daughter heard the shouts below and saw the torches in the garden. It was no use dissembling. The tower was littered with evidence of vile deeds, besides what the woman kept in a chest beneath her unknowing husband's bed. She understood it was all up with her, and she understood, too, how witchcraft was punished hereabouts. She snatched a knife from the altar.

The girl shrieked when she realized what her mother was at. The woman caught the girl by her red hair and shook her.

"Listen to me, my daughter," she cried, "and listen carefully, for the minutes are short. If you do as I tell you, you can escape their wrath and only I need die. And if you live I am satisfied, for you can carry on my labour after me. My vengeance I shall leave you, and my witchcraft to exact it by. Indeed, I promise you stronger powers than mine. I will beg my lord Satanas for it, and he will not deny me, for he is just, in his fashion, and I have served him well. Now will you attend?"

"I will," said the girl.

So the woman advised her, and swore her to the fellowship of Hell. And then the woman forced the knife into her own heart and dropped dead on the floor of the tower.

When the men burst in with their swords and staves and their torches and their madness, the girl was ready for them.

She stood blank-faced, blank-eyed, with her arms hanging at her sides. When one touched her, she dropped down at his feet.

"Surely she is innocent," this man said. She was lovely enough that it was hard to accuse her. Then her father went to her and took her hand and lifted her. At that, the girl opened her eyes, and she said, as if terrified: "How did I come here? I was in my chamber and sleeping ..."

"The woman has bewitched her," her father said.

He desired very much that this be so. And when the girl clung to his hand and wept, he was certain of it. They showed her the body with the knife in it. The girl screamed and seemed to lose her senses totally.

She was put to bed. In the morning, a priest came and questioned her. She answered steadfastly. She remembered nothing, not even of the great books she had been observed reading. When they told her what was in them, she screamed again and apparently would have thrown herself from the narrow window, only the priest stopped her.

Finally, they brought her the holy cross in order that she might kiss it and prove herself blameless.

Then she knelt, and whispered softly, that nobody should hear but one: "Lord Satanas, protect thy handmaid." And either that gentleman has more power than he is credited with or else the symbols of God are only as holy as the men who deal in them, for she embraced the cross and it left her unscathed.

At that, the whole household thanked God. The whole household saving, of course, the woman's daughter. She had another to thank.

The woman's body was burned and the ashes put into unconsecrated ground beyond the city gates. Though they had discovered her to be a witch, they had not discovered the direction her witchcraft had selected. Nor did they find the wax image with its limbs all twisted and stuck through with needles. The girl had taken that up and concealed it. The duke continued in his distress, but he did not die. Sometimes, in the dead of night, the girl would unearth the image from under a loose brick by the hearth and gloat over it, but she did nothing else. Not yet. She was fourteen, and the cloud of her mother's acts still hovered over her. She knew what she must do next.

The period of mourning ended.

"Daughter," said the silk merchant to her, "why do you not remove your black? The woman was malign and led you into wickedness. How long will you mourn her, who deserves no mourning?"

"Oh, my father," she said, "never think I regret my wretched mother. It is my own unwitting sin I mourn," and she grasped his hand and spilled her tears on it. "I would rather live in a convent," said she, "than mingle with proper folk. And I would seek a convent too, if it were not that I cannot bear to be parted from you."

Do you suppose she smiled secretly as she said this? One might suppose it. Presently she donned a robe of sackcloth and poured ashes over her red-copper hair. "It is my penance," she said. "I am glad to atone for my sins."

People forgot her beauty. She was at pains to obscure it. She slunk about like an aged woman, a rag pulled over her head, dirt smeared on her cheeks and brow. She elected to sleep in a cold cramped attic and sat all day by a smoky hearth in the kitchens. When someone came to her and begged her to wash her face and put on suitable clothes and sit in the rooms of the house, she smiled modestly, drawing the rag of a piece of hair over her face. "I swear, " she said, "I am glad to be humble before God and men."

They reckoned her pious and they reckoned her simple. Two years passed. They mislaid her beauty altogether and reckoned her ugly. They found it hard to call to mind who she was exactly, as she sat in the ashes or shuffled unattended about the streets like a crone.

At the end of the second year, the silk merchant married again. It was inevitable, for he was not a man who liked to live alone.

On this occasion, his choice was a harmless widow. She already had two daughters, pretty in an unremarkable style. Perhaps the merchant hoped they would comfort him for what had gone before, this normal cheery wife and the two sweet, rather silly daughters, whose chief interests were clothes and weddings. Perhaps he hoped also that his deranged daughter might be drawn out by company. But that hope floundered. Not that the new mother did not try to be pleasant to the girl. And the new sisters, their hearts grieved by her condition, went to great lengths to enlist her friendship. They begged her to come from the kitchens or the attic. Failing in that, they sometimes ventured to join her, their fine silk dresses trailing on the greasy floor. They combed her hair, exclaiming, when some of the ash and dirt were removed, on its color. But no sooner had they turned away than the girl gathered up handfuls of soot and ash and rubbed them into her hair again. Now and then, the sisters attempted to interest their bizarre relative in a bracelet or a gown or a current song. They spoke to her of the young men they had seen at the suppers or the balls which were then given regularly by the rich families of the city. The girl ignored it all. If she ever said anything, it was to do with penance and humility. At last, as must happen, the sisters wearied of her and left her alone. They had no cares and did not want to share in hers. They came to resent her moping grayness, as indeed the merchant's second wife had already done.

"Can you do nothing with that girl?" she demanded of her husband. "People will say that I and my daughters are responsible for her condition and that I ill-treat the maid from jealousy of her dead mother."

"Now how could anyone say that," protested the merchant, "when you are famous as the epitome of generosity and kindness?"

Another year passed, and saw no difference in the household.

A difference there was, but not visible.

The girl who slouched in the corner of the hearth was seventeen. Under the filth and grime she was, impossibly, more beautiful, although no one could see it.

And there was one other invisible item: her power (which all this time she had nurtured, saying her prayers to Satanas in the black of midnight), her power rising like a dark moon in her soul.

Three days after her seventeenth birthday, the girl straggled about the streets, as she frequently did. A few noted her and muttered it was the merchant's ugly simple daughter and paid no more attention. Most did not know her at all. She had made herself appear one with the scores of impoverished flotsam which constantly roamed the city, beggars and starvelings. Just outside the city gates, these persons congregated in large numbers, slumped around fires of burning refuse or else wandering to and fro in search of edible seeds, scraps, the miracle of a dropped coin. Here the girl now came, and began to wander about as they did. Dusk gathered and the shadows thickened. The girl sank to her knees in a patch of earth as if she had found something. Two or three of the beggars sneaked over to see if it were worth snatching from her—but the girl was only scrabbling in the empty soil. The beggars, making signs to each other that she was touched by God—mad—left her alone. But very far from mad, the girl presently dug up a stoppered urn. In this urn were the ashes and charred bones of her mother. She had got a clue as to the location of the urn by devious questioning here and there. Her occult power had helped her to be sure of it.

296

In the twilight, padding along through the narrow streets and alleys of the city, the girl brought the urn homeward. In the garden, at the foot of the old tower, gloom-wrapped, unwitnessed, she unstoppered the urn and buried the ashes freshly. She muttered certain unholy magics over the grave. Then she snapped off the sprig of a young hazel tree and planted it in the newly turned ground.

I hazard you have begun to recognize the story by now. I see you suppose I tell it wrongly. Believe me, this is the truth of the matter. But if you would rather I left off the tale ... no doubt your carriage will soon be here—No? Very well. I shall continue.

I think I should speak of the duke's son at this juncture. The prince was nineteen, able, intelligent, and of noble bearing. He was of that rather swarthy type of looks one finds here in the north, but tall and slim and clear-eyed. There is an ancient square where you may see a statue of him, but much eroded by two centuries and the elements. After the city was sacked, no care was lavished on it.

The duke treasured his son. He had constant delight in the sight of the young man and what he said and did. It was the only happiness the invalid had.

Then, one night, the duke screamed out in his bed. Servants came running with candles. The duke moaned that a sword was transfixing his heart, an inch at a time. The prince hurried into the chamber, but in that instant the duke spasmed horribly and died. No mark was on his body. There had never been a mark to show what ailed him.

The prince wept. They were genuine tears. He had nothing to reproach his father with, everything to thank him for. Presently, they brought the young man the seal ring of the city, and he put it on.

It was winter, a cold blue-white weather with snow in the streets and countryside and a hard wizened sun that drove thin sharp blades of light through the sky but gave no warmth. The duke's funeral cortege passed slowly across the snow: the broad open chariots, draped with black and silver; the black-plumed horses; the chanting priests with their glittering robes, their jeweled crucifixes and golden censers. Crowds lined the roadways to watch the spectacle. Among the beggar women stood a girl. No one noticed her. They did not glimpse the expression she veiled in her ragged scarf. She gazed at the bier pitilessly. As the young prince rode by in his sables, the seal ring on his hand, the eyes of the girl burned through her ashy hair, like a red fox through grasses.

The duke was buried in the mausoleum you can visit to this day, on the east side of the city. Several months elapsed. The prince put his grief from him and took up the business of the city competently. Wise and courteous he was, but he rarely smiled. At nineteen, his spirit seemed worn. You might think he guessed the destiny that hung over him.

The winter was a hard one too. The snow had come and, having come, was loath to withdraw. When at last the spring returned, flushing the hills with color, it was no longer sensible to be sad.

The prince's name day fell about this time. A great banquet was planned, a ball. There had been neither in the palace for nigh on three years, not since the duke's fatal illness first claimed him. Now the royal doors were to be thrown open to all men of influence and their families. The prince was liberal, charming, and clever even in this. Aristocrat and rich trader were to mingle in the beautiful dining room, and in this very chamber, among the frescoes, the marble, and the candelabra. Even a merchant's daughter, if the merchant was notable in the city, would get to dance on the sea-green floor, under the white eye of the fearful clock.

The clock. There was some renewed controversy about the clock. They did not dare speak to the young prince. He was a skeptic, as his father had been. But had not a death already occurred? Was the clock not a flying in the jaws of fate? For those disturbed by it, there was a dim writing in their minds, in the dust of the street or the pattern of blossoms. *When the clock strikes—* But people do not positively heed these warnings. Man is afraid of his fears. He ignores the shadow of the wolf thrown on the paving before him, saying: It is only a shadow.

The silk merchant received his invitation to the palace, and to be sure, thought nothing of the clock. His house had been thrown into uproar. The most luscious silks of his workshop were carried into the house and laid before the wife and her two daughters, who chirruped and squealed with excitement. "Oh, Father," cried the two sisters, "may I have this one with the gold piping?" "Oh, Father, this one with the design of pineapples?" Later a jeweler arrived and set out his trays. The merchant was generous. He wanted his women to look their best. It might be the night of their lives. Yet all the while, at the back of his mind, a little dark spot, itching, aching. He tried to ignore the spot, not scratch at it. His true daughter, the mad one. Nobody bothered to tell her about the invitation to the palace. They knew how she would react, mumbling in her hair about her sin and her penance, paddling her hands in the greasy ash to smear her face. Even the servants avoided her, as if she were just the cat seated by the fire. Less than the cat, for the cat saw to the mice—just a block of stone. And yet, how fair she might have looked, decked in the pick of the merchant's wares, jewels at her throat. The prince himself could not have been unaware of her. And though marriage was impossible, other, less holy though equally honorable, contracts might have been arranged, to the benefit of all concerned. The merchant sighed. He had scratched the darkness after all. He attempted to comfort himself by watching the two sisters exult over their apparel. He refused to admit that the finery would somehow make them seem but more ordinary than they were by contrast.

The evening of the banquet arrived. The family set off. Most of the servants sidled after. The prince had distributed largess in the city; oxen roasted in the squares, and the wine was free by royal order.

The house grew somber. In the deserted kitchen, the fire went out.

By the hearth, a segment of gloom rose up.

The girl glanced around her, and she laughed softly and shook out her filthy hair. Of course, she knew as much as anyone, and more than most. This was to be her night too.

A few minutes later she was in the garden beneath the old tower, standing over the young hazel tree which had thrust up from the earth. It had become strong, the tree, despite the harsh winter. Now the girl nodded to it. She chanted under her breath. At length a pale light began to glow, far down near where the roots of the tree held to the ground. Out of the pale glow flew a thin black bird, which perched on the girl's shoulder. Together, the girl and the bird passed into the old tower. High up, a fire blazed that no one had lit. A tub steamed with scented water that no one had drawn. Shapes that were not real and barely seen flitted about. Rare perfumes, the rustle of garments, the glint of gems as yet invisible, filled and did not fill the restless air.

Need I describe further? No. You will have seen paintings which depict the attendance upon a witch of her familiar demons. How one bathes her, another anoints her, another brings clothes and ornaments. Perhaps you do not credit such things in any case. Never mind that. I will tell you what happened in the courtyard before the palace.

Many carriages and chariots had driven through the square, avoiding the roasting oxen, the barrels of wine, the cheering drunken citizens, and so through the gates into the courtyard. Just before ten o'clock (the hour, if you recall the clock, of the magician), a solitary carriage drove through the square and into the court. The people in the square gawped at the carriage and pressed forward to see who would step out of it, this latecomer. It was a remarkable vehicle that looked to be fashioned of solid gold, all but the domed roof, that was transparent flashing crystal. Six black horses drew it. The coachman and postilions were clad in crimson, and strangely masked as curious beasts and reptiles. One of these beast-men now hopped down and opened the door of the carriage. Out came a woman's figure in a cloak of white fur, and glided up the palace stair and in at the doors.

There was dancing in the ballroom. The whole chamber was bright and clamorous with music and the voices of men and women. There, between those two pillars, the prince sat in his chair, dark, courteous, seldom smiling. Here the musicians played, the deep-throated viol, the lively mandolin. And there the dancers moved up and down on the sea-green floor. But the music and the dancers had just paused. The figures on the clock were themselves in motion. The hour of the magician was about to strike.

As it struck, through the doorway came the figure in the fur cloak. And as if they must, every eye turned to her.

For an instant she stood there, all white, as though she had brought the winter snow back with her. And then she loosed the cloak from her shoulders, it slipped away, and she was all fire.

300

She wore a gown of apricot brocade embroidered thickly with gold. Her sleeves and the bodice of her gown were slashed over ivory satin sewn with large rosy pearls. Pearls, too, were wound in her hair, that was the shade of antique burnished copper. She was so beautiful that when the clock was still, nobody spoke. She was so beautiful that it was hard to look at her for very long.

The prince got up from his chair. He did not know he had. Now he started out across the floor, between the dancers, who parted silently to let him through. He went toward the girl in the doorway as if she drew him by a chain.

The prince had hardly ever acted without considering first what he did. Now he did not consider. He bowed to the girl.

"Madam," he said. "You are welcome, Madam," he said. "Tell me who you are."

She smiled.

"My rank," she said. "Would you know that, my lord? It is similar to yours, or would be were I now mistress in my dead mother's palace. But, unfortunately, an unscrupulous man caused the downfall of our house."

"Misfortune indeed," said the prince. "Tell me your name. Let me right the wrong done you."

"You shall," said the girl. "Trust me, you shall. For my name, I would rather keep it secret for the present. But you may call me, if you will, a pet name I have given myself—Ashella."

"Ashella . . . But I see no ash about you," said the prince, dazzled by her gleam, laughing a little, stiffly, for laughter was not his habit.

"Ash and cinders from a cold and bitter hearth," said she. But she smiled again. "Now everyone is staring at us, my lord, and the musicians are impatient to begin again. Out of all these ladies, can it be you will lead me in the dance?"

"As long as you will dance," he said. "You shall dance with me."

And that is how it was.

There were many dances, slow and fast, whirling measures and gentle ones. And here and there, the prince and the maiden were parted. Always then he looked eagerly after her, sparing no regard for the other girls whose hands lay in his. It was not like him, he was usually so careful. But the other young men who danced on that floor, who clasped her fingers or her narrow waist in the dance, also gazed after her when she was gone. She danced, as she appeared, like fire. Though if you had asked those young men whether they would rather tie her to themselves, as the prince did, they would have been at a loss. For it is not easy to keep pace with fire.

The hour of the hag struck on the clock.

The prince grew weary of dancing with the girl and losing her in the dance to others and refinding her and losing her again.

Behind the curtains there is a tall window in the east wall that opens on the terrace above the garden. He drew her out there, into the spring night. He gave an order, and small tables were brought with delicacies and sweets and wine. He sat by her, watching every gesture she made, as if he would paint her portrait afterward.

In the ballroom, here, under the clock, the people murmured. But it was not quite the murmur you would expect, the scandalous murmur about a woman come from nowhere that the prince had made so much of. At the periphery of the ballroom, the silk merchant sat, pale as a ghost, thinking of a ghost, the living ghost of his true daughter. No one else recognized her. Only he. Some trick of his heart had enabled him to know her. He said nothing of it. As the stepsisters and wife gossiped with other wives and sisters, an awful foreboding weighed him down, sent him cold and dumb.

And now it is almost midnight, the moment when the page of the night turns over into day. Almost midnight, the hour when the figure of Death strikes the golden bell of the clock. And what will happen when the clock strikes? Your face announces that you know. Be patient; let us see if you do.

"I am being foolish," said the prince to Ashella on the terrace. "But perhaps I am entitled to be foolish, just once in my life. What are you saying?" For the girl was speaking low beside him, and he could not catch her words.

"I am saying a spell to bind you to me," she said.

"But I am already bound."

"Be bound, then. Never go free."

"I do not wish it," he said. He kissed her hands, and he said, "I do not know you, but I will wed you. Is that proof your spell has worked? I will wed you, and get back for you the rights you have lost."

"If it were only so simple," said Ashella, smiling, smiling. "But the debt is too cruel. Justice requires a harsher payment."

And then, in the ballroom, Death struck the first note on the golden bell.

The girl smiled and she said:

"I curse you in my mother's name."

The second stroke.

"I curse you in my own name."

The third stroke.

"And in the name of those that your father slew."

The fourth stroke.

"And in the name of my Master, who rules the world."

As the fifth, the sixth, the seventh strokes pealed out, the prince stood nonplussed. At the eighth and ninth strokes, the strength of the malediction seemed to curdle his blood. He shivered and his brain writhed. At the tenth stroke, he saw a change in the loveliness before him. She grew thinner, taller. At the eleventh stroke, he beheld a thing in a ragged black cowl and robe. It grinned at him. It was all grin below a triangle of sockets of nose and eyes. At the twelfth stroke, the prince saw Death and knew him.

In the ballroom, a hideous grinding noise, as the gears of the clock failed. Followed by a hollow booming, as the mechanism stopped entirely.

The conjuration of Death vanished from the terrace.

Only one thing was left behind. A woman's shoe. A shoe no woman could ever have danced in. It was made of glass.

Did you intend to protest about the shoe? Shall I finish the story, or would you rather I did not? It is not the ending you are familiar with. Yes, I perceive you understand that now.

I will go quickly, then, for your carriage must soon be here. And there is not a great deal more to relate.

The prince lost his mind. Partly from what he had seen, partly from the spells the young witch had netted him in. He could think of nothing but the girl who had named herself Ashella. He raved that Death had borne her away but he would recover her from Death. She had left the glass shoe as token of her love. He must discover her with the aid of the shoe. Whomsoever the shoe fitted would be Ashella. For there was this added complication, that Death might hide her actual appearance. None had seen the girl before. She had disappeared like smoke. The one infallible test was the shoe. That was why she had left it for him.

His ministers would have reasoned with the prince, but he was past reason. His intellect had collapsed totally as only a profound intellect can. A lunatic, he rode about the city. He struck out at those who argued with him. On a particular occasion, drawing a dagger, he killed, not apparently noticing what he did. His demand was explicit. Every woman, young or old, maid or married, must come forth from her home, must put her foot into the shoe of glass. They came. They had no choice. Some approached in terror, some weeping. Even the aged beggar women obliged, and they cackled, enjoying the sight of royalty gone mad. One alone did not come.

Now it is not illogical that out of the hundreds of women whose feet were put into the shoe, a single woman might have been found that the shoe fitted. But this did not happen. Nor did the situation alter, despite a lurid fable that some, tickled by the idea of wedding the prince, cut off their toes that the shoe might fit them. And if they did, it was to no avail, for still the shoe did not.

Is it really surprising? The shoe was sorcerous. It constantly changed itself, its shape, its size, in order that no foot, save one, could ever be got into it.

Summer spread across the land. The city took on its golden summer glaze, its fetid summer spell.

What had been a whisper of intrigue swelled into a steady distant thunder. Plots were hatched.

One day the silk merchant was brought, trembling and gray of face, to the prince. The merchant's dumbness had broken. He had unburdened himself of his fear at confession, but the priest had not proved honest. In the dawn, men had knocked on the door of the merchant's house. Now he stumbled to the chair of the prince.

Both looked twice their years, but if anything, the prince

looked the elder. He did not lift his eyes. Over and over in his hands he turned the glass shoe.

The merchant, stumbling, too, in his speech, told the tale of his first wife and his daughter. He told everything, leaving out no detail. He did not even omit the end: that since the night of the banquet the girl had been absent from his house, taking nothing with her — save a young hazel from the garden beneath the tower.

The prince leapt from his chair.

His clothes were filthy and unkempt. His face was smeared with sweat and dust ... it resembled, momentarily, another face.

Without guard or attendant, the prince ran through the city toward the merchant's house, and on the road, the intriguers way-laid and slew him. As he fell, the glass shoe dropped from his hands and shattered in a thousand fragments.

There is little else worth mentioning.

Those who usurped the city were villains and not merely that but fools. Within a year, external enemies were at the gates. A year more, and the city had been sacked, half burned out, ruined. The manner in which you find it now is somewhat better than it was then. And it is not now anything for a man to be proud of. As you were quick to note, many here earn a miserable existence by conducting visitors about the streets, the palace, showing them the dregs of the city's past.

Which was not a request, in fact, for you to give me money. Throw some from your carriage window if your conscience both-ers you. My own wants are few.

No, I have no further news of the girl Ashella, the witch. A devotee of Satanas, she has doubtless worked plentiful woe in the world. And a witch is long-lived. Even so, she will die eventually. None escapes Death. Then you may pity her, if you like. Those who serve the gentleman below — who can guess what their final lot will be? But I am very sorry the story did not please you. It is not, maybe, a happy choice before a journey.

And there is your carriage at last.

What? Ah, no, I shall stay here in the ballroom, where you came on me. I have often paused here through the years. It is the clock. It has a certain — what shall I call it? — power to draw me back.

Is it Arabella?

I am not trying to unnerve you. Why should you suppose that? Because of my knowledge of the city, of the story? You think that I am implying that I myself am Death? Now you laugh. Yes, it is absurd. Observe the twelfth figure on the clock. Is he not as you always heard Death described? And am I in the least like that twelfth figure?

Although, of course, the story was not as you have heard it, either.

THE TALE OF THE HANDKERCHIEF

Emma Donoghue

THE reason I would have killed you to stay a queen is that I have no right to be a queen. I have been a fraud from the beginning.

I was born a maid, daughter to a maid, in the court of a widow far across the mountains. How could you, a pampered princess, know what it's like to be a servant, a pair of hands, a household object? To be no one, to own nothing, to owe every last mouthful to those you serve?

All our queen loved in the world was her horse and her daughter.

The horse was white, a magnificent mare with a neck like an oak. The princess was born in the same month of the same year as I was. But where I was dark, with thick brows that overshadowed my bright eyes, the princess was fair. Yellowish, I thought her; slightly transparent, as if the sun had never seen her face. All she liked to do was walk in the garden, up and down the shady paths between the hedges. Once when I was picking nettles for soup, I saw her stumble on the gravel and bruise her knee. The queen ran into the garden at the first cry, lifted her onto her lap and wiped two jeweled tears away with her white handkerchief. Another time I was scrubbing a hearth and stood up to stretch my back, when laughter floated through the open window. I caught sight of the two of them cantering past on the queen's horse, their hands dancing in its snowy mane.

My own mother died young and tired, having made me promise to be a good maid for the rest of my days. I kissed her waxy forehead and knew that I would break my word.

But for the moment I worked hard, kept my head low and my apron clean. At last I was raised to the position of maid to the princess. Telling me of my good fortune, the queen rested her smooth hand for half a moment on my shoulder. If your mother only knew, she said, how it would gladden her heart.

The young princess was a gentle mistress, never having needed to be anything else. The year she came of age, the queen received ambassadors from all the neighboring kingdoms. The prince she chose for her daughter lived a long day's ride away. He was said to be young enough. The girl said neither yes nor no; it was not her question to answer. She stood very still as I tried the bridal dresses on her for size. My hands looked like hen's claws against the shining brocade. The queen told her daughter not to be sad, never to be willful, and always to remember her royal blood. I listened, my mouth full of pins.

If I had had such a mother I would never have left her to journey into a strange country. I would have fought and screamed and clung to the folds of her cloak. But then, my blood is not royal.

Ahead of her daughter the queen sent gold and silver and a box full of crystals. She took the princess into the chamber where I was packing furs, and there she took out a knife and pressed the point into her own finger. I could hardly believe it; I almost cried out to stop her. The queen let three drops of blood fall onto her lawn handkerchief. She tucked this into the girl's bosom, saying that as long as she kept the handkerchief, she could come to no great harm.

And then the queen led her daughter out into the courtyard, and swung her up onto her own great horse. I would come with you myself, she said, if only my kingdom were secure. In these troubled times you will be safer where you're going. In my place, you will have my own horse to carry you, and your own maid to ride behind you.

This was the first I had heard of it. I went to pack my clean linen. The rest of my bits and pieces I left under the mattress for the next maid; I had nothing worth taking into a far country. In the courtyard, a stableman hoisted me onto a nag weighed down with all the princess's paraphernalia.

I watched the queen and the princess kiss good-bye in the

early-morning sunlight. The horse's mane shone like a torch, but where the mother's forehead rested against the daughter's, the sun behind them was blotted out.

We trotted along for some hours without speaking; the princess seemed lost in daydreams, and my mother had taught me never to be the first to break a silence. The day grew hotter as the sun crawled up the sky. Sweat began to break through the princess's white throat, trickling down the neck of her heavy gold dress. My thin smock was scorching through.

Suddenly there was a glint in the trees. The princess brought her great white horse to a halt and said, without looking at me, Please fill my golden cup with some cool water from that stream.

The heat in my head was a hammer on an anvil, pounding a sword into shape. It was the first order I had ever disobeyed in my life. If you're thirsty, I told her, get it yourself.

The princess turned her milky face and stared at me. When my eyes refused to fall she climbed down, a little awkwardly, and untied her cup. She pulled back her veil as she walked to the stream. I was thirsty myself, but I didn't move. The white horse looked round at me with its long eyes that seemed to say, If her mother only knew, it would break her heart. When the princess walked back from the stream, her mouth was wet and her cheeks were pale.

We rode on for several hours until the sun was beginning to sink. The princess reined in at the edge of a river and asked me again, more shyly, if I would fetch her some water. I did mean to say yes this time, now that I had taught her a lesson; I was not plotting anything. But when I opened my mouth the sound that came out was No. If you want to drink, I said hoarsely, you have to stoop down for it.

I held her gaze until her eyes fell. She got down and stepped through the rushes to the water. The horse tossed its foam-colored head and neighed as if warning of an enemy approach. My lips were cracked; my tongue rasped against them as I watched the princess. She bent over the stream to fill her cup, and something fluttered from the curve of her breast into the water. My handkerchief, she cried, as it slid away. As if saying what it was would bring it back.

With that I leapt down from my knock-kneed horse and

waded into the river. I found the square of linen caught in a knot of reeds, mud silting over the three brown drops. I turned and shook it in the princess's face. A drop of water caught on her golden sleeve. You know nothing, I told her. Do you even know how to wash a handkerchief?

She shook her head. Her face was marked with red, like faint lines on a map.

You scrub it on a rock like this, I told her, and scrub again, and scrub harder, and keep scrubbing until your fingers are numb. Look, the spots are coming out. Your mother's royal blood is nearly gone.

The princess made a small moan.

Look, there are only three faint marks left, I said. And then you find somewhere off the ground and leave it to bleach in the sun, I instructed her, tossing the handkerchief up into the high branches of a tree.

The princess's eyes left the handkerchief and came back. Hers was the look of the rabbit, and it brought out all the snake in me. Take off your dress, I told her.

She blinked.

Take off your dress or I'll strip it from your body with my bare hands.

She reached behind to unfasten the hooks. I didn't help. I watched. Then I slipped my own plain dress over my head. The air felt silken on my shoulders. The dresses lay crumpled at our feet like snakeskins. Look, I said. Where is the difference between us now?

The princess had no answer.

I picked up the golden cup and filled it from the stream. I drank until my throat hurt. I splashed my face and arms and breasts until I shivered despite the sun. Then I stepped into the stiff golden dress and turned my back on the girl. After a moment she understood, and began to do up the hooks and eyes. When she was finished, she hesitated, then pulled on the smock I had left in a heap by the rushes. It suited her. Her fair hair hung around her dry lips. I filled the cup again and passed it to her. She drank without a word.

When I got onto the white horse, it reared under me, and I had to give it a kick to make it stand still. I waited until I could hear the girl settling in the saddle of the old nag, and then I wheeled around. I am the queen's daughter, I told her, and you are my maid, and if you ever say otherwise I will rip your throat open with my bare hands.

Her eyes slid down to my fingers. The skin was angry, with calluses on the thumbs; anyone who saw it would know. I rummaged around in the saddlebag until I found a pair of white gloves and pulled them on. The girl was looking away. I moved my great horse alongside hers, until I was so close I could have struck her. Swear by the open sky, I whispered, that you will never tell anyone what has happened by this river.

I swear by the open sky, she repeated doubtfully, raising her eyes to it.

We rode on. The gold dress was heavier than I could have imagined. My bones felt as if they had been made to bear this burden, as if they had found their one true dress at last.

It was dark by the time we reached the palace. They had lit a double row of torches for us to follow. The prince came to the foot of the steps and lifted me down from my horse. Through the hard brocade I couldn't feel whether he was warm or cold. He was pale with nerves, but he had a kind face. At the top of the steps I made him put me down. I said, The maid I brought with me.

Yes? His voice was thin but not unpleasant.

She does not know anything about waiting on ladies. Could you set her to some simpler task?

Perhaps she could mind the geese, suggested the prince.

I gave a single nod and walked beside him toward the great doors. My back prickled. If the girl was going to denounce me this would be the moment for it. But I heard nothing except the clinking harnesses as they led the horses away.

I found that I knew how to behave like a princess, from my short lifetime of watching. I snapped my fan; I offered my gloved hand to be kissed; I never bent my back. At times, I forgot for a moment that I was acting.

But I never forgot to be afraid. I had wanted to be married at once, but the pace of royal life is stately. There were pigs to be fattened, spices to wait for, the king and his army to come safely home. I was given a broad chamber with a view of the city arch and all the fields beyond.

The first week slid by. The goose girl seemed to go about her duties without a word. I had never eaten such good food in my life, but my stomach was a knotted rope. Every day I made some excuse to pass by the stables and catch a glimpse of the great white horse in its box. Its eyes grew longer as they fixed on me; If the queen her mother only knew, they seemed to say.

I became convinced that it was the horse who would betray me. It was not scared the way the goose girl was. In the dreams that came to ride me in my gilt feather bed, the horse drew pictures in the mud under the city arch with its hoof, illustrating my crime for all the court to see. Sometimes it spoke aloud in my head, its voice a deep whistle, telling all it knew. I woke with my knees under my chin, as if I were packed in a barrel, as we punish thieves in the mountains. That evening at dinner I said to my pale fiancé, That brute of a horse I rode here tried to throw me on the journey.

Then we will have it destroyed, he assured me.

His eyes were devoted, the shape of almonds. He looked as if he would believe every word that slipped from my mouth.

The next day, I passed by the stableyard, and the box was empty. Back in my chamber, I threw the window open to the delicate air. My eye caught sight of something bright, nailed to the city arch. Something in the shape of a horse's head. Below it stood a girl, geese clacking at her skirts. From this distance I couldn't be sure if her lips were moving.

She must have bribed the knacker to save the horse's head and nail it up where she would pass by. She must have guessed the exact shape of my fears. I watched her make her way through the arch and out into the open fields.

Another week crawled by. Every day I looked out for the girl pausing under the arch with her noisy flock, and tried to read her face. I wore my finest dresses, but my heart was drumming under their weight. I kept my white gloves buttoned, even on the hottest days.

I began to worry that the queen might come to the wedding after all, as a surprise for her daughter, despite the danger of leaving her kingdom unguarded. In the dreams that lined up along my bed, the queen pointed at me across the royal dining table and slapped the crown from my head. She ripped the glove from my hand and held up my finger, pressing it to the point of her knife, till dark drops stained the tablecloth: See, she cried, there is nothing royal about this blood, common as dirt. When I woke, doubled up, I felt as if they were driving long spikes through the sides of the barrel, into my skin.

One day I heard that a messenger had come from the kingdom of my birth. I couldn't get to him before the prince did. I sat in my chamber, waiting for the heavy tramp of the guards. But the step, when it came at last, was soft. The prince said, The queen your mother has fallen in battle.

So she will not be coming to the wedding? I asked, and only then understood his words. I bent over to hide my face from him; his gentle eyes shamed me. I hoped my laughter would sound like tears. And then the tears did come, and I hoped they were for her, a queen dead in her prime, and not just for my own treacherous self.

I don't know who told the goose girl. I hadn't the courage. I suppose she heard it in the kitchen, or from a goose boy. I thought that the moment of hearing might be the moment she would run through the court to denounce me. But the next morning she was standing under the arch in the usual way, her face turned up as if in conversation with the rotting head above her. She paused no longer than usual before walking her flock into the fields.

The day before the wedding I rode out into the country. I found myself near the river where it all began, this fantastical charade. I stopped beside the bank, and there in the tree above my head was a flash of white.

I had to take off my dress to climb, or I would have got stuck in the branches. The tree left red lashes on my arms and thighs. At last my hand reached the handkerchief. It was washed through by the dew and bleached stiff by the sun, but there were still three faint brown marks.

I saw then that the end was coming. When I had dressed myself I rode straight for the fields around the castle to find the goose girl. All at once I knew it would be tonight she would tell them; she was waiting till the last minute, so my hopes would be at their highest just before the guards came to take me away to a walled-up, windowless room.

There she was with the breeze blowing her yellow hair out of its bonds and across her sunburnt face. I rode up to her, then jumped down. I held out the handkerchief; my hand was shaking. It still bears the marks of your mother's royal blood, I told her. If I give it to you now, will you let me run away before you tell them?

She tucked the handkerchief into her rough dress and said, Tell what?

I stared at her. Your fear of me will die away, I said. Your need to speak the truth will swell within you. You will be overheard lamenting as you sleep beside the stove; you will confide in the reeds and they will sing it back.

Her eyes flicked upward. She said, By the open sky, I swear I will never tell what is not true.

But you are the royal princess, I reminded her.

A little time passed before she spoke. No, she said, I don't think so, not anymore. The horse helped me to understand.

What?

When it was alive, it seemed to be a proud and stern horse, she said. After you had it killed, I could hear it talking in my head, and what it had to say surprised me.

My mouth was hanging open.

I've grown accustomed to this life, the goose girl went on. I have found the fields are wider than any garden. I was always nervous, when I was a princess, in case I would forget what to do. You fit the dresses better; you carry it off.

My mouth was dry; I shut it. I could hardly believe her words, this unlooked-for reprieve. If your mother only knew, I protested, it would break her heart.

My mother is dead, said the girl, and she knows everything now.

As I heard her, the barrel I felt always about my ribs seemed to crack open, its hoops ringing about my feet. I could breathe. I could stretch.

That night at dinner the prince filled my goblet with the best wine, and I gave him a regal smile. He had very clean fingernails, and the blue pallor of true royalty. He was all I needed. Perhaps I would even grow to love him in the end, once I was truly safe;

stranger things had happened. Once I had the crown settled on my head and a baby or two on my lap, who knew what kind of woman I might turn out to be? That night I slept deep and dreamless.

During the wedding, my mind wandered. I looked out the chapel window, onto the rooftops. From here I couldn't see the city arch, or the wide yellow fields. I wondered how the goose girl had felt when she heard the wedding bells. I thought of how both of us had refused to follow the paths mapped out for us by our mothers and their mothers before them, but had perversely gone our own ways instead, and I wondered whether this would bring us more or less happiness in the end.

Then I heard a tiny cough. When the prince took his lace handkerchief away from his mouth, there was a spatter of blood on it. I gave my husband a proper, searching look for the first time. I saw the red rims of his eyes, the hollows of his cheeks. Once more I seemed to feel the barrel locked around me, the spikes hammering through. I knew if I was not with child in a month or two, I would have nothing to hold on to. The day after my husband's funeral I would be wandering the world again in search of a crown I could call my own.

THE THREE LITTLE PIGS

James Finn Garner

ONCE there were three little pigs who lived together in mutual respect and in harmony with their environment. Using materials that were indigenous to the area, they each built a beautiful house. One pig built a house of straw, one a house of sticks, and one a house of dung, clay, and creeper vines shaped into bricks and baked in a small kiln. When they were finished, the pigs were satisfied with their work and settled back to live in peace and self-determination.

But their idyll was soon shattered. One day, along came a big, bad wolf with expansionist ideas. He saw the pigs and grew very hungry, in both a physical and an ideological sense. When the pigs saw the wolf, they ran into the house of straw. The wolf ran up to the house and banged on the door, shouting, "Little pigs, little pigs, let me in!"

The pigs shouted back, "Your gunboat tactics hold no fear for pigs defending their homes and culture."

But the wolf wasn't to be denied what he thought was his manifest destiny. So he huffed and puffed and blew down the house of straw. The frightened pigs ran to the house of sticks, with the wolf in hot pursuit. Where the house of straw had stood, other wolves bought up the land and started a banana plantation.

At the house of sticks, the wolf again banged on the door and shouted, "Little pigs, little pigs, let me in!"

The pigs shouted back, "Go to hell, you carnivorous, imperialistic oppressor!"

At this, the wolf chuckled condescendingly. He thought to himself: "They are so childlike in their ways. It will be a shame to see them go, but progress cannot be stopped."

So the wolf huffed and puffed and blew down the house of sticks. The pigs ran to the house of bricks, with the wolf close at their heels. Where the house of sticks had stood, other wolves built a time-share condo resort complex for vacationing wolves, with each unit a fiberglass reconstruction of the house of sticks, as well as native curio shops, snorkeling, and dolphin shows.

At the house of bricks, the wolf again banged on the door and shouted, "Little pigs, little pigs, let me in!"

This time in response, the pigs sang songs of solidarity and wrote letters of protest to the United Nations.

By now the wolf was getting angry at the pigs' refusal to see the situation from the carnivore's point of view. So he huffed and puffed, and huffed and puffed, then grabbed his chest and fell over dead from a massive heart attack brought on from eating too many fatty foods.

The three little pigs rejoiced that justice had triumphed and did a little dance around the corpse of the wolf. Their next step was to liberate their homeland. They gathered together a band of other pigs who had been forced off their lands. This new brigade of *porcinistas* attacked the resort complex with machine guns and rocket launchers and slaughtered the cruel wolf oppressors, sending a clear signal to the rest of the hemisphere not to meddle in their internal affairs. Then the pigs set up a model socialist

democracy with free education, universal health care, and afford-
able housing for everyone.

*Please note: The wolf in this story was a metaphorical construct. No
actual wolves were harmed in the writing of the story.*

POETRY

ONE relatively recent innovation in the world of fairy tale is the
growing body of poetry that either re-interprets one or other of
the classic tales or explores the general significance of fairy tale in
our society. This interest may be due in part to the greater understanding and appreciation of the fairy tale that can be attributed to
such creative minds as those of J. R. R. Tolkien and Joseph Campbell and also, in part, to the controversies that have swirled about
the tale, particularly in relation to sexual stereotyping. It becomes
quickly apparent, indeed, that in poetry as in prose, the modern
perspective is characteristically darker. Implicit in many of these
poems is a juxtaposition of an idealized past (expressed either in
terms of childhood or of an earlier, perhaps even edenic, existence) and a disillusioned present: in other words, a re-statement
of the contrary states defined by the Romantic poet William
Blake as Innocence and Experience.

In addition, the poetic form reflects modern preoccupations in
that it invites a much more personal, intimate perspective. Plot
becomes a secondary consideration, as our attention is now much
more focused upon the poet-narrator's voice. In this respect, one
might suggest that this shift in emphasis parallels the importance
of the teller in the context of the *oral* tale, an importance that is all
but lost when the tale is in literary form.

Lisel Mueller's poem "Reading the Brothers Grimm to Jenny"
deals with this difference of perception in a context made the
more effective by its familiarity: a parent re-discovering a simpler,
brighter world in the daughter's love of fairy tale. A similar
parental perspective is used in John Ower's poem "The Gingerbread House," but to very different effect. Here both adult and
child are caught up in a re-enactment of the tale, which, in its
emotional intensity, offers an insight into the *resilience* of the fairy

tale, since there is no missing the realization that fantasy provides a means by which we can come to grips with some of life's critical moments.

One of the most remarkable qualities of the fairy tale is what might be termed its resonance. This can be seen very clearly if one compares "The Gingerbread House" with "Gretel in Darkness" by Louise Glück. Both poems are based on the same fairy tale, yet deal with entirely different realms of human (and inhuman) experience. To achieve a powerful immediacy of effect in her poem, Glück chooses to observe her world through Gretel's eyes—but this is an older, disillusioned Gretel, burdened with the unbearable weight of memory. Traditionally, it is the woman who remembers and shares her experience through such means as the old wives' tale. When that experience is beyond imagining, however, it brings with it a terrible loneliness.

Interestingly, three other poems in our selection also adopt the first-person point of view, leading one to speculate that the introspectiveness of this approach is particularly appealing to the modern writer (and particularly suited to the poetic medium), perhaps because characters in the original tales are so *lacking* in reflection. Today we are interested in what a character thinks, what he or she is like inside, and so a whole new angle on the fairy tale emerges. Like Glück, Gwen Strauss chooses to confront horror by means of the first-person perspective in her poem "Bluebeard," but this time the speaker is the perpetrator rather than the victim. We commented in our introduction to "Villains" upon "our ongoing fascination with the mysteries of the aberrant mind," and it is clear that this is the challenge that Strauss has set herself here: to explore the pathology of wickedness and perhaps to unsettle us by rejecting the facile category of "monster." In her hands, (as in those of Angela Carter in her story "The Bloody Chamber"), Bluebeard is all the more disturbing for the unimaginable loneliness of his cruelty.

It is surely the sheer oddity of perspective that explains why "The Frog Prince" is so often re-told in the first person; of all the transformations that take place in fairy tale, none is stranger than from frog to prince (not to mention the manner in which it is accomplished). When the tale was first told, one can only think that to be turned into a frog was seen unequivocally as a curse. Yet, in Susan Mitchell's "From the Journals of the Frog Prince," we come across a radically different interpretation—one that appears to challenge the confident anthropocentrism of the traditional tale. The same revisionist spirit is to be found in Sara Henderson Hay's poem, "One of the Seven Has Somewhat to Say," which suggests that Snow White's expertise with mop and duster (a matter of celebration from Grimm to Disney) may not have been regarded so enthusiastically by the "seven old bachelors" themselves.

Thus far, none of the poems in our selection are what we might term re-tellings of classic tales—point of view has taken precedence over plot. The longer poems by Anne Sexton and Roald Dahl certainly pay more attention to plot, but not at the expense of point of view. Both may be described as parodies, and yet we are quickly aware of a marked difference in tone. Sexton brings a bitter irony to her re-telling of "Cinderella"; it is as if she is venting her anger at fairy tales for creating a world so much at odds with our own imperfect existence. Indeed, her technique of exposing the fantasy of the tale to her sardonic brand of realism is curiously reminiscent of such puritanical critics as Sarah Trimmer (see Introduction, p. xxi). While Sexton is clearly wrestling with a fierce love/hate relationship with fairy tales, Roald Dahl's approach is considerably lighter; his verse has an irreverent bounce to it, culminating in an outrageous piece of revisionism that surely owes something to an earlier parody of the same story by James Thurber. Even as he pokes fun at the tale, however, Dahl acknowledges its value by giving us a heroine who—in more ways than one—knows the story. (It is useful to compare her with the girl in Angela Carter's "The Company of Wolves.") Behind Dahl's comic exuberance is the critical notion that Little Red Riding Hood has acquired the self-awareness to step outside the story, while the Wolf is trapped within it—a postmodern perspective, if there ever was one!

We conclude this brief selection of fairy-tale poetry with a piece that strikes an entirely different note. Wilfred Owen is remembered almost exclusively for his war poetry in which he described the horrors of combat for a public still caught up in a fantasy of patriotism and comic-book bravado. Written in 1914, "The Sleeping Beauty" is undeniably old-fashioned in its tender lyricism and archaic diction; yet, here too, a moment of human experience is illuminated and perhaps comprehended through the fantasy of a fairy tale.

READING THE BROTHERS GRIMM TO JENNY

Lisel Mueller

Dead means somebody has to kiss you.

Jenny, your mind commands
kingdoms of black and white:
you shoulder the crow on your left,
the snowbird on your right;
for you the cinders part
and let the lentils through,
and noise falls into place
as screech or sweet roo-coo,
while in my own, real world
gray foxes and gray wolves
bargain eye to eye,
and the amazing dove
takes shelter under the wing
of the raven to keep dry.

Knowing that you must climb,
one day, the ancient tower
where disenchantment binds
the curls of innocence,
that you must live with power
and honor circumstance,
that choice is what comes true —
O, Jenny, pure in heart,
why do I lie to you?

Why do I read you tales
in which birds speak the truth
and pity cures the blind,

319

and beauty reaches deep
to prove a royal mind?
Death is a small mistake
there, where the kiss revives;
Jenny, we make just dreams
out of our unjust lives.

Still, when your truthful eyes,
your keen, attentive stare,
endow the vacuous slut
with royalty, when you match
her soul to her shimmering hair,
what can she do but rise
to your imagined throne?
And what can I, but see
beyond the world that is
when, faithful, you insist
I have the golden key —
and learn from you once more
the terror and the bliss,
the world as it might be?

THE GINGERBREAD HOUSE

John Ower

We made our little girl
A gingerbread house.
Despite sweet cement
It leaned as if it yielded
To a hurricane wind.
Our baby took one look at it,
Said it was a witch's house,
And burst into tears.
She was a prophet in her way.
During our estrangement
The witch flew out the window
Riding on the storm.

She cast a wicked spell
That made us hate each other.
And now between the two of us
In the finest fashion
Of the old fairy-tales
We gobble up our child.

GRETEL IN DARKNESS

Louise Glück

This is the world we wanted.
All who would have seen us dead
are dead. I hear the witch's cry
break in the moonlight through a sheet
of sugar: God rewards.
Her tongue shrivels into gas ...

  Now far from women's arms
and memory of women, in our father's hut
we sleep, are never hungry.
Why do I not forget?
My father bars the door, bars harm
from this house, and it is years.

No one remembers. Even you, my brother,
summer afternoons you look at me as though
you meant to leave,
as though it never happened.
But I killed for you. I see armed firs,
the spires of that gleaming kiln come back, come back...

Nights I turn to you to hold me
but you are not there.
Am I alone? Spies
hiss in the stillness, Hansel,
we are there still and it is real, real,
that black forest and the fire in earnest.

BLUEBEARD

Gwen Strauss

Come, love, and show me
the small key to my turret-chamber.
Yesterday, in a far off place,
I heard a door scrape a threshold
and the cold clank of metal on stone.

Today, I am returned.
And what, my bride, is this? A stain?
Blood? Again betrayal.

When you arrived in my castle yard,
a country virgin dressed in Paris silks,
I opened all rooms to you but that one,
trusted you with my keys to leave untouched
the one dark corner where I go alone.

Each woman I destroyed, I loved
with infinite tenderness.
Each woman gave herself complete
to me in death, because, as you will find,
there is no freedom greater.

Pain and pleasure are but a moment to either.
Remember this.
Remember our wedding night. In the end,
I will leave no part of you untouched.

In that far place, remember me,
how I remain a prisoner of a little room,
searching for one who loves me as I love.

FROM THE JOURNALS OF
THE FROG PRINCE

Susan Mitchell

In March I dreamed of mud,
sheets of mud over the ballroom chairs and table,
rainbow slicks of mud under the throne.
In April I saw mud of clouds and mud of sun.
Now in May I find excuses to linger in the kitchen
for wafts of silt and ale,
cinnamon and river bottom,
tender scallion and sour underlog.

At night I cannot sleep.
I am listening for the dribble of mud
climbing the stairs to our bedroom
as if a child in a wet bathing suit ran
up them in the dark.

Last night I said, "Face it, you're bored
How many times can you live over
with the same excitement
that moment when the princess leans
into the well, her face a petal
falling to the surface of the water
as you rise like a bubble to her lips,
the golden ball bursting from your mouth?"
Remember how she hurled you against the wall,
your body cracking open,
skin shrivelling to the bone,
the green pod of your heart splitting in two,
and her face imprinted with every moment of your
transformation?

I no longer tremble.

Night after night I lie beside her.
"Why is your forehead so cool and damp?" she asks.

Her breasts are soft and dry as flour.
The hand that brushes my head is feverish.
At her touch I long for wet leaves,
the slap of water against rocks.

"What were you thinking of? she asks.
How can I tell her
I am thinking of the green skin
shoved like wet pants behind the Directoire desk?
Or tell her I am mortgaged to the hilt
of my sword, to the leek-green tip of my soul?
Someday I will drag her by her hair
to the river — and what? Drown her?
Show her the green flame of my self rising at her feet?
But there's no more violence in her
than in a fence or a gate.

"What are you thinking of?" she whispers.
I am staring into the garden.
I am watching the moon
wind its trail of golden slime around the oak,
over the stone basin of the fountain.
How can I tell her
I am thinking that transformations are not forever?

ONE OF THE SEVEN HAS SOMEWHAT TO SAY

Sara Henderson Hay

Remember how it was before she came —?
The picks and shovels dropped beside the door,
The sink piled high, the meals any old time,
Our jackets where we'd flung them on the floor?
The mud tracked in, the clutter on the shelves.
None of us shaved, or more than halfway clean ...
Just seven old bachelors, living by ourselves?
Those were the days, if you know what I mean.

She scrubs, she sweeps, she even dusts the ceilings:
She's made us build a tool shed for our stuff.
Dinner's at eight, the table setting's formal
And if I weren't afraid I'd hurt her feelings
I'd move, until we get her married off,
And things can gradually slip back to normal.

CINDERELLA

Anne Sexton

You always read about it:
the plumber with twelve children
who wins the Irish Sweepstakes.
From toilets to riches.
That story.

Or the nursemaid,
some luscious sweet from Denmark
who captures the oldest son's heart.
From diapers to Dior.
That story.

Or a milkman who serves the wealthy,
eggs, cream, butter, yogurt, milk,
the white truck like an ambulance
who goes into real estate
and makes a pile.
From homogenized to martinis at lunch.

Or the charwoman
who is on the bus when it cracks up
and collects enough from the insurance.
From mops to Bonwit Teller.
That story.

Once
the wife of a rich man was on her deathbed

and she said to her daughter Cinderella:
Be devout. Be good. Then I will smile
down from heaven in the seam of a cloud.
The man took another wife who had
two daughters, pretty enough
but with hearts like blackjacks.
Cinderella was their maid.
She slept on the sooty hearth each night
and walked around looking like Al Jolson.
Her father brought presents home from town,
jewels and gowns for the other women
but the twig of a tree for Cinderella.
She planted that twig on her mother's grave
and it grew to a tree where a white dove sat.
Whenever she wished for anything the dove
would drop it like an egg upon the ground.
The bird is important, my dears, so heed him.

Next came the ball, as you all know.
It was a marriage market.
The prince was looking for a wife.
All but Cinderella were preparing
and gussying up for the big event.
Cinderella begged to go too.
Her stepmother threw a dish of lentils
into the cinders and said: Pick them
up in an hour and you shall go.
The white dove brought all his friends;
all the warm wings of the fatherland came,
and picked up the lentils in a jiffy.
No, Cinderella, said the stepmother,
you have no clothes and cannot dance.
That's the way with stepmothers.

Cinderella went to the tree at the grave
and cried forth like a gospel singer:
Mama! Mama! My turtledove,
send me to the prince's ball!
The bird dropped down a golden dress

and delicate little gold slippers.
Rather a large package for a simple bird.
So she went. Which is no surprise.
Her stepmother and sisters didn't
recognize her without her cinder face
and the prince took her hand on the spot
and danced with no other the whole day.

As nightfall came she thought she'd better
get home. The prince walked her home
and she disappeared into the pigeon house
and although the prince took an axe and broke
it open she was gone. Back to her cinders.
These events repeated themselves for three days.
However on the third day the prince
covered the palace steps with cobbler's wax
and Cinderella's gold shoe stuck upon it.
Now he would find whom the shoe fit
and find his strange dancing girl for keeps.
He went to their house and the two sisters
were delighted because they had lovely feet.
The eldest went into a room to try the slipper on
but her big toe got in the way so she simply
sliced it off and put on the slipper.
The prince rode away with her until the white dove
told him to look at the blood pouring forth.
That is the way with amputations.
They don't just heal up like a wish.
The other sister cut off her heel
but the blood told as blood will.
The prince was getting tired.
He began to feel like a shoe salesman.
But he gave it one last try.
This time Cinderella fit into the shoe
like a love letter into its envelope.

At the wedding ceremony
the two sisters came to curry favor
and the white dove pecked their eyes out.

327

Two hollow spots were left
like soup spoons.

Cinderella and the prince
lived, they say, happily ever after,
like two dolls in a museum case
never bothered by diapers or dust,
never arguing over the timing of an egg,
never telling the same story twice,
never getting a middle-aged spread,
their darling smiles pasted on for eternity.
Regular Bobbsey Twins.
That story.

LITTLE RED RIDING HOOD
AND THE WOLF

Roald Dahl

As soon as Wolf began to feel
That he would like a decent meal,
He went and knocked on Grandma's door.
When Grandma opened it, she saw
The sharp white teeth, the horrid grin,
And Wolfie said, "May I come in?"
Poor Grandmamma was terrified,
"He's going to eat me up!" she cried.
And she was absolutely right.
He ate her up in one big bite.
But Grandmamma was small and tough,
And Wolfie wailed, "That's not enough!
I haven't yet begun to feel
That I have had a decent meal!"
He ran around the kitchen yelping,
"I've *got* to have a second helping!"
Then added with a frightful leer,
"I'm therefore going to wait right here
Till Little Miss Red Riding Hood

Comes home from walking in the wood."
He quickly put on Grandma's clothes,
(Of course he hadn't eaten those).
He dressed himself in coat and hat.
He put on shoes and after that
He even brushed and curled his hair,
Then sat himself in Grandma's chair.
In came the little girl in red.
She stopped. She stared. And then she said,

"What great big ears you have, Grandma."
"All the better to hear you with," the Wolf replied.
"What great big eyes you have, Grandma,"
said Little Red Riding Hood.
"All the better to see you with," the Wolf replied.

He sat there watching her and smiled.
He thought, I'm going to eat this child.
Compared with her old Grandmamma
She's going to taste like caviar.
Then Little Red Riding Hood said, *"But Grandma,
what a lovely great big furry coat you have on."*

"That's wrong!" cried Wolf. "Have you forgot
To tell me what BIG TEETH I've got?
Ah well, no matter what you say,
I'm going to eat you anyway."
The small girl smiles. One eyelid flickers.
She whips a pistol from her knickers.
She aims it at the creature's head
And *bang bang bang*, she shoots him dead.
A few weeks later, in the wood,
I came across Miss Riding Hood.
But what a change! No cloak of red,
No silly hood upon her head.
She said, "Hello, and do please note
My lovely furry wolfskin coat."

THE SLEEPING BEAUTY

Wilfred Owen

Sojourning through a southern realm in youth,
I came upon a house by happy chance
Where bode a marvellous Beauty. There, romance
Flew faerily until I lit on truth —
For lo! the fair Child slumbered. Though, forsooth,
She lay not blanketed in drowsy trance,
But leapt alert of limb and keen of glance,
From sun to shower; from gaiety to ruth;
Yet breathed her loveliness asleep in her:
For, when I kissed, her eyelids knew no stir.
So back I drew tiptoe from that Princess,
Because it was too soon, and not my part,
To start voluptuous pulses in her heart,
And kiss her to the world of Consciousness.

ILLUSTRATION

No publisher nowadays would dream of trying to sell a volume of fairy tales not accompanied by illustrations; indeed, one might be forgiven for thinking that the illustrator is sometimes of greater importance than the tales, which are chosen primarily as suitable vehicles for his or her artistic prowess. Indeed, the modern fairy-tale book consists, as often as not, of a single tale told primarily in pictures; the text has become a secondary consideration. It's an intriguing question, whether the inclusion of illustrations stifles the reader's imagination by imposing an "expert's" visual representation upon it, or whether the pictures actually enhance the reader's imaginative response to the story. Clearly there are many factors involved, such as the age of the reader, the ability of the artist, and the quality of the book itself. Yet even if we were able somehow to calculate relative values for such factors, how could we then compare the quality of the reader's response with and without the presence of illustrations? Calculations aside, there can be no question but that pictures add one more dimension to the various imaginative experiences of reading a tale, being read a tale, and being *told* a tale.

Thus the encounter between the text and the reader's imagination is made more complex by the arrival of the illustrator, who imposes his or her particular vision and tone upon the narrative. Just how completely the reading of a tale can be influenced by different artists' interpretations will be demonstrated in the following pages: though the words may remain the same, the pictures tell us a different story. Without a teller there is no tale; without an illustrator, the text is still there on the printed page. Yet, as Perry Nodelman points out in his instructive book *Words About Pictures*, our imaginations can rarely achieve the vividness and specificity that can be found in a good illustration. To achieve these qualities, both teller and illustrator must give something of themselves to the tale in order to infuse it with new life, since in its "basic" form, the tale leaves ample scope for the inventiveness of both contributors, as they work within the familiar framework of the story to create something new.

One significant challenge for the artist is the depiction of characters familiar in name but not in image; he or she presumes thus to make explicit what the tale leaves largely to our imagination (we are told no more than that Little Red Riding Hood is a "pretty little girl," or that Rumpelstiltskin is "a little man"). Alternatively, the artist may choose to concentrate upon the setting of the tale, giving a specificity to time and place denied by the traditional beginning of "once upon a time." Indeed, the opportunity to expand has also been exploited by recorders of the tales, for as we noted earlier, Perrault and the Grimms were quite prepared to leave their imprint on the tales, in the process of making them more suitable for their respective audiences. There is, of course, no guarantee that the embellishment provided by teller or artist will necessarily enrich the tale; we all know how painful an experience it can be to listen to a flat, indifferent reading of a tale, or how short-changed we feel when confronted by illustrations that do little more than fill space on the page.

We are told that every picture tells a story; an illustration tells at least two, for not only does it provide a visual dimension for the story it accompanies, but it also reveals something of the assumptions and values of the artist and of the culture to which he or she belongs. In that sense, the pictures that accompany fairy tales are often as much a mirror as are the tales themselves. Thus, in the case of the illustrations, we are seeing the tale through the eyes of yet another intermediary, behind whom there is a further influence in the publisher, whose decisions are ultimately dictated by market forces. In recent years, for instance, it has become common practice to publish editions of individual tales rather than collections. The justification for this innovation is clearly the expanded role of the artist, who has now become the primary consideration.

At the outset we commented that no modern publisher would seriously consider producing a book of fairy tales without illustrations; we might now add that few would publish such a book without illustrations in color. At the same time, the black-and-white originals included in our selection provide convincing evidence that the artist's decision not to use color does not signify a lesser commitment to the story. We have chosen examples of illustrative work that range from the last century to the present day. It is admittedly a very partial selection, since the number of illustrated versions of fairy tales has increased so dramatically in recent years. However, it may serve to give some indication of the variety of approaches that certain artists have adopted over the years and hopefully will provide the student with some stimulus to seek out the work of others.

LITTLE RED RIDING HOOD

As we pointed out in our introduction to this tale, there is more to the story than a simple warning to children not to speak to strangers. One artist whose work manifests abundant awareness of that fact is Gustave Doré (1832-83). The fact that Doré's work (published in 1867) is the earliest example in our selection makes his insight into Perrault's tales all the more remarkable, not least because his engravings are of course without the benefit (or is it the distraction?) of color. Like many other artists since, he illustrates a critical moment in this story: the meeting between Little Red Riding Hood and the wolf (p.362). Absent, however, is the anthropomorphic interpretation of the wolf that many subsequent illustrators have adopted; this wolf is every inch a wolf. Nevertheless, Doré provides us with a carefully detailed portrait of the relationship between the two characters that foreshadows the outcome of their encounter. As is often the case in his work, the eyes are the focal point of the picture, in this instance, the fascinated gaze that binds prey to predator. Doré makes this a claustrophobic picture, as the little girl finds herself hemmed in by the wolf, whose proximity appears at first glance to be protective; its impact is all the more effective because the observer alone knows that deception and malice are at work here. Subtler still is the detail of the girl's unfastened shoe-strap, indicative of her vulnerability, her unpreparedness for harsh experience. As the little girl gazes up at the wolf as if hypnotized, her whole body expresses a naive trust and uncertainty. Although the wolf is depicted from a highly unusual perspective creating the effect of an upright human stance, Doré still manages to include his penetrating stare. That, together with the half-protective, half-suggestive movement of his hindquarters toward Little Red Riding Hood, reveals to the discerning eye what is to follow.

Sarah Moon focuses on the same fateful moment in her illustration (1983, pp.356-7), only this time in very different surroundings. The reader's expectations are frustrated at first by both the modern urban context and the "truthful" medium of photography, but once the associative leap is made, the story's impact is irresistible, so striking and apposite is Moon's imagery. The girl is a startled creature caught in the glare of the car's headlights, the darkness of the street creates the same claustrophobic effect as Doré's forest, and the menace implicit in the shiny, cold anonymity of the car—a familiar modern symbol of male status and power—is perhaps more meaningful for a contemporary reader than the sight of the "wolf" himself. In fact, Moon's black-and-white photo-journalistic treatment of this very familiar story capitalizes on our ever-increasing dependence on the visual medium, rendering the text all but extraneous. It also reminds us how familiar we are with the story that these particular images tell, as a brief glance at today's newspapers or magazines will confirm.

A third visualization of this same scene is to be found in the work of Beni Montresor (1991, pp.344-5). Montresor openly acknowledges his debt to Gustave Doré, to the extent of including in his book adapted versions of the three Doré illustrations for this tale (two of which are reproduced here). As a review of page 362 will reveal, the major change introduced by Montresor (apart from the use of color) is in the appearance of the wolf—as urbane as Doré's is feral. What is particularly appealing, at least to the *adult* reader, is the visual pun that the artist (an occasional resident of New York City) makes at the expense of another well-known New Yorker, the writer and man-about-town Tom Wolfe (!). The topicality of this allusion may be compared to the flexibility of the oral tale, as the teller adds a reference to impress and amuse his or her immediate audience. The disadvantage, of course, is that such an addition can only have a temporary appeal: what is familiar today may be forgotten tomorrow.

We return to another Doré illustration (pp.360-1) for the simple reason that it is another masterpiece of psychological insight. Once again, our attention is drawn to eyes, the windows of the soul. As on page 362, we observe the girl's expression of intermingled fear and fascination, not only in her eyes but also in her ambivalent body posture, but now the central focus of the image is surely the wolf. He lies inert, paying no attention to the girl, the granny cap pulled absurdly over his ears, apparently lost in his own gloomy thoughts. Is Doré not implying a certain "sympathy for the Devil" here, as the wolf considers the base indignities to which his appetites have brought him? He will fulfill his destiny as a predator, but he will have no illusions about his shame and depravity. Angela Carter expresses a startlingly similar insight in "The Company of Wolves":

There is a vast melancholy in the canticles of the wolves, melancholy infinite as the forest, endless as these long nights of winter, and yet that ghastly sadness, that mourning for their own, irremediable appetites, can never move the heart, for not one phrase in it hints at the possibility of redemption; grace could not come to the wolf from its own despair, only through some external mediator, so that, sometimes, the beast will look as if he half welcomes the knife that dispatches him. (p.282)

Thus the imminent catastrophe is rendered all the more disturbing by the psychological depth and intensity that Doré brings to the image.

HANSEL AND GRETEL

Arthur Rackham (1867-1939) remains the most popular artist of what has become known as the Golden Age of children's book illustration (1860-1930). He created an appealing fairy world that is delicate and evanescent, an airy, unthreatening place, where the contest between good and evil is played out with little fear of the consequences. His approach is evident in his illustration from "Hansel and Gretel" (1903, p.346), in which the encounter between the children and the witch reveals a Dickensian combination of the realistic and the grotesque, represented by the apparently well-fed, rosy-cheeked children on the one hand, and the spectacularly ugly witch on the other. (Given their desperate plight, it is intriguing how seldom Hansel and Gretel are depicted as manifesting any signs of malnutrition and misery.) Although Rackham's focus is clearly on the *human* drama, the observer is equally drawn in by the picturesque setting: the soothing quality of the sepia tones and the intricate delicacy of the details of wood, leaf, and stone. The attraction of the cottage is certainly not in the sweetness of its candy composition (which Rackham all but ignores) as in its romantic quaintness. We, like the children, long to see what lies beyond the antique bottle panes of the open window. It is not surprising to learn that Rackham's work, which was as popular in the United States as it was in Europe, subsequently provided a source of inspiration for Walt Disney.

Kay Nielsen's visualization (1925, p.347) of almost the same moment in the story produces a very different picture. If Rackham is interested in carefully depicting the bare feet of the children and each hair on the witch's chin, Nielsen (1886–1957) is far more attracted by the nightmarish glamor of the scene with its unearthly cottage, crouching like a fluorescent spider in the middle of a web composed of sinuous, oppressive trees. Here the children are reduced to observers, sharing our own fascination at the otherworldly scene that lies before them. Despite the highly stylized approach, Nielsen's view draws us effectively into the story: the unindividualized children are here cast as our representatives — we too are waiting for that door to open.

Like Sarah Moon in her version of "Little Red Riding Hood" (pp.356-7), Anthony Browne takes the considerable risk of giving "Hansel and Gretel" a modern setting: this family lives in a brick house containing many of the household items that populate our world also. Both artists, however, have been careful to evoke a contemporary setting that is nevertheless distant enough (vaguely mid-twentieth century) not to be exactly identifiable, thereby combining the open-endedness of "once upon a time" with the here and now. In Browne's opening illustration of the parlor

(1981, p.348), the familiar look of modern poverty is immediately apparent in the dirty, peeling wallpaper, the threadbare rug, and in the father's face and demeanor as he looks in vain through what is clearly the "Want" ad section of the newspaper. More arresting, however, is the manner in which Browne manages to underline the crucial aspect of family dynamics and the stepmother's role in the lives of her husband and children. Browne sets her apart from the rest of her family: glamorous and comfortable, she watches a passenger jet take off on television. Through the symbols that permeate the picture—the abandoned "Gretel" doll, the bird mark on the ceiling— Browne paints us a story as meaningful as the words themselves. Illustrators such as Browne and Moon remind us that folk tales, like Shakespeare's dramas, are as pertinent today as they ever were.

It takes no more than a glance at the work of Tony Ross (1989, p.349) to realize that his approach is quite different from that of the other artists in this section: the contemporary cartoon style, the bright colors, the characterization all add to the slapstick mood of this version. (Not surprisingly, Ross also re-writes the text, since it's clear that his style of illustration is not compatible with the serious tone of the Grimms' narrative.) In their different ways, all three of the previous illustrations are relatively static; we are invited to savor (or to absorb) the moment. In this case, however, the moment is fleeting, since the action in Ross's picture is little short of manic; the witch is clearly no stranger to the concept of fast food. In keeping with this frenetic pace, the jokes come thick and fast: the *un*happy face on the mug, the tadpole jelly, the animal entourage ready and willing to partake of the feast—all add to the atmosphere of heedless self-gratification. If Browne's picture conveys a mood of silence and withdrawal, here all is noise and bonhomie, as the witch takes wicked pleasure in beguiling her innocent victims. Ross's approach may lack the historical detail or psychological complexity that dignifies other artists' versions of these tales, but his sense of the absurd provides a vivid reminder of the fairy tale's enduring ability to entertain.

BEAUTY AND THE BEAST

Walter Crane (1845-1915) was one of three particularly talented artists (the other two being Kate Greenaway and Randolph Caldecott) who had the good fortune to collaborate with an equally talented and innovative printer, Edmund Evans. Crane was also very much involved, along with such contemporaries as William Morris, in the Arts and Crafts Movement in England, which sought to re-assert the role of the craftsman in a world that was quickly succumbing to the new phenomenon of mass production. Consequently, we may find in his illustration of "Beauty and the Beast" (1900, pp.350-1) a greater concern with style than with the substance of the story: the flatness of the picture is reminiscent of a Classical frieze, the Beast's more modern attire notwithstanding. Crane freely acknowledged that the timelessness of fairy tales allowed him an artistic licence that he was quite prepared to take advantage of: "I was in the habit of putting in all sorts of subsidiary detail that interested me, and often made them the vehicle for my ideas in furniture and decoration."[1] The preoccupation with decoration and various artistic styles makes this an elegant but at the same time rather detached, even distracting illustration; there is simply no room for the emotional tension that surely fills this encounter.

In strong contrast to the decorous *sang-froid* of Crane's illustration is the ferocity and passion in Alan Barrett's depiction of the Beast (1972, p.343). Over the years, artists have depicted the Beast in a variety of ways, ranging from leonine to monstrous, yet he frequently is given the kind of savage nobility we associate with certain large animals. Barrett's intention, on the other hand, is to provoke a more visceral reaction — something closer to the terror inspired by a Beast that appears irrational, alien, and cruel. From our voyeuristic position as reader, we turn the page only to be confronted by the open jaws of the enraged Beast and thus find ourselves in Beauty's position. For a moment, our identification with the heroine is complete. Curiously enough, Barrett's illustration bears a striking resemblance to the most memorable image from Steven Spielberg's highly successful movie *Jaws* (1975), which might itself be regarded as an important example of the urban legend phenomenon.

A quite different contrast, this time to all the "subsidiary detail"

---

1. Rodney K. Engen, *Walter Crane as a Book Illustrator* (London: Academy Editions, 1975) 5.

in Crane's picture, may be found in the work of Barry Moser (1992, p.359), whose minimalist approach produces an illustration as stark as Crane's is elaborate. It is a trademark of Moser's style to look for the key moments in the story and then reduce them to the specific character — or even gesture — that represents the crux of that particular episode. All distractions of color, descriptive detail, and movement are rejected, and out of the darkness an image emerges that arrests our attention: Beauty and the Beast are playing the strategic and intellectual game of chess. Nancy Willard, the author of the text of this version, clearly intends the chess-game as a metaphor for the psychological intricacy and uncertainty of a developing relationship: "She tried not to show her horror as his claws groped for the pieces, and she had to help him make his moves..."[1] There may be horror, but Moser also conveys tenderness and compassion in Beauty's guiding hand.

SLEEPING BEAUTY

The sophistication of the work of some modern illustrators once again raises the issue of audience: to whom are these pictures addressed? Do they represent another reminder of the anomaly of fairy tales: that although these tales are commonly perceived as children's literature, the artist intuitively responds to their symbolism, which, as we have already seen, can result in a startlingly different interpretation? Examine, for instance, the illustration by Michael Foreman (1978, p.358) for "Briar Rose; or, The Sleeping Beauty," in which the sexual imagery is, to adult eyes, nothing short of startling. In the tradition of the finest illustrators, Foreman acknowledges the depth of the fairy tale by, in effect, providing two pictures in one, since it contains both a narrative and a symbolic level. As with the tale itself, however, the reader sees what he or she is ready to see. There may well be those who object to such an overtly Freudian interpretation, but it is undeniable that such controversy breathes new life into the fairy tale.

It should be noted that this is the only illustration that Foreman provided for the tale (some years later, he illustrated the Perrault version more fully). One may therefore assume that he chose his

---

1. Nancy Willard, *Beauty and the Beast* (New York: Harcourt, 1992) 42.

moment carefully, in order to communicate his interpretation of the tale as eloquently as possible. If we turn to Trina Schart Hyman's depiction of the same tale (1977, pp.352-3), we find ourselves at the other end of the illustrative spectrum, so to speak, in that she tells the tale *primarily* in pictures; as we observed at the outset, this is an instance of the text being given equal, if not secondary consideration, as it is carefully integrated into the design of the double-page spread. There is no single climactic picture, since the intention here is to maintain a continuity of illustration, with the result that setting, characterization, and interpretation are given ample consideration. Thus, while Hyman creates an effective quasi-medieval context for the tale through a combination of architectural and costume detail, it is not at the expense of the human drama. Although there is a modern, positively Technicolor glamor to the principal characters depicted here, there is no denying the excitement that Hyman infuses into this courtyard scene. As we pointed out in our introduction to "Sleeping Beauty," the fate of the princess has a profound effect on the greater community, a fact that Hyman expresses very effectively in this illustration.

We have already seen some evidence, in the shape of James Finn Garner's story from *Politically Correct Bedtime Stories* and Roald Dahl's poem from *Revolting Rhymes*, to suggest that the fairy tale has entered the postmodern age. If further proof is necessary, it can surely be found in *The Stinky Cheese Man and other Fairly Stupid Tales*, by Jon Scieszka and Lane Smith (1992, p.354-5). (The cheerful cynicism of these titles tells a story in itself.) The sophistication of both text and illustration is remarkable; "Giant Story" is little short of a deconstruction of the fairy tale, of storytelling, perhaps even of the book itself. Smith's chaotic collage provides a visual representation of J.R.R. Tolkien's seminal image of the Cauldron of Story, suggesting the ever-bubbling, ever-replenished mixture of human experience and imagination that manifests itself in the fairy tale.

POSTSCRIPT

Nowhere is the role of the visual artist more obvious than in the popular medium of film, synonymous in the world of fairy tale with the work of Walt Disney. Indeed, our familiarity with fairy tales today is attributable almost exclusively to more than half a century of Disney's animated productions.

The transfer from book to screen represents an important qualitative leap in the recipient's experience of the tale. Quality and quantity of the illustrations notwithstanding, the book still provides the reader (or listener) with the text of the story and, thus, imaginative ownership of the material. The reader still has some ability to decide how much of an influence the visual images will have on his or her experience of the narrative. Nevertheless, the number, if not the quality, of pictures is bound to make a difference and, as we have seen, the growing tendency to illustrate fairy tales ever more profusely can have the effect of relegating the text to secondary importance. This predominance of the visual image at the expense of the text is, however, made complete in the medium of film. The most obvious contrast, of course, is the *complete* reliance on the visual image to re-create the story; without any text, each and every detail must be graphically represented and many more details have to be invented, since the fairy tale leaves much to the imagination.

Not least is the problem of how to make the inherently dark side of fairy tales—their violence and cruelty—visually acceptable to a child audience. In *Snow White* (1937), his first animated tale, Disney had to deal with the stepmother's cannibalism, her three attempts to kill Snow White, and her subsequent horrific death. (Such a gruesome "happy ending" is not untypical of the fairy tale. Much of our satisfaction, in fact, derives from the inexorable working-out of justice in the tales, however harsh it may be.) Disney's solution was to reduce or eliminate as much of the violent and cruel material as possible: the diminution of the stepmother's role, the comic characterization of the dwarfs, the addition of domestic scenes with cute animal helpers, and the romantic ending, all to the accompaniment of cheerful song and dance, provide a radical departure from the spirit and essence of the original fairy tale. While Disney was quick to recognize and exploit the visually exciting potential of "scary" scenes which he added to the stories—one of the most memorable scenes from *Sleeping Beauty* (1959) is the battle between the Prince and Maleficent during which she transforms herself into a fire-breathing dragon—the effect was to replace the disturbing or complex elements of the tale with the titillation of violence as spectacle, something Hollywood has always excelled at.

As Jack Zipes makes clear in his discussion of Disney's work (p.427), its shortcomings have less to do with his alteration of the story—the prerogative of every artist— than with his departure from the *spirit* of the fairy tale. As we pointed out at the beginning of this section, in re-working the raw material, the artist's response must be sensitive to its depth of meaning. In the process of translating these stories from book to screen, Disney reduced them to the romantic stereotypes and cliches that have given fairy tales a bad name, especially among feminist critics. Be that as it may, the enormous popularity of his productions makes a statement which surely reveals more about our own attitudes and aspirations than about fairy tale. In this respect, it can be argued that Walt Disney was as much a man of his time as were the Brothers Grimm and Charles Perrault before him; they too manipulated the fairy tale to suit the tastes and expectations of their audience.

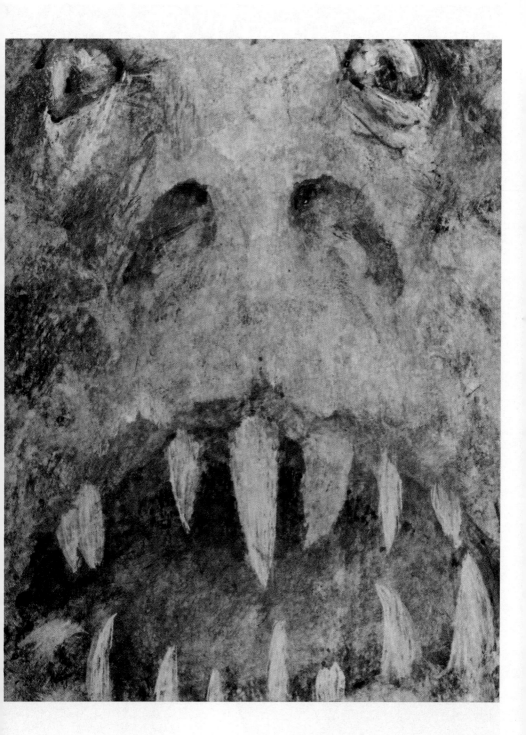

Beauty and the Beast, Alan Barrett

343

Little Red Riding Hood, Beni Montresor

Hansel and Gretel, Arthur Rackham

Hansel and Gretel, Kay Nielsen

Hansel and Gretel, Anthony Browne

Hansel and Gretel, Tony Ross

Beauty and the Beast, Walter Crane

Sleeping Beauty, Trina Schart Hyman

After a little while, they went down from the tower together, hand in hand. Where one drop of blood drains a castle of life, so one kiss can bring it alive again. Then the King and Queen woke up, and so did all their knights and ladies, and everyone looked at each other with astonishment in their sleepy eyes. The horses in the stable stood up and shook themselves, and the grooms scratched their heads and stretched their legs. The hounds began to leap about, barking at nothing and wagging their tails.

THE END

of the evil Stepmother

said "I'll HUFF and SNUFF and

give you three wishes."

The beast changed into

SEVEN DWARVES

HAPPILY EVER AFTER

for a spell had been cast by a Wicked Witch

Once upon a time

"That's your story?" said Jack.
"You've got to be kidding. That's not a
Fairly Stupid Tale. That's an Incredibly Stupid Tale.
That's an Unbelievably Stupid Tale. That is
the Most Stupid Tale I Ever— *awwwk!*"
The Giant grabbed Jack and dragged him to the next page.

Giant Story, Lane Smith

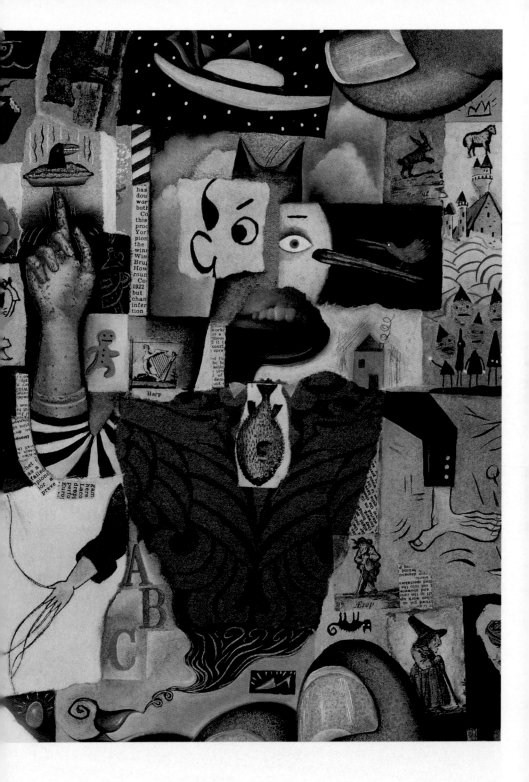

355

Little Red Riding Hood, Sarah Moon

Sleeping Beauty, Michael Foreman

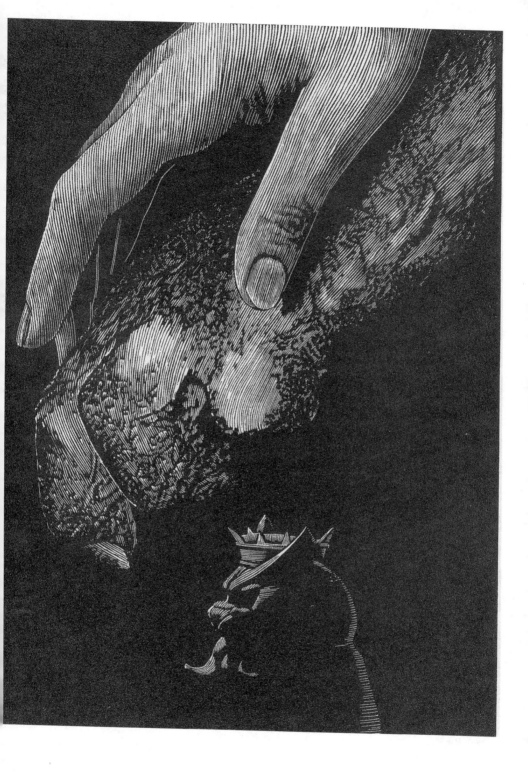

Beauty and the Beast, Barry Moser

Little Red Riding Hood, Gustav Doré

Little Red Riding Hood, Gustav Doré

CRITICISM

SERIOUS critical attention to the folk-fairy tale is essentially a phenomenon of the twentieth century. As we have noted in our introduction, discussion prior to that tended to be dismissive, even condemnatory, despite the more positive testimonials of various literary figures. In the English-speaking world, a breakthrough of sorts came with the publication of the *Blue Fairy Book*, edited by the eminent scholar Andrew Lang, which was received with such enthusiasm as to inspire numerous additional volumes in the "color" fairy book series. As a folklorist, Lang was a representative of a new field of study that seized upon the folk tale as a repository of valuable information about traditional beliefs, superstitions, and customs. This field of knowledge was gradually absorbed into the larger discipline of anthropology, culminating in the monumental project, initiated in Finland by Antti Aarne and later taken on by the American Stith Thompson, to produce a comprehensive index of types and motifs to be found in the entire *corpus* of folk tale.

Folk-fairy tale scholarship has long prospered in the German-speaking world, in part as the legacy of the Grimm Brothers and their Romantic colleagues. Much of this valuable work remains unavailable in English, but fortunately several works by the Swiss scholar Max Lüthi have been translated, an excerpt from one of which is included here. Lüthi's major concern is to demonstrate the folk-fairy tale's preoccupation with, and relevance for, humanity; his goal is to remedy the fact that "[t]he grownup, still under the influence of the Enlightenment and realism, quickly turns away from the fairy tale with a feeling of contempt." The error in this reaction, claims Lüthi, can be seen in the fact that "... in modern art, fascination with the fairy tale is everywhere evident" (p.375).

Bruno Bettelheim's interest in the folk-fairy tale is not so much literary as psychological. As a renowned child psychologist, Bettelheim came to write his influential work *The Uses of Enchantment* (1976) in the conviction that "... more can be learned from [folk-fairy tales] about the inner problems of human beings, and of the right solutions to their predicaments in any society, than from any other type of story within a child's comprehension" (p.378). It has been argued that in his desire to demonstrate the psychic merits of the folk-fairy tale, Bettelheim is selective not only in the tales he chooses to discuss, but even in the *versions* thereof: what may hold true for version A may well be contradicted by version B. Nevertheless, there is no denying that the publication of his book renewed interest in, and appreciation of, the folk-fairy tale.

The controversial role of gender, both in characterization and in reader-reception, is the topic that Kay Stone considers in "The Misuses of Enchantment" (her choice of title should be noted as itself a comment on Bettelheim's book). Sexual stereotyping in the folk-fairy tale has been a contentious issue for feminist scholars for several decades. Stone's approach to the subject is illuminating in that she balances discussion of theory with her findings "in the field," so to speak. While it is fascinating to explore the historical, psychological, or cultural aspects of the tale, it is salutary to be reminded of the views of "the common reader," which may cause us to stop and reflect upon the distance we have come.

Like Stone, Marina Warner approaches fairy tales from a feminist perspective, but while Stone is interested in the contemporary response to well-established versions of a classic tale, Warner explores the manner in which a tale has continued to evolve as writers, artists, and film-makers identify and exploit aspects of the tale that speak to current preoccupations — in this case, the abiding fascination with the wild man. As Warner points out: "... in the cascade of deliberate revisions of ["Beauty and the Beast"], Beauty stands in need of the Beast, rather than vice versa, and the

Beast's beastliness is good, even adorable" (p.416). Her discussion testifies to the extraordinary energy that remains in these stories and also to the extent to which each re-telling reveals our ever-changing views about ourselves and the world we live in.

Nobody can deny that the name most closely connected to the fairy tale in the twentieth century has been that of Walt Disney; it is hardly an exaggeration to say that for many children, the term "fairy tale" signifies a cartoon rather than a book. As a critic who has long been interested in the social context of the fairy tale, Jack Zipes sees Disney's influence as nothing less than "a cultural stranglehold" and demonstrates in this provocative article the extent to which Disney's personal values and attitudes are conveyed through his movies. While much the same observation could be made of the publications of Charles Perrault and the Grimm Brothers, it is Zipes's contention that in exploiting the new medium of film, Disney gained access to an extraordinarily powerful means of communication—and the fairy tale was changed for ever.

THE FAIRY-TALE HERO: THE IMAGE OF MAN IN THE FAIRY TALE

Max Lüthi

Is it mere chance that the principal characters we have encountered in our studies are more often female than male: Sleeping Beauty; the Greek princess who kneaded a husband for herself out of groats, sugar, and almonds; good little Anny in the story of the little earth-cow; Rapunzel; the riddle princesses; and the clever peasant girls? The only corresponding male figures we have seen in the European fairy tales are the dragon slayer and that clever poser of riddles, Petit-Jean. Is this preponderance of women typical? Does our sampling reflect the true situation? If we are asked just which fairy-tale figures are generally best known, we immediately think of Sleeping Beauty, Cinderella, Snow White, Little Red Riding Hood, Rapunzel, The Princess in Disguise, and Goldmarie in "Mother Hulda"—all female figures. In "Hansel and Gretel" and in "Brother and Sister," the girl also plays the leading role. We find ourselves nearly at a loss when called upon for the names of male protagonists: Iron Hans and Tom Thumb, perhaps; the Brave Little Tailor, Strong Hans, and Lucky Hans — but here we are already in the realm of the folktale jest. How can one explain this peculiar predominance of women and girls? All the names mentioned are taken from the Grimm brothers' collection. Despite the existence of innumerable other collections, this one today is, in German-speaking countries, almost the sole surviving source for the public at large of real contact with the fairy tale. Now the Grimm brothers' informants were predominantly women. And today children learn fairy tales mainly from their mothers, grandmothers, aunts, and female kindergarten and school teachers. Thus, it is natural that the principal figures are mostly women. Moreover, the child — whether boy or girl — is basically closer to the feminine than the masculine, living in the domain of the mother and female teachers and not yet that of the father and male teachers. The fairy tales which grownups remember are those of their childhood. Furthermore, our era, whose character, despite everything, is still determined by men, feels the strong and clear need for a complementary antipole. The woman is assigned a privileged position, not only by social custom; in art and literature, as well, she has occupied a central position since the time of the troubadours and the Mariology of the late Middle Ages. In painting and in the novel, she has been the subject of persistent interest and loving concern. Thus, it comes as no surprise that she also plays a significant role in the fairy tale — which for centuries was one of the most vital and indirectly influential art forms in Europe — the feminine component, that part of man closer to nature, had to come to the forefront to compensate for the technological and economic system created by the masculine spirit, which dominated the external world of reality.

However, that was a peculiarity of the era. Tellers of fairy tales were not always predominantly women, and not always was existence influenced so strongly by the masculine spirit that the antipole asserted itself with such conspicuous force in art. If we go beyond *Grimm's Fairy Tales* and leaf through the many volumes of the *Märchen der Weltliteratur* (Fairy Tales of World Literature), *Das Gesicht der Völker* (The Face of the Peoples), or Richard M. Dorson's *Folktales of the World*, we see that there are at least as many masculine as feminine protagonists, and that, in general, the masculine figures may even predominate, as they do in the myths. But one thing is quite clear: at the focal point in the fairy tale stands *man*. One cannot say this of the local legend and saint's legend: they portray the intrusion of another world upon our own existence; myths tell of gods; and among primitive peoples, animal stories predominate. The hero of the European fairy tale, however, is *man*. In the minds of the ancient Greeks, the earlier animal gods assumed human form. The humanism of the Greek classical period became a basic element of European culture. Thus, a connection no doubt exists between this European or Indo-European attribute and our fairy tales, which, in the main, concern not animals, as in the stories of primitive peoples, but men.

The European fairy tale draws a picture of man and shows him in his confrontation with the world. Since our children are interested in fairy tales in their most receptive years, and since even today almost all children have a considerable number of fairy tales which are told or read to them or which they read themselves, it is worthwhile to ask what sort of picture of man they find there. Can one say that the large number of fairy tales present a coherent picture? In a certain sense, yes. The fairy-tale hero, or heroine, to be sure, is sometimes a rollicking daredevil and sometimes a silent sufferer; at times a lazybones and at times a diligent helper; often sly and wily but just as often open and honest. At times he is a shrewd fellow, an undaunted solver of riddles, a brave fighter; at others, he is a stupid person or one who sits down and begins to cry every time he encounters difficulty. There are friendly and compassionate fairy-tale heroes, but others that are merciless and perfidious. To say nothing of the differences in social class: princess and Cinderella, prince and swineherd. Or must we perhaps say something about them? Are we not perplexed by something we see at just this point? Surprisingly, the difference in social class is often only apparent. The goosegirl, in reality, is not at all one of the common folk but a princess forced into her lowly role by her servant girl. And the gardener boy with the mangy hair, whom the beautiful princess observes every morning, is, in reality, a prince who has tied an animal hide over his golden hair.

Thus, in the fairy tale, one and the same person can abruptly change from a mangy-headed youth into one with golden hair, and the despised Cinderella can suddenly turn into a dancer in a radiant gown at whom all gaze in wonder. The one considered to be stupid or loutish often turns out to be the wisest and cleverest of all. In addition, the real swineherd can unexpectedly become the princess's husband, and the poor girl can marry the prince or the king and thus be raised to royal status.

In the fairy tale, all things are possible, not just in the sense that all sorts of miracles occur, but in the sense just mentioned: the lowest can rise to the highest position, and those in the highest position—evil queens, princes, princesses, government ministers—can fall and be destroyed. It has therefore been said that fairy tales derive from the wishful thinking of poor people or those who have been unsuccessful or slighted. But such psychological and sociological interpretations are too limited. Wish dreams and wishful thinking play a part in fairy tales, just as they do in all human matters, and social tensions and yearnings also are reflected in them.

Yet these are only superficial aspects. Fairy-tale figures have an immediate appeal. The king, the princess, a dragon, a witch, gold, crystal, pitch, and ashes—these things are, for the human imagination, age-old symbols for what is high, noble, and pure or dangerous, bestial, and unfathomable; what is genuine and true, or what is sordid and false. The fairy tale often depicts how a penniless wretch becomes wealthy, a maid becomes queen, a disheveled man is changed into a youth with golden hair, or a toad, bear, ape, or dog is transformed into a beautiful maiden or handsome youth. Here, we feel at once the capacity for change of man in general. The focal point is not the rise of the servant to his position of master, not the esteem and recognition accorded the former outcast child; these are images for something more fundamental: man's deliverance from an unauthentic existence and his commencement of a true one. When the real princess lets herself be forced into the role of a goose girl while the lowly maid arrogates to herself the dominant position, this means that a false, ignoble side of the total personality gains control and suppresses that which is truly regal. When the prince marries the witch's ugly daughter instead of his bride-to-be, he has lost the way to his own soul and given himself up to a strange demon. The psychologist views things in this way, assuming that the fairy tale depicts processes within the mind. Although such specialized interpretations are often risky, it is evident that more is involved for both the author and his hearers than mere external action when the fairy tale tells how the hero conquers the dragon, marries the princess, and becomes king.

In general, one can say that the fairy tale depicts processes of development and maturation. Every man has within him an ideal image, and to be king, to wear a crown, is an image for the ascent to the highest attainable realms. And every man has within him his own secret kingdom. The visible kingdom, the figure of the princess and her bridegroom, are fascinating, influential, and oft-cited even in democratic societies because they have a symbolic force. To be king does not mean just to have power; in the modern world, kings and queens have been relieved of almost all their material power. One might say they have been freed of it and by this have acquired even greater symbolic appeal. To be a king is an image for complete self-realization; the crown and royal robe which play such a great role in the fairy tale make visible the splendor and brilliance of the great perfection achieved inwardly. They call to mind an analogous phenomenon in the saint's legend, the halo, which likewise renders visible the inward brilliance. When Goldmarie, after proving herself in the realm of Mother Hulda, is showered with gold, no one doubts that this is an image—one which reveals the girl's good soul. And when other fairy-tale heroines comb golden flowers out of their hair, or when a flower shoots out of the ground at their every step, we likewise immediately take it to be symbolic. Not only alchemists, but people generally feel gold to be a representative for a higher human and cosmic perfection. Kingship, like gold and the royal robe, has symbolic significance and power in the fairy tale. It may well be—as psychologists of the Jungian school assert—that the marriage with the animal bride or animal prince, the union of the king with the armless mute lost in the forest, and the wedding of the princess and the goatherd are images for the union of disparities in the human soul, for the awareness of a hitherto unrecognized spiritual strength, and for the maturation into a complete human personality. In any event, the fairy tale depicts over and over an upward development, the overcoming of mortal dangers and seemingly insoluble problems, the path toward marriage with the prince or princess, toward kingship or gold and jewels. The image of man portrayed in the fairy tale—or, rather, one aspect of this image—is that of one who has the capability to rise above himself, has within him the yearning for the highest things, and is also able to attain them. We can be sure that children, engrossed in the story as it is told to them, do not understand this in all its implications; but, what is more important, they can sense it. The child, at the fairy-tale age, is fascinated not by the upward social movement but by the overcoming of dangers and entry into the realm of glory, whether this is depicted as the realm of the sun and stars or as an earthly kingdom of unearthly splendor.

But the image of man as it appears in the fairy tale can be defined from yet another aspect upon closer examination. The fairy-tale hero is essentially a wanderer. Whereas the events in the local legend usually take place in the hometown or its vicinity, the fairy tale time and again sends its heroes out into the world. Sometimes the parents are too poor to be able to keep their children, at times the hero is forced away by a command or enticed away by a contest, or it may be merely that the hero decides to go out in search of adventure. In a Low German fairy tale, the father sends his two eldest sons out into the world as punishment, but does the same thing to his youngest son as a reward. Nothing shows more clearly that the fairy tale will use any excuse to make its hero a wanderer and lead him far away, often to the stars, to the bottom of the sea, to a region below the earth, or to a kingdom at the end of the world. The female protagonist is also frequently removed to a distant castle or abducted to that place by an animal-husband. This wandering, or soaring, over great distances conveys an impression of freedom and ease that is further strengthened by other characteristics in the fairy tale which also convey a feeling of freedom. Whereas in the local legends man is endowed from the very beginning with something stifling and unfree by stagnation in the ancestral village and dumbfounded gazing at the frightful phenomenon, the fairy-tale hero appears as a free-moving wanderer. In the local legend, man is an impassioned dreamer, a visionary; the fairy-tale hero, however, strides from place to place without much concern or astonishment. The other worldly beings which he encounters interest him only as helpers or opponents and do not inspire him with either curiosity, a thirst for knowledge, or a vague fear of the supernatural. The fairy tale depicts its heroes not as observing and fearful but as moving and active. In the local legend, man is embedded in the society of his village, not only that of the living, but also that of the dead. He is also rooted in the countryside or town in which he lives. The wild people in the forest and the mountains and the water sprites and poltergeists inhabit the general surroundings. The fairy-tale hero, however, breaks away from his home and goes out into the world. He is almost always alone; if there are two brothers, they separate at a certain crossroads and each experiences the decisive adventure alone. Frequently the fairy-tale hero does not return to his home town. When he sets forth to save a king's daughter or accomplish a difficult task, he usually does not know how he will accomplish his purpose. But along the way he meets a little old man, shares his bread with him, and gets from him the advice that will lead him to his goal. Or he meets a wild animal, pulls out a thorn that was hurting it, and thus gains the help of the thankful beast, whose abilities just suffice to solve his problem. In the local legend, people summon the priest or Capuchin to help in conjuring spirits, but the fairy-tale hero enters strange lands all alone and there has the decisive confrontation. The priest or Capuchin is not only a member of the village community, everyone knows the source of his helping powers: the salvation of the Christian church, the grace of God. The helping animals and other supernatural beings in the fairy tale are, however, usually just as isolated as the fairy-tale hero himself. The latter takes their advice and magic gifts nonchalantly, uses them at the decisive moment, and then no longer thinks about them. He doesn't ponder over the mysterious forces or where his helpers have come from; everything he experiences seems natural to him and he is carried along by this help, which he has earned often without his knowledge. The fairy-tale hero quite frequently is the youngest son, an orphan, a despised Cinderella or poor goatherd, and this all contributes to making the hero appear isolated; the prince, princess, and king, as well, at the very pinnacle of society, are in their own way detached, absolute, and isolated.

Local legends and fairy tales, which have existed for centuries side by side among the common folk, complement one another. Local legends originate among the common people half spontaneously and half under the influence of simple traditions and ask, we might say, the anxious question, "What is man, what is the world?" Fairy tales certainly do not originate among simple folk but with great poets, perhaps the so-called "initiated," or religious, poets; and, in a sense, they provide an answer. In the local legend, one senses the anxiety of man, who, though apparently a part of the community of his fellow men, finds himself ultimately confronted with an uncanny world which he finds hard to comprehend and which threatens him with death. The fairy tale, however, presents its hero as one who, though not comprehending ultimate relationships, is led safely through the dangerous, unfamiliar world. The fairy-tale hero is gifted, in the literal sense of the word. Supernatural beings lavish their gifts on him and help him through battles and perils. In the fairy tale, too, the ungifted, the unblessed, appear. Usually, they are the older brothers or sisters of the hero or heroine. They are often deceitful, wicked, envious, cold-hearted, or dissolute—though this is by no means always the case. It may be that they just don't come across any helping animal or little man; they are the unblessed. The hearer does not, however, identify with them, but with the hero, who makes his way through the world alone—and for just this reason is free and able to establish contact with essential things. Usually, it is his unconsciously correct behavior that gains him the help of the animal with the magic powers or some other supernatural creature. This behavior, however, need not be moral in the strict sense. The idler is also a favorite of the fairy tale; it may be that he is given the very thing he wants and needs most: that his every wish is fulfilled without his having to move a finger. In the fairy tale about the frog-king, the heroine who repeatedly tries to avoid keeping her promise and finally flings the irksome frog against the wall in order to kill it is neither kind, compassionate, nor even dutiful. But by flinging the frog against the wall, she has, without knowing it, fulfilled the secret conditions for the release of the enchanted prince who had been transformed into a frog. The hero and heroine in the fairy tale do the right thing, they hit the right key; they are heaven's favorites. The local legend, provided it is not jesting in tone, usually portrays man as unblessed, unsuccessful, and as one who, despite his deep involvement in the community, must face life's ultimate questions alone and uncertain. The fairy tale sees man as one who is essentially isolated but who, for just this reason—because he is not rigidly committed, not tied down—can establish relationships with anything in the world. And the world of the fairy tale includes not just the earth, but the entire cosmos. In the local legend, man is seemingly integrated in the community, but inwardly, essentially, he is alone. The fairy-tale hero is seemingly isolated, but has the capacity for universal relationships. Certainly, we can say that both are true portrayals of man. The local legend expresses a basic human condition: although deeply entrenched in human institutions, man feels abandoned, cast into a threatening world which he can neither understand nor view as a whole. The fairy tale, however, which also knows of failure and depicts it in its secondary characters, shows in its heroes that, despite our ignorance of ultimate things, it is possible to find a secure place in the world. The fairy-tale hero also does not perceive the world as a whole, but he puts his trust in and is accepted by it. As if led by an invisible force and with the confidence of a sleepwalker, he follows the right course. He is isolated and at the same time in touch with all things. The fairy tale is a poetic vision of man and his relationship to the world, a vision that for centuries inspired the fairy tale's hearers with strength and confidence because they sensed the fundamental truth of this vision. Even though man may feel outcast and abandoned in the world, like one groping in the dark, is he not in the course of his life led from step to step and guided safely by a thousand aids? The fairy tale, however, not only inspires trust and confidence; it also provides a sharply defined image of man: isolated, yet capable of universal relationships. It is salutary that in our era, which has experienced the loss of individuality, nationalism, and impending nihilism, our children are presented with just such an image of man in the fairy tales they hear and absorb. This image is all the more effective for having proceeded naturally from the over-all style of the fairy tale. The fairy-tale technique—the sharp lines, the two-dimensional, sublimating portrayal we have so often observed as well as the encapsulating of the individual episodes and motifs—this entire technique is isolating, and only for this reason can it interconnect all things so effortlessly. The image of man in the fairy tale, the figure of the hero, grows out of its over-all style; this gives it a persuasive power which cannot fail to impress even the realistically minded listener.

Every type of fairy tale portrays events which can safely be interpreted as images for psychological or cosmic processes. Every single fairy tale has a particular message. A beautiful girl's eyes are cruelly torn out and then, one year and a day later, are replaced and can see seven times as clearly as before. Another fairy-tale heroine is locked up in a box by her wicked mother-in-law and hung in the chimney, where she remains without nourishment until her husband returns from the war; yet the smoked woman does not die of hunger — indeed, she emerges from her box younger and more beautiful. Such stories make the listener feel how suffering can purify and strengthen. In speaking of the wisdom in fairy tales, one is usually thinking of similar passages in particular fairy tales. Much more powerful, however, is the overall image of man and the world as portrayed in folk fairy tales generally. This image recurs in a large number of tales and makes a profound impression on the listener — formerly, illiterate grownups; today, children. Is this image in accord with our present-day view of life and the world?

Modern literature, narrative as well as dramatic, is characterized by a strange turning away from the heroic figure. This begins as far back as Naturalism, where the coachman or the cleaning woman takes the place of the tragic hero, the kings and noble ladies, and where the masses — the weavers, for example — can take the place of the individual. In the modern novel, interest centers on impersonal forces, subconscious powers, and processes transcending the individual. If an individual does become the center of attention, he is often an anti-hero, or, as he is sometimes called, the passive or negative hero. The stories of Franz Kafka, which influence so much of present-day literature, have been characterized as out-and-out anti-fairy tales. And yet they have much in common with fairy tales. Their figures, like those of the fairy tale, are not primarily individuals, personalities, characters, but simply figures: doers and receivers of the action. They are no more masters of their destiny than are the figures in the fairy tale. They move through a world which they do not understand but in which they are nevertheless involved. This they have in common with the figures of the fairy tale: they do not perceive their relationship to the world about them. Whereas Kafka's figures stand helpless and despairing amidst the confusion of relationships they do not understand, the fairy-tale hero is happy in his contacts. The fairy tale is the poetic expression of the confidence that we are secure in a world not destitute of sense, that we can adapt ourselves to it and act and live even if we cannot view or comprehend the world as a whole. The preference of modern literature for the passive hero, the negative hero, is not without parallel in the fairy tale. The simpleton or dejected person who sits down on a stone and cries is not able to help himself, but help comes to him. The fairy tale, too, has a partiality for the negative hero: the insignificant, the neglected, the helpless. But he unexpectedly proves to be strong, noble, and blessed. The spirit of the folk fairy tale parallels that in modern literature to a degree, but then the listener is relieved of his feeling of emptiness and filled with confidence. The grownup, still under the influence of the Enlightenment and realism, quickly turns away from the fairy tale with a feeling of contempt. But in modern art, fascination with the fairy tale is everywhere evident. The turning away from descriptive realism, from the mere description of external reality in itself, implies an approach to the fairy tale. The same can be said of the fantastic mixtures of human, animal, vegetable, and mineral, which, like the fairy tale, bring all things into relationship with one another. Modern architecture has a great preference for what is light, bright, and transparent; one often refers to the dematerialization in architecture, the sublimation of matter. The sublimation of all material things, however, is one of the basic characteristics of fairy-tale style. We find crystal-clear description combined with elusive, mysterious meaning in fairy tales, in modern lyric poetry, and in Ernst Jünger and Franz Kafka, who has said that true reality is always unrealistic. The modern American writer W.H. Auden has said, "The sort of pleasure we get from folk fairy tales seems to me similar to that which we derive from Mallarmé's poems or from abstract painting." We are not surprised at such a statement. The fairy tale is a basic form of literature, and of art in general. The ease and calm assurance with which it stylizes, sublimates, and abstracts makes it the quintessence of the poetic process, and art in the twentieth century has again been receptive to it. We no longer view it as mere entertainment for children and those of childlike disposition. The psychologist, the pedagogue, knows that the fairy tale is a fundamental building block and an outstanding aid in development for the child; the art theorist perceives in the fairy tale—in which reality and unreality, freedom and necessity, unite—an archetypal form of literature which helps lay the groundwork for all literature, for all art. We have attempted to show, in addition, that the fairy tale presents an image of man which follows almost automatically from its over-all style. The fairy-tale style isolates and unites: its hero is thus isolated and, for this very reason, capable of entering into universal relationships. The style of the fairy tale and its image of man are of timeless validity and, at the same time, of specific significance in our age. Thus, we must hope that despite the one-sided rationalistic outlook of many grownups, it will not be neglected and forgotten by our children and by the arts.

THE STRUGGLE FOR MEANING

Bruno Bettelheim

IF we hope to live not just from moment to moment, but in true consciousness of our existence, then our greatest need and most difficult achievement is to find meaning in our lives. It is well known how many have lost the will to live, and have stopped trying, because such meaning has evaded them. An understanding of the meaning of one's life is not suddenly acquired at a particular age, not even when one has reached chronological maturity. On the contrary, gaining a secure understanding of what the meaning of one's life may or ought to be—this is what constitutes having attained psychological maturity. And this achievement is the end result of a long development: at each age we seek, and must be able to find, some modicum of meaning congruent with how our minds and understanding have already developed.

Contrary to the ancient myth, wisdom does not burst forth fully developed like Athena out of Zeus's head; it is built up, small step by small step, from most irrational beginnings. Only in adulthood can an intelligent understanding of the meaning of one's existence in this world be gained from one's experiences in it. Unfortunately, too many parents want their children's minds to function as their own do—as if mature understanding of ourselves and the world, and our ideas about the meaning of life, did not have to develop as slowly as our bodies and minds.

Today, as in times past, the most important and also the most difficult task in raising a child is helping him to find meaning in life. Many growth experiences are needed to achieve this. The child, as he develops, must learn step by step to understand himself better; with this he becomes more able to understand others, and eventually can relate to them in ways which are mutually satisfying and meaningful.

To find deeper meaning, one must become able to transcend the narrow confines of a self-centered existence and believe that one will make a significant contribution to life — if not right now, then at some future time. This feeling is necessary if a person is to be satisfied with himself and with what he is doing. In order not to be at the mercy of the vagaries of life, one must develop one's inner resources, so that one's emotions, imagination, and intellect mutually support and enrich one another. Our positive feelings give us the strength to develop our rationality; only hope for the future can sustain us in the adversities we unavoidably encounter.

As an educator and therapist of severely disturbed children, my main task was to restore meaning to their lives. This work made it obvious to me that if children were reared so that life was meaningful to them, they would not need special help. I was confronted with the problem of deducing what experiences in a child's life are most suited to promote his ability to find meaning in his life; to endow life in general with more meaning. Regarding this task, nothing is more important than the impact of parents and others who take care of the child; second in importance is our cultural heritage, when transmitted to the child in the right manner. When children are young, it is literature that carries such information best.

Given this fact, I became deeply dissatisfied with much of the literature intended to develop the child's mind and personality, because it fails to stimulate and nurture those resources he needs most in order to cope with his difficult inner problems. The preprimers and primers from which he is taught to read in school are designed to teach the necessary skills, irrespective of meaning. The overwhelming bulk of the rest of so-called "children's literature" attempts to entertain or to inform, or both. But most of

377

these books are so shallow in substance that little of significance can be gained from them. The acquisition of skills, including the ability to read, becomes devalued when what one has learned to read adds nothing of importance to one's life.

We all tend to assess the future merits of an activity on the basis of what it offers now. But this is especially true for the child, who, much more than the adult, lives in the present and, although he has anxieties about his future, has only the vaguest notions of what it may require or be like. The idea that learning to read may enable one later to enrich one's life is experienced as an empty promise when the stories the child listens to, or is reading at the moment, are vacuous. The worst feature of these children's books is that they cheat the child of what he ought to gain from the experience of literature: access to deeper meaning, and that which is meaningful to him at his stage of development.

For a story truly to hold the child's attention, it must entertain him and arouse his curiosity. But to enrich his life, it must stimulate his imagination; help him to develop his intellect and to clarify his emotions; be attuned to his anxieties and aspirations; give full recognition to his difficulties, while at the same time suggesting solutions to the problems which perturb him. In short, it must at one and the same time relate to all aspects of his personality — and this without ever belittling but, on the contrary, giving full credence to the seriousness of the child's predicaments, while simultaneously promoting confidence in himself and in his future.

In all these and many other respects, of the entire "children's literature" — with rare exceptions — nothing can be as enriching and satisfying to child and adult alike as the folk fairy tale. True, on an overt level fairy tales teach little about the specific conditions of life in modern mass society; these tales were created long before it came into being. But more can be learned from them about the inner problems of human beings, and of the right solutions to their predicaments in any society, than from any other type of story within a child's comprehension. Since the child at every moment of his life is exposed to the society in which he lives, he will certainly learn to cope with its conditions, provided his inner resources permit him to do so.

Just because his life is often bewildering to him, the child needs even more to be given the chance to understand himself in this complex world with which he must learn to cope. To be able to do so, the child must be helped to make some coherent sense out of the turmoil of his feelings. He needs ideas on how to bring his inner house into order, and on that basis be able to create order in his life. He needs—and this hardly requires emphasis at this moment in our history—a moral education which subtly, and by implication only, conveys to him the advantages of moral behavior, not through abstract ethical concepts but through that which seems tangibly right and therefore meaningful to him.

The child finds this kind of meaning through fairy tales. Like many other modern psychological insights, this was anticipated long ago by poets. The German poet Schiller wrote: "Deeper meaning resides in the fairy tales told to me in my childhood than in the truth that is taught by life." (*The Piccolomini*, III, 4.)

Through the centuries (if not millennia) during which, in their retelling, fairy tales became ever more refined, they came to convey at the same time overt and covert meanings—came to speak simultaneously to all levels of the human personality, communicating in a manner which reaches the uneducated mind of the child as well as that of the sophisticated adult. Applying the psychoanalytic model of the human personality, fairy tales carry important messages to the conscious, the preconscious, and the unconscious mind, on whatever level each is functioning at the time. By dealing with universal human problems, particularly those which preoccupy the child's mind, these stories speak to his budding ego and encourage its development, while at the same time relieving preconscious and unconscious pressures. As the stories unfold, they give conscious credence and body to id pressures and show ways to satisfy these that are in line with ego and super-ego requirements.

But my interest in fairy tales is not the result of such a technical analysis of their merits. It is, on the contrary, the consequence of asking myself why, in my experience, children—normal and abnormal alike, and at all levels of intelligence—find folk fairy tales more satisfying than all other children's stories.

The more I tried to understand why these stories are so successful at enriching the inner life of the child, the more I realized that these tales, in a much deeper sense than any other reading material, start where the child really is in his psychological and emotional being. They speak about his severe inner pressures in a way that the child unconsciously understands, and—without belittling the most serious inner struggles which growing up entails—offer examples of both temporary and permanent solutions to pressing difficulties.

FAIRY TALES AND THE EXISTENTIAL PREDICAMENT

In order to master the psychological problems of growing up—overcoming narcissistic disappointments, oedipal dilemmas, sibling rivalries; becoming able to relinquish childhood dependencies; gaining a feeling of selfhood and of self-worth, and a sense of moral obligation—a child needs to understand what is going on within his conscious self so that he can also cope with that which goes on in his unconscious. He can achieve this understanding, and with it the ability to cope, not through rational comprehension of the nature and content of his unconscious, but by becoming familiar with it through spinning out daydreams—ruminating, rearranging, and fantasizing about suitable story elements in response to unconscious pressures. By doing this, the child fits unconscious content into conscious fantasies, which then enable him to deal with that content. It is here that fairy tales have unequaled value, because they offer new dimensions to the child's imagination which would be impossible for him to discover as truly on his own. Even more important, the form and structure of fairy tales suggest images to the child by which he can structure his daydreams and with them give better direction to his life.

In child or adult, the unconscious is a powerful determinant of behavior. When the unconscious is repressed and its content denied entrance into awareness, then eventually the person's conscious mind will be partially overwhelmed by derivatives of these unconscious elements, or else he is forced to keep such rigid, compulsive control over them that his personality may become severely crippled. But when unconscious material *is* to some degree permitted to come to awareness and worked through in imagination, its potential for causing harm—to ourselves or others—is much reduced; some of its forces can then be made to serve positive purposes. However, the prevalent parental belief is that a child must be diverted from what troubles him most: his

formless, nameless anxieties, and his chaotic, angry, and even violent fantasies. Many parents believe that only conscious reality or
pleasant and wish-fulfilling images should be presented to the
child—that he should be exposed only to the sunny side of
things. But such one-sided fare nourishes the mind only in a one-
sided way, and real life is not all sunny.

There is a widespread refusal to let children know that the
source of much that goes wrong in life is due to our very own
natures—the propensity of all men for acting aggressively, asocial-
ly, selfishly, out of anger and anxiety. Instead, we want our children
to believe that, inherently, all men are good. But children know
that *they* are not always good; and often, even when they are, they
would prefer not to be. This contradicts what they are told by
their parents, and therefore makes the child a monster in his own
eyes.

The dominant culture wishes to pretend, particularly where
children are concerned, that the dark side of man does not exist,
and professes a belief in an optimistic meliorism. Psychoanalysis
itself is viewed as having the purpose of making life easy—but
this is not what its founder intended. Psychoanalysis was created
to enable man to accept the problematic nature of life without
being defeated by it, or giving in to escapism. Freud's prescription
is that only by struggling courageously against what seem like
overwhelming odds can man succeed in wringing meaning out of
his existence.

This is exactly the message that fairy tales get across to the child
in manifold form: that a struggle against severe difficulties in life is
unavoidable, is an intrinsic part of human existence—but that if
one does not shy away, but steadfastly meets unexpected and often
unjust hardships, one masters all obstacles and at the end emerges
victorious.

Modern stories written for young children mainly avoid these
existential problems, although they are crucial issues for all of us.
The child needs most particularly to be given suggestions in symbolic form about how he may deal with these issues and grow
safely into maturity. "Safe" stories mention neither death nor
aging, the limits to our existence, nor the wish for eternal life. The
fairy tale, by contrast, confronts the child squarely with the basic
human predicaments.

For example, many fairy stories begin with the death of a mother or father; in these tales the death of the parent creates the most agonizing problems, as it (or the fear of it) does in real life. Other stories tell about an aging parent who decides that the time has come to let the new generation take over. But before this can happen, the successor has to prove himself capable and worthy. The Brothers Grimm's story "The Three Feathers" begins: "There was once upon a time a king who had three sons.... When the king had become old and weak, and was thinking of his end, he did not know which of his sons should inherit the kingdom after him." In order to decide, the king sets all his sons a difficult task; the son who meets it best "shall be king after my death."

It is characteristic of fairy tales to state an existential dilemma briefly and pointedly. This permits the child to come to grips with the problem in its most essential form, where a more complex plot would confuse matters for him. The fairy tale simplifies all situations. Its figures are clearly drawn; and details, unless very important, are eliminated. All characters are typical rather than unique.

Contrary to what takes place in many modern children's stories, in fairy tales evil is as omnipresent as virtue. In practically every fairy tale good and evil are given body in the form of some figures and their actions, as good and evil are omnipresent in life and the propensities for both are present in every man. It is this duality which poses the moral problem, and requires the struggle to solve it.

Evil is not without its attractions — symbolized by the mighty giant or dragon, the power of the witch, the cunning queen in "Snow White" — and often it is temporarily in the ascendancy. In many fairy tales a usurper succeeds for a time in seizing the place which rightfully belongs to the hero — as the wicked sisters do in "Cinderella." It is not that the evildoer is punished at the story's end which makes immersing oneself in fairy stories an experience in moral education, although this is part of it. In fairy tales, as in life, punishment or fear of it is only a limited deterrent to crime. The conviction that crime does not pay is a much more effective deterrent, and that is why in fairy tales the bad person always loses out. It is not the fact that virtue wins out at the end which promotes morality, but that the hero is most attractive to the child, who identifies with the hero in all his struggles. Because of this identification the child imagines that he suffers with the hero his trials and tribulations, and triumphs with him as virtue is victorious. The child makes such identifications all on his own, and the inner and outer struggles of the hero imprint morality on him.

The figures in fairy tales are not ambivalent—not good and bad at the same time, as we all are in reality. But since polarization dominates the child's mind, it also dominates fairy tales. A person is either good or bad, nothing in between. One brother is stupid, the other is clever. One sister is virtuous and industrious, the others are vile and lazy. One is beautiful, the others are ugly. One parent is all good, the other evil. The juxtaposition of opposite characters is not for the purpose of stressing right behavior, as would be true for cautionary tales. (There are some amoral fairy tales where goodness or badness, beauty or ugliness play no role at all.) Presenting the polarities of character permits the child to comprehend easily the difference between the two, which he could not do as readily were the figures drawn more true to life, with all the complexities that characterize real people. Ambiguities must wait until a relatively firm personality has been established on the basis of positive identifications. Then the child has a basis for understanding that there are great differences between people, and that therefore one has to make choices about who one wants to be. This basic decision, on which all later personality development will build, is facilitated by the polarizations of the fairy tale.

Furthermore, a child's choices are based, not so much on right versus wrong, as on who arouses his sympathy and who his antipathy. The more simple and straightforward a good character, the easier it is for a child to identify with it and to reject the bad other. The child identifies with the good hero not because of his goodness, but because the hero's condition makes a deep positive appeal to him. The question for the child is not "Do I want to be good?" but "Who do I want to be like?" The child decides this on the basis of projecting himself wholeheartedly into one character. If this fairy-tale figure is a very good person, then the child decides that he wants to be good, too.

Amoral fairy tales show no polarization or juxtaposition of good and bad persons; that is because these amoral stories serve an

383

entirely different purpose. Such tales or type figures as "Puss in Boots," who arranges for the hero's success through trickery, and Jack, who steals the giant's treasure, build character not by promoting choices between good and bad, but by giving the child the hope that even the meekest can succeed in life. After all, what's the use of choosing to become a good person when one feels so insignificant that he fears he will never amount to anything? Morality is not the issue in these tales, but rather, assurance that one can succeed. Whether one meets life with a belief in the possibility of mastering its difficulties or with the expectation of defeat is also a very important existential problem.

The deep inner conflicts originating in our primitive drives and our violent emotions are all denied in much of modern children's literature, and so the child is not helped in coping with them. But the child is subject to desperate feelings of loneliness and isolation, and he often experiences mortal anxiety. More often than not, he is unable to express these feelings in words, or he can do so only by indirection: fear of the dark, of some animal, anxiety about his body. Since it creates discomfort in a parent to recognize these emotions in his child, the parent tends to overlook them, or he belittles these spoken fears out of his own anxiety, believing this will cover over the child's fears.

The fairy tale, by contrast, takes these existential anxieties and dilemmas very seriously and addresses itself directly to them: the need to be loved and the fear that one is thought worthless; the love of life, and the fear of death. Further, the fairy tale offers solutions in ways that the child can grasp on his level of understanding. For example, fairy tales pose the dilemma of wishing to live eternally by occasionally concluding: "If they have not died, they are still alive." The other ending—"And they lived happily ever after"—does not for a moment fool the child that eternal life is possible. But it does indicate that which alone can take the sting out of the narrow limits of our time on this earth: forming a truly satisfying bond to another. The tales teach that when one has done this, one has reached the ultimate in emotional security of existence and permanence of relation available to man; and this alone can dissipate the fear of death. If one has found true adult love, the fairy story also tells, one doesn't need to wish for eternal life. This is suggested by another ending found in fairy tales:

"They lived for a long time afterward, happy and in pleasure."

An uninformed view of the fairy tale sees in this type of ending an unrealistic wish-fulfillment, missing completely the important message it conveys to the child. These tales tell him that by forming a true interpersonal relation, one escapes the separation anxiety which haunts him (and which sets the stage for many fairy tales, but is always resolved at the story's ending). Furthermore, the story tells, this ending is not made possible, as the child wishes and believes, by holding on to his mother eternally. If we try to escape separation anxiety and death anxiety by desperately keeping our grasp on our parents, we will only be cruelly forced out, like Hansel and Gretel.

Only by going out into the world can the fairy-tale hero (child) find himself there; and as he does, he will also find the other with whom he will be able to live happily ever after; that is, without ever again having to experience separation anxiety. The fairy tale is future-oriented and guides the child—in terms he can understand in both his conscious and his unconscious mind—to relinquish his infantile dependency wishes and achieve a more satisfying independent existence.

Today children no longer grow up within the security of an extended family, or of a well-integrated community. Therefore, even more than at the times fairy tales were invented, it is important to provide the modern child with images of heroes who have to go out into the world all by themselves and who, although originally ignorant of the ultimate things, find secure places in the world by following their right way with deep inner confidence.

The fairy-tale hero proceeds for a time in isolation, as the modern child often feels isolated. The hero is helped by being in touch with primitive things—a tree, an animal, nature—as the child feels more in touch with those things than most adults do. The fate of these heroes convinces the child that, like them, he may feel outcast and abandoned in the world, groping in the dark, but, like them, in the course of his life he will be guided step by step, and given help when it is needed. Today, even more than in past times, the child needs the reassurance offered by the image of the isolated man who nevertheless is capable of achieving meaningful and rewarding relations with the world around him.

THE FAIRY TALE: A UNIQUE ART FORM

While it entertains the child, the fairy tale enlightens him about himself, and fosters his personality development. It offers meaning on so many different levels, and enriches the child's existence in so many ways, that no one book can do justice to the multitude and diversity of the contributions such tales make to the child's life.

This book attempts to show how fairy stories represent in imaginative form what the process of healthy human development consists of, and how the tales make such development attractive for the child to engage in. This growth process begins with the resistance against the parents and fear of growing up, and ends when youth has truly found itself, achieved psychological independence and moral maturity, and no longer views the other sex as threatening or demonic, but is able to relate positively to it. In short, this book explicates why fairy tales make such great and positive psychological contributions to the child's inner growth.

If this book had been devoted to only one or two tales, it would have been possible to show many more of their facets, although even then complete probing of their depths would not have been achieved; for this, each story has meanings on too many levels. Which story is most important to a particular child at a particular age depends entirely on his psychological stage of development, and the problems which are most pressing to him at the moment. While in writing the book it seemed reasonable to concentrate on a fairy tale's central meanings, this has the shortcoming of neglecting other aspects which might be much more significant to some individual child because of problems he is struggling with at the time. This, then, is another necessary limitation of this presentation.

For example, in discussing "Hansel and Gretel," the child's striving to hold on to his parents even though the time has come for meeting the world on his own is stressed, as well as the need to transcend a primitive orality, symbolized by the children's infatuation with the gingerbread house. Thus, it would seem that this fairy tale has most to offer to the young child ready to make his first steps out into the world. It gives body to his anxieties, and offers reassurance about these fears because even in their most exaggerated form—anxieties about being devoured—they prove unwarranted: the children are victorious in the end, and a most threatening enemy — the witch — is utterly defeated. Thus, a good case could be made that this story has its greatest appeal and value for the child at the age when fairy tales begin to exercise their beneficial impact, that is, around the age of four or five.

But separation anxiety — the fear of being deserted — and starvation fear, including oral greediness, are not restricted to a particular period of development. Such fears occur at all ages in the unconscious, and thus this tale also has meaning for, and provides encouragement to, much older children. As a matter of fact, the older person might find it considerably more difficult to admit consciously his fear of being deserted by his parents, or to face his oral greed; and this is even more reason to let the fairy tale speak to his unconscious, give body to his unconscious anxieties, and relieve them, without this ever coming to conscious awareness.

Other features of the same story may offer much-needed reassurance and guidance to an older child. In early adolescence a girl had been fascinated by "Hansel and Gretel," and had derived great comfort from reading and rereading it, fantasizing about it. As a child, she had been dominated by a slightly older brother. He had, in a way, shown her the path, as Hansel did when he put down the pebbles which guided his sister and himself back home. As an adolescent, this girl continued to rely on her brother; and this feature of the story felt reassuring. But at the same time she also resented the brother's dominance. Without her being conscious of it at the time, her struggle for independence rotated around the figure of Hansel. The story told her unconscious that to follow Hansel's lead led her back, not forward, and it was also meaningful that although Hansel was the leader at the story's beginning, it was Gretel who in the end achieved freedom and independence for both, because it was she who defeated the witch. As an adult, this woman came to understand that the fairy tale had helped her greatly in throwing off her dependence on her brother, as it had convinced her that an early dependence on him need not interfere with her later ascendancy. Thus, a story which for one reason had been meaningful to her as a young child provided guidance for her at adolescence for a quite different reason.

The central motif of "Snow White" is the pubertal girl's surpassing in every way the evil stepmother who, out of jealousy, denies her an independent existence — symbolically represented by the stepmother's trying to see Snow White destroyed. The story's deepest meaning for one particular five-year-old, however, was far removed from these pubertal problems. Her mother was cold and distant, so much so that she felt lost. The story assured her that she need not despair: Snow White, betrayed by her step-mother, was saved by males — first the dwarfs and later the prince. This child, too, did not despair because of the mother's desertion, but trusted that rescue would come from males. Confident that "Snow White" showed her the way, she turned to her father, who responded favorably; the fairy tale's happy ending made it possible for this girl to find a happy solution to the impasse in living into which her mother's lack of interest had projected her. Thus, a fairy tale can have as important a meaning to a five-year-old as to a thirteen-year-old, although the personal meanings they derive from it may be quite different.

In "Rapunzel" we learn that the enchantress locked Rapunzel into the tower when she reached the age of twelve. Thus, hers is likewise the story of a pubertal girl, and of a jealous mother who tries to prevent her from gaining independence — a typical ado-lescent problem, which finds a happy solution when Rapunzel becomes united with her prince. But one five-year-old boy gained quite a different reassurance from this story. When he learned that his grandmother, who took care of him most of the day, would have to go to the hospital because of serious illness — his mother was working all day, and there was no father in the home — he asked to be read the story of Rapunzel. At this critical time in his life, two elements of the tale were important to him. First, there was the security from all dangers in which the substi-tute mother kept the child, an idea which greatly appealed to him at that moment. So what normally could be viewed as a represen-tation of negative, selfish behavior was capable of having a most reassuring meaning under specific circumstances. And even more important to the boy was another central motif of the story: that Rapunzel found the means of escaping her predicament in her own body — the tresses on which the prince climbed up to her room in the tower. That one's body can provide a lifeline reas-sured him that, if necessary, he would similarly find in his own body the source of his security. This shows that a fairy tale —

because it addresses itself in the most imaginative form to essential human problems, and does so in an indirect way — can have much to offer to a little boy even if the story's heroine is an adolescent girl.

These examples may help to counteract any impression made by my concentration here on a story's main motifs, and demonstrate that fairy tales have great psychological meaning for children of all ages, both girls and boys, irrespective of the age and sex of the story's hero. Rich personal meaning is gained from fairy stories because they facilitate changes in identification as the child deals with different problems, one at a time. In the light of her earlier identification with a Gretel who was glad to be led by Hansel, the adolescent girl's later identification with a Gretel who overcame the witch made her growth toward independence more rewarding and secure. The little boy's first finding security in the idea of being kept within the safety of the tower permitted him later on to glory in the realization that a much more dependable security could be found in what his body had to offer him, by way of providing him with a lifeline.

As we cannot know at what age a particular fairy tale will be most important to a particular child, we cannot ourselves decide which of the many tales he should be told at any given time or why. This only the child can determine and reveal by the strength of feeling with which he reacts to what a tale evokes in his conscious and unconscious mind. Naturally a parent will begin by telling or reading to his child a tale the parent himself or herself cared for as a child, or cares for now. If the child does not take to the story, this means that its motifs or themes have failed to evoke a meaningful response at this moment in his life. Then it is best to tell him another fairy tale the next evening. Soon he will indicate that a certain story has become important to him by his immediate response to it, or by his asking to be told this story over and over again. If all goes well, the child's enthusiasm for this story will be contagious, and the story will become important to the parent too, if for no other reason than that it means so much to the child. Finally there will come the time when the child has gained all he can from the preferred story, or the problems which made him respond to it have been replaced by others which find better expression in some other tale. He may then temporarily lose interest in this story and enjoy some other one much more. In the telling of fairy stories it is always best to follow the child's lead.

Even if a parent should guess correctly why his child has become involved emotionally with a given tale, this is knowledge best kept to oneself. The young child's most important experiences and reactions are largely subconscious, and should remain so until he reaches a much more mature age and understanding. It is always intrusive to interpret a person's unconscious thoughts, to make conscious what he wishes to keep preconscious, and this is especially true in the case of a child. Just as important for the child's well-being as feeling that his parent shares his emotions, through enjoying the same fairy tale, is the child's feeling that his inner thoughts are not known to his parent until he decides to reveal them. If the parent indicates that he knows them already, the child is prevented from making the most precious gift to his parent of sharing with him what until then was secret and private to the child. And since, in addition, a parent is so much more powerful than a child, his domination may appear limitless — and hence destructively overwhelming—if he seems able to read the child's secret thoughts, know his most hidden feelings, even before the child himself has begun to become aware of them.

Explaining to a child why a fairy tale is so captivating to him destroys, moreover, the story's enchantment, which depends to a considerable degree on the child's not quite knowing why he is delighted by it. And with the forfeiture of this power to enchant goes also a loss of the story's potential for helping the child struggle on his own, and master all by himself the problem which has made the story meaningful to him in the first place. Adult interpretations, as correct as they may be, rob the child of the opportunity to feel that he, on his own, through repeated hearing and ruminating about the story, has coped successfully with a difficult situation. We grow, we find meaning in life, and security in ourselves by having understood and solved personal problems on our own, not by having them explained to us by others.

Fairy-tale motifs are not neurotic symptoms, something one is better off understanding rationally so that one can rid oneself of them. Such motifs are experienced as wondrous because the child feels understood and appreciated deep down in his feelings, hopes, and anxieties, without these all having to be dragged up and investigated in the harsh light of a rationality that is still beyond him. Fairy tales enrich the child's life and give it an enchanted quality just because he does not quite know how the stories have worked their wonder on him.

THE MISUSES OF ENCHANTMENT: CONTROVERSIES ON THE SIGNIFICANCE OF FAIRY TALES

Kay F. Stone

LITTLE did we realize while reading our childhood fairy tales how controversial these seemingly simple and amusing stories were. Adults were enthusiastically engaged in determining whether such tales were damaging because of their violence or irrationality, or whether they instead furnished powerful fantasies good for developing psyches. The battle over the significance of fairy tales has been raging in various forms for some time. As early as the 1700s we find a writer of children's stories referring to fairy tales as "frolicks of a distempered mind," a sentiment still very much alive today (Kiefer 1948:87).[1]

In recent times the battle has spread to a new front, where opposing forces clash over the issue of sexual stereotyping. There are those who feel that fairy tales are unsuitable because they reinforce sexist stereotyping for both boys and girls, others who feel that fairy tales challenge such stereotyping, and still others who insist that these stories have neither a negative nor a positive impact in terms of gender. Because a major premise of folklorists studying women's folklore has been that gender is indeed significant in terms of interaction between people and material, I would

---

1. The early controversy on fairy tales is discussed by Elizabeth Stone (n.d.). A more contemporary opponent of fairy tales is Lucy Sprague Mitchell, who feels that their irrational fantasy might "delay a child's rationalizing of the world and leave him longer than desirable without the beginnings of scientific standards" (1984:24). The most eloquent proponent of fairy tales thus far is Bruno Bettelheim, who suggests "Nothing can be as enriching and satisfying to child and adult alike as the folk fairy tale" (1976:5).

like to examine the arguments in this controversy and describe actual rather than theoretical connections between fairy tales and their readers, both male and female.

I have found no clear statements on sexism in fairy tales from the suffragist movement of past decades, probably because feminist efforts then were devoted to legal and economic problems. Writers from more recent decades, however, have expressed themselves clearly on the issue of sexual stereotyping in all forms of literature. Simone de Beauvoir complains that "everything still encourages the young girl to expect fortune and happiness from some Prince Charming rather than to attempt by herself their difficult and uncertain conquest" (Beauvoir 1953:126). She mentions "Cinderella," "Snow White," and "Sleeping Beauty" as the stories most widely read and therefore most pervasive in their influence. Bullough and Bullough, in *The Subordinate Sex*, provide a scenario for a modern heroine who has read the stories carefully:

> The most obvious example of this today is the beautiful girl with the right measurements who catches the attention of a rich sponsor and simply by being female in a male–dominated society can advance far beyond her own social origins. Men, on the other hand, are more likely to have to earn their status through hard work. (Bullough and Bullough 1973:53)

These observations cited from Beauvoir and from the Bulloughs appear in the context of much longer works dealing with the broader problem of male-female roles. In 1972, however, we find a lengthy article devoted to the impact of fairy tales in sexual stereotyping. After examining tales in a number of Andrew Lang's fairy-tale books, Marcia Lieberman states:

> Millions of women must surely have formed their psycho-sexual selfconcepts, and their ideas of what they could or could not accomplish, what sort of behavior would be rewarded, and of the nature of the reward itself, in part from their favorite fairy tales. These stories have been made the repositories of the dreams, hopes and fantasies of generations of girls. (1972:385)

Lieberman's pointed remarks are a reaction to the positive comments of Alison Lurie, who writes that "the traditional folktale ... is one of the few sorts of classic children's literature of which a radical feminist would approve" (1970:42), emphasizing that the bulk of the tales portray strong and positive women:

> These stories suggest a society in which women are as competent and active as men, at every age and in every class.... The contrast is greatest in maturity, where women are often more powerful than men. Real help for the hero or heroine comes most frequently from a fairy godmother or wise woman; and real trouble from a witch or wicked stepmother. (Lurie 1970:42)

A professional folklorist, Stith Thompson, also seems to define märchen (or fairy tales) in terms of heroines when he states (about various translations of the term), "What they are all trying to describe is such tales as 'Cinderella,' 'Snow White,' or 'Hansel and Gretel'" (Thompson 1946:8). Similarly, another folktale scholar, Max Lüthi, reminds us that a great many of the Grimms' fairy tales have heroines, that fairy tales are most often told by women, and that "today children learn fairy tales mainly from their mothers, grandmothers, aunts, and female kindergarten and grade school teachers" (Lüthi 1970:136).[1] He concludes from this:

> The woman is assigned a privileged position, not only by social custom; in art and literature, as well, she has occupied a central position since the time of the troubadours and the Mariology of the late Middle Ages. In painting and in the novel, she has been the subject of persistent interest and loving concern. (Lüthi 1970:136)

Lurie, Lüthi, and Thompson all emphasize that fairy tales demonstrate the power of women simply because these stories are

---

1. Not all scholars agree that tale narration is female-dominated. For example, folktale specialist Linda Dégh observes that the reverse is true in Hungary (1969:92-93), and this seems to be the case in North America as well, judging by material in Anglo-American collections.

dominated by women, both as protagonists and as narrators. None of them mentions that most of the heroines are pretty and passive rather than powerful. Thompson and Lüthi almost immediately move on to describe tales with male protagonists only, and Lurie apologetically observes: "Even in the favorite fairy tales of the Victorians it is only the young girls who are passive and helpless. In the older generation, women often have more power and are more active than the men" (Lurie 1971:6). More power, yes—and most often it is of a kind destructive to both heroines and heroes, because the older women are often wicked stepmothers or witches.

The favorable reactions noted above make an interesting contrast to the reaction of a young mother who did not want her daughter to read fairy tales precisely because they are so dominated by women and because the so-called "privileged position" emphasized by Lüthi is really a very restricted one (Minard 1975:vii). Her comment inspired Rosemary Minard to compile a collection of traditional tales with active heroines, because she felt these stories were too valuable to give up. In contrast to Lüthi and Lurie, Minard observes:

> Many of us ... are ... concerned today that *woman* be recognized as a full-fledged member of the human race. In the past she has not often been accepted as such, and her role in traditional literature reflects her second-rate position. Fairy tales abound with bold, courageous, and clever heroes. But for the most part female characters, if they are not witches or fairies or wicked stepmothers, are insipid beauties waiting for Prince Charming. (1975:viii)

Minard's relatively modest statement was sharply attacked by Susan Cooper, who objected both to "that uncomfortable title" (*Womenfolk and Fairy Tales*) and to "the motive behind the collecting" (1975:8):

> It's a false premise: an adult neurosis foisted upon children. I don't believe little Jane gives a damn that Jack the Giant Killer is a boy. Lost in the story, she identifies with him as a *character*, just as little John shares Red Riding Hood's terror

of the wolf without reflecting that, of course, she's only a girl. (Cooper 1975:8)

Cooper, a writer of science fiction fantasy rather than an expert on either fairy tales or neuroses, expresses an opinion shared by many scholars who are interested in the psychological interpretation of fairy tales.[1]

N.J. Girardot, for example, presents a detailed study of "Snow White" in support of his view that fairy tales are essentially non-sexist. He suggests that many fairy tales echo the general outlines of *rites de passage*, thus offering listeners the possibility of a religious experience during which they can recognize "that life itself is a story, a story told by God or the gods, to accomplish the happy passage of men and women through a dark and dangerous world" (Girardot 1977:300). He feels that the difference between male and female acts in fairy tales is superficial and deceptive: "Heroes and heroines in fairy tales, more so than in epic and saga, do not ordinarily succeed because they act, but because they allow themselves to be acted upon—helped, protected, saved, or transformed—by the magic of the fairy world" (1977:284).[2] In Girardot's opinion, fairy tales reflect the struggle for maturity and enlightenment, and both hero and heroine are engaged equally in this struggle. The manner in which they "allow themselves to be acted upon" might be different in degree, but not in its basic essence. Both seek an awakening rather than a mate.

Bruno Bettelheim makes an even more forceful statement in his lengthy and detailed comment on fairy tales, *The Uses of*

1. Marie-Louise von Franz deals with the Jungian *animus/anima* (male/female) concept in *Problems of the Feminine in Fairytales* and proposes that the real function of the fairy tale for both females and males is gaining "individuation—the attainment of that subtle rightness which is the far-away goal of the fairy tale put before us" (1972:194).

2. Here he also chides me for overemphasizing female passivity in Stone (1975): "In this way Kay Stone's comments on what she considers to be the insipid and uninspiring 'passivity' of female characters in the Grimm tales, while not entirely unfounded, do seem to miss the point that ultimately initiation is the fortuitous work of the gods (however they are disguised)." See also the exchange of letters between Steven Jones (1979) and Girardot (1979).

Enchantment. I reproduce the following passage in full to avoid possible misrepresentation:

> Recently it has been claimed that the struggle against child-
> hood dependency and for becoming oneself in fairy tales is
> frequently described differently for the girl than for the boy,
> and that this is the result of sexual stereotyping. Fairy tales
> do not render such one-sided pictures. Even when a girl is
> depicted as turning inward in her struggle to become her-
> self, and a boy as aggressively dealing with the external
> world, these two *together* symbolize the two ways in which
> one has to gain selfhood: through learning to understand
> and master the inner as well as the outer world. In this sense
> the male and the female heroes are again projections onto
> two different figures of two (artificially) separated aspects of
> one and the same process which *everybody* has to undergo in
> growing up. While some literal-minded parents do not real-
> ize it, children know that, whatever the sex of the hero, the
> story pertains to their own problems. (Bettelheim 1976:226)

Like Girardot, Bettelheim feels that gender is irrelevant in the tales' ultimate significance for young readers, and he suggests that only misguided adults fail to see beneath the surface. Children, he maintains, react unconsciously and positively, regardless of any possible surface stereotyping of the characters.

We can assume from the intensity of the statements both attacking and supporting fairy tales that these stories are regarded as meaningful for both children and adults rather than as merely quaint and amusing. Moreover, fairy tales apparently have the power to affect readers deeply, either negatively or positively, in ways that other forms of children's literature generally do not. The fact that these multilevel stories are usually read early in life when a child is struggling to find a place in the world, and a sexu-al identity, can be used to support the arguments of both propo-nents and opponents of fairy tales.

Thompson, Lüthi, and Lurie seem to feel that fairy tales offer strongly positive images for both boys and girls; Girardot and Bet-telheim suggest that gender differences are less important than the psychological significance of the tales; Beauvoir, Lieberman, and

Minard insist that significant differences in heroes and heroines exist and that these are important because they contribute to differential socializing of boys and girls in contemporary Western society.

While the authors discussed here argue that fairy tales are negatively or positively significant, none has given the readers themselves much of a voice. Even the mother concerned about sexism described in Rosemary Minard's book speaks *for* her daughter, not from her daughter. Bettelheim does occasionally refer to some of his patients, but only to support his own views. The others speak only in general terms about the effects and the meanings of fairy tales for a hypothetical and therefore silent audience. In the following section I will draw on the reactions of readers of various ages and backgrounds, both male and female. Their varied responses demonstrate that there is no single truth about either the meaning or the impact of fairy tales that is applicable to all readers, but there are some definite patterns.

For several years I have questioned people informally and formally about their memories of and reactions to fairy tales. Formal interviews were conducted with forty-four people individually and in small groups.[1] Of these forty-four, twenty-three were girls between the ages of seven and seventeen. Only six of the total number were males, ranging in age from nine to sixty-eight. This

---

1. I conducted interviews (in Winnipeg, Minneapolis, and Miami, during 1972–1973) with adults and children of both sexes and of differing backgrounds. Twenty-five people were interviewed individually, and nineteen were interviewed in groups sharing the same age. In addition to forty-four formal interviews, countless other children and adults have informally responded to the basic question: "Do you remember anything about fairy tales, and do you feel they have affected you in any way?" I have also received material from students and colleagues. Most notably, Linda Dégh showed me the responses to a similar question she asked students in her course in European folktales, taught at the University of California at Berkeley in the spring of 1978. Karen Rowe, of U.C.L.A., recently sent me a detailed questionnaire on fairy tales now being handed out to students in a number of classes. Michael Taft also shared student responses from his classes at the University of Saskatchewan.

small number of male respondents is a result of the inability of male informants *of any age* to recall fairy tales at all. Many males, questioned informally, could not even remember if they had ever read fairy tales. With females, on the other hand, I found that all could remember clearly having read and reacted to fairy tales, and several in different age groups accurately recalled specific stories—even when they had disliked and rejected them. At first I assumed that boys simply did not read these stories, but parents, teachers, and librarians have assured me that they did. The mother of a nine-year-old boy who had just claimed he had no favorite fairy tales told me she had read him "Jack and the Beanstalk" only the night before. She suggested that he was embarrassed to admit that he read "those girls' stories." Another nine-year-old boy was willing to admit that he had read such stories but had since rejected them:

> I like that one ["Jack and the Beanstalk"] a lot better than those other stories, like "Snow White" and "Cinderella." Those are all girls' stories. They're about girls and not boys. I like the ones with boys a lot better because they're not boring, like the girls' ones. The only one I like with a girl in it is "Molly Whuppee,"[1] because she does things, sort of like Jack.

A male student-teacher of a fifth-grade class described the same pattern of boys' rejecting and girls' accepting fairy tales, at least in part because of the dominance of heroine tales in popular collections. But his description of boys' and girls' reactions indicates that the situation is more complex than boys' rejecting and girls' identifying with protagonists because they are female, for the boys seem to have forgotten the tales altogether.

> In the winter of 1978, while discussing fairy tales with a group of grades five and six students, an interesting phenomenon arose. When the discussion centered on the subject of

---

1. The Scottish tale "Molly Whuppee," in which the heroine saves herself and her two sisters from the giant and then steals his treasures, is reprinted in one of the third-grade reader series in Canada.

"Cinderella," it became apparent from student remarks that there was a definite difference between boys' and girls' attitudes to the story. The boys' remarks, "It's boring," or "It's a kids' story," reflected a definite lack of interest. The girls, however, said it was one of their favorites. In fact, the majority of girls seemed to feel that someday their prince would come and they too would live happily ever after. From this difference in attitudes I am theorizing that fairy tales like "Cinderella," while being enchanting and entertaining in their own right, also serve another purpose entirely. (Spiller 1979)

Apparently the female-dominated tales extolled by Lurie and Lüthi fail to retain the interest of male readers as they mature. We cannot know for sure whether boys consciously reject them because they are viewed as girls' stories, or whether choices were made on the basis of the passivity or aggressiveness of protagonists rather than strictly on the basis of gender. We cannot even be certain whether this was a conscious decision, or whether boys did work through childhood problems in the way that Bettelheim suggests, thus leaving enchantment with no further uses for them. In any case, the pattern for girls and for boys here is clearly different.

A few girls and women seemed to agree with males in their rejection of heroines who were too passive to be interesting, but these readers did not give up fairy tales. They attempted to compensate for disappointing heroines in other ways. A nine-year-old, for example, decided that she preferred heroes to heroines:

My favorite people now are boys named Jack. I remember "Cinderella" too, but I didn't like it as much as some others. The ones with boys in them are more exciting. They usually go out and do things. "Cinderella" doesn't have that.

A twelve-year-old reported that she had usually identified with the older sisters "who never got anything and made stupid mistakes like not giving bread to the birds in the woods." Negative as such characters were, they were more interesting to her than "the ones who just sit by the fireside and never do anything, and then one day blossom into beautiful girls." Similarly, a thirty-one-year-old woman observed:

> I certainly identified with the women in the stories, but the ones I remember are the ones where the woman was dominant — like in "The Snow Queen," where the woman is sort of all-powerful. She may be meant to be a negative figure, but I didn't see her that way. But looking back, I suppose it was the boys who had the action and did things in most of the stories.

While choosing the active but negative women in fairy tales provided these readers with a less passive model, it did not free them from the knowledge that these women were punished in the end for their aggressiveness. The woman just quoted, for example, stated later in the interview:

> I wanted to be beautiful like in the stories but I didn't think I was or would be. It just seemed ridiculous. So I was more inclined to the stories where ghastly things would happen to bad little girls. I hated them but I would read them over and over.

The twelve-year-old admitted that, as an older sister herself, she was frustratingly aware that in her life, as in fairy tales, it was the younger sister "who got all the goodies."

These sentiments are more clearly expressed by a twenty-nine-year-old mother who said:

> I remember a feeling of being left out in the fairy stories. Whatever the story was about, it wasn't about me. But this feeling didn't make me not interested in them. I knew there was something I was supposed to do or be to fit in there, but I couldn't do it, and it bothered me.

Others were more definite about why they felt left out, and clearly resented the apparent fact that boys "went out and did things" and girls did not. Said one fifteen-year-old:

I don't think it's really fair that in all the fairy tales, it's usually the princess who's locked away. Or someone's bartering her off. In the ones with boys — I only remember "Jack and the Beanstalk" — Jack being a boy meant that he had more curiosity. I don't think I could imagine a girl being Jack, in that kind of story.

Some echoed the sentiments of the thirteen-year-old who was annoyed by the disparity between heroines and heroes ("Big Joe Tough") and insisted, "You know, there are some girls who can cope better with things than boys can!"

Not all females felt restricted by the seemingly narrow choice of models offered by fairy tale heroines. I would like to examine one especially popular story in greater depth to see how both the acceptance and the rejection of fairy tales on the basis of gender relates to the observations of the writers quoted in the first section of this chapter. The issues raised here revolve around the possibilities of fairy tales as either problem-solving stories, as Bettelheim and Girardot suggest, or as problem-creating stories, as feminist writers insist.

While the Cinderella story is found orally in all parts of the world, most North American readers will be familiar with only two versions, from printed sources. The first of these, and by far the most popular, is Perrault's 1697 reworking, complete with fairy godmother, pumpkin coach, and glass slipper. The less popular but more dynamic Grimm version has a more resourceful heroine who does without fairy godmothers and coaches and who makes her own curfew. She does not reward her sisters at the end, as does the Perrault heroine, but neither is she responsible for their mutilation, which occurs first at their own hands (cutting off pieces of their feet to force them into the slipper) and then as punishment from the vengeful doves, who blind them for their treachery. Apparently this popular story expresses an entire range of hopes, fears, and possibilities for both narrators and audiences.[1] Signifi-

---

1. Michael Taft, now at the University of Saskatchewan recently sent me twenty-seven versions of "Cinderella" written by students of his folklore class in Newfoundland: "They had no prior warning of the assignment and I gave

cantly, it is the more passive variant (Type 510A rather than Type 510B) that is strongly favored in the books and unanimously chosen by those I interviewed.

Like most good folktales, "Cinderella" functions on a number of levels of meaning and has several possible interpretations even at surface level.[1] In the Grimm version, Cinderella's stepsisters equal her in beauty but are "vile and black of heart" (Grimm and Grimm, 1974:121). More significant, they are interested in getting ahead and hope to do so by marrying the prince. They do not consider their stepsister a serious competitor—although their mother is more perceptive on this score. Cinderella herself is not primarily interested in meeting the prince or in gaining any material benefits—her handsome clothing cannot be purchased at any price—but wishes to escape the confines of her painfully narrow existence. She is rewarded with magic objects because she follows precisely the instructions of her dying mother. She wins the prince at least in part because she is *not* a man-chaser, as are her stepsisters. One interpreter of the tale insists that the prince is merely a symbol for Cinderella's well-deserved freedom and that marriage is not at all the point of the story (Kavablum 1973). In any case, her marriage signifies that she has managed to reject her subservient position and to take action in getting herself to the outside world, and that she has demonstrated her acceptance of maturity by entering into marriage.

Among those interviewed, only three theorized about the possible psychoanalytic significance of the "Cinderella" story. A sixty-eight-year-old male said:

> I liked all these stories because in that time of life [childhood] you feel you can't accomplish anything by yourself. And if you're the youngest and trampled on, like Cinderella,

---

them half an hour to complete this in-class assignment." Not a single student failed to re-create the story in detail—although Taft unfortunately does not indicate the gender of the respondents. The success of Taft's experiment is not surprising to me, because almost all my informants, including some of the males, named this story either as one they definitely remembered or as their favorite story.

1. For a discussion of different narrative levels, see Jason (1977:99-139).

you really need to have impossible dreams and read impossible fairy tales.

A seventeen-year-old female adds, "You can take the stories like 'Cinderella' from two points of view, for the very serious aspect or for the face value. It depends on what you want at the time. That's what you get out of it." Similarly, a fifteen-year-old girl noted that she didn't expect to see fairy godmothers, witches, dragons, or giants walking on the street, but knew people who took similar roles in real life. For these readers, gender is of little importance, because they are reacting to the tales on an abstract level. The sixty-eight-year-old male, for example, identified Cinderella as an early favorite of his because as a child he identified with her feeling of powerlessness — though his later preferences were for heroic fairy tales, epics, and myths. The two girls likewise did not feel that the sex of the protagonist was significant to them, though they all noted in their interviews that there was a definite difference between heroes and heroines.

For other readers, however, the story of Cinderella was interpreted more literally as a model for feminine behavior as well as a depiction of the rewards to be gained. A ten-year-old girl, for example, stated:

> "Cinderella" is my favorite. She's a happy person, when she gets away from her family. People could live like that, like Cinderella. I guess I'd like to live like that, like the happy part. Not in a castle, though. And I wouldn't want to marry a prince, but maybe somebody *like* a prince.

The emphasis here is not on the unpleasant aspects of Cinderella's ordeal, but on her rewards — and on the fact that she "gets away from her family." Here we meet a modern Cinderella, a model for the maturing girl who dreams of escaping with her boyfriend from her restrictive family situation, acquiring a fine wardrobe, a steady income (from her "prince," not from her own efforts), and a suburban castle, all of which will presumably allow her to live happily ever after with glamour and material comfort. An eleven-year-old said, "I really liked 'Cinderella.' Yeah, when I was about five I guess I wanted to grow up and be a princess, or something like that." Her friend added: "I used to like 'Cinderella' too, like, it should be *my* story. She starts off very poor and then she gets rich and very successful, and I used to think of myself that way. I thought I'd just sit around and get all this money."

The eleven- and twelve-year-old girls described by the fifth-grade student-teacher quoted above were less cynical (or perhaps just less defensive about romantic fantasies), for they had not yet rejected the happily-ever-after ending promised by "Cinderella." But in contrast to the ten-year-old who still expects to marry "someone *like* a prince," the eleven-year-olds seem to be more realistic. However, the eleven-year-olds' responses reflect the fact that they have only recently stopped reading fairy tales (few children read them beyond the age of ten, if my sampling is any indication) and are on the defensive about "childish" things. More significant, older women who might have expressed the same somewhat cynical tone at eleven years of age were not so certain upon reconsidering their reactions. For example, a twenty-six-year-old mother of two, now divorced, said:

> I figured Cinderella was pretty lucky. First I felt sorry for her, and then she went to the dance and got the guy, and I thought this was going to apply to my life. I really figured you just sit around and wait, and something fantastic is going to happen. You go to the right dance and you've got it made! It was definitely "Cinderella" I liked best. She was gorgeous. I was homely, and I kept thinking it would happen to me too — I'd bloom one day. But it's never happened. I'm still waiting!

Those readers who identify with Cinderella are definitely interested in the dance and in the prince. A university student comments:

> My favorite fairy tales were the romantic ones, like "Cinderella," "Snow White," and "Sleeping Beauty." The romantic, "prince and princess live happily ever after" ones. I easily put myself in the princess' role, waiting for Prince Charming.

Thus the message of the Cinderella story that seems most relevant for modern girls and women concerns the rewards one is supposed to receive for being pretty, polite, and passive; the primary reward, of course, is marriage, and marriage to not just anyone but to a "prince," someone who can provide status and the material benefits of the beautiful life.[1] As Simone de Beauvoir asks, "How, indeed, could the myth of Cinderella not keep all its vitality?" (1953:126). Thus for this group the message of the tale shifts from Cinderella's growing independence and maturity to the rewards she receives and how she receives them. In this kind of narrow interpretation, success for the female comes from being beautiful and from sitting around and waiting. It is ironic that Cinderella, the ultimate in humility and selflessness, becomes for such readers a woman who uses her beauty and personality to gain material success—and at the expense of other women. In this interpretation, there is little difference between Cinderella and her stepsisters, except that she is more "feminine": unlike her openly ambitious sisters, she masks her real hopes for the future by just "sitting and waiting" for everything to turn out happily ever after for all eternity. In *Transformations*, a poetic reworking of several Grimm tales, Anne Sexton captures this frighteningly static aspect of the tale in her poem "Cinderella," which concludes:

> Cinderella and the prince
> lived, they say, happily ever after,
> like two dolls in a museum case
> never bothered by diapers and dust,
> never arguing over the timing of an egg,
> never telling the same story twice,
> never getting a middle-aged spread,
> their darling smiles pasted on for eternity.

---

1. In a recent interview in Winnipeg, Anne Bowden, who is preparing a book on the history of marriage in Manitoba, observed that the wedding as the high point in a girl's life seems to be a post-World War II phenomenon. She agreed that girls easily identified with the "happily ever after" conclusion of many fairy tales that end in marriage and suggested that many girls have never thought beyond the wedding ceremony.

Regular Bobbsey Twins.

That story.

(Sexton 1971:56-57)

Another aspect of the story commented on by readers was the competition between the women, a competition our society seems to accept as natural. Sisters in particular reacted to this conflict, which they reluctantly accepted as inevitable. One thirty-two-year-old still recalls her sibling relations clearly:

> I always felt my sister was making it more than I was. She was blond, blue-eyed, and as a child this was always commented upon. She was the sweet baby girl. I suppose those fairy tales with elder sisters are the ones I have identified with most.

A twelve-year-old (quoted earlier) agrees: "You know, being the oldest daughter like me is sort of ... well, I didn't want to be a princess, or anything, but I didn't want to be the bad one, either." This supposed inevitability of female competition is commented on by a junior high school guidance counselor:

> It's just amazing! The conflicts that occur between girls at this stage are even much greater than the conflicts between the boys.... I don't know why, for sure, but I guess they're preparing to compete for male attention even when they don't know it.

It would be simplistic to blame fairy tales for encouraging females to see their lives primarily in terms of competing for and winning male attentions, when many other aspects of North American culture reinforce this same ideal. The popular interpretation of the Cinderella story can be identified in disguised form in popular magazines and books, in films, and on television. Psychologist Eric Berne has suggested that one's favorite fairy tale, reinforced by other aspects of culture, could set a lifelong pattern of behavior. "The story will then be his script and he will spend the rest of his life trying to make it come to pass" (Berne 1973:95). Despite the masculine pronoun intended to encompass all humanity, Berne provides only female examples when it comes to fairy tales. He describes two "scripts" in detail, one of which is Cinderella, to whom he devotes an entire chapter. Her story, he says, is adopted by women who feel themselves to be unjustly treated or generally unrecognized for their better qualities. They learn to put on a sweet outer personality to improve their chances of getting more recognition and may, when they succeed, taunt other women whom they have bested. Such women, according to Berne, might be unable to give up the exciting game of "Try and Catch Me," first played with the prince and later continued with various adulterous lovers (Berne 1973:238).

Berne might be exaggerating in suggesting such a firm connection between stories like "Cinderella" and later behavior, but it would be a mistake to pass fairy tales off as "child's play." If one agrees that childhood is a critically impressionable time of life, especially in terms of forming sexual identity, and if popular fairy tales consistently present an image of heroines that emphasize their beauty, patience, and passivity, then the potential impact of such tales cannot be ignored. Certainly some who once favored Cinderella will later find her irrelevant, but many others will continue unconsciously or consciously to strive for her ideal femininity — or will be annoyed with themselves for failing to attain her position. The remarks of a twenty-nine-year-old woman indicate that the fairy tale model undermined her desire for independence:

> I couldn't really say whether the impact of stories is stronger when you're an adolescent or when you're younger; but the impact in both cases was harmful to me, I think, because instead of making me feel confident or able to develop my strengths or anything, they made me feel there was something in me I had to stamp out.

A thirty-six-year-old mother of four felt that fairy tales were good stimulation for the imagination but also encouraged impossible expectations, especially for girls:

> I never felt I would ever fit in, but I wanted to. There was a nice romantic thing about fairy tales that was misleading, just like Sunday school was misleading. I identified with them

very much. Now I know they didn't relate much to people I knew then ... well, on the other hand, the men seemed to be able to handle themselves, but the women didn't. Lots of things came together to prevent them. Outside forces controlled their lives, so the only way they could solve it was with some kind of magic. It doesn't say anywhere in the fairy tales I remember that if they just got off their ass and thought about their situation they could maybe do something—except for the ones who were already aggressive and mean.

Several others of various ages mentioned the emphasis on beauty and expressed disappointment in their own inability to measure up, and one astutely observed: "I was troubled by the fact that these women were, first of all, very beautiful, and second, virtuous enough not to care about it. So it was sort of a double insult to those of us who worried about our appearance."

Does it all matter? It would be simplistic, as noted earlier, to credit fairy tales with full power as a socializing force, when everything from early nursery rhymes, school texts and other books, television and movies, and personal contacts contribute to our particular system of differential socialization for girls and boys. Still, many adult female informants felt that fairy tales in particular had definitely affected their lives to some degree, and "Cinderella" in particular was the story remembered best. Why "Cinderella," and why such a materialistic interpretation of a story in which the main point is that Cinderella is *not* materialistic or even man-hungry? Judging by the comments of these respondents, Cinderella seems to present the clearest image of our idealized perfect woman—beautiful, sweet, patient, submissive, and an excellent housekeeper and wife. She also represents the female version of the popular rags-to-riches story that can be found at all levels of North American culture, one which assures us that the small can become the great and that we all have a chance to do so. For only one example, here is a *Newsweek* article describing the "Cinderella Story" of the British model, Twiggy:

Once upon a time, back in the 1960's a wisp of a Cockney lass named Lesley Hornby parlayed her bean-stalk figure and

408

wide-eyed air into fame and fortune as Twiggy, one of the world's most photographed fashion models. She became an international celebrity and a movie star. There haven't been many real-life Cinderella stories to match it — and if the slipper fits that well, why not wear it? The Twig is turning into Cinderella in her stage debut, when she will play the fairy-tale heroine in pantomime. (Anonymous 1974:72)

Certainly, if the slipper fits, it is likely to be worn, but it should not be forced. Julius E. Heuscher emphasizes this aspect of the story in his study of myths and fairy tales: "Finally, Cinderella is the individual who is able willingly to restrict her enjoyment of the prince's palace and feast, until she has grown sufficiently, until the slipper fits perfectly" (1974:55).

But for many women it *does* not fit, though they try to wear it anyway. And that is why it does matter how and why readers, male and female, interpret and reinterpret fairy tales that they feel were significant to them as children. The few males who mentioned "Cinderella" concentrated solely on the fact that she was a mistreated and powerless person who later obtained position and power. Women, however, concentrated on Cinderella's innate goodness, on her mistreatment at the hands of her own family (a familiar complaint for adolescents of both sexes), her initial lack of beauty and proper clothing followed by her "blooming," and finally the rewards she received for at last being recognized as the ideal female, in contrast to her ambitious stepsisters.[1] Many of the women who remembered her story recognized, either early or late, that the shoe did not fit. For example, a twenty-eight-year-old divorced mother of three complained:

I remember "Cinderella" and "Snow White." Now I don't think they show the ideal woman — at least not for me, or

1. In my current folklore class I asked students to describe in one sentence what they considered to be the main point of the "Cinderella" story. The men overwhelmingly responded that it was a "rags-to-riches" story, emphasizing the heroine's positive actions and her reward. The women characterized it as a "good-over-evil" story, concentrating on the heroine's inherent and unchanging nature and her need to find outside recognition of her goodness.

for my daughter, but I liked them at her age [nine]. It's too glamorous. A man is supposed to solve all your problems. I thought this would be the answer to what I'd been growing up and waiting for. What a bunch of bullshit! Fantasy is okay, but not if it puts patterns into kids' heads about what to expect from life.

This woman's statement, made in response to a simple query concerning what she remembered about fairy tales in general, returns us to the issues raised in the first section of this chapter. She responded as a girl, and continues to respond as a woman, to heroines rather than heroes in fairy tales. Furthermore, she now views her initial positive response to these tales as problem-creating rather than as problem-solving.

Perhaps her response reflects only the surface level of meaning and neglects the psychoanalytic level emphasized first by Bettelheim and then by Girardot, who insist that the "real" meaning of the tales cannot be taken from the surface story alone. Perhaps as a young child she, like other children, unconsciously reacted to this deeper meaning but was later distracted from it by other aspects of socialization and her responses to them. In any case, emphasis on the surface level of these stories by this reader and others has been carried into later life, even though fairy tales may no longer be read or even clearly remembered. Furthermore, it is females and not males who continue to be troubled by the view of women presented in fairy tales. It would seem, then, that gender is indeed significant, both in the protagonists of fairy tales and in the readers. Still, the question of the importance of gender is not a simple one.

Bettelheim's observation that fairy tales help certain children work through certain problems at certain times of their lives is undoubtedly correct, though it is difficult to demonstrate this precisely because the working-out process is an unconscious one. For males, fairy tales apparently cease to function at an early age, but for many females these stories continue to function on some level well past childhood. Whatever positive functions the tales have for girls in their early lives apparently become less positive for them in later life. The fact that all the adult females I questioned easily recalled fairy tales both generally and specifically seems to indicate this. That a girl at the age of seven, perhaps, may react to fairy tales as initiatory rites, as Girardot suggests, or as psychoanalytically valid, as Bettelheim suggests, does not prevent them from later interpreting the same tales as literal models for ideal female behavior in later years.

The emphasis on ideal female beauty, passivity, and dependence on outside forces suggested in the fairy tales is supported by Western culture in general. The women and girls who felt uncomfortable with this model, or even those who challenged it, were not fully certain that they had the right to do so. Even when they felt they did not fit in, they did not give up the tales that on the surface suggested they *should* fit in. Similarly, even those who claim to have accepted the ideal feminine model at some time in their lives were defensive. The women often claimed that they had envied and admired Cinderella at an early age, leading one to assume that this was no longer so—but these readers generally did not clearly admit that they had indeed rejected their earlier model of behavior. Often women who said they still felt that the fairy tales projected a positive model for women expressed some doubts about the universal truth of such a model—especially with regard to their own real or hypothetical daughters. A thirty-one-year-old mother of two sons and one daughter, for example, told me:

> I guess I would say that the image of stories like "Snow White" and "Cinderella" would be good for a little girl. I gave my daughter a fairy tale book for Christmas once, I think. But then when you get down to it, maybe Cinderella and Snow White were too goody-goody. Everyone's doing things to them and they never say anything. Not exactly like real life!

I am not suggesting that men cease to be concerned with the problem of ideal masculine roles, but simply that they cease to use fairy tales as a model, while women who have not read these stories since they were children have not left them completely behind. Even when they think they have done so, as did the mother above, they are still struggling with the problem of female roles as they are presented in fairy tales, if not for themselves then projected onto their daughters (or onto other females). The surface message of popular tales like "Cinderella," "Snow White," and "Sleeping Beauty" is that nice and pretty girls have the problems of life worked out once they have attracted and held Prince Charming. Girls and women who have felt that in some way they cannot or will not fit themselves into this idealized role, into an image that does not suit their individual characters and needs, still cannot free themselves fully from the fairy tale princess. Her power is indeed strong.

Thus fairy tales, as they are presented through popular collections in which passive heroines outnumber more active heroines or heroes, do not continue to function in the problem-solving manner ideally suggested by Girardot and Bettelheim. For many females they become instead problem-creating as "purveyors of the romantic myth" (as discussed by Rowe n.d.). In this myth love conquers all, and one who is not loved is incomplete. While there are certainly male versions of this "myth," fairy tales generally do not figure in them. Thus gender does indeed seem significant in terms of readers' reactions to fairy tales. Males and females at some stage of their lives (and not only as the "literal minded adults" conjured up by Bettelheim) clearly view fairy tale heroines and heroes as providing different kinds of idealized behavior, and both males and females react to these differences in different ways. Most important, females continue to react to them even when they consciously feel that the problem was left behind in childhood. For women, the problem-creating aspect of the tales is the attempted identification with the ideal woman, or the guilt if one fails to identify with her, and the expectation that one's life will be transformed dramatically and all one's problems solved with the arrival of a man. Females who once reacted strongly to the problem-creating aspect might continue to reinterpret their responses at various ages, but often without solving the problem. Life is not a "happily ever after" affair for either males or females, nor can anyone else make it so, regardless of how princely they might be. Certainly women understand this as well as males, but they are still held back rather than released, disturbed by the stagnant "museum case" image created by Anne Sexton's poem.

But if women remember fairy tales, consciously or unconsciously, they can reinterpret them as well. It is the possibility of such reinterpretation that gives hope that women can eventually free themselves from the bonds of fairy tale magic, magic that transforms positively at one age and negatively at another. Such reinterpretation, conscious or unconscious, can occur at any age, of course. I offer here a spontaneous and conscious reworking of "Cinderella" by the nine-year-old girl who earlier claimed that she preferred Jack to Cinderella. Despite her rejection, she did not give up "Cinderella," but came back to the story later in the inter-view and re-created it in a more pleasing manner for herself.

> I like "Cinderella," but I think it should be more exciting. Well, Cinderella goes to the dance, finally, and then she loses her slipper and the prince gets it. Then the prince comes with the slipper but her mother won't let him try it on her. Cinderella comes in and sees that it's her slipper, but she doesn't say anything. So that night she sneaks out and she goes to the prince's palace when he's sleeping, and she gets the slipper back. And maybe she doesn't marry him, but she gets a lot of money anyway, and she gets a job. It would be more fun that way, if she had to work for it, wouldn't it?

This girl is coming to grips with a problem. She revises for herself a story she dislikes but cannot abandon. Such personal reworkings, whether conscious or unconscious, are bound to have more impact than those imposed by well-meaning adaptors.[1] As Heuscher reminds us, echoing the observations of other scholars, the dynamic possibilities of such stories in meaning and impact, understanding and response, are richly varied: "The fairy tale is not static, is not a rigid image of an immutable situation. It is sub-ject to all kinds of modifications which depend on the psycholog-

---

1. In an attempt to make the Cinderella story more rational, one concerned psy-chologist has his "Cinderelma" reject the prince and palace life, set up her own dress shop, and fall for the nextdoor printer. However, his ending is even more romantic than the original: "They never seemed to get bored with one another. They never seemed to get tired of doing things together. In time, they married and had children and lived together until the end of their days" (Gardner 1974:96).

ical makeup of the narrator [and audience] as well as on his [their] cultural environment" (Heuscher 1974:389).

Thus, while fairy tales are not inherently sexist, many readers receive them as such. This study indicates that many females find in fairy tales an echo of their own struggles to become human beings. Gender of both reader and protagonist is indeed significant in this struggle.

References

Beauvoir, Simone de. 1953. *The Second Sex,* trans. H.M. Parshley. New York: Knopf.

Berne, Eric. 1973. *What Do You Say After You Say Hello? The Psychology of Human Destiny.* New York: Bantam.

Bettelheim, Bruno. 1976. *The Uses of Enchantment: The Meaning and Importance of Fairy Tales.* New York: Knopf.

Bullough, Vern L. and Bullough, Bonnie. 1973. *The Subordinate Sex: A History of Attitudes Toward Women.* Urbana: University of Illinois Press.

Cooper, Susan. 1975. Review of *Womenfolk and Fairy Tales,* by Rosemary Minard. *New York Times Book Review* April 13, p.8.

Girardot, N.J. 1977. "Initiation and Meaning in the Tale of Snow White and the Seven Dwarfs." *Journal of American Folklore* 92:73-76.

Grimm, Jacob, and Grimm, Wilhelm. 1974. *The Complete Grimm's* [sic] *Fairy Tales,* trans. Margaret Hunt and James Stern, intro. Padraic Colum, folkloristic commentary Joseph Campbell. New York: Pantheon.

Heuscher, Julius E. 1974. *A Psychiatric Study of Myths and Fairy Tales: Their Origin, Meaning and Usefulness,* 2d ed. Springfield, Ill.: Charles C. Thomas.

Kavablum, Lea. 1973. *Cinderella: Radical Feminist, Alchemist.* Guttenberg, N.J.: The author.

Kiefer, Monica. 1948. *American Children Through Their Books, 1700-1835.* Philadelphia: University of Pennsylvania Press.

Lieberman, Marcia R. 1972. "'Some Day My Prince Will Come': Female Acculturation Through The Fairy Tale." *College English* 34: 383-395.

Lurie, Alison. 1970. "Fairy Tale Liberation." *New York Review of Books* December 17, pp. 42-44.

—. 1971. "Witches and Fairies: Fitzgerald to Updike." *New York Review of Books* December 2, pp. 6, 8-11.

Lüthi, Max. 1970. *Once Upon A Time: On The Nature of Fairy Tales.* trans. Lee Chadeayne and Paul Gottwald. Bloomington and London: Indiana University Press.

Minard, Rosemary, ed. 1975. *Womenfolk and Fairy Tales.* Boston: Houghton Mifflin.

Sexton, Anne. 1971. *Transformations.* Boston: Houghton Mifflin.

Spiller, Harley. 1979. "Cinderella in the Schools." Unpublished paper.

Thompson, Stith. 1946. *The Folktale.* New York: Dryden Press.

GO! BE A BEAST:
BEAUTY AND THE BEAST

Marina Warner

FOR a fabulous *divertissement* given at Versailles in 1664, the king's troupes of dancers and musicians and artists and actors assembled for his entertainment and staged allegories of the seasons with the additional help of wild animals from the king's menagerie: Winter was accompanied by a bear. A skit was included in an interlude. Written by Molière, it featured a bear-fight between a certain wild man of the woods, 'Moron', who is playing with an echo when a bear comes upon him. Trying to appease the animal, Moron exclaims: 'Oh, my lord! How delightful, how lissom your highness is! Your highness has altogether the most gallant looks and the most handsome figure in the world! Oh! what lovely fur! What beautiful looks! ... Help, help!'

Charles Perrault himself may have been involved in devising the tableaux, and in producing the sumptuous feast book of engravings which commemorated the occasion. No beast in fairy tale at the time would have excited anything less than Moron's squirming terror; no courtier would have cooed and gurgled at the appearance of the bear in the manner of children today. The threat of animals was a real and frightening one in the seventeenth and eighteenth centuries; in times of scarcity and hard winters, bears and wolves came in from the wild to prey on towns and villages.

The narrators of earlier versions of 'Beauty and the Beast' frequently avoid giving precise indications of the Beast's horrible features, and generally describe his enchanted shape in the vaguest terms. D'Aulnoy is typically fanciful about her beasts; Villeneuve adds the unusual detail that Beauty's father was terrified by 'a horrible beast ... It had a trunk resembling an elephant's which it placed on the merchant's neck'; as he approaches Beauty later, his scales clank. Beaumont confines herself to saying that he looked so dreadful, Beauty's father felt he was going to faint.

In the literary fairy tale of the *ancien régime*, the Beast's low, animal nature is more usually revealed by his muteness, uncouthness, inability to meet Beauty as a social and intellectual equal. In Villeneuve's version, Beauty sighs that, though he treats her well, she finds him boring because he can utter only a few words and repeats them endlessly. In these secular romances the valued arts of conversation and storytelling remain beyond him.

Authors, often keen to emphasize the unreliability of outward appearances, could hardly press the disagreeable Platonic and Christian equation of deformity of body with deformity of soul. But the illustrators needed to choose an appropriate physical form: the Beast had to be represented. The word 'monster', from the Latin *monstrare*, to show, even suggests that monstrousness is above all visible. But monstrousness is a condition in flux, subject to historical changes in attitudes. One volatile current, carrying ideas of ugliness, abnormality, abominable deformation, converges with another, carrying ideas about nature and man, and in their confluence the beastliness of the Beast diminishes....

The attraction of the wild, and of the wild brother in twentieth-century culture, cannot be overestimated; as the century advances, in the cascade of deliberate revisions of the tale, Beauty stands in need of the Beast, rather than vice versa, and the Beast's beastliness is good, even adorable. Or at least, this has become the drift of the story. She has not mistaken a human lover for a monster, like Psyche, or failed to see a good man beneath the surface, like Belle; on the contrary, the Beast's beastliness will teach her something. Her need of him may be reprehensible, a moral flaw, a part of her carnal and materialist nature; or, it can represent her understanding of love, her redemption. He no longer stands outside her, the threat of male sexuality in bodily form, or of male authority with all its fearful amorality and social legitimacy, as in D'Aulnoy's stories, but he holds up a mirror to the force of nature within her, which she is invited to accept and allow to grow. In one sense the Beast has returned to define Beauty in the early medieval feminine character of seductive concupiscence; only now, the stigma has been lifted. The Beast as a beast has become the object of desire.

Part of Angela Carter's boldness — which made her unpopular in some quarters of the feminist movement in the 1970s — was that she dared to look at women's waywardness. and especially at their attraction to the Beast in the very midst of repulsion. The early novel *The Magic Toyshop*, already tells the story of a beast's defeat: the puppet master makes a monstrous swan automaton to assault his niece in play-acting. But she rejects him, refuses the part in his puppet show, and eventually escapes, with the whole family, from his designs. *The Bloody Chamber* followed two years after a dry and adept translation she made of Perrault, and offers her answer to Perrault's vision of better things. Angela Carter returned to the theme of Beauty and the Beast again and again, turning it inside out and upside down; in a spirit of mischief, she was seizing the chance to mawl governessy moralizers. Rather like the heroines of the Grimms' animal bridegroom tale, 'Snow White and Rose Red', her Beauties choose to play with the Beast precisely because his animal nature excites them and gives their desires licence:

> They tugged his hair with their hands, put their feet on his back and rolled him about, or they took a hazel switch and beat him, and when he growled, they laughed. But the bear took it all in good part, only when they were too rough he called out, 'Leave me alive, children. Snow White, Rose Red, will you beat your wooer dead?'

Deliberately flouting conventional ladylike aspirations (the love of the prince), with which, since the nineteenth century, fairy tales had been identified, Carter places her protagonists in the shoes of

Red Riding Hood, of Beauty, of Snow White, of Bluebeard's
bride. 'The Courtship of Mr. Lyon', 'The Tiger's Bride', 'The
Werewolf', 'The Company of Wolves' lift the covers from the
body of carnal knowledge usually more modestly draped in fairy
tales. For 'The Company of Wolves', she re-imagined familiar
tales in a spiny, springing prose which borrows elements from
Symbolism and pornography, Gothic romance, street slang and
Parnassian preciousness all at once, to conjure young girls' sexual
hunger and the lure of the wild. The wolf stirs desire here far
more profoundly than would the pattern of princes:

> Carnivore incarnate, only immaculate flesh appeases him.
> She will lay his fearful head on her lap and she will pick
> out the lice from his pelt and perhaps she will put the lice
> into her mouth and eat them, as he will bid her, as she would
> do in a savage marriage ceremony.
> The blizzard will die down ...
> See! sweet and sound she sleeps in granny's bed, between
> the paws of the tender wolf.

As the English critic Lorna Sage writes:

> [Carter] produced her own haunting, mocking—sometimes
> tender—variations on some of the classic motifs of the
> genre ... in retelling these tales she was deliberately drawing
> them out of their set shapes, out of the separate space of
> 'children's stories' or 'folk art' and into the world of change.
> It was yet another assault on Myth ... done caressingly and
> seductively. The monsters and the princesses lose their places
> in the old script, and cross forbidden boundary lines.

But Carter could also be love's votary in more traditional fashion.
Another of the tales, almost an ekphrasis of the Cocteau film,
describes the Beast's rescue:

> 'I'm dying, Beauty,' he said in a cracked whisper of his for-
> mer purr. 'Since you left me, I have been sick ...'
> She flung herself upon him, so that the iron bedstead

groaned, and covered his poor paws with her kisses.

'Don't die, Beast! If you'll have me, I'll never leave you.'

When her lips touched the meat-hook claws, they drew back into their pads and she saw how he had always kept his fists clenched but, painfully, tentatively, at last began to stretch his fingers. Her tears fell on his face like snow and, under their soft transformation, the bones showed through the pelt, the flesh through the wide, tawny brow ...

The narrator's voice can be urgent, addressing the reader in the first person: 'My father lost me to the Beast at cards' is the opening line of 'The Tiger's Bride'; this story ends with the heroine's own transformation, under the Beast's caresses, into a furry, naked creature like him.

'East o' the Sun and West o' the Moon' was invoked by Carter as 'one of the most lyrically beautiful and mysterious of all Northern European fairy tales'. It closely reworks the Cupid and Psyche material, and in it a White Bear taking the role of Eros abducts the heroine, asking as he does so, 'Are you afraid?' She says, 'No,' and climbs eagerly on to his back to go forth into a new life with him. Carter also noted the hypocritical evasions of so many modern versions of 'Beauty and the Beast', commenting caustically that the tale had been increasingly employed 'to house-train the id'.

A contemporary artist who also shows Surrealist affinities, Paula Rego, has been inspired by seemingly innocuous English nursery rhymes to plumb darker sides to women's fantasy life than is openly admitted. She too manages to stir some of the same depths when she illustrates 'Baa baa black sheep', for instance, with an image of a little girl provocatively accepting the embrace of a giant ram as she waves to the little boy in the lane.

Beauty's attraction to the Beast before his regeneration inspires fantasies about abduction in pulp fiction, and echoes pornography's conjuration of sadism and rape. The territory is thickly sown with land mines; both Angela Carter's and Paula Rego's work excites contradictory and powerful feelings in their audience, because, while openly challenging conventional misogyny in the very act of speaking and making images, they also refuse the wholesome or pretty picture of female gender (nurturing, caring) and deal plainly with erotic dominance as a source of pleasure for men—and for women.

In 1982, the poet Ted Hughes dramatized 'Beauty and the Beast' for television. His script developed the fantasy, implicit in the classical myth of Cupid and Psyche, that Beauty's passionate desiring summons the Beast to her side, and that, after she has lost him, her yearning for him brings about their reunion. The Hughes version, though it was made for children, does not scant the heroine's erotic fantasy as the dynamic of the story. It begins with the father crazed with worry that every night his beloved daughter the princess is visited by a monstrous and unnameable terror which takes possession of her; invisible, with a huge voice, this phenomenon occupies her dreams and her bed. Doctors are put to watch by her side, and they too are overcome with horror at what they feel, though they see nothing—one specialist's hair turns white overnight. Then a wandering musician with a performing bear comes to the palace at the king's wish, to entertain the melancholy and even mad princess—and the bear charms her. She dances with the beast, and the king her father rejoices that the bear seems to have lifted the mad darkness that was oppressing her. But then, as they are dancing, the bear seizes her in his arms and carries her off.

When, after a long search, the hunting party tracks them down, the princess begs them not to hurt her bear. They wound him, and she weeps—and then, as in other versions, her tears, the proof of her love, fall on his pelt and he stands up, transfigured.

Ted Hughes's intuition that Beauty is stirred by love for the Beast, even when he terrorizes her in the night, reappeared in a more definite form in the popular 1987 CBS series for television, which was also shown in Britain, in which the Beast never casts off his hybrid form. A roaring, rampaging half-lion, half-human creature, he reigns over the subway system of New York as a defender of women and beggars, an urban Robin Hood, who was born from an immaculate virgin and the seed of two fathers, the double lord of the underworld, one a good magus, the other a wicked wizard. Beauty in this case works as an investigator in the District Attorney's of office, but communicates secretly with her saviour Beast; their love is passionate, chivalrous and ... illicit. He is 'the monster of her dreams' and she likes him just as he is.

The disenchantments of the Beast take many forms, not all of them benign; women have remained consistently intrigued. As Karel Capek has commented: 'The same fiction of evil which quickens events in fairy stories also permeates our real lives.' It would be easy to dismiss these visions of the Beast's desirability as male self-flattery, and female collusion with subjection, or, even more serious, as risky invitations to roughness and even rape. But to do so misses the genuine attempt of the contemporary versions of the fairy tale, in certain metamorphoses of its own, to face up to the complicated character of the female erotic impulse. From the post-Utopian vantage point of the 1990s, we cannot rejoice unequivocally in the sexual liberation Surrealism and its aftermath offered women: the experiences of the last decades have given former flower children pause. But what threatens women consumers — and makers — of fairy tale above all is the identification of the Beast with some exclusively male positive area of energy and expression.

The journey the story has itself taken ultimately means that the Beast no longer needs to be disenchanted. Rather, Beauty has to learn to love the beast in him, in order to know the beast in herself. Beauty and the Beast stories are even gaining in popularity over 'Cinderella' as a site for psychological explorations along these lines, and for pedagogical recuperation. Current interpretations focus on the Beast as a sign of authentic, fully realized sexuality, which women must learn to accept if they are to become normal adult heterosexuals. Bettelheim argues:

> Eventually there comes a time when we must learn what we have not known before — or, to put it psychoanalytically, to undo the repression of sex. What we had experienced as dangerous, loathsome, something to be shunned, must change its appearance so that it is experienced as truly beautiful.

Belle had to learn to be a loving wife in the eighteenth century; in the late twentieth, she has to learn to be game in bed. But the Bettelheimian argument takes the exuberance and the energy from female erotic voices, and effects one last transformation of the Beast, by turning him into a mistaken illusion in unawakened female eyes. In this, the psychoanalyst works his way back, in more solemn vein, to the Hellenistic romance, in which Psyche was at fault for fearing her lover was an ogre and not trusting him in bed.

The cuddliness of the teddy bear, the appeal of domesticated sexuality, also informs the present trend towards celebrating the male. In Tim Burton's film *Edward Scissorhands* (1990), the outcast hero does harm, entirely inadvertently: like Frankenstein's monster, he has been made by a mad scientist but left half finished, with cutlery for hands. As a metonymy of maleness and its fumbling connection to the world of others, the scissorhands capture eloquently the idea of the redeemed male beast in current circulation. By the 1990s, the perception of the social outcast, the exile from humankind in the form of a beast, had undergone such a sea-change that any return to full human shape might have degraded rather than redeemed the hero, limited his nobility rather than restored it.

In the same year, the Disney film animation, *Beauty and the Beast*, one of the biggest box-office draws of all time, ran the risk of dramatic collapse when the Beast changed into the prince. No child in my experience preferred the sparkling candy-coloured human who emerged from the enchanted monster; the Beast had won them. Linda Woolverton and the team who collaborated on the film had clearly steeped themselves in the tale's history, on and off screen; prolonged and intense production meetings, turning over every last detail of representation and narrative, can almost be heard over the insouciant soundtrack. This fairytale film is more vividly aware of contemporary sexual politics than any made before; it consciously picked out a strand in the tale's history and deliberately developed it for an audience of mothers who grew up with Betty Friedan and Gloria Steinem, who had daughters who listened to Madonna and Sinead O'Connor. Linda Woolverton's screenplay put forward a heroine of spirit who finds romance on her own terms. Beneath this prima facie storyline, the interpretation contained many subtexts, both knotty and challenging, about changing concepts of paternal authority and rights, about permitted expressions of male desire, and prevailing notions in the quarrel about nature/nurture. Above all, the film placed before the 1990s audience Hollywood's cunning domestication of feminism itself.

Knowing as the film is, it could not avoid the trap that modern retellings set: the Beast steals the show. While the Disney version ostensibly tells the story of the feisty, strong-willed heroine, and carries the audience along on the wave of her dash, her impatient ambitions, her bravery, her self-awareness, and her integrity, the principal burden of the film's message concerns maleness, its various faces and masks, and, in the spirit of romance, it offers hope of regeneration from within the unregenerate male. The graphic intensity given to the two protagonists betrays the weight of interest: Beauty is saucer-eyed, dainty, slender, and wears a variation on the pseudo-medieval dresses of both Cinderella and Snow White, which, as in *Cinderella*, turn into *ancien régime* crinolines-cum-New Look débutante gowns for the scene of awakening love when she dances with the Beast. Her passage from repugnance to attraction also follows a movement from village hall to castle gate, in the conventional upwardly mobile style of the twentieth-century fairy tale. The animators have introduced certain emancipated touches: she is dark-haired, a book worm and walks with a swing. The script even contains a fashionable bow in the direction of self-reflexiveness, for Belle likes reading fairy tales more than any other kind of book, and consequently recognizes, when she finds herself in the Beast's castle, the type of story she is caught in.

But next to the Beast, this Belle is a lacklustre creature. He held the animators' full attention: the pneumatic signature style of Disney animation suited the Beast's character as male desire incarnate. He embodies the Eros figure as phallic toy. The Beast swells, he towers, he inflates, he tumesces. Everything about him is big, and apt to grow bigger: his castle looms, its furnishings dwarfed by its Valhalla-like dimensions. His voice thunders, his anger roars to fill the cavernous spaces of his kingdom. We are shown him enraged, crowding the screen, edge to edge, like a face in a comic strip; when he holds Belle he looks as if he could snap her between his teeth like a chicken wing. His body too appears to be constantly burgeoning; poised on narrow hooves and skimpy legs, the Disney Beast sometimes lollops like a big cat, but more often stands erect, rising to an engorged torso, with an enormous, craggy, bull-like head compacted into massive shoulders, maned and shaggy all

over, bristling with fangs and horns and claws that almost seem
belittled by the creature's overall bulk.

The Beast's sexual equipment was always part of his charm—
hidden or otherwise (it is of course scattered by synecdoche all
over his body in the Disney cartoon). When Titania fell in love
with Bottom the weaver, the associations of the ass were not lost
on the audience. But the comic—and its concomitant, the
pathetic—have almost entirely slipped away from this contemporary representation of virility.

Whereas Bottom, even in his name, was a figure of fun, and the
Golden Ass, his classical progenitor, a ruefully absurd icon of
(male) humanity, the contemporary vision of the Beast tends to
the tragic. The new Disney Beast's nearest ancestor is the Minotaur, the hybrid offspring of Phaedra and the bull, and an ancient
nightmare of perverted lust, and it is significant that Picasso adopted the Minotaur as his alter ego, as the embodiment of his pri-
apism, in the vigour of youth as well as the impotence of old age.
But the real animal which the Disney Beast most resembles is the
American buffalo, and this tightens the Beast's connections to current perceptions of natural good—for the American buffalo, like
the grizzly, represents the lost innocence of the plains before man
came to plunder. So the celluloid Beast's beastliness thrusts in two
contradictory directions; though he is condemned for his 'animal'
rages, he also epitomizes the primordial virtues of the wild.

The Beast's longstanding identity with masculine appetite nevertheless works for him rather than against him, and interacts with
prevailing ideas of healthy male sexuality. The enterprise of the
earlier fairytale writers, to try to define their own desires by making up stories about beasts who either denied them or fulfilled
them, has been rather lost to sight. The vindication of the Beast
has become the chief objective; the true lovableness of the good
Beast the main theme. The Disney cartoon has double-knotted
the lesson in contemporary ecological and sexual politics, by
introducing a second beast, another suitor for Belle's love, the
human hunk Gaston. Gaston is a killer—of animals—and
remains one; he is a lyncher, who preys on social outcasts (suspected lunatics and marginals), he wants to breed (he promises Belle
six or seven children), and he is capable of deep treachery in pursuit of his own interests. The film wastes no sympathy on Gas-

424

ton—though his conceit inspires some of its cleverest and funniest lyrics.

The penalty for Gaston's brutishness is death: he falls off a high crag from the Beast's castle. In the film, he takes the part of the real beast, the Calvinist unredeemed damned beast: socially deviant in his supremacist assumptions, unsound on ecology in both directions, abusing the natural (the forest) and culture (the library). What is above all significant about this caricature is that he is a man in a man's shape, Clark Kent as played by Christopher Reeve. The Disney version is pitiless towards Gaston; self-styled heart throbs who fancy themselves Supermen are now the renegades, and wild men in touch with nature and the beast within the exemplars.

He is moreover one of the rustics whom the sophisticated Belle despises in her opening song ('I want much more than they've got planned'), an anthem for the Me-generation; this Disney, like its predecessors, does not question the assumption that the Beast's princeliness must be material and financial. His credit card, with his social status, is no doubt bigger than Gaston's, too.

In *Edward Scissorhands*, the heroine also acts quickly, with gallantry and courage, to save this outcast from a mob; but he is fatally hampered by his hybrid form, halfway between the automaton and the creaturely; his weapon hands encumber him with manmade technology and cut him off from the desirable aspects of the human, which derive from what is perceived as natural, as animal. The further the cinematic outcast lies from the machine, the more likely his redemption; the Beast as cyborg, as in the *Terminator* movies, represents the apocalyptic culmination of human ingenuity and its diabolical perversion. Whereas, to a medieval spectator, the Devil was represented as close to the animal order in his hooved hairiness, and a bloodless and fleshless angel in gleaming armour approximated the divine artefact, the register of value has been turned topsy-turvy since the eighteenth century and the wild man has come into his own as an ideal. The evolution of the Beast in fairy tale and his portraits in film illustrate this profound shift in cultural values as well as sexual expectations.

The most significant plot change to the traditional story in the Disney film concerns the role of Beauty's father, and it continues the film's trend towards granting Beauty freedom of movement and responsibility for the rescue of the Beast and for his restoration to fundamental inner goodness. The traditional fairy tale often includes the tragic motif that, in return for his life, the father promises the Beast the first thing to greet him when he returns home; as in the story of Jephthah in the Bible (Jg. 11: 12), his daughter, his youngest and most dear, rushes to the gate to meet him, and the father has to sacrifice her. In the eighteenth-century French fairy story, which focussed on the evils of matrimonial customs, the father hands over Belle to the Beast in exactly the same kind of legal and financial transaction as an arranged marriage, and she learns to accept it. Bruno Bettelheim takes a governessy line on the matter: Beauty, learning to relinquish her Oedipal attachment to her father, should be grateful to her father for giving her away and making the discovery of sexuality possible.

Linda Woolverton's script sensibly sets such patriarchal analysis aside, and instead provides subplots to explain away the father's part in Beauty's predicament, as well as supplying Beauty herself with all the wilfulness and determination to make her mistress of her own fate. The Disney studio, sensitive to the rise of children's rights, has replaced the father with the daughter as the enterprising authority figure in the family. The struggle with patriarchal plans underlies ... the plots of many other familiar tales.

In popular versions, 'Beauty and the Beast' offers a lesson in female yielding and its satisfactions. The Beast stirs desire, Beauty responds from some deep inner need which he awakens. (There are echoes here of 'Sleeping Beauty' too.) The Beast, formerly the stigmatizing envelope of the fallen male, has become a badge of the salvation he offers; Beauty used to grapple with the material and emotional difficulties of matrimony for young women; now she tends to personify female erotic pleasures in matching and mastering a man who is dark and hairy, rough and wild, and, in the psychotherapist Robert Bly's phrase, in touch with the Inner Warrior in himself.

In her encounter with the Beast, the female protagonist meets her match, in more ways than one. If she defeats him, or even kills him, if she outwits him, banishes or forsakes him, or accepts him and loves him, she arrives at some knowledge she did not possess; his existence and the challenge he offers is necessary before she can grasp it. The ancient tale of 'Cupid and Psyche' told of their love; apart from the child Pleasure whom Psyche bore, their other descendants—the tales in the Beauty and the Beast group—number among the most eloquent testaments to women's struggles, against arranged marriage, and towards a definition of the place of sexuality in love. The enchantments and disenchantments of the Beast have been a rich resource in stories women have made up, among themselves, to help, to teach, to warn.

BREAKING THE DISNEY SPELL

Jack Zipes

IT was not once upon a time, but in a certain time in history, before anyone knew what was happening, Walt Disney cast a spell on the fairy tale, and it has been held captive ever since. He did not use a magic wand or demonic powers. On the contrary, Disney employed the most up-to-date technological means and used his own "American" grit and ingenuity to appropriate the European fairy tales. His technical skills and ideological proclivities were so consummate that his signature has obfuscated the names of Charles Perrault, the Brothers Grimm, Hans Christian Andersen, and Collodi. If children or adults think of the great classical fairy tales today, be it *Snow White*, *Sleeping Beauty*, or *Cinderella*, they will think Walt Disney. Their first and perhaps lasting impressions of these tales and others will have emanated from a Disney film, book, or artefact. Though other filmmakers and animators produced remarkable fairy-tale films, Disney managed to gain a cultural stranglehold on the fairy tale, tightened by the recent productions of *Beauty and the Beast* (1991) and *Aladdin* (1992). The man's spell over the fairy tale seems to live on even after his death.

But what does the Disney spell mean? Did Disney achieve a complete monopoly of the fairy tale during his lifetime? Did he imprint a particular *American* vision on the fairy tale through his animated films that dominates our perspective today? And, if he did manage to cast his mass-mediated spell on the fairy tale so that we see and read the classical tales through his lens, is that so terrible? Was Disney a nefarious wizard of some kind that we should lament his domination of the fairy tale? Wasn't he just more inventive, more skillful, more in touch with the American spirit of the times than his competitors, who also sought to animate the classical fairy tale for the screen?

Of course, it would be a great exaggeration to maintain that Disney's spell totally divested the classical fairy tales of their meaning and invested them with his own. But it would not be an exaggeration to assert that Disney was a radical filmmaker who changed our way of viewing fairy tales, and that his revolutionary technical means capitalized on American innocence and utopianism to reinforce the social and political status quo. His radicalism was of the right and the righteous. The great "magic" of the Disney spell is that he animated the fairy tale only to transfix audiences and divert their potential utopian dreams and hopes through the false promises of the images he cast upon the screen. But before we come to a full understanding of this magical spell, we must try to understand what he did to the fairy tale that was so revolutionary and why he did it.

In order to grasp the major impact of film technology on the fairy tale and to evaluate Disney's role during the pioneer period of fairy-tale animation, it is first necessary to summarize the crucial functions that the literary fairy tale as institution had developed in middle-class society by the end of the nineteenth century:

1. It introduced notions of elitism and separatism through a select canon of tales geared to children who knew how to read.

2. Though it was also told, the fact that the fairy tale was printed and in a book with pictures gave it more legitimacy and enduring value than an oral tale which disappeared soon after it was told.

3. It was often read by a parent in a nursery, school, or bedroom to soothe a child's anxieties, for the fairy tales for children were optimistic and were constructed with the closure of the happy end.

4. Although the plots varied and the themes and characters were altered, the classical fairy tale for children and adults reinforced the patriarchal symbolical order based on rigid notions of sexuality

and gender.

5. In printed form the fairy tale was property and could be taken by its owner and read by its owner at his or her leisure for escape, consolation, inspiration.

6. Along with its closure and reinforcement of patriarchy, the fairy tale also served to encourage notions of rags to riches, pull yourself up by your bootstraps, dreaming, miracles, and such.

7. There was always tension between the literary and oral traditions. The oral tales continued and continue to threaten the more conventional and classical tales because they can question, dislodge, and deconstruct the written tales. Moreover, within the literary tradition itself, there were numerous writers such as Charles Dickens, George MacDonald, Lewis Carroll, Oscar Wilde, and Edith Nesbit who questioned the standardized model of what a fairy tale should be.

8. It was through script that there was a full-scale debate about what oral folk tales and literary fairy tales were and what their respective functions should be. By the end of the nineteenth century, the fairy tale had expanded as a high art form (operas, ballets, dramas) and low art form (folk plays, vaudevilles, and parodies) and a form developed classically and experimentally for children and adults. The oral tales continued to be disseminated through communal gatherings of different kinds, but they were also broadcast by radio and gathered in books by folklorists. Most important in the late nineteenth century was the rise of folklore as an institution and various schools of literary criticism that dealt with fairy tales and folk tales.

9. Though many fairy-tale books and collections were illustrated and some lavishly illustrated in the nineteenth century the images were very much in conformity with the text. The illustrators were frequently anonymous and did not seem to count. Though the illustrations often enriched and deepened a tale, they were more subservient to the text.

However, the domination of the word in the development of the fairy tale as genre was about to change. The next great revolution in the institutionalization of the genre was the film, for the images now imposed themselves on the text and formed their own text in violation of print but also with the help of the print culture. And here is where Walt Disney and other animators enter the scene.

By the turn of the twentieth century there had already been a number of talented illustrators such as Gustav Doré, George Cruikshank, Walter Crane, Charles Folkard, and Arthur Rackham who had demonstrated great ingenuity in their interpretations of fairy tales through their images....

During the early part of the twentieth century Walter Booth, Anson Dyer, Lotte Reiniger, Walter Lantz, and others all used fairy-tale plots in different ways in trick films and cartoons, but none of the early animators ever matched the intensity with which Disney occupied himself with the fairy tale. In fact, it is noteworthy that Disney's very first endeavors in animation (not considering the advertising commercials he made) were the fairy-tale adaptations that he produced with Ub Iwerks in Kansas City between 1922-1923: *The Four Musicians of Bremen, Little Red Riding Hood, Puss in Boots, Jack and the Beanstalk, Goldie Locks and the Three Bears,* and *Cinderella.* To a certain degree, Disney identified so closely with the fairy tales he appropriated that it is no wonder his name virtually became synonymous with the genre of the fairy tale itself....

We have already seen that one of the results stemming from the shift from the oral to the literary in the institutionalization of the fairy tale was a loss of live contact with the storyteller and a sense of community or commonality. This loss was a result of the social-industrial transformations at the end of the nineteenth century with the *Gemeinschaft* (community) giving way to the *Gesellschaft* (society). However, it was not a total loss, for industrialization brought about greater comfort, sophistication, and literacy and new kinds of communication in public institutions. Therefore, as I have demonstrated, the literary fairy tale's ascent corresponded to violent and progressive shifts in society and celebrated individualism, subjectivity, and reflection. It featured the narrative voice of the educated author and publisher over communal voices and set new guidelines for freedom of speech and expression. In addition, proprietary rights to a particular tale were established, and the literary tale became a commodity that paradoxically spoke out in the name of the unbridled imagination. Indeed, because it was born out of alienation, the literary fairy tale fostered a search for new "magical" means to overcome the instrumentalization of the imagination....

In the case of the fairy-tale film at the beginning of the twentieth century, there are "revolutionary" aspects that we can note, and they prepared the way for progressive innovation that expanded the horizons of viewers and led to greater understanding of social conditions and culture. But there were also regressive uses of mechanical reproduction that brought about the cult of the personality and commodification of film narratives. For instance, the voice in fairy-tale films is at first effaced so that the image totally dominates the screen, and the words or narrative voice can only speak through the designs of the animator who, in the case of Walt Disney, has signed his name prominently on the screen. In fact, for a long time, Disney did not give credit to the artists and technicians who worked on his films. These images were intended both to smash the aura of heritage and to celebrate the ingenuity, inventiveness, and genius of the animator. In most of the early animated films, there were few original plots, and the story lines did not count. Most important were the gags, or the technical inventions of the animators, ranging from introducing live actors to interact with cartoon characters to improving the movement of the characters so that they did not shimmer to devising ludicrous and preposterous scenes for the sake of spectacle. It did not matter what story was projected so long as the images astounded the audience, captured its imagination for a short period of time, and left the people laughing or staring in wonderment. The purpose of the early animated films was to make audiences awestruck and to celebrate the magical talents of the animator as demigod. As a result, the fairy tale as story was a vehicle for animators to express their artistic talents and develop the technology. The animators sought to impress audiences with their abilities to use pictures in such a way that they would forget the earlier fairy tales and remember the images that they, the new artists, were creating for them. Through these moving pictures, the animators appropriated

431

literary and oral fairy tales to subsume the word, to have the final word, often through image and book, for Disney began publishing books during the 1930s to complement his films.

Of all the early animators, Disney was the one who truly revolutionized the fairy tale as institution through the cinema. One could almost say that he was obsessed by the fairy-tale genre, or, put another way, Disney felt drawn to fairy tales because they reflected his own struggles in life. After all, Disney came from a relatively poor family, suffered from the exploitative and stern treatment of an unaffectionate father, was spurned by his early sweetheart, and became a success due to his tenacity, cunning, and courage and his ability to gather talented artists and managers like his brother Roy around him.

One of his early films, *Puss in Boots*, is crucial for grasping his approach to the literary fairy tale and for understanding how he used it as self-figuration that would mark the genre for years to come. Disney did not especially care whether one knew the original Perrault text of *Puss in Boots* or some other popular version. It is also unclear which text he actually knew. However, what is clear is that Disney sought to replace all versions with his animated version and that his cartoon is astonishingly autobiographical.

If we recall, Perrault wrote his tale in 1697 to reflect upon a cunning cat whose life is threatened and who manages to survive by using his brains to trick a king and an ogre. On a symbolical level, the cat represented Perrault's conception of the role of the haute bourgeoisie (his own class), who comprised the administrative class of Louis XIV's court and who were often the mediators between the peasantry and aristocracy. Of course, there are numerous ways to read Perrault's tale, but whatever approach one chooses, it is apparent that the major protagonist is the cat.

This is not the case in Disney's film. The hero is a young man, a commoner, who is in love with the king's daughter, and she fondly returns his affection. At the same time, the hero's black cat, a female, is having a romance with the royal white cat, who is the king's chauffeur. When the gigantic king discovers that the young man is wooing his daughter, he kicks him out of the palace, followed by Puss. At first, the hero does not want Puss's help, nor will he buy her the boots that she sees in a shop window. Then they go to the movies together and see a film with "Rudolph

Vaselino" as a bull-fighter that spurs the imagination of Puss. Consequently, she tells the hero that she now has an idea which will help him win the king's daughter, providing that he will buy her the boots.

Of course, the hero will do anything to obtain the king's daughter. Puss explains to him that he must disguise himself as a masked bullfighter, and she will use a hypnotic machine behind the scenes so he can defeat the bull and win the approval of the king. When the day of the bullfight arrives, the masked hero struggles but eventually manages to defeat the bull. The king is so overwhelmed by his performance that he offers his daughter's hand in marriage, but first he wants to know who the masked champion is. When the hero reveals himself, the king is enraged, but the hero grabs the princess and leads her to the king's chauffeur. The white cat jumps in front with Puss, and they speed off with the king vainly chasing after them.

Although Puss as cunning cat is crucial in this film, Disney focuses most of his attention on the young man who wants to succeed at all costs. In contrast to the traditional fairy tale, the hero is not a peasant, nor is he dumb. Read as a "parable" of Disney's life at that moment, the hero can be seen as young Disney wanting to break into the industry of animated films (the king) with the help of Ub Iwerks (Puss). The hero upsets the king and runs off with his prize possession. Thus, the king is dispossessed, and the young man outraces him with the help of his friends.

But Disney's film is also an attack on the literary tradition of the fairy tale. He robs the literary tale of its voice and changes its form and meaning. Since the cinematic medium is a popular form of expression and accessible to the public at large, Disney actually returns the fairy tale to the majority of people. The images (scenes, frames, characters, gestures, jokes) are readily comprehensible for young and old alike from different social classes. In fact, the fairy tale is practically infantilized, just as the jokes are infantile. The plot records the deepest oedipal desire of every young boy: the son humiliates and undermines the father and runs off with his most valued object of love, the daughter/wife. By simplifying this complex semiotically in black and white drawings and making fun of it so that it had a common appeal, Disney also touched on other themes:

1. Democracy. The film is very *American* in its attitude towards royalty. The monarchy is debunked, and a commoner causes a kind of revolution.

2. Technology: It is through the new technological medium of the movies that Puss's mind is stimulated. Then she uses a hypnotic machine to defeat the bull and another fairly new invention, the automobile, to escape the king.

3. Modernity: The setting is obviously the twentieth century, and the modern minds are replacing the ancient. The revolution takes place as the king is outpaced and will be replaced by a commoner who knows how to use the latest inventions.

But who is the commoner? Was Disney making a statement on behalf of the masses? Was Disney celebrating "everyone" or "every man"? Did Disney believe in revolution and social change in the name of socialism? The answer to all these questions is simply — no.

Disney's hero is the enterprising young man, the entrepreneur who uses technology to his advantage. He does nothing to help the people or the community. In fact, he deceives the masses and the king by creating the illusion that he is stronger than the bull. He has learned, with the help of Puss, that one can achieve glory through deception. It is through the artful uses of images that one can sway audiences and gain their favor. Animation is trickery — trick films — for still images are made to seem as if they move through automatization. As long as one controls the images (and machines) one can reign supreme, just as the hero is safe as long as he is disguised. The pictures conceal the controls and machinery. They deprive the audience of viewing the production and manipulation, and in the end, audiences can no longer envision a fairy tale for themselves as they can when they read it. The pictures deprive the audience now of visualizing their own characters, roles, and desires. At the same time, Disney offsets the deprivation with the pleasure of scopophilia and inundates the viewer with delightful images, humorous figures, and erotic signs. In general, the animator, Disney, projects the enjoyable fairy tale of his life through his own images, and he realizes through animated stills his basic oedipal dream that he was to play out time and again in most of his fairy-tale films. It is the repetition of Disney's infantile quest—the core of American mythology—that enabled him to strike a chord in American viewers from the 1920s to the present.

However, it was not through *Puss in Boots* and his other early animated fairy tales that he was to captivate audiences and set the "classical" modern model for animated fairy-tale films. They were just the beginning. Rather, it was in *Snow White and the Seven Dwarfs* that Disney fully appropriated the literary fairy-tale and made his signature into a trademark for the most acceptable type of fairy tale in the twentieth century. But before the making of *Snow White*, there were important developments in his life and in the film industry that illustrate why and how *Snow White* became the first definitive animated fairy-tale film—definitive in the sense that it was to define the way other animated films in the genre of the fairy tale were to be made.

After Disney had made several Laugh-O-Gram fairy-tale films, all ironic and modern interpretations of the classical versions, he moved to Hollywood in 1923 and was successful in producing 56 *Alice* films, which involved a young pubescent girl in different adventures with cartoon characters. By 1927 these films were no longer popular, so he and Ub Iwerks developed Oswald the Lucky Rabbit cartoons that also found favor with audiences. However, in February of 1928, while Disney was in New York trying to rene- gotiate a contract with his distributor Charles Mintz, he learned that Mintz, who owned the copyright to Oswald, had lured some of Disney's best animators to work for another studio. Disney faced bankruptcy because he refused to capitulate to the exploita- tive conditions that Mintz set for the distribution and production of Disney's films.[1] This experience sobered Disney in his attitude toward the cutthroat competition in the film industry, and when he returned to Hollywood, he vowed to maintain complete con- trol over all his productions—a vow that he never broke.

In the meantime, he and Iwerks had to devise another character for their company if they were to survive, and they conceived the idea for films featuring a pert mouse named Mickey. By Septem-

---

1. See Leonard Mosley, *Disney's World* (New York: Stein and Day, 1985), 85-140.

ber of 1928, after making two Mickey Mouse shorts, Disney, similar to his masked champion in *Puss in Boots*, had devised a way to gain revenge on Mintz and other animation studios by producing the first animated cartoon with sound, *Steamboat Willie*, starring Mickey Mouse. From this point on, Disney became known for introducing all kinds of new inventions and improving animation so that animated films became almost as realistic as films with live actors and natural settings. His next step after sound was color, and in 1932 he signed an exclusive contract with Technicolor and began producing his *Silly Symphony Cartoons* in color. More important, Disney released *The Three Little Pigs* in 1933 and followed it with *The Big Bad Wolf* and *The Three Little Wolves*, all of which involved fairy-tale characters and stories that touched on the lives of people during the depression, for as Bob Thomas has remarked, "*The Three Little Pigs* was acclaimed by the Nation. The wolf was on many American doorsteps, and 'Who's Afraid of the Big Bad Wolf?' became a rallying cry."[1]

Not only were wolves on the doorsteps of Americans but also witches, and to a certain extent, Disney with the help of his brother Roy and Iwerks, had been keeping "evil" connivers and competitors from the entrance to the Disney Studios throughout the 1920s. Therefore, it is not by chance that Disney's next major experiment would involve a banished princess, loved by a charming prince, who would triumph over deceit and regain the rights to her castle. *Snow White and the Seven Dwarfs* was to bring together all the personal strands of Disney's own story with the destinies of desperate Americans, who sought hope and solidarity in their fight for survival during the Depression of the 1930s.

Of course, by 1934 Disney was, comparatively speaking, wealthy, and now that he had money and had hired Don Graham, a professional artist, to train his own animators at the Disney Art School, founded in November 1932, he could embark on ventures to stun moviegoers with his ingenuity and talents as organizer, storyteller, and filmmaker. Conceived sometime in 1934, *Snow White* was to take three years to complete, and Disney did not leave one stone unturned in his preparations for the first full-

---

1. *Disney's Art of Animation: From Mickey Mouse to Beauty and the Beast* (New York: Hyperion, 1991), 49.

length animated fairy-tale film ever made in history. Disney knew he was making history.

During the course of the next three years, Disney worked closely with all the animators and technicians assigned to the production of *Snow White*. By now, Disney had divided his studio into numerous departments such as animation, layout, sound, music, and storytelling, and there were even subdivisions so that certain animators were placed in charge of developing the characters of Snow White, the prince, the dwarfs, and the queen/crone. Disney spent thousands of dollars on a multiplane camera to capture the live action depictions that he desired, the depth of the scenes, and close-ups. In addition he had his researchers experiment with colored gels, blurring focus, and filming through frosted glass, and he employed the latest inventions in sound and music to improve the synchronization with the characters on the screen. Throughout the entire production of this film, Disney had to be consulted and give his approval for each stage of development. After all, *Snow White* was his story that he had taken from the Grimm Brothers and changed completely to suit his tastes and beliefs. He cast a spell over this German tale and transformed it into something peculiarly American.

Just what were the changes he induced? In Disney's version, Snow White is an orphan. Neither her father nor her mother are alive, and she is at first depicted as a kind of Cinderella, cleaning the castle as a maid in a patched dress. In the Grimms' version there is the sentimental death of her mother. Her father remains alive, and she was never forced to do the work of commoners such as wash the steps of the castle. Also, Disney has the Prince appear at the very beginning of the film on a white horse and sing a song of love and devotion to Snow White, though he plays a negligible role in the Grimms' version. In the Disney film, the queen not only is jealous that Snow White is more beautiful than she is, but also sees the prince singing to Snow White and is envious because her stepdaughter has such a handsome suitor. Though the forest and the animals do not speak, they are anthromorphologized by Disney. In particular the animals befriend Snow White and become her protectors. Disney's dwarfs are hardworking and rich miners, and he gave them names — Doc, Sleepy, Bashful, Happy, Sneezy, Grumpy, Dopey — representative of certain human characteristics. His dwarfs are fleshed-out so that they become the star attractions of the film. Their actions are what counts in defeating evil. In the Grimms' tale, the dwarfs are anonymous and play a humble role. Disney's queen only comes to the cottage Snow White shares with the dwarfs one time instead of three as in the Grimms' version, and she is killed while trying to destroy the dwarfs by rolling a huge stone down a mountain to crush them. The punishment in the Grimms' tale is more horrifying: she must dance in red-hot iron shoes at Snow White's wedding. Finally, Disney's Snow White does not return to life when a dwarf stumbles while carrying the glass coffin as in the Grimms' tale. She returns to life when the prince, who has searched far and wide for her, arrives and bestows a kiss on her lips. His kiss of love is the only antidote to the queen's poison.

At first glance, it would seem that the changes that Disney made were not momentous. If we recall Sandra Gilbert and Susan Gubar's stimulating analysis in their book, *The Madwoman in the Attic*,[1] the film follows the classic "sexist" narrative about the framing of women's lives through a male discourse. Such male framing drives women to frustration and some women to the point of madness. It also pits women against women in competition for male approval (the mirror) of their beauty that is short-lived. No matter what they may do, women cannot chart their own lives without male manipulation and intervention, and in the Disney film, the prince plays even more of a framing role since he is introduced at the beginning while Snow White is singing, "I'm Wishing for the One I Love To Find Me Today." He will also appear at the end as the fulfillment of her dreams.

There is no doubt that Disney retained key ideological features of the Grimms' fairy tale that reinforce nineteenth-century patriarchal notions which Disney shared with the Grimms. In some way, he can even be considered their descendant, for he preserves and carries on many of their benevolent attitudes toward women. For instance, in the Grimms' tale, when Snow White arrives at the cabin, she pleads with the dwarfs to allow her to remain and promises that she will wash the dishes, mend their clothes, and

---

1. See *The Woman Writer and the Nineteenth-Century Literary Imagination* (New Haven: Yale University Press, 1979).

clean the house. In Disney's film, she arrives and notices that the house is dirty. So, she convinces the animals to help her make the cottage tidy so that the dwarfs will perhaps let her stay there. Of course, the house for the Grimms and Disney was the place where good girls remained, and one aspect of the fairy tale and the film is about the domestication of women.

However, Disney went much further than the Grimms to make his film more memorable than the tale, for he does not celebrate the domestication of women so much as the triumph of the banished and the underdogs. That is, he celebrates his destiny, and insofar as he had shared marginal status with many Americans, he also celebrated an American myth of Horatio Alger: it is a male myth about perseverance, hard work, dedication, loyalty, and justice.

It may seem strange to argue that Disney perpetuated a male myth through his fairy-tale films when, with the exception of *Pinocchio*, they all featured young women as "heroines." However, despite their beauty and charm, Sleeping Beauty, Cinderella, and the other heroines are pale and pathetic compared to the more active and demonic characters in the film. The witches are not only agents of evil but represent erotic and subversive forces that are more appealing both for the artists who drew them and for the audiences.[1] The young women are like helpless ornaments in need of protection, and when it comes to the action of the film, they are omitted.

In *Snow White and the Seven Dwarfs*, the film does not really become lively until the dwarfs enter the narrative. They are the mysterious characters who inhabit a cottage, and it is through their hard work and solidarity that they are able to maintain a world of justice and restore harmony to the world. The dwarfs can be interpreted as the humble American workers, who pull together during a depression. They keep their spirits up by

---

1. Cf. Charles Solomon, "Bad Girls Finish First in Memory of Disney Fans," *Milwaukee Journal*, TV Section (August 17, 1980): 28. This article cites the famous quote by Woody Allen in *Annie Hall*: "You know, even as a kid I always went for the wrong women. When my mother took me to see 'Snow White,' everyone fell in love with Snow White; I immediately fell for the Wicked Queen."

singing a song, "Hi Ho, it's home from work we go," or "Hi Ho, it's off to work we go," and their determination is the determination of every worker, who will succeed just as long as he does his share while women stay at home and keep the house clean. Of course, it is also possible to see the workers as Disney's own employees, on whom he depended for the glorious outcome of his films. In this regard, the prince can be interpreted as Disney, who directed the love story from the beginning. If we recall, it is the prince who frames the narrative. He announces his great love at the beginning of the film, and Snow White cannot be fulfilled until he arrives to kiss her. During the major action of the film, he, like Disney, is lurking in the background and waiting for the proper time to make himself known. When he does arrive, he takes all the credit as champion of the disenfranchised, and he takes Snow White to his castle while the dwarfs are left as keepers of the forest.

But what has the prince actually done to deserve all the credit? What did Disney actually do to have his name flash on top of the title — "Walt Disney's *Snow White and the Seven Dwarfs*" — in big letters and later credit his co-workers in small letters? Disney never liked to give credit to the animators who worked with him, and they had to fight for acknowledgment. Disney always made it clear that he was the boss and owned total rights to his products. He himself had struggled for his independence against his greedy and unjust father and against fierce and ruthless competitors in the film industry. As producer of the fairy-tale films and major owner of the Disney studios, he wanted to figure in the film, and he sought, as Crafton has noted, to create a more indelible means of self-figuration. He accomplished this by stamping his signature as owner on the frame with the title of the film and then by having himself embodied in the figure of the prince. It is the prince Disney who made inanimate figures come to life through his animated films, and it is the prince who is to be glorified in *Snow White and the Seven Dwarfs* when he resuscitates the heroine with a magic kiss. Afterwards he holds Snow White in his arms, and in the final frame, he leads her off on a white horse to his golden castle on a hill. His golden castle — every woman's dream — supersedes the dark, sinister castle of the queen. The prince becomes her reward, and his power and wealth are glorified in the end.

There are obviously mixed messages or multiple messages in *Snow White and the Seven Dwarfs*, but the overriding sign, in my estimation, is the signature of Disney's self-glorification in the name of justice. Disney wants the world *cleaned up*, and the pastel colors with their sharply drawn ink lines create images of cleanliness, just as each sequence reflects a clearly conceived and preordained destiny for all the characters in the film. For Disney, the Grimms' tale is not a vehicle to explore the deeper implications of the narrative and its history.[1] Rather, it is a vehicle to display what he can do as an animator with the latest technological and artistic developments in the industry. The story is secondary, and if there is a major change in the plot, it centers on the power of the prince, the only one who can save Snow White, and he becomes the focal point by the end of the story.

In Disney's early work with fairy tales in Kansas City, he had a wry and irreverent attitude toward the classical narratives, and there was a strong suggestion in the manner in which he and Iwerks rewrote and filmed the tales that they were "revolutionaries," the new boys on the block, who were about to introduce innovative methods of animation into the film industry and speak

---

1. See Karen Merritt, "The Little Girl/Little Mother Transformation: The American Evolution of 'Snow White and the Seven Dwarfs,'" in *Storytelling in Animation: The Art of the Animated Image*, ed. John Canemaker (Los Angeles: American Film Institute, 1988), 105-21. Merritt makes the interesting point that

> Disney's *Snow White* is an adaptation of a 1912 children's play (Disney saw it as a silent movie during his adolescence) still much performed today, written by a male Broadway producer under a female pseudonym; this play was an adaptation of a play for immigrant children from the tenements of lower East Side New York; and that play, in turn, was a translation and adaptation of a German play for children by a prolific writer of children's comedies and fairy tale drama. Behind these plays was the popularity of nineteenth and early twentieth century fairy tale pantomimes at Christmas in England and fairy tale plays in German and America. The imposition of childish behavior on the dwarves, Snow White's resulting mothering, the age ambiguities in both Snow White and the dwarves, the "Cinderella" elements, and the suppression of any form of sexuality were transmitted by that theatrical tradition,

for the outcasts. However, in 1934, Disney is already the kingpin of animation, and he uses all that he had learned to reinforce his power and command of fairy-tale animation. The manner in which he copied the musical plays and films of his time, and his close adaptation of fairy tales with patriarchal codes indicate that all the technical experiments would not be used to foster social change in America, but to keep power in the hands of individuals like himself, who felt empowered to design and create new worlds. As Richard Schickel has perceptively remarked, Disney "could make something his own, all right, but that process nearly always robbed the work at hand of its uniqueness, of its soul, if you will. In its place he put jokes and songs and fright effects, but he always seemed to diminish what he touched. He came always as a conqueror, never as a servant. It is a trait, as many have observed, that many Americans share when they venture into foreign lands hoping to do good but equipped only with knowhow instead of sympathy and respect for alien traditions."[1]

Disney always wanted to do something new and unique just as long as he had absolute control. He also knew that novelty would depend on the collective skills of his employees, whom he had to

_____

which embodied a thoroughly developed philosophy of moral education in representations for children.... By reading Disney's *Snow White*
by the light of overt didacticism of his sources, he no longer appears
the moral reactionary disdained by contemporary critics. Rather, he is
the entertainer who elevates the subtext of play found in his sources
and dares once again to frighten children (106).

Though it may be true that Disney was more influenced by an American theatrical and film tradition, the source of all these productions, one acknowledged by Disney, was the Grimms' tale. And, as I have argued, Disney was not particularly interested in experimenting with the narrative to shock children or provide a new perspective on the traditional story. For all intents and purposes his film reinforces the didactic messages of the Grimms' tale, and it is only in the technical innovations and designs that he did something startlingly new. It is not the object of critique to "disdain" or "condemn" Disney for reappropriating the Grimms' tradition to glorify the great design-er but to understand those cultural and psychological forces that led him to map out his narrative strategies in fairy-tale animation.

1. *The Disney Version* (New York: Simon and Schuster, 1968), 227.

keep happy or indebted to him in some way. Therefore, from 1934 onward, about the time that he conceived his first feature-length fairy-tale film, Disney became the orchestrator of a corporate network that changed the function of the fairy-tale genre in America. The power of Disney's fairy-tale films does not reside in the uniqueness or novelty of the productions, but in Disney's great talent for holding antiquated views of society *still* through animation and his use of the latest technological developments in cinema to his advantage.

Disney's adaptation of the literary fairy tale for the screen led to a number of changes in the institution of the genre. Technique now takes precedence over the story, and the story is used to celebrate the technician and his means. The carefully arranged images narrate through seduction and imposition of the animator's hand and the camera. The images and sequences engender a sense of wholeness, seamless totality, and harmony that is orchestrated by a savior/technician on and off the screen. Though the characters are fleshed out to become more realistic, they are also one-dimensional and are to serve functions in the film. There is no character development because the characters are stereotypes, arranged according to a credo of domestication of the imagination. The domestication is related to colonization insofar as the ideas and types are portrayed as models of behavior to be emulated. Exported through the screen as models, the "American" fairy tale colonizes other national audiences. What is good for Disney is good for the world, and what is good in a Disney fairy tale is good in the rest of the world. The thematic emphasis on cleanliness, control, and organized industry reinforces the technics of the film itself: the clean frames with attention paid to every detail; the precise drawing and manipulation of the characters as real people; the careful plotting of the events that focus on salvation through the male hero. Private reading pleasure is replaced by pleasurable viewing in an impersonal cinema. Here one is brought together with other viewers not for the development of community but to be diverted in the French sense of *divertissement* and American sense of diversion. The diversion of the Disney fairy tale is geared toward nonreflective viewing. Everything is on the surface, one-dimensional, and we are to delight in one-dimensional portrayal

443

and thinking, for it is adorable, easy, and comforting in its simplicity.

Once Disney realized how successful he was with his formula for feature-length fairy tales, he never abandoned it, and in fact, if one regards two recent Disney Studio productions, *Beauty and the Beast* and *Aladdin*, Disney's contemporary animators have continued in his footsteps. There is nothing but the "eternal return of the same" in *Beauty and the Beast* and *Aladdin* that makes for enjoyable viewing and delight in techniques of these films as commodities but nothing new in the exploration of narration, animation, and signification.

There is something sad in the manner in which Disney "violated" the literary genre of the fairy tale and packaged his versions in his name through the merchandising of all sorts of books, articles, clothing, and records. Instead of using technology to enhance the communal aspects of narrative and bring about major changes in viewing stories to stir and animate viewers, he employed animators and technology to stop thinking about change, to return to his films, and to long nostalgically for neatly ordered patriarchal realms. Fortunately, the animation of the literary fairy tale did not stop with Disney, but that is another tale to tell, a tale about breaking Disney's magic spell.

SELECTED BIBLIOGRAPHY

Anthologies / Collections

NINETEENTH CENTURY AND EARLIER

Andersen, Hans Christian. *Hans Andersen: His Classic Fairy Tales*. Trans. Erik Haugaard. New York: Doubleday, 1974.

Auerbach, Nina, and U.C. Knoepflmacher, eds. *Forbidden Journeys: Fairy Tales and Fantasies by Victorian Women Writers*. Chicago: University of Chicago Press, 1992.

Basile, Giambattista. *The Pentamerone of Giambattista Basile*. Trans. Benedetto Croce. Ed. N.M. Penzer. 2 vols. London: John Lane the Bodley Head, 1932.

Calvino, Italo, comp. *Italian Folktales*. Trans. George Martin. New York: Pantheon, 1980.

Cott, Jonathan, comp. *Beyond the Looking Glass: Extraordinary Works of Fantasy and Fairy Tale*. New York: Stonehill, 1973.

Grimm, Jacob, and Wilhelm Grimm. *Grimms' Tales for Young and Old: The Complete Stories*. Trans. Ralph Mannheim. Garden City: Anchor Press, 1977.

Hearn, Michael P., comp. *The Victorian Fairy Tale Book*. New York: Pantheon, 1988.

Minard, Rosemary, comp. *Womenfolk and Fairy Tales*. Boston: Houghton Mifflin, 1975.

Opie, Iona, and Opie, Peter, comp. *The Classic Fairy Tales*. London: Oxford University Press, 1974.

Tatar, Maria, ed. *The Classic Fairy Tales*. New York: W.W. Norton, 1999.

Tully, Carol, ed. *Romantic Fairy Tales*. Harmondsworth: Penguin, 2000.

Zipes, Jack D., comp. *Beauties, Beasts and Enchantment: Classic French Fairy Tales*. New York: North American Library, 1989.

—. *The Complete Fairy Tales of Oscar Wilde*. New York: Signet, 1990.

—. *Victorian Fairy Tales: The Revolt of the Fairies and Elves.* New York: Methuen, 1987.

—. *Spells of Enchantment: the Wondrous Fairy Tales of Western Culture.* New York: Viking, 1991.

TWENTIETH CENTURY AND LATER

Carter, Angela. *The Bloody Chamber and Other Stories.* London: Gollancz, 1979.

Datlow, Ellen, and Terri Windling, eds. *Snow White, Blood Red.* New York: Morrow/Avon, 1993.

—. *Black Thorn, White Rose.* New York: Morrow/Avon, 1995.

—. *Ruby Slippers, Golden Tears.* New York: Morrow/Avon, 1996.

—. *Black Swan, White Raven.* New York: Morrow/Avon, 1998.

—. *Silver Birch, Blood Moon.* Toronto: Hearst, 1999.

—. *Black Heart, Ivory Bones.* Toronto: Hearst, 2000.

Donoghue, Emma. *Kissing the Witch: Old Tales in New Skins.* New York: HarperCollins, 1997.

Lee, Tanith. *Red as Blood, or Tales of the Sisters Grimmer.* New York: Daw, 1983.

Zipes, Jack, ed. *The Outspoken Princess and the Gentle Knight.* New York: Bantam, 1994.

POETRY

Dahl, Roald. *Revolting Rhymes.* London: Jonathan Cape, 1982.

Hay, Sara Henderson. *Story Hour.* Garden City: Doubleday, 1963.

Mieder, Wolfgang, ed. *Disenchantments: An Anthology of Modern Fairy Tale Poetry.* Hanover, NH: University Press of New England, for University of Vermont, 1985.

Sexton, Anne. *Transformations.* Boston: Houghton Mifflin, 1971.

Strauss, Gwen. *Trail of Stones.* London: Julia McRae Books, 1990.

Critical / General

Bacchilega, Cristina. *Postmodern Fairy Tales: Gender and Narrative Strategies.* Philadelphia: University of Pennsylvania Press, 1997.

Baker, Donald. *Functions of Folk and Fairy Tales.* Washington, DC: Association for Childhood Education International, 1981.

Bottigheimer, Ruth B., ed. *Fairy Tales and Society: Illusion, Allusion and Paradigm.* Philadelphia: University of Pennsylvania Press, 1986.

Canepa, Nancy, ed. *Out of the Woods: The Origins of the Literary Fairy Tale in Italy and France*. Detroit: Wayne State University Press, 1997.

De Vos, Gail, and Anna E. Altmann. *New Tales for Old: Folktales as Literary Fictions for Young Adults*. Englewood, CO: Teacher Ideas Press, 1999.

Dundes, Alan, ed. *Cinderella: A Casebook*. Madison: University of Wisconsin Press, 1988.

—. *Little Red Riding Hood: A Casebook*. Madison: University of Wisconsin Press, 1989.

Houghton, Rosemary. *Tales from Eternity: the World of Fairy Tales and the Spiritual Search*. New York: Seabury Press, 1973.

Hearne, Betsy G. *Beauty and the Beast: Visions and Revisions of an Old Tale*. Chicago: University of Chicago Press, 1989.

Jones, Steven Swann. *The Fairy Tale: The Magic Mirror of Imagination*. New York: Twayne, 1995.

Knoepflmacher, U.C. *Ventures into Childland: Victorians, Fairy Tales and Femininity*. Chicago: University of Chicago Press, 1999.

Lane, Marcia. *Picturing the Rose: A Way of Looking at Fairy Tales*. New York: H.W. Wilson Co., 1994.

Lüthi, Max. *Once Upon a Time: On the Nature of Fairy Tales*. Trans. Lee Chadeayne and Paul Gottwald. New York: Frederick Ungar, 1970.

—. *The European Folktale: Form and Nature*. Trans. John D. Niles. Bloomington: Indiana University Press, 1982.

—. *The Fairy Tale as Art Form and Portrait of Man*. Trans. Jon Erickson. Bloomington: Indiana University Press, 1984.

McGlathery, James M. *Fairy Tale Romance: The Grimms, Basile and Perrault*. Urbana: University of Illinois Press, 1991.

Rohrich, Lutz. *Folktales and Reality*. Trans. Peter Tokofsky. Bloomington: Indiana University Press, 1991.

Sale, Roger. *Fairy Tales and After: From Snow White to E.B. White*. Cambridge, Mass.: Harvard University Press, 1978.

Schectman, Jacqueline M. *The Stepmother in Fairy Tales*. Boston: Sigo Press, 1991.

Tatar, Maria M. *Off with Their Heads!: Fairy Tales and the Culture of Childhood*. Princeton, NJ: Princeton University Press, 1992.

Thomas, Joyce. *Inside the Wolf's Belly: Aspects of the Fairy Tale*. Sheffield, UK: Sheffield Academic Press, 1989.

Tolkien, J.R.R. *Tree and Leaf*. Boston: Houghton Mifflin, 1965.

Warner, Marina. *From the Beast to the Blonde*. London: Chatto and Windus, 1994.

447

Zipes, Jack D. *Breaking the Magic Spell: Radical Theories of Folk and Fairy Tales*. Austin: University of Texas Press, 1979.

—. *Fairy Tale as Myth : Myth as Fairy Tale*. Lexington: University Press of Kentucky, 1994.

—. *Fairy Tales and the Art of Subversion: The Classic Genre for Children and the Process of Civilization*. New York: Methuen, 1983.

—. *Happily Ever After: Fairy Tales, Children, and the Culture Industry*. New York: Routledge, 1997.

—. *The Trials and Tribulations of Little Red Riding Hood: Versions of the Tale in Sociocultural Context*. South Hadley, Mass.: Bergin and Garvey, 1983.

—. *When Dreams Came True: Classical Fairy Tales and Their Tradition*. New York: Routledge, 1998.

BROTHERS GRIMM

Bottigheimer, Ruth B. *Grimms' Bad Girls and Bold Boys: The Moral and Social Vision of the Tales*. New Haven: Yale University Press, 1987.

Ellis, John M. *One Fairy Story Too Many: The Brothers Grimm and Their Tales*. Chicago: University of Chicago Press, 1983.

Haase, Donald, ed. *The Reception of Grimms' Fairy Tales: Responses, Reactions, Revisions*. Detroit: Wayne State University Press, 1993.

Kamenetsky, Christa. *The Brothers Grimm and Their Critics: Folk Tales and the Quest for Meaning*. Athens: Ohio University Press, 1992.

McGlathery, James M., ed. *The Brothers Grimm and Folk Tale*. Urbana: University of Illinois Press, 1988.

—. *Grimms' Fairy Tales: A History of Criticism on a Popular Classic*. Columbia, SC: Camden House, 1993.

Michaelis-Jena, Ruth. *The Brothers Grimm*. New York: Praeger, 1970.

Murphy, G. Ronald. *The Owl, the Raven and the Dove: The Religious Meaning of the Grimms' Magic Fairy Tales*. Oxford: Oxford University Press, 2000.

Peppard, Murray. *Paths Through the Forest: A Biography of the Brothers Grimm*. New York: Holt, Rinehart and Winston, 1971.

Rusch-Feja, Diann. *The Portrayal of the Maturation Process in Girl Figures in Selected Tales of the Brothers Grimm*. Frankfurt-am-Mein: Peter Lang, 1995.

Tatar, Maria. *The Hard Facts of the Grimms' Fairy Tales*. Princeton, NJ: Princeton University Press, 1987.

Zipes, Jack. *The Brothers Grimm: From Enchanted Forests to the Modern World*. New York: Routledge, 1988.

PERRAULT AND THE FRENCH

Barchilon, Jacques, and Peter Flinders. *Charles Perrault*. Boston: Twayne Publishers, 1981.

Darnton, Robert. *The Great Cat Massacre and Other Episodes in French Cultural History*. New York: Basic Books, 1984.

Lewis, Philip. *Seeing Through the Mother Goose Tales: Visual Turns in the Writings of Perrault*. Stanford: Stanford University Press, 1996.

Morgan, Jeanne. *Perrault's Morals for Moderns*. New York: Peter Lang, 1985.

Seifert, Lewis. *Fairy Tales, Sexuality and Gender in France, 1690-1715: Nostalgic Utopias*. New York: Cambridge University Press, 1996.

ANDERSEN / WILDE

Bredsdorff, Elias. *Hans Christian Andersen*. New York: Charles Scribner's Sons, 1975.

Gronbech, Bo. *Hans Christian Andersen*. Boston: Twayne Publishers, 1980.

Lederer, Wolfgang. *The Kiss of the Snow Queen: Hans Christian Andersen and Man's Redemption by Woman*. Berkeley: University of California Press, 1986.

Spink, Reginald. *Hans Christian Andersen and His World*. New York: G.P. Putnam's Sons, 1972.

Roditi, Edouard. *Oscar Wilde*. Norfolk, Conn.: New Directions Books, 1947.

PSYCHOLOGICAL

Bettelheim, Bruno. *The Uses of Enchantment: The Meaning and Importance of Fairy Tales*. New York: Alfred Knopf, 1976.

Bly, Robert. *Iron John: A Book About Men*. New York: Vintage, 1992.

Campbell, Joseph. *The Hero with a Thousand Faces*. Princeton: Princeton University Press, 1970.

Cashdan, Sheldon. *The Witch Must Die: How Fairy Tales Shape Our Lives*. New York: HarperCollins, 2000.

Chinen, Allan B. *In the Ever After: Fairy Tales and the Second Half of Life*. Wilmette, Ill.: Chiron Publications, 1989.

—. *Once Upon a Midlife: Classical Stories and Mythic Tales to Illuminate the Middle Years.* Los Angeles: Jeremy Tarcher, 1992.

Dieckmann, Hans. *Twice-Told Tales: The Psychological Use of Fairy Tales.* Wilmette, IL: Chiron, 1986.

Estes, Clarissa Pinkola. *Women Who Run with the Wolves: Myths and Stories of the Wild Woman Archetype.* New York: Ballantyne, 1992.

Franz, Marie Louise von. *An Introduction to the Psychology of Fairy Tales.* 3rd ed. Zurich: Spring Publications, 1975.

—. *Individuation in Fairy Tales.* Zurich: Spring Publications, 1977.

—. *Problems of the Feminine in Fairy Tales.* Irving, TX.: Spring Publications, 1979.

Fromm, Erich. *The Forgotten Language: An Introduction to the Understanding of Dreams, Fairy Tales and Myths.* New York: Grove Press, 1951.

Heuscher, Julius. *A Psychiatric Study of Myths and Fairy Tales: Their Origin, Meaning and Usefulness.* Springfield, Ill.: Thomas, 1974.

Livo, Norma. *Who's Afraid...? Facing Children's Fears with Folktales.* Englewood, CO: Teacher Ideas Press, 1994.

Mallet, Carl-Heinz. *Fairy Tales and Children: The Psychology of Children Revealed through Four of Grimms' Fairy Tales.* New York: Schocken Books, 1984.

Metzger, Michael, and Mommsen, Katherina, eds. *Fairy Tales as Ways of Knowing: Essays on Märchen in Psychology, Society and Literature.* Bern: P. Lang, 1981.

ANTHROPOLOGICAL / FOLKLORIC / LINGUISTIC

Aarne, Antti, and Stith Thompson. *The Types of the Folktale: A Classification and Bibliography.* Helsinki: FF Communications #184, 1961.

Dégh, Linda. *Folktales and Society: Storytelling in a Hungarian Peasant Community.* Trans. Emily M. Schossberger. Bloomington: Indiana University Press, 1969.

Dundes, Allan. ed. *Analytic Essays in Folklore.* The Hague: Mouton, 1975.

—. *The Study of Folklore.* Englewood Cliffs, NJ: Prentice-Hall, 1965.

Hartland, E.S. *The Science of Fairy Tales: An Enquiry into Fairy Mythology.* Detroit: Singing Tree Press, 1968.

Propp, Vladimir. *The Morphology of the Folktale.* Austin: University of Texas Press, 1968.

Thompson, Stith. *The Folktale.* New York: Holt, Reinhart and Winston, 1946.

Yearsley, Percival M. *The Folklore of Fairy Tale*. Detroit: Singing Tree Press, 1968.

FEMINIST

Farrer, Claire, ed. *Women and Folklore*. Austin: University of Texas Press, 1975.

Kolbenschlag, Madonna. *Kiss Sleeping Beauty Goodbye*. Garden City, NY: Doubleday, 1979.

Rusch-Feja, Diann. *The Portrayal of the Maturation Process in Girl Figures in Selected Tales of the Brothers Grimm*. Frankfurt-am-Mein: Peter Lang, 1995.

Walker, Barbara. *Feminist Fairy Tales*. New York: HarperCollins, 1997.

Zipes, Jack D., comp. *Don't Bet on the Prince: Contemporary Feminist Fairy Tales in North America and England*. New York: Methuen, 1986.

ILLUSTRATION AND FILM

Engen, Rodney K. *Walter Crane as a Book Illustrator*. London: Academy Editions, 1975.

Holliss, Richard, and Brian Sibley. *Walt Disney's "Snow White and the Seven Dwarfs" and the Making of the Classic Film*. New York: Simon and Schuster, 1987.

Meyer, Susan E. *A Treasury of the Great Children's Book Illustrators*. New York: Harry Abrams, 1987.

Lanes, Selma C. *The Art of Maurice Sendak*. New York: Harry Abrams, 1984.

Nodelman, Perry. *Words About Pictures: The Narrative Art of Children's Picture Books*. Athens: University of Georgia Press, 1988.

Schickel, Richard. *The Disney Version: The Life, Times, Art and Commerce of Walt Disney*. New York: Simon Schuster, Inc., 1985.

Journals

Canadian Children's Literature (CanCL)
Children's Literature (CL)
Children's Literature Association Quarterly (ChLAQ)
Children's Literature in Education (CLE)
Horn Book
The Lion and the Unicorn (LU)
Signal

SOURCES

"The Story of Grandmother" from *The Borzoi Book of French Folktales* by Paul Delarue, copyright © 1956 by Alfred A. Knopf, a division of Random House Inc. Used by permission of Alfred A. Knopf, a division of Random House, Inc.

"The Wolf and the Three Girls" from *Italian Folktales: Selected and Retold by Italo Calvino*, copyright © 1956 by Giulio Einaudi, s.p.a., English translation by George Martin copyright © 1980 by Harcourt, Inc., reprinted by permission of Harcourt, Inc.

"Bluebeard" from *Trail of Stones* by Gwen Strauss, copyright © 1990 by Gwen Strauss. Used by permission of Alfred A. Knopf Children's Books, a division of Random House, Inc.

"Little Red Cap," "Brier Rose," "Ashputtle," "Snow White," "Rapunzel," "The Goose Girl," "Clever Gretel," "The Frog King or Iron Heinrich," "Bearskin," "Hansel and Gretel," "The Brave Little Tailor," "Rumpelstiltskin," and "The Blue Light" from *Grimm's Tales for Young and Old* by Jakob & Wilhelm Grimm, translated by Ralph Manheim, copyright © 1977 by Ralph Manheim. Used by permission of Doubleday, a division of Random House, Inc.

"The Tinderbox," "The Ugly Duckling," "The Nightingale," "The Little Mermaid," and "The Swineherd" from *Hans Christian Anderson: His Classic Fairy Tales* by Erik Haugaard, copyright © 1974 Erik Christian Haugaard. Used by permission of Doubleday, a division of Random House, Inc.

"The Company of Wolves" from *The Bloody Chamber* by Angela Carter. Copyright © Angela Carter 1979. Reproduced by permission of the Estate of Angela Carter c/o Rogers, Coleridge & White Ltd., 20 Powis Mews, London W11 1JN.

452